DUDLEY PUBLIC LIBRARIES

The loan of this book may be renewed if not required by other readers, by contacting the library from which it was borrowed.

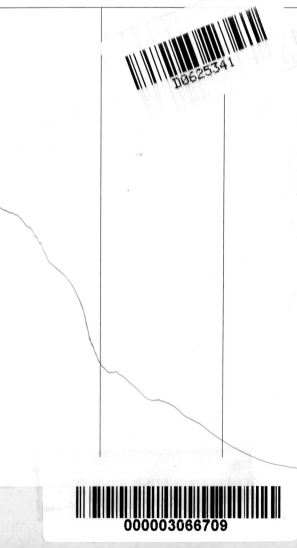

Mavericks

Mavericks: Bringing Home the Billionaire

BARBARA DUNLOP

VICTORIA PADE

LUCY RYDER

MIX
Paper from
responsible sources
FSC
FSC C007464

This book is produced from independently certified FSC™ paper
to ensure responsible forest management

For more information visit: www.harpercollins.co.uk/green

Printed and bound in Spain
by CPI, Barcelona

MILLS & BOON

First Published in Great Britain 2020
By Mills & Boon, an imprint of HarperCollins*Publishers*
1 London Bridge Street, London, SE1 9GF

MAVERICKS: BRINGING HOME THE BILLIONAIRE
© 2020 Harlequin Books S.A.

His Stolen Bride © 2016 Barbara Dunlop
To Catch a Camden © 2014 Victoria Pade
Resisting Her Rebel Hero © 2014 Bev Riley

ISBN: 978-0-263-29838-3

HIS STOLEN BRIDE

BARBARA DUNLOP

To Mom with love

One

A heavy metal door clanged shut behind Jackson Rush, echoing down the hallway of the Riverway State Correctional Institute in northeast Illinois. He paused to mentally brace himself as he took in the unfamiliar surroundings. Then he walked forward, his boot heels clacking against the worn linoleum. He couldn't help thinking the prison would make a perfect movie set, with its cell bars, scarred gray cinder blocks, flickering fluorescent lights and the scattered shouts from connecting rooms and hallways.

His father, Colin Rush, had been locked up here for nearly seventeen years, ever since he was caught stealing thirty-five million dollars from the unsuspecting investors in his personal Ponzi scheme.

His dramatic arrest had taken place on Jackson's thirteenth birthday. The police rushed the backyard pool party, sending guests shrieking and scattering. Jackson could still see the two-tiered blue-and-white layer cake sliding from the table, splattering on the grass, obliterating his name as it oozed into a pile of goo.

At first, his father had stridently proclaimed his innocence. Jackson's mother had taken Jackson to the courtroom every day of the trial, where they'd sat stoically and supportively behind the defense. But it soon became clear that Colin was guilty. Far from being a brilliant investor, he was a common thief.

When one of his former clients committed suicide, he lost all public sympathy and was sentenced to twenty years in jail. Jackson hadn't seen his father since.

Now he rounded the corner to the visiting area, prepared for stark wooden benches, Plexiglas partitions and hardwired black telephone receivers. Instead, he was surprised to find himself in a bright, open room that looked like a high school cafeteria. A dozen round red tables were positioned throughout, each with four stools connected by thick metal braces directly to the table base. The hall had high rectangular windows and checkerboard tile floors. A few guards milled around while the other visitors seemed to be mostly families.

A man stood up at one of the tables and made eye contact. It took Jackson a moment to recognize his father. Colin had aged considerably, showing deep wrinkles around his eyes and along his pale, hollow cheeks. His posture was stooped, and his hairline had receded. But there was no mistaking it was him, and he smiled.

Jackson didn't smile back. He was here under protest. He didn't know why his father had insisted he come, only that the emails and voice messages had become increasingly frequent and sounded more and more urgent. He'd eventually relented in order to make them stop.

Now he marched toward the table, determined to get the visit over and done with.

"Dad," he greeted flatly, sticking out his hand, preempting what would surely be the most awkward hug in history.

"Hello, son," said Colin, emotion shimmering in his eyes as he shook Jackson's hand.

His grip was firmer than Jackson had expected.

Jackson's attention shifted to a second man seated at the round table, half annoyed by his presence, but half curious as well.

"It's good to see you," said Colin.

Jackson didn't respond, instead raising his brow inquiringly at the stranger.

Colin cleared his throat and released Jackson's hand. "Jackson, this is Trent Corday. Trent and I have been cell mates for the past year."

It seemed more than strange that Colin would bring a

friend to this meeting. But Jackson wasn't about to waste time dwelling on the question.

He looked back to his father. "What is it you want?"

He could only guess there must be a parole hearing coming up. If there was, Colin was on his own. Jackson wouldn't help him get out of prison early. Colin had three years left on his sentence, and as far as Jackson was concerned, he deserved every minute.

His selfish actions had harmed dozens of victims, not the least of which was Jackson's mother. She'd been inconsolable after the trial, drinking too much, abusing prescription painkillers, succumbing to cancer five years later just as Jackson graduated from high school.

Colin gestured to one of the stools. "Please, sit."

Jackson perched himself on the small metal seat.

"Trent has a problem," said Colin, sitting down himself.

What Trent's problem could possibly have to do with Jackson was the first question that came to mind. But he didn't ask—instead, he waited.

Trent filled the silence. "It's my daughter. I've only been inside for three years. A misunderstanding, really, I—"

"Save it," said Jackson.

Seventeen years ago, he'd listened to Colin protest endlessly about how he'd been framed, then railroaded, then misunderstood. Jackson wasn't here to listen to the lies of a stranger.

"Yes, well…" Trent glanced away.

Jackson looked at his watch.

"She's fallen victim," said Trent. He fished into the pocket of his blue cotton shirt. "It's the Gerhard family. I don't know if you've heard of them."

Jackson gave a curt nod.

Trent put a photograph on the table in front of Jackson. "Isn't she beautiful?"

Jackson's gaze flicked down.

The woman in the picture was indeed beautiful, likely

in her midtwenties, with rich auburn hair, a bright, open smile, shining green eyes. But her looks were a moot point.

"She's getting married," said Trent. "To Vern Gerhard. They hide it well. But that family's known to a lot of the guys in here. Vern is a con artist and a crook. So is his father, and his father before that."

The woman obviously had questionable taste in men. Jackson found that less than noteworthy. In his line of work, he'd come across plenty of women who'd married the wrong guy, even more whose husbands didn't meet with the approval of their fathers. Again, this had nothing to do with him.

He looked back to Colin. "What is it *you* want from me?"

"We want you to stop the wedding," said Colin.

It took a second for the words to compute inside Jackson's head. "Why would I do anything like that?"

"He's after her money," said Trent.

"She's a grown woman." Jackson's glance strayed to the photo again.

She looked to be twenty-six or twenty-seven. He doubted she was thirty. With a face like that and any kind of money in the mix, she had to know she was going to attract a few losers. If she didn't recognize them herself, there wasn't anything Jackson could do about it.

Colin spoke up again. "She can't possibly know she's being conned. The girl places a huge value on honesty and integrity, has done her entire life. If she knew the truth, she wouldn't have anything to do with him."

"So tell her."

"She won't speak to me," said Trent. "She sure won't listen to me. She doesn't trust me as far as she can throw me."

"I'm sure you can relate to that particular viewpoint," said Colin, an edge to his voice.

"*That's* what you want to say to me?" Jackson rose to his feet. No way, no how was he buying into a guilt trip from his old man.

"Sit down," said Colin.

"Please," said Trent. "Year ago, I put something in her name, shares in a diamond mine."

"Lucky for her."

The woman might well be picking the wrong husband, but at least she'd have a comfortable lifestyle.

"She doesn't know about it," said Trent.

For the first time since he'd walked in, Jackson's curiosity was piqued. "She doesn't know she owns a diamond mine?"

Both men shook their heads.

Jackson looked at the picture again, picking it up from the table. She didn't appear naive. In fact, if he had to guess, he'd say she looked intelligent. But she was drop-dead gorgeous. In his eight years as a private detective, he'd discovered features like that made women targets.

"Hear us out," said Colin. "Please, son."

"Don't call me that."

"Okay. Fine. Whatever you want." Colin was nodding again.

"You hear things in here. And the Gerhards are dangerous," said Trent.

"More dangerous than you two felons?" Jackson didn't like that he'd become intrigued by the circumstances, but he had.

"Yes," said Trent.

Jackson hesitated for a beat, but then he sat back down. Another ten minutes wouldn't kill him.

"They found out about the mine," said Trent, his tone earnest.

"You know this for sure?" asked Jackson.

"I do."

"How?"

"A friend of a friend. The Borezone Mine made a promising new discovery a year ago. Only days later, Vern Gerhard made contact with my daughter. Final assaying is about to be announced, and the value will go through the roof."

"Is it publicly traded?" asked Jackson.

"Privately held."

"Then how did Gerhard know about the discovery?"

"Friends, industry contacts, rumors. It's not that hard if you know where to ask."

"It could be a coincidence."

"It's not." There was cold anger in Trent's voice. "The Gerhards are bottom-feeders. They heard about the discovery. They targeted her. And as soon as the ink is dry on the marriage certificate, they'll rob her blind and dump her like last week's trash."

Jackson traced his index finger around the woman's face. "You have proof of that? You have evidence that he's not in love with her?"

With that fresh-faced smile and those intelligent eyes, Jackson could imagine any number of men could simply fall in love, money or no money.

"That's what we need you for," said Colin.

"Expose their con," said Trent. "Look into their secret, slimy business dealings and tell my Crista what you find. Convince her she's being played and stop that wedding."

Crista. Her name was Crista. It suited her.

Despite himself, Jackson was beginning to think his way through the problem, calculate the time he'd need for a cursory look into the Gerhard family's business. At the moment, things weren't too busy in the Chicago office of Rush Investigations. He'd planned to use the lull to visit the Boston office and discuss a possible expansion. But if push came to shove, he could make some time for this.

She was pretty. He'd give her that. Nobody in the Boston office was anywhere near this pretty.

"Will you do it?" asked Colin.

"I'll scratch the surface," said Jackson, pocketing the photo.

Trent opened his mouth, looking like he might protest

Jackson taking the picture. But he obviously thought better of it and closed his mouth again.

"Keep us posted?" asked Colin.

For a split second, Jackson wondered if this was all a ruse to keep him in contact with his father. Did Colin plan to string him along for a while for some hidden reason of his own? He was, after all, a gifted con artist.

"The wedding's Saturday," said Trent.

That diverted Jackson's attention. "*This* Saturday?"

"Yes."

That was three days away.

"Why didn't you start this sooner?" Jackson demanded. What did they expect him to accomplish in only three days?

"We did," Colin said quietly.

Jackson clamped his jaw. Yeah, his father had been trying to get hold of him for a month. He'd been studiously ignoring the requests, just like he'd been doing for years. He owed Colin nothing.

He stood. "It's not much time, but I'll see what I can find."

"She *cannot* marry him." Trent's undertone was rock hard with vehemence.

"She's a grown woman," Jackson repeated.

He'd look into the Gerhards. But if Crista Corday had fallen for a bad boy, there might be nothing her daddy or anyone else could do to change her mind.

Crista Corday swayed back and forth in front of the full-length mirror, her strapless lace and tulle wedding gown rustling softly against her legs. Her hair was swept up in a profusion of curls and braids. Her makeup had been meticulously applied. Even her underwear was white silk perfection.

She stifled a laugh at the absurdity of it all. She was a struggling jewelry designer, living in a basement suite off Winter Street. She didn't wear antique diamonds. She didn't get married in the magnificent Saint Luke's Cathedral with a reception at the Brookbend Country Club. And she didn't get swept off her feet by the most eligible prince charming in all of greater Chicago.

Except for the part where she did, and she had.

Cinderella had nothing on her.

There was a knock on the Gerhard mansion's bedroom door.

"Crista?" the male voice called out. It was Vern's cousin Hadley, one of the groomsmen.

"Come in," she called in return.

She liked Hadley. He was a few years younger than Vern, laid-back by Gerhard standards, fun-loving and friendly. Taller than most of the men in the family, he was athletic and good-looking, with a jaunty swath of dark blond hair that swooped across his forehead.

He lived in Boston rather than Chicago, but he visited often, sometimes staying at the mansion, sometimes using a hotel. Crista assumed he preferred a hotel when he had a date. Vern's mother, Delores, was staunchly religious and would not have allowed Hadley to have an overnight guest.

The door opened, and he stepped into the spacious, sumptuously decorated guest room. Crista had spent the night here, while Vern had stayed in his apartment downtown. Maybe it was Dolores's influence, but Crista had been feeling old-fashioned the past few weeks, insisting she and Vern sleep apart until the honeymoon. Vern had reluctantly agreed.

Hadley halted. Then he pushed the door shut behind him and seemed to take in her ensemble.

"What?" she asked, checking herself out, wondering if she'd missed some glaring flaw.

"You look amazing," he said.

Crista scoffed. "I sure hope I do." She spread her arms. "Do you have any idea how much this all cost?"

Hadley grinned. "Aunt Delores wouldn't have it any other way."

"I feel like an impostor." Crista's stomach fluttered with a resurgence of apprehension.

"Why?" he asked. His tone was gentle, and he moved closer.

"Because I grew up on the lower west side."

"You don't think we're your people?"

She turned back to the mirror and gazed at her reflection. The woman staring back was her, but not her. It was a surreal sensation.

"Do you think you're my people?" she asked him.

"If you want us to be," he said.

Their gazes met in the mirror.

"But it's not too late," he added.

"Too late for what?"

"To back out." He looked serious, but he had to be joking.

"You're wrong about that." Not that she wanted to back out. Not that she'd even consider backing out. In fact, she couldn't imagine how their conversation had come to this.

"You look scared," he said.

"Of the wedding, sure. I'm probably going to trip on my way down the aisle. But I'm not afraid of the marriage."

It was Vern. She was marrying smart, respectful, polite Vern. The man who'd stepped up to invest in her jewelry design company, who'd introduced her to the finer things, who'd swept her away for a fantasy weekend in New York City and another in Paris. There wasn't much about Vern that wasn't fantastic.

"The future in-laws?" Hadley asked.

Crista quirked a smile. "Intimidated, not afraid."

The intensity left his expression, and he smiled in return. "Who wouldn't be intimidated by them?"

"Nobody I know, that's for sure."

Manfred Gerhard was a humorless workaholic. He was exacting and demanding, with a cutting voice and an abrupt manner. His wife, Delores, was prim and uptight, excruciatingly conscious of the social hierarchy, but skittish whenever Manfred was in the room, constantly catering to his whims.

If Vern ever acted like his father, Crista would kick him to the curb. No way, no how would she put up with that. Then the thought brought her up short. Vern wasn't at all like his father. She'd never seen anything to even suggest he might behave like Manfred.

"He's very close to them," said Hadley.

He was watching her intently again, and for a split second Crista wondered if he could read her thoughts.

"He's talking about buying an apartment in New York City." She liked the idea of putting some distance between Vern and his family. He loved them dearly, but she couldn't see spending every Sunday evening at the mansion the way Vern seemed to like.

"I'll believe that when it happens," said Hadley.

But Crista knew it was already decided. "It's so I can expand the business," she elaborated.

"Are you having second thoughts?" asked Hadley.

"No." She turned to face him. She wasn't. "What makes you say that? What makes you ask that?"

"Maybe I want you for myself."

"Very funny."

He hesitated for a moment then gave an unconcerned shrug. "I'm not sure I'd marry into this family."

"Too bad you're already in this family."

He looked her straight in the eyes. "So, you're sure?"

"I'm sure. I love him, Hadley. And he loves me. Everything else will work itself out around that."

He gave a nod of acquiescence. "Okay. If I can't get you to call off the wedding, then I'm here to tell you the limos have arrived."

"It's time?" The flutter in her stomach turned into a spasm.

It was perfectly normal, she told herself. She was about to walk down the aisle in front of hundreds of people, including her future in-laws and a who's who list of notable Chicagoans. She'd be a fool to be calm under these circumstances.

"You just turned pale," said Hadley.

"I told you, I'm afraid of tripping halfway down the aisle."

"You want me to walk you?"

"That's not how we rehearsed it."

Crista's father was in prison, and she didn't have a close male relative to escort her down the aisle. And in this day and age, it seemed ridiculous to scramble for a figurehead to "give her away" to Vern. She was walking down the aisle alone, and she was perfectly fine with that.

"I could still do it," said Hadley.

"No, you can't. You need to stand up front with Vern. Otherwise the numbers will be off, more bridesmaids than groomsmen. Dolores would faint dead away."

Hadley straightened the sleeves of his tux. "You got that right."

Crista pictured her six bridesmaids at the front of the cathedral in their one-shoulder crisscross aqua dresses. Their bouquets would be plum and white, smaller versions of the dramatic rose-and-peony creation Delores had ordered for Crista. It was going to be heavy, but Delores had said with a congregation that large, people needed to see it from a distance. They could probably see it from Mars.

"The flowers are here?" asked Crista, half hoping they hadn't arrived so she wouldn't have to lug the monstrosity around.

"Yes. They're looking for you downstairs to get some pictures before you leave."

"It's time," said Crista, bracing herself.

"It's not too late," said Hadley. "We can make a break for it through the rose garden."

"You need to shut up."

He grinned. "Shutting up now."

Crista was getting married today. It might have happened fast. The ceremony might be huge. And her new family might be overwhelming. But all she had to do was put one foot in front of the other, say, "I do," and smile in all the right places.

By tonight, she'd be Mrs. Vern Gerhard. By this time tomorrow, she'd be off on a Mediterranean honeymoon. A posh private jet would take them to a sleek private yacht for a vacation in keeping with the stature of the Gerhard family.

Hadley offered her his arm, and she took it, feeling a sudden need to hang on tight.

"I'll see you at the church," he said.

She could do this. She would do this. There was no downside. Any woman would be thrilled by such a complete and total change in her lifestyle.

Dressed in a crisp tuxedo, freshly shaved, his short hair neatly trimmed, Jackson stood outside Saint Luke's Cathedral north of Chicago in the Saturday afternoon sunshine pretending he belonged. It was a picture-perfect June wedding day. The last of the well-heeled guests had just been escorted inside, and the groomsmen now stood in a cluster on the outside stairs. Vern Gerhard was nowhere to be seen, likely locked up in an anteroom with the best man waiting for Crista Corday to arrive.

Jackson had learned a lot about Crista over the past three days. He'd learned she was beautiful, creative and reputedly hardworking.

As a girl, she'd grown up in a modest neighborhood, living with her single mother, her father, Trent, having visitation rights and apparently providing some small amount of financial support. She'd attended community college, taking a diploma in fine arts. It was during that time that she'd lost her mother in a car accident.

After graduation she'd found a job in women's clothing in a local department store. He assumed she must have worked on her jewelry designs in her off hours.

So far, she seemed exactly as she appeared, an ordinary,

working-class Chicago native who'd been living a perfectly ordinary life until she'd met her fiancé. The most remarkable thing about her seemed to be her father's conviction on fraud charges. Then again, maybe it wasn't so remarkable. This was Chicago, and Jackson was definitely familiar with having a convicted criminal in the family.

Vern and the Gerhards had proven harder for him to gauge. Their public and social media presence was slick and heavily controlled. Their family company, Gerhard Incorporated, was privately held, having been started as a hardware store by Vern's great-grandfather during the Depression. It now centered on commercial real estate ownership and development.

Their estimated net worth was high, but Jackson hadn't found anything illegal or shady in their business dealings. They did seem to have incredible timing, often buying up properties at fire sale prices in the months before corporate mergers, gentrification or zoning changes boosted their value. It was enough to make Jackson curious, but the individual instances weren't overly suspicious, and what he had so far didn't come close to proving they were conning Crista.

Despite Trent's suspicions, Vern Gerhard and Crista's romance seemed to be just that, a romance.

"I say more power to him." One of the groomsmen's voices carried from the cathedral staircase, catching Jackson's attention.

"I almost told her at the house," said another groomsman. This one looked younger. He had the trademark Gerhard brown eyes, but he was taller than most, younger than Vern. His flashy hairstyle made him look like he belonged in a boy band.

"Why would you do that?" asked a third. This man was shorter, balding, and his bow tie was already askew. Jackson recognized him as a brother-in-law to Vern.

"You don't think she deserves to know?" asked the younger one.

"Who cares? She's hot," said the bald one. "That body, hoo boy."

"Such a sweet ass," said the first groomsman, grinning.

"Nice," Jackson muttered under his breath. The Gerhards might be rich, but they didn't seem to have much in the way of class.

"So, why does he need Gracie?" asked the younger groomsman, glancing around the circle for support. "He should break it off already."

"You want to stick to just one ice cream flavor?" asked the balding man.

"For the rest of your life?" asked the first groomsman.

"Some days I feel like praline pecan. Some days I feel like rocky road," said the heavyset one with a chortle.

"And *that's* why you're sleeping with Lacey Hanniberry."

"Lumpy Lacey."

The other men laughed.

"Vern hit the jackpot." The first groomsman made a rude gesture with his hips.

"On both fronts," said the bald one. "Crista's the lady, Gracie's the tramp."

"She's going to find out," said the younger man with the flashy hair.

"Not if you don't tell her she won't," said the first man, a warning in his tone.

Jackson had half a mind to tell her himself. Vern sounded like a pig. And most of his friends didn't seem any better.

"Gracie won't last, anyway," said the heavyset man.

"Vern will trade up," said the balding one.

"Uncle Manfred's girlfriends have been twenty-five for the past thirty years."

"Wives age, girlfriends don't."

They all laughed, except for the young guy. He frowned instead. "Crista's different."

"No, she's not." The first groomsman slapped him on the

back. "You're young, naive. All your girlfriends are twenty-five."

"I don't cheat on them."

"Then you're not trying hard enough."

"Get with the program."

Out of the corner of his eye, Jackson saw two white limos pull up to the curb. The groomsmen spotted them, too, and they turned to head up the wide staircase to the cathedral entrance, their voices and laughter fading with the distance.

So, Vern was cheating on Crista. It was a coldhearted and idiotic move, but it was none of Jackson's business. Maybe she knew and accepted it. Or maybe she wasn't as smart as everyone seemed to think, and she was oblivious. Or maybe—and this was a real possibility—she was only marrying the guy for his money and didn't care about his fidelity one way or the other.

The limo doors opened and a group of pretty bridesmaids spilled out of one. The driver of the other vehicle quickly hopped to the back door, helping the bride step onto the sidewalk.

Crista straightened and rose in the bright sunshine, looking absolutely stunning. Her auburn hair was swept up in braids, thick at the nape of her neck, wispy and delicate around her beautiful face. Her shoulders were bare and looked creamy smooth. The white dress was tight across her breasts and her waist, showing off an amazing figure. The lace and beading on the full skirt glittered with every little movement.

Jackson didn't normally fantasize about brides. But if he had, they'd look exactly like her. His annoyance at Vern redoubled. What was the man's problem? If Jackson had someone like Crista in his bed, he'd never so much as look at another woman.

The bridesmaids giggled and clustered around her while the drivers returned to their cars to move them from the busy street.

"This is it," said one bridesmaid, fussing with Crista's bouquet and taking a critical look at her face and hairdo.

"I'm okay?" Crista asked.

"You're perfect."

Crista drew in a deep breath.

The women started for the staircase that led to the cathedral's big front doors. Jackson's first instinct was to step forward and offer his arm, but he held back.

Crista spotted him. She looked puzzled at first, as if she was struggling to recognize him. Their gazes locked, and he felt a shot to his solar plexus.

Her eyes were green as a South Pacific sea and just as deep, flickering in the sunshine. She looked honest. She looked honorable. In that split second, he knew her father's words had been true. She wouldn't put up with a cheating husband, which meant she didn't know about Vern and Gracie.

Jackson wanted to shout at her to stop, to get out of here. She might not know it, but she was making a mistake. Deep down in his gut, he knew she was making a terrible mistake.

Maybe he should tell her the truth about Vern, just call out, right here, right now. Then at least she'd know what she was getting herself into. He told himself to do it. He owed Vern absolutely nothing. He formed the words inside his head, opened his mouth and was ready to blurt it out.

But then a bridesmaid whispered to Crista. She laughed, and her gaze broke from Jackson's, releasing him from the spell.

The women moved up the staircase, and the moment was lost.

He shook himself. It was time for him to leave. There was nothing more he could do here, nothing he could do for Trent except hope the man was wrong. The Gerhards seemed like a singularly distasteful family, and if they really were after her diamond mine, she had herself some trouble. But it wasn't Jackson's trouble to borrow. He'd done as he'd promised, and he'd found nothing concrete, nothing that said the Gerhards were nefarious criminals.

The bridesmaids filed in through the doorway, chattering among themselves. Crista hung back, touching each of her earrings, fingering her necklace then grasping her large bouquet in both hands and tipping up her chin.

Then, unexpectedly, she twisted her head to look back again. He felt that same rush of emotion tighten his chest cavity. He knew with an instant certainty that she deserved better than Vern. It might be none of his business, but surely she wouldn't tolerate a husband who'd sneak off and sleep with a string of mistresses.

The heavy door swung shut behind the bridesmaids.

Just he and Crista were left outside.

Jackson glanced around and confirmed that for these short seconds, they were alone.

Before his brain could form a thought, his feet were moving. He was striding toward her.

Her green eyes went wide, and she drew her head back in obvious surprise.

"Crista Corday?" he asked.

"Are you a friend of Vern's?" Her sexy voice seemed to strum along his nervous system.

"Not for long," he said. He scooped her into his arms and began walking.

"What?" she squeaked, one of her hands pushing on his shoulder, the other gripping the big bouquet.

"I'm not going to hurt you." He lengthened his stride to the sidewalk.

"You're not...*what* are you doing?"

"There are things you don't know about Vern."

"*Put me down!*" She started to squirm, glancing frantically around.

"I will," he promised, speeding up his pace. "In a moment."

He reached out and opened the driver's door of his SUV.

He shoved her across to the passenger side. Before she had a chance to react, he jumped in behind her, cranked the engine and gunned the accelerator, peeling away from the curb, narrowly missing a taxi, which responded with a long blast from its horn.

"You can't do this," Crista cried, twisting her neck to look back at the church.

"I only want to talk."

"I'm *getting married.*"

"After you hear me out if you still want to get married, I'll take you back to him."

And, he would. Trent was a criminal. He could easily be lying about the Gerhards for reasons of his own. So, if Crista was okay with infidelity, Jackson would return her to Vern. It would go against every instinct inside him, but he'd do it.

Two

"Take me back *now*," Crista shouted at the stranger who seemed to be abducting her. Her mind raced to make some sense out of the situation.

"As soon as you hear me out." His jaw was tight, his eyes straight ahead, his hands firm on the wheel as they gathered speed.

"Who *are* you?" She struggled not to panic.

She'd always considered herself a smart, sensible, capable woman. But in this scenario she had no idea what to do.

"Jackson Rush. I'm an investigator."

"Investigating what?" She struggled to stay calm. What was he doing? Why had he taken her?

Then she saw a red light coming up. He'd have to stop for it. When he did, she'd jump from the vehicle. She quickly glanced at the passenger door to locate the handle.

She'd open the door, jump out and run to… She scanned the businesses along the section of the street. The Greek restaurant might be closed. The apartment building doors would be locked. But the drug store. That would be open, and it would be crowded. Surely one of the clerks would lend a bride a phone.

She realized she was still holding onto her bouquet, and she let it slip from her hand to the floor. She didn't need it slowing her down. Vern's mother would flip. Then again, Vern's mother, along with everyone else, was probably flipping already. Had anyone seen this man, Jackson, take her?

She surreptitiously slanted a glance his way. He was maybe thirty. He looked tough and determined, maybe a little world-weary. But there was no denying he was attractive. He was obviously fit under the tux, and very well-groomed.

The vehicle was slowing. She lifted her hand, ready to grab the handle.

But suddenly he hit the accelerator, throwing her back in her seat and sideways as he made a hard right. Another car honked as their tires squealed against the pavement.

"What are you *doing*?" she demanded.

"How well do you know Vern Gerhard?"

What a ridiculous question. "He's my fiancé."

"Would it surprise you to know he was cheating on you?"

Crista's jaw dropped. "Where did that come from?"

"Would it surprise you?" Jackson repeated.

"Vern's not cheating on me." The idea was preposterous.

Vern was sweet and kind and loyal. He made no secret of the fact that he adored Crista. They were about to be married. And his family was extremely old-fashioned. Vern would never risk disappointing his mother by cheating.

No, scratch that. Vern wouldn't cheat because Vern wouldn't cheat. It had nothing to do with Delores.

"Okay," said Jackson, the skepticism clear in his tone.

"Take me back," she said.

"I can't do that. Not yet."

"There are three hundred people in that church. They're all waiting for me to walk down the aisle."

She could only imagine the scene as the guests grew more restless and Vern grew more confused. She wasn't wearing a watch, and she didn't have her cell phone. But what time was it? Exactly how late was she to her own wedding?

She scanned the dashboard for a clock. Traffic was light, and Jackson seemed able to gauge the stoplights and adjust his speed, making sure he didn't have to come to a halt.

"Would you care if he was cheating?" asked Jackson, eyeing her quickly. "Would that be a deal breaker for you?"

"He's not cheating." It didn't look like she'd have a chance to bail out anytime soon. "Do you want money? Will you call in a ransom demand? They'll probably pay. They'll probably pay more if you take me back there right away."

"This isn't about money."

"Then what's it about?" She struggled to keep her tone even but panic was creeping in.

He seemed to hesitate over his answer. "You deserve to be sure. About Vern."

"You don't even know me." She stared at him more closely. "Do you? Have we met?"

Could he be some long-lost person from her past?

"We haven't met," he said.

She racked her brain for an explanation. "Then do you know Vern? Did he do something bad to you?"

She realized she ought to be frightened. She'd been kidnapped—*kidnapped*. This stranger was holding her hostage and wouldn't let her go.

"I've never met Vern," he said.

"Then are you crazy? Though I suppose that's a stupid question. Crazy people never question their own sanity." She realized she was babbling, but she couldn't seem to help herself.

"I'm beginning to think I am," he said.

"A sure sign that you're not."

He gave a chopped laugh and seemed to drop his guard.

She tried to take advantage. "Will you let me go? Please, just pull over and drop me off. I'll find my own way back to the church."

It had to be at least fifteen minutes now. Vern would be frantic. Delores would be incensed. Unless someone saw Jackson grab her, they probably thought she ran away.

Now she wondered what Hadley was thinking. He might guess she'd taken his advice, changed her mind, that she didn't want to marry Vern after all. She scrunched her eyes shut and shook her head. How had things gotten so mixed up?

"He's cheating on you, Crista. Why would you want to marry a man who's cheating on you?"

"First of all, he's not. And…" She paused, experienced

a moment of clarity. "Wait a minute. If I say I don't care if he's cheating, will you let me go?"

"If you honestly don't care and you want to marry him anyway, yeah, I'll let you go."

"Then I don't care." Why hadn't she thought of this sooner? "It's fine. No problem." She waved a dismissive hand. "He can cheat away. I still want to marry him."

"You're lying."

"I'm not." She was.

"I don't believe you."

"You've never met me. You don't know a thing about me."

He shook his head. "I can tell you have pride."

"I have no pride. Maybe I like to share. Maybe I'm into polygamy. After this wedding, Vern might find another wife. We'll all live happily ever after."

"As if."

"Let me go!"

"I'm here because somebody out there cares about you, Crista."

"I know somebody cares about me. His name is Vern Gerhard. Do you have any idea how upset he is right now?"

Jackson's tone went dry. "Maybe Gracie could console him."

The name set a shiver through Crista's chest. "*What* did you say?"

"Gracie," Jackson repeated, doing a double take at Crista's face. "You okay?"

"I'm fine. No, I'm not. I've been kidnapped!"

"Do you know someone named Gracie?"

Crista did know Gracie Stolt. Or at least she knew *of* a Gracie Stolt. Vern had once used that name during a phone call. He'd said it was business. It *had* been business, making the name irrelevant to this conversation.

"I don't know any Gracie," she said to Jackson, her tone tart.

"He's sleeping with Gracie."

"Stop saying that."

The vehicle bounced, and she grabbed the armrest to steady herself. She realized they'd turned off the main roads and onto a tree-lined lane.

A new and horrible thought crossed her mind, and her throat went dry. Was Jackson some sicko with a thing for brides?

"Are you going to hurt me?" she rasped.

"What?" He did another double take. "No. I told you. I'm not going to harm you at all."

"I bet every psychopathic murderer says that."

The corner of his mouth tipped up, but then quickly disappeared. "We have a mutual acquaintance. The person who sent me is someone who cares about you."

"Who?"

"I can't reveal my client."

"I bet every psychopathic murderer says that, too."

She was vacillating between genuine fear and disbelief that any of this could be real.

"I'm sorry you're frightened right now, but I'm not going to hurt you. You'll figure that out soon enough, I promise."

They rounded a corner, and a lake fanned out before them, the gravel beach dotted with weathered docks. He pulled to the side of a small, deserted parking lot.

"Are we there?" she asked.

"Almost." He nodded toward one of the docks.

A tall white cabin cruiser bobbed against its moor lines.

Crista shrank back against the seat, her voice going up an octave. "You're going to dump my body in the lake?"

He extracted a cell phone from his inside jacket pocket. "I'm going to call my staff."

"You have a phone?"

"Of course I have a phone."

"You should make a ransom call. My fiancé is from a rich family. They'll pay you."

At least she hoped the Gerhards would pay to get her back. She was certain Vern would be willing. His father, maybe not so much.

Jackson hated that he was frightening Crista. But he was operating on the fly here. Taking her a quarter mile offshore on Lake Michigan was the best he could come up with to keep her safe but under wraps. He wasn't about to tie her up in a basement while Mac and some of his other guys looked into Vern Gerhard's love life.

"You're going to jail, you know," she said for about the twenty-fifth time.

She stood on the deck of the boat, gazing back at the mansions along the coastline, their lights coming up as the sun sank away. Her extravagant white wedding gown rustled in the breeze. The intricate lace-and-bead-covered skirt was bell shaped, billowing out from a tight waist, while the strapless top accentuated her gorgeous figure.

She was right. He was taking a very stupid risk. But the alternative had been to let the wedding go ahead. Which he could have done. In fact, he should have done. He owed nothing to her father and nothing to his own father. And Crista was all but a stranger to him. She was an intelligent adult, and she'd made her choice in Vern. He should have walked away.

"I'm hoping you won't press charges," he said, moving to stand beside her.

"In what universe would I not press charges?"

Though he knew she was frightened, her expression was defiant. He couldn't help but be impressed with her spirit.

"In the universe where I did you a favor."

"You destroyed my wedding. Do you have any idea how important this was to my mother-in-law? How much she planned and spent?"

"To your mother-in-law?"

"Yes."

"Not to you?"

Her expression faltered. "Well, me, too, of course. It was my wedding."

"It was an odd way to put it, worrying about your mother-in-law first."

"What I meant was, from my own perspective, I can get married any old time, in the courthouse, in Vegas, whatever. But she has certain expectations, a certain standing in the community. She wants to impress her friends and the rest of the family."

"She sounds charming."

"It comes with the Gerhard territory." There was a resignation to her tone.

"What about Vern? How did he feel about the opulent wedding?"

"He was all for it. He's close to his family. He wants them to be happy."

"Does he want you to be happy?"

Crista glanced sharply up at Jackson. "Yes, he wants me to be happy. But he knows I don't sweat the small stuff."

Jackson lifted a brow. "The small stuff being your own wedding?"

She shrugged her bare shoulders, and he was suddenly seized by an urge to run his palms over them, to test the smoothness of her skin. Was she cold out here on the lake?

"It'll work just as well with three hundred people in the room as it would with two witnesses and a judge."

Jackson stifled a chuckle. "You sure don't sound like the average bride."

Her tone turned dry. "The average bride doesn't have a five-hundred-dollar wedding bouquet."

"Seriously?"

"I don't know for sure, but I think that's in the ballpark."

Jackson drew back to take in the length of her. "And the dress?"

She spread her arms. "Custom-made in Paris."

"You flew to Paris for a wedding dress."

"Don't be ridiculous. The designer flew to Chicago."

This time Jackson did laugh. "You have got to be kidding."

"And that was only the start. I'm wearing antique diamonds." She tilted her head to show him her ears.

He wanted to kiss her neck. It was ridiculous, given the circumstances, but there was something incredibly sensual about the curve of her neck, the line of her jaw, the lush red of her lips.

"And you should see my underwear," she said.

Their gazes met. She took in his stare and obviously saw a flare of desire. Those gorgeous green eyes widened in surprise, and she took a step back.

He wanted to tell her he'd give pretty much anything to see her underwear. But he kept his mouth firmly shut.

"You wouldn't," she said, worry in her tone.

"I wouldn't," he affirmed. "I won't. I'm not going to try anything out of line." He turned his attention to the shoreline.

"Will you take me back?" she asked.

"I doubt there's anybody left at the church."

"They'll be crazy with worry," she said. "They'll have called the police by now."

"The police won't take a missing-person report for twenty-four hours."

"You don't know my future in-laws."

"I know the Chicago Police Department."

"Why are you doing this?"

"I was hired to look into Vern Gerhard's integrity."

"By who?"

Jackson shook his head. "I have a strict policy of client confidentiality."

Given their understandably fractured relationship, bringing Trent's name into it would be the fastest way to completely lose her trust. Not that he'd blame her. He felt the same about anything his own father touched.

"But you don't have a strict policy against kidnapping innocent people?" she asked.

"To be honest, this is the first time it's come up."

"I *am* going to press charges." It was clear she was serious.

There was no denying that the situation had spiraled out of control. But there was also nothing to do but keep moving forward. If he took her back now, the Gerhards would definitely have him arrested. His only hope was to find proof of Vern's infidelity and turn Crista against her fiancé.

His phone rang. He kept eye contact with her as he reached for it.

It was Mac, his right-hand man.

"Hey," Jackson answered.

"Everything okay so far?" asked Mac.

"Yeah." Jackson turned away from Crista and moved along the deck toward the bridge. "You come up with anything?"

"Rumors, yes. But nothing that gives us proof. Norway's looking into Gracie."

"Pictures would be good."

"Videotape better."

"I'd take videotape," said Jackson. "Is somebody on the family?"

"I am."

"And?"

"They've contacted the police, but they're being waved off until morning. I guess runaway brides aren't that unusual."

"If Vern Gerhard is a typical example of our gender, I don't blame them."

Mac coughed out a laugh.

"I guess we've got till morning," said Jackson.

It was less time than he would have liked. But that's what happened when you threw a plan together at the last minute.

"And then?" asked Mac. "Have you thought through what happens in the morning?"

He had, and most of the options were not good. "We better have something concrete by then."

"Otherwise she's a liability," said Mac.

Jackson had to agree. "At that point, she's going to be a huge liability."

Crista was predictably angry at having her posh wedding ruined. If they didn't find something to incriminate Vern, Jackson's career if not his freedom would be at stake.

He heard a sudden splash behind him.

He spun to find the deck empty, Crista gone. His gaze moved frantically from corner to corner as he rushed to the stern and spotted her in the water. "You gotta be kidding me!"

"What?" asked Mac.

"Call you back." Jackson dropped his phone.

She was flailing in the choppy waves, obviously hampered by the voluminous white dress. She gasped and went under.

He immediately tossed two life jackets overboard, as close to her as he could.

"Grab one!" he shouted. Then he stripped off his jacket, kicked off his shoes and dived in.

The water closed icy cold around him. He surfaced and gasped in a big breath. She was twenty feet away, and he kicked hard. He dug in with his arms, propelling himself toward her.

When he looked up again, she was gone. He twisted his head, peering in all directions, spotting a wisp of white below the surface. He dived under, groping in the dark until he caught hold of her arm. He clamped his hand tight and hauled her upward, breaking the surface and wrapping his arm firmly around her chest.

She coughed and sputtered.

"Relax," he told her. "Just relax and let me do the work."

She coughed again.

He grabbed one of the life jackets and tucked it beneath her. The boat was close, but the water was frigid. He wasn't going to be able to swim for long. Her teeth were already chattering.

He found another life jacket and looped it around the arm that supported her. He used his legs and free arm to move them through the water.

"You okay?" he asked her. "You breathing?"

She nodded against his chest.

"Don't fight me," he cautioned.

"I won't," she rasped.

The side of the boat loomed closer. He aimed for the stern where there was a small swimming platform. It was a relief to grasp on to something solid. His muscles throbbed from the effects of the cold water, and his limbs were starting to shake.

He unceremoniously cupped her rear end and shoved her onto the platform. She scrambled up, her dress catching and tearing. He kept her braced until she was stable. Then he looped both forearms over the platform and hoisted himself up, sitting on the edge, dragging in deep breaths.

"What the heck?" he demanded.

She was breathing hard. "I thought I could make it."

"To the beach?"

"It's not that far."

"It's a quarter mile. And you're dressed in an anchor."

"The fabric is light."

"Maybe when it's bone-dry." He reached up and pulled himself to his feet. His legs trembled, and his knees felt weak, but he put an arm around her waist and lifted her up beside him.

With near-numb fingers, he released the catch on the deck gate and swung it open.

"Careful," he cautioned as he propelled her back onto the deck.

She held on and stepped shakily forward. "It tangled around my legs."

"You could have killed us both." He followed her.

"It'd serve you right."

"To be *dead*? You'd be dead, too."

"I'm going to be dead anyway."

"What?" He was baffled now.

She was shivering. "I heard you on the phone. You said tomorrow morning I'd be a liability. We both know what that means."

"One of us obviously doesn't."

"Don't bother to deny it."

"Nobody's killing anyone." He gazed out at the dark water. "Despite your best attempt."

"You can't let me live. I'll turn you in. You'll go to jail."

"You might not turn me in."

"Would you actually believe me if I said I wouldn't?"

"At the moment, no."

Right now, she was having a perfectly normal reaction to the circumstances. Proof of the truth might mitigate her anger eventually, but they didn't have that yet.

"Then that was a really stupid statement," she said.

"What I am going to prove is that I mean you no harm."

It was the best he could come up with for the moment. The breeze was chilling, and he ushered her past the bridge, opening the door to the cabin.

"How are you going to do that?"

"For starters by not harming you. Let's find you something dry."

She glared at him. "I'm not taking off my dress."

He pointed inside. "You can change in the head—the bathroom. I've got some T-shirts on board and maybe some sweatpants, though they'd probably drop right off you."

"This is your boat?"

"Of course it's my boat. Whose boat did you think it was?"

She passed through the door and stopped between the sofa and the kitchenette. "I thought maybe you stole it."

"I'm not a thief."

"You're a kidnapper."

He realized she'd made a fair point. "Yeah, well, that's the sum total of my criminal activity to date." He started working on his soggy tie. "If you let me get past you, I'll see what I can find."

She shrank out of his way against the counter.

He turned sideways to pass her, and their thighs brushed together. She arched her back to keep her breasts from touching his chest. It made things worse, because her wet cleavage swelled above the snug, stiff fabric.

Reaction slammed through his body, and he faltered, unable to stop himself from staring. She was soaked to the skin, her auburn hair plastered to her head, her makeup smeared. And yet she was still the most beautiful woman he'd ever seen.

"Jackson," she said, her voice coming out a whisper.

He lifted his gaze to meet hers. It was all he could do to keep his hands by his sides. He wanted to smooth her hair, brush the droplets from her cheeks and run his thumb across her lips.

"Thank you," she said.

The words took him by surprise. "You're welcome," he automatically answered.

For a minute, it seemed that neither of them could break eye contact. Longing roiled inside him. He wanted to kiss her. He wanted to do so much more. And he wanted it very, very badly.

Finally, she looked away. "You better, uh…"

"Yeah," he said. "I'd better." He moved, but the touch of her thighs made him feel like he'd been branded.

Crista reached and twisted. She stretched her arms in every direction, but no matter how she contorted, she couldn't push the tiny buttons through the loops on the back of her dress.

"Come on," she muttered. Then she whacked her elbow against a small cabinet. "Ouch!"

"You okay?" came Jackson's deep voice.

He was obviously only inches from the other side of the small door, and the sound made her jerk back. Her hip caught the corner of the vanity, and she sucked in a sharp breath.

"Fine," she called back.

"I'm getting changed out here."

"Thanks for the warning." An unwelcome picture bloomed in her mind of Jackson peeling off his dress shirt, revealing what had to be washboard abs and muscular shoulders. She'd clung to him in the ocean and again climbing onto the boat. She'd felt what was under his dress shirt, and her brain easily filled in the picture.

She shook away the vision and redoubled her efforts with the buttons. But it wasn't going to happen. She couldn't get out of the dress alone. She had two choices—stay in the soaking-wet garment or ask him for help. Both were equally disagreeable.

She caught a glimpse of herself in the small mirror. The wedding gown was stained and torn. She crouched a little, cringing at the mess of her hair. It was stringy and lopsided. If she didn't undo the braids and rinse out the mess from the lake water she'd probably have to shave it off in the morning.

"Are you decent?" she called through the door.

"Sure," he answered.

She opened the small door, stepped over the sill, and Jackson filled her vision. The cabin was softly lit around him. His hair was damp, and his chest was bare. A pair of worn gray sweatpants hung on his hips. As she'd expected, his abs were washboard hard.

"What happened?" he asked, taking in her dress.

"I can't reach the buttons."

He gave an eye roll and pulled a faded green T-shirt over his head. "I'll give you a hand."

She turned her back and steeled herself for his touch. The only reason she was letting him near her was that it was foolish to stay cold and uncomfortable in a ruined dress. She told herself that if he was going to kill her, he would have just let her go under. Instead, he'd saved her life.

His footfalls were muffled against the teak floor as he came up behind her. The sound stopped, and he drew in an audible breath. Then his fingertips grazed her skin above the top button, sending streaks of sensation up her spine. Her muscles contracted in reaction.

What was the matter with her? She wasn't attracted to him. She was appalled by him. She wanted to get away from him, to never see him again.

But as his deft fingers released each button, there was no denying her growing arousal. It had to be some pathetic version of Stockholm syndrome. If she'd paid more attention in her psychology elective, she might know how to combat it.

The dress came loose, and she clasped her forearms against her chest to keep it in place.

"That should do it," he said.

There was a husky timbre to his voice—a sexy rasp that played havoc with her emotions.

"Thanks," she said before she could stop herself. "I mean…" She turned to take the sentiment back, and her gaze caught with his. "That is…"

They stared at each other.

"I don't usually do this," he said.

She didn't know what he meant. He didn't usually kidnap women, or he didn't unbutton their wedding gowns?

She knew she should ask. No, she shouldn't ask. She should move now, lock herself in the bathroom until her emotions came under control.

But he slowly lifted his hand. His fingertips grazed her shoulder. Then his palm cradled her neck, slipping up to her hairline. The touch was smooth and warm, his obvious strength couched by tenderness.

She couldn't bring herself to pull away. In fact, it was a fight to keep from leaning into his caress.

He dipped his head.

She knew what came next. Anybody would know what came next.

His lips touched hers, kissing her gently, testing her texture and then her taste. Arousal instantly flooded her body. He stepped forward, his free arm going around her waist, settling at the small of her back, strong and hot against her exposed skin.

He pressed harder, kissed her deeper. She met his tongue, opening, drowning in the sweet sensations that enveloped her.

Good thing she didn't marry Vern today.

The thought brought her up short.

She let out a small cry and jerked away.

What was the matter with her?

"What are you doing?" she demanded, tearing from his hold.

Her dress slipped, and she struggled to catch the bodice. She was a second too late, and she flashed him her bare breasts.

His eyes glowed, and his nostrils flared.

"Back off," she ordered, quickly covering up.

"You kissed me too," he pointed out.

"You took me by surprise."

"We both know that's a lie."

"We do not," she snapped, taking a step away.

"Whatever you say."

"I'm *engaged*."

"So I've heard," he drawled. "Are you sure that's what you want?"

She couldn't seem to frame an answer.

If not for Jackson, she'd already be married to Vern.

They'd be at the reception, cutting the enormous cake and dancing to Strauss's *Snowdrops*, Delores's favorite waltz. Crista's knees suddenly felt weak, and she sat down on the padded bench beside her.

"The thought of being married makes you feel faint?" Jackson asked.

"I'm worried about my mother-in-law. I can't even imagine how she reacted. All those guests. All that planning. What did they do when I didn't show up? Did they all just go home?"

"You're not worried about Vern?"

"Yes, I'm worried about Vern. Quit putting words in my mouth."

"You never said his name."

"Vern, Vern, Vern. I'm worried sick about Vern. He's going through hell." Then a thought struck her. "You should call him. *I* should call him. I can at least let him know I'm all right."

"I can't let you use my phone."

"Because then they'd discover it was you. And they'd arrest you. And you'd go to jail. You know, sooner than you're already going to jail after I tell the police everything you did." Crista paused. Maybe she wouldn't tell them *everything*. Better to keep certain missteps off the public record.

"I've got five guys working on this." Jackson lowered himself to the bench opposite, the compact table between them.

"Five guys working on what?" Her curiosity was piqued.

"Vern's infidelity."

"Vern wasn't unfaithful."

Jackson smirked. "Right. And you never kissed me too."

Crista wasn't about to lie again. "Just tell me what you want. Whatever is going on here, let's please get this over with so I can go home."

"I want you to wait here with me while I find out exactly what your husband-to-be has been up to with Gracie."

"Gracie's a business acquaintance." Crista immediately realized her slipup.

Jackson caught it, too. "So, you do know her."

Crista wasn't about to renew the debate. She knew what she knew, and she trusted Vern.

"Why are you doing this?" she asked Jackson again.

"So you can decide whether or not you want to marry him."

"I *do* want to marry him."

His gaze slipped downward, and she realized her grip on her dress had relaxed. She was showing cleavage—a lot of cleavage. She quickly adjusted.

"Maybe," he said softly.

"There's no maybe about it."

"What's the harm in waiting?" he asked, sounding sincere. "The wedding's already ruined."

"Thanks to you."

"My point is there's no harm in waiting a few more hours."

"Except for my frantic fiancé."

Jackson seemed to think for a moment. "I can have someone call him, tell him you're okay."

"From a pay phone?" she mocked.

"Who uses pay phones? We've got plenty of burner phones."

"Of course you do."

"You want me to call?"

"Yes!" But then she thought about it. "No. Hang on. What are you going to tell him?"

"What do you want me to tell him?"

"The truth."

"Yeah, that's not going to happen."

"Then tell him I'm okay. Tell him something unexpected came up. I'm…uh…" She bit down on her lower lip. "I don't know. Other than the truth, what can I possibly say that doesn't sound terrible?"

"You got me."

"He'll think I got cold feet."

"He might."

"No, he won't." She shook her head firmly. Vern knew her better than that. He knew she was committed to their marriage.

But Jackson would never send a message that incriminated himself. And anything else could make it sound like it had been her decision to run off. Maybe it was better to keep silent.

"How long do you think this will take?" she asked. "To clear Vern's name?"

Jackson gave a shrug. "It could go pretty fast. My guys are good."

Crista rose to her feet. "Then don't call him. I'm going to change."

"Good idea."

"It doesn't mean I've capitulated."

"I took it to mean you wanted to be dry."

"That's exactly what it means."

"Okay," he agreed easily.

She turned away from his smug expression, gripping the front of her ruined wedding dress, struggling to hold on to some dignity as she made her way into the bathroom. She could feel his gaze on her back, taking in the expanse of bare skin. He knew she wasn't wearing a bra, and he could probably see the white lace at the top of her panties.

A rush of heat coursed through her. She told herself it was anger. She didn't care where he looked, or what he thought. It was the last he'd see of her that was remotely intimate.

Three

Jackson recognized Mac's number and put his phone to his ear. "Find something?"

"Norway talked to the girl," said Mac.

"Did she admit to the affair?"

"She says there's nothing between them. But she's lying. And she's doing it badly. Norway got thirty seconds alone with her phone and grabbed some photos."

That was encouraging. "Anything incriminating?"

"No nudity, but they do look intimate. Gerhard's got an arm around her shoulders, and his expression says he slept with her. We're combing through social media now."

"Good. Keep me posted."

"How are things at your end?"

Crista emerged from the bathroom. Her hair was still wet but combed straight. She'd washed her face, and she was dressed in Jackson's white and maroon U of Chicago soccer jersey. It hung nearly to her knees, which were bare, as were her calves.

"Pants didn't fit?" he asked.

"Huh?" asked Mac.

"Fell off," she said.

"Stay safe," Jackson said to Mac, setting down his phone.

"Who's that?" asked Crista, moving to the sofa. She took the end opposite to Jackson and tucked the hem of the jersey over her knees.

"Mac."

"He works for your agency?"

"He does."

She nodded. She looked curious but stayed silent.

"Are you afraid to ask?" he guessed.

She flicked back her damp hair. "I'm not afraid to ask anything."

"They found some pictures of Vern and Gracie."

"You're bluffing."

"They're not specifically incriminating—"

"I know they're not."

"But they are suggestive of more than a business relationship."

"If suggestive is all you've got, then let me go."

"It's all we've got *so far*." He glanced at his watch. "We've only been chasing this lead for five hours."

She heaved an exaggerated sigh.

"You hungry?" he asked.

He was, and he doubted brides were inclined to eat heartily before their weddings.

"No," she said.

"You really need to stop lying."

"*You're* criticizing *my* behavior?"

"You're not going to help anything by starving."

He rose, taking the few steps to the small kitchen and popping open a high cupboard.

"You're not going to make me like you," she said from behind him.

"Why would I want to make you like me?"

He wanted to convince her not to marry Vern. No, scratch that. He couldn't care less if she married Vern. No, scratch that, too. Vern didn't deserve her. If Jackson was sure of one thing in all this, it was that Vern didn't deserve a woman like Crista.

"To make me more docile and easy to manipulate."

Jackson located a stray bag of tortilla chips. "Docile? You? Are you kidding me?"

Her tone turned defensive. "I'm really quite easy to get along with. I mean, under normal circumstances."

He also found a jar of salsa. It wasn't much, but it would

keep them from starving. If they were lucky, they'd find a few cans of beer in the mini fridge.

He turned back.

She froze, her expression a study in guilt, his phone pressed to her ear.

He swore, dropping the food, taking two swift steps to grab it from her. How could he have made such an idiotic mistake?

"Nine-one-one operator," came a female voice through the phone. "What is your emergency?"

He hit the end button. "What did you do?"

"Tried to get help." Her words were bold, but she shrank back against the sofa.

Jackson hit the speed dial for Mac.

"Yeah?" Mac answered immediately.

"I have to move. This phone is compromised. Tuck's dock, zero eight hundred."

"Roger that," said Mac.

Jackson pushed open a window and tossed the phone overboard.

"That was stupid," he said to Crista.

"I was trying to escape. How was that stupid?"

"*You* were reckless. *I* was stupid."

He grasped her arm and pulled her to her feet.

"Hey," she cried.

"Listen, I'm still not going to hurt you, but you had no way of knowing that for sure. I could have been a vengeful jerk." He tugged her to the bridge, holding fast to her upper arm while he started the engine and engaged the anchor winch.

Her tone turned mulish. "I had to try."

"I shouldn't have given you the chance."

"You let your guard down."

"I did. And that was stupid."

Not to mention completely unprofessional. He wasn't sure

what had distracted him. Their kiss? Her legs? The sight of her in his jersey?

He'd have to worry about it later. Right now, he couldn't take a chance on an overzealous 911 operator tracing their location. Anchor up, he opened the throttle, and they surged forward.

She swayed, but he held her steady.

"You were trying to be nice," she said.

He struggled not to laugh at that. "You're trying to make me feel better about being stupid?"

"I'm saying… I'm not unappreciative of you offering me something to eat."

"Well, I'm definitely unappreciative of you compromising our location."

He set a course north along the coastline. His friend Tuck Tucker owned a beach house north of the city. Tuck wouldn't mind Jackson using his dock. He might mind the kidnapping part, but Jackson didn't plan to mention that. And if Mac and the others didn't come through with proof positive by morning, Tuck's reaction would be the least of Jackson's worries.

"Where are we going?" Crista asked.

Jackson did chuckle at that. "Yeah, sure. I'm going to tell you."

"It's not like we still have a phone." As she spoke, her gaze flicked to the radio.

"I'll be disconnecting the battery to that long before I take my eyes off you," he told her.

"What are you talking about?"

"You just looked at the radio. You might as well be wearing a neon sign that says it's your next move."

She drew an exasperated sigh and shifted her feet.

"You probably don't want to consider a life of crime," he said.

She lifted her chin and gave her damp hair a little toss. "I'm surprised you did."

"It's been a surprising day."

"Not exactly what I expected, either."

He'd have to hand her the win on that one.

He switched screens on the GPS, orienting himself to the shoreline.

"I'm hoping you'll thank me later," he said.

"Hoping? You don't seem as confident as before."

"The stakes just keep getting higher and higher. Now we're headed for the state line."

Her attention swung from the windshield to him. "You're taking me to *Wisconsin*?"

"What's wrong with Wisconsin?"

"It's a long way from Chicago. Why are you taking me there? What's happening?" She struggled to get away from him.

He regretted frightening her again. They weren't really going all the way to Wisconsin.

"I didn't plan to grab you today," he told her. "I was only there to get a look at Gerhard."

"Why?"

"To take his measure."

"I mean why do you care about us at all?"

"It's a job."

"Who hired you?"

"It doesn't matter. What matters to you is that your fiancé is already having an affair. You can't marry a man like that." Jackson wasn't ready to tell her more. Mention of her father would likely alienate her further. He didn't yet have proof of Trent's accusations. And if she was having trouble accepting that Vern would cheat, she'd never believe he was conning her.

"He's not like that. I don't know where you even came up with that idea."

She'd stopped struggling against his grip, and that was good. Her fear seemed to have been replaced by anger. Jackson's guilt eased off.

"Wedding guests," he said, opening the throttle to increase their speed. It was a clear, relatively calm night, thank goodness. They needed to put distance between them and the position where Crista had made the call.

"*My* wedding guests?"

"Technically, I would say they were Vern's wedding guests. They seemed to know him, and they were joking about his relationship with Gracie. I realized I couldn't in good conscience let you marry him, so I took the opportunity and grabbed you."

She was silent for a moment. "So this isn't so much crime as altruism."

"Yes. The easiest thing for me would have been to walk away."

"You can still walk away."

"We're on a boat."

"Swim away, then. Or drop me off onshore and drive away—motor away? Float away? What do you call it?"

"Navigate away. And no, I'm not dropping you off onshore." He made a show of looking her up and down, enjoying the view far too much. "You're not dressed, for one thing."

"I'll put my wedding dress back on. It might be uncomfortable, but it's better than staying here."

"I'd get thrown in jail," he said.

"Darn right. But that's going to happen anyway."

"Not for a few hours." And hopefully not ever, although Jackson's worry factor was steadily rising.

"How long until we get there?" she asked.

"Get where?"

"To the secret location, wherever it is you're taking me. How long until we stop navigating?"

"Why?"

"Because I'm hungry."

"Oh, now you're hungry. Well, you're going to have to wait."

"I can eat while you navigate."

"I'm not letting go of you."

"I'm not going to jump."

"That's what I thought last time."

"We're way too far from shore."

"Yeah, but I'm sure you've got another brilliant plan in mind already. Sabotage the engine, harpoon me from behind."

"You have harpoons on board?"

"Give me strength," he muttered.

She leaned close to him. "Am I annoying you? Frustrating you?"

"Yes on both counts."

Her argumentative nature was annoying, but his frustration came from a whole other place. She was stimulating and exciting. She was a beautiful, feisty, apparently complex and intelligent woman, and he was battling hard against his sexual attraction to her. He didn't want to be rushing from a crime scene with her as his captive, contemplating the best way to stay out of jail. He wanted to be on a date with her, somewhere great in the city, contemplating how best to get her into his bed.

"There's a simple solution," she told him.

It took a second for him to get his brain back on track. "Let you go?" he guessed.

"Bingo."

"Not until we meet up with Mac tomorrow."

"You'll let me go then?"

He knew he was being cornered, but there really was no choice. He could only hope Mac could come up with definitive proof by morning.

"Yes," said Jackson.

Crista's mouth curved into a dazzling smile. They hit a swell, and she pressed against him. Her curves were soft, and her scent was fresh. For a moment the risk of jail seemed almost worth it.

* * *

When Crista awoke, she was disoriented. It took a few seconds to realize the warm body beside her wasn't Vern. She was in bed with someone bigger, harder, with a deeper breathing pattern and an earthier scent. And the bed was moving beneath them.

Then reality came back in a rush. Long after midnight, she'd given in and laid down on the bed in the bow of Jackson's boat. He was still up, and she'd hugged one edge of the massive, triangular shape in case he decided to join her. At some point he obviously had, and in her sleep she must have moved to the middle.

Now she was cradled by his strong arm, hers thrown across his chest. And her leg…uh-oh. Her leg was draped across his thighs. The jersey had ridden up to her waist. Luckily, he was wearing sweatpants. Otherwise, there'd be nothing between them but the lacy silk of her white panties.

She knew she should move. She had to move. And she needed to do it before he woke up and caught her in such a revealing position. Now that she thought about it, she should have recoiled from him the second she was conscious.

Staying put like this was bad. The fact that she liked it was even worse. She was an engaged woman. She was all but married. She had absolutely no business enjoying the intimate embrace of another man, no matter how fit his body, no matter how handsome his face and no matter how sexy his warm palm felt against her hip.

It was all she could do not to groan out loud.

Jackson moved and she drew a sharp breath.

"Hey, there," he whispered lazily in her ear, obviously only half-awake himself, obviously believing she was someone else.

Then he kissed her hairline.

"I—" she began. But he kissed her mouth. And his arms closed around her.

Before she could gather her wits enough to struggle, the

kiss deepened. A fog of desire invaded her brain, blocking out the real world.

He was one fantastic kisser.

His hand slipped down to cradle her rear. Pulling her to him, his thigh wedged between her legs. Arousal fanned through her, hot, heavy and demanding.

She had to make this stop. She so had to shut this down.

"Jackson," she gasped. "I'm not your date. Wake up. It's me. It's Crista."

"I know." He drew back, gazing at her with dark eyes. "I know who you are."

"But—"

"And you know I'm not Gerhard."

She wanted to deny it. She desperately wanted to lie and say that, of course, she'd thought he was her fiancé. What kind of a woman would behave like this with another man? But she couldn't bring herself to lie, not with his sharp stare only inches away, and their hearts beating together.

"I was confused," she replied instead.

He answered with a knowing smile. "Confused about what?"

"Who you were."

He shook his head. "Crista, Crista. There's no real harm in not being truthful with me. But I hope you're being honest with yourself."

"I am being honest with myself."

"You claim you love Gerhard, yet you're in bed with a stranger."

"I'm not in bed with you." She immediately realized how ridiculous the protest sounded. "I mean, not like that. We didn't... We aren't..."

He glanced down between them, noting without words that they were in each other's arms.

She quickly pulled back, wriggling to get away from him.

A pained expression came over his face. "Uh, Crista, don't—"

"What?" Had she hurt him?

"The way you're moving."

And then she realized what he meant. They might be mostly dressed, but she could feel every nuance of his body. Raw arousal coursed through her all over again. She felt her face heat in embarrassment.

"However you have to move. Whatever you have to do. Just do it," she demanded hoarsely.

He cupped a palm under her knee, lifting her leg from his body and lowering it to the mattress. But his hand lingered on her thigh.

She closed her eyes, steeling herself. What was the matter with her? "Please," she whispered.

"You're going to have to be more specific." His husky voice amped up her arousal.

"We can't." But she wanted to. She couldn't remember ever wanting a man so intensely.

"We won't," he said and gathered her into his arms all over again.

She didn't protest. Instead, she reveled in the security of his strength. Yesterday had been a nightmare of fear, disappointment and confusion. It had all been Jackson's fault. But for some reason that didn't seem to matter. He was still a comfort.

"Mac will be here in a few minutes," said Jackson.

"Is he going to swim?" she asked.

"I docked the boat last night after you fell asleep."

"You mean I could have escaped?"

"You'd have had to get out of my bed without waking me. But, yeah, you could have escaped."

Crista heaved a sigh. "This isn't normal. My reaction to these circumstances," she said.

"It doesn't feel normal to me, either." He scooted to the end of the bed and stood.

"Jackson?" A man's voice came from beyond the small hatch door.

She jerked back, quickly adjusting her jersey over her thighs.

"We'll be right out," Jackson called. To Crista he said, "You didn't do anything wrong."

"Yes, I did."

He was right about one thing—she should stop lying to herself. She might love Vern, but she'd just kissed the heck out of another man. Maybe fear and stress had combined to mess with her hormones, but what she'd done was absolutely, fundamentally wrong.

Jackson slipped a T-shirt over his head. "Forget about it."

"Are you really going to let me go?" She forced herself to think ahead.

If she could make a phone call, Vern would pick her up. She didn't have her purse, no cash or credit cards or her phone. She'd have to change back into her ruined wedding dress before he got here. Man, was he going to be ticked off about that.

"After you look at what Mac found, yes, I'll let you go."

"Good." She struggled to summon her pride as she rose from the bed.

She followed Jackson up a couple of steps and ducked through the hatch to the main cabin. There she found Mac, a tall, bulky man with broad shoulders, who had a heavy brow and a military hairstyle. Jackson looked almost urbane by comparison. The contrast to Vern would be startling.

"Mac," said Jackson with a nod. "This is Crista Corday."

"Miss Corday," said Mac. His voice was as rugged as his appearance.

"I think we can skip the formality of *Miss* Corday, since you participated in my kidnapping."

"Mac had nothing to do with it," said Jackson.

"He does now," said Crista. She was telling Vern and the police everything. Jackson and his gang of men should not be allowed to roam free.

"I've got the photos," said Mac, stepping forward.

He held out his phone so she could see the screen. The first one was taken on a busy street. It was Vern, all right. Despite herself, she leaned in for a closer look.

He walking side by side with a woman, presumably Gracie. They seemed to be exiting a restaurant. The woman was tall, with a bouncy mane of wavy blond hair. Her makeup was dark—thick, sparkly liner and a coating of mascara emphasizing her bright blue eyes. Her lips were full, her bust fuller, and her waist was tiny beneath a white tank top. The next photo showed that she wore blue leather pants and black, spike–heeled ankle boots.

"They're just walking," said Crista.

She'd allow that Gracie didn't look like your average commercial real estate client, but looks could be deceiving. One thing was for certain, she was a polar opposite of Crista.

"Wait for it," said Mac. He scrolled to another picture.

Here they were holding hands, then cuddling, then Vern was kissing her on the cheek. It was persuasive, but Crista had played with Photoshop software. She knew that pictures could be manipulated. There were also other logical problems.

"Why would he marry me?" she asked.

Gracie was drop-dead, glamour-magazine, movie star–material stunning.

"What do you mean?" asked Jackson, looking genuinely puzzled.

Crista gestured to the photo. "If there's really something romantic between them, why not marry her? She's a knock-out. And he seems to like her well enough." The two were smiling and laughing in most of the pictures.

Both Mac and Jackson were frowning at her.

"What?" she asked, looking from one to the other.

"He wants you," said Jackson.

"Which means he isn't involved with her," Crista said slowly, making sure he could understand each of her words.

"Look at this," said Mac.

He produced a picture where the two were embracing. It was nighttime, and they were dressed differently. It had been taken in front of a hotel.

"April of this year," said Mac. "It's date stamped."

Crista would admit it looked damning. *If* she believed it hadn't been altered, and *if* she believed the date stamp was valid. She was about to mount another argument in Vern's defense when she realized this was her ticket home. If Jackson thought he'd won, he'd let her go.

She gave herself a moment. She had to deliver this just right.

She took the phone from Mac's hand. She stared at the photo for a long time, pretending she was having an emotional reaction. Then she gripped the back of the bench seat that curved around the table. She lowered herself down.

"It looks bad," she said in a hushed voice.

"It is what it seems," said Mac. "I also have some emails."

Crista gave what she hoped was a shaky nod, still playacting. As if emails weren't even easier to fake than photos.

She made a show of swallowing, then she set the phone down on the table. She tried to put a catch into her voice. "I guess you were right."

"I wish I could say I was sorry."

"Don't you start lying."

To her surprise, Jackson put a comforting hand on her shoulder. "He doesn't deserve you, Crista."

"I never would have believed it," she said. "He cheated on me. He's been cheating on me the entire time. I'm such an idiot." For good measure, she pulled off her engagement ring and squeezed it in her palm.

"It's not your fault," said Jackson.

She didn't answer. If she had Jackson convinced that she'd bought his story, it was time to shut up and let it lay. It was also time to get herself out of here and back to Vern. He had to be frantic. She'd reassure him she was safe, and then she'd tell him everything. Jackson and Mac deserved whatever they got.

"Will you let me go now?" she asked.

She could feel their hesitation, but she was afraid to look up and gauge their expressions. Had she seemed too easy to convince? She hoped she hadn't overplayed her hand.

It was Jackson who spoke. "I'll drive you home."

Four

Crista had asked to be taken directly to the Gerhard mansion. Fine by Jackson. He looked forward to seeing the expression on Gerhard's face when she dumped him.

Once she'd broken it off, he'd report the success to Colin and Trent and go back to his regular life. At least, he ought to go directly back to his regular life. But he wasn't sure how quickly he wanted to walk away from her.

He found himself strongly attracted to her. But more than that, he was intrigued by her. She couldn't have had an easy life. Her father was a criminal like Jackson's. Yet, here she was, running a business, hobnobbing with Chicago's elite, almost marrying into one of the city's wealthy families.

She was obviously a survivor, and from what he'd seen of her, she was tough. She'd jumped into the bay, for goodness' sake, planning to swim for it to save herself. Okay, so maybe she was more reckless than clever. But the same could be said of him.

"Their driveway is the next right," she said.

She'd redressed in her damp wedding gown, which was now stark against the black leather seat of the Rush Investigations SUV. Jackson appreciated the drama of the visual—breaking your engagement in a ruined wedding gown—but he doubted she was thinking about that. She likely just wanted to get it over with. He couldn't say he blamed her.

He swung the vehicle into the driveway, passing a pair of brick pillars. They had lions on them. Who did that? Then he steered around the curves of a smooth, oak-lined driveway.

A quarter mile in, the mansion came into view. It was a rambling stone building, three stories high, sprawling in the center of manicured lawns and colorful flower beds. The driveway circled around a cherub fountain. Water spurted from three statues, foaming into a concrete pond.

"I should tell you," said Crista, her tone flat as he pulled to the curb and stopped in front of the grand staircase. "Just so you understand what's coming next." She angled her body to look at him. "I didn't buy it, not for a second."

He shifted to Park, his brain sorting through her words for some kind of logic. "Buy what?"

"The fake pictures of Vern. I'm sure the fake emails were just as creative."

Jackson saw where she was going, and it was nowhere good.

"I'm turning you in," she continued. Then she made a show of shoving her engagement ring back on her finger. "I'm telling them everything, and I'm not sorry." She swung open the door.

He lunged for her, but the shoulder belt brought him up short.

"Don't do that." He tore off his seat belt and leaped out of the car.

She moved fast considering her spiky shoes and the awkward dress. He rushed to catch up with her.

"They weren't fake," he said, kicking himself for having been taken in like a chump. He'd let his mind get ahead of events instead of properly focusing on the moment. He'd let himself project forward, debating whether to offer her comfort right away or wait a decent period of time before asking her out on a date. Distracted by his attraction to her, he'd missed the signs that she was lying.

At the top of the stairs, she rounded on him. "You think I don't know my own fiancé."

"Crista—"

"No."

"Crista?" A man spoke from the doorway behind her.

"Vern," she gasped in obvious relief, a smile coming over her face.

Her steps quickened, and her arms went out, obviously expecting to rush into his embrace.

But Gerhard was frowning.

"Wait until I tell—" she began.

"What were you *thinking*?" he demanded on a roar. "And who is this guy?"

She stopped short. Jackson's instincts told him to leave. His duty was done. He was risking arrest and imprisonment by staying.

"Your dress is absolutely ruined." Gerhard gestured to the soiled and torn gown.

And your fiancée is safe, Jackson wanted to shout out.

Crista drew back, obviously shocked by the reaction. "I—"

"Do you have any idea what Mother has been through?" asked Gerhard.

Jackson waited for Crista to say that she'd been through something, too. He took a reflexive step away, telling himself to make good his escape before she could tell the story of how she'd been kidnapped and held against her will.

"Mother was *mortified*," said Vern. "She nearly collapsed right there in the church. She hasn't come out of her room all morning. The doctor's with her now."

"It wasn't my—"

"Three hundred people," Gerhard interjected. "The mayor was there, for God's sake. And who is this?" Vern's beady black eyes peered in Jackson's direction.

Jackson stepped forward, his sense of justice winning over his instinct for self-preservation. "Do you even want to know what happened?"

"It doesn't take a rocket scientist to figure out what *happened*." Gerhard's attention turned back to Crista. "She got scared. Well, sweetheart, we all get scared. But you don't get scared two minutes before the wedding. You do it the day before, and we talk about it. Or do you do it the day after, and we get a divorce."

Crista's posture sagged. "A divorce?"

Jackson took her elbow, afraid she might go down.

"You'd want a divorce?" she asked Gerhard in a tone of amazement.

"There are ways to do this," he answered. "And this wasn't one of them."

"That's not what happened," said Jackson.

She grasped the hand on her elbow. "Don't."

"Crista didn't get scared," he said. "I'm the one who stopped your wedding."

"Let it go," she whispered. "Don't do it."

He glanced down at her expression. It looked like she'd changed her mind and didn't want him to confess. Well, that worked fine for him.

"Just who are you?" Gerhard demanded again.

"I'm an old boyfriend," he said, crafting a story on the fly. "I showed up at the church. I begged her for another chance. I told her she couldn't marry you until we'd talked."

Vern's jaw went tight. There was anger in his expression, but it didn't exactly look like jealousy. "You ran off with another man?"

"I insisted," said Jackson, bracing for Vern to come at him. If the tables had been turned and Crista had been his bride, Jackson would have taken the man's head off.

Gerhard didn't move. His attention swung back to Crista. "What do you expect me to do?"

"I don't care what you do," she said, determination returning to her tone.

Gerhard took a step forward, and Jackson stepped between them. "Don't touch her."

"Crista, get in the house."

Jackson countered. "Crista, get in the car."

"Mother and Father are owed an explanation," said Gerhard.

"You weren't even interested in her explanation," said Jackson.

"Get out of my way."

"No." Jackson had no intention of leaving Crista behind.

"This is none of your business."

"I'm making it my business."

Gerhard took another step.

Jackson braced his feet apart, willing the guy to take a swing. All he needed was an excuse, and he'd wipe the cocky confidence right off Gerhard's face.

"Please don't hurt him," said Crista.

"Okay," said Jackson.

"She's talking to me," said Gerhard.

Jackson couldn't help but smile at that.

"Please," Crista repeated.

"Get in the car," said Jackson.

"You won't?" she asked.

"I won't," he promised.

"We are not done talking," Gerhard called to Crista.

"Oh, yes, you are." Jackson listened to her footfalls until she slammed the passenger door.

"Make any move, and I'll defend myself," he told Gerhard.

Gerhard didn't look like he was going to try.

Still, Jackson kept an eye over his shoulder as he returned to the vehicle. Half of him hoped Gerhard would come at him. But the smarter half just wanted to get Crista away from this family.

He planted himself behind the wheel.

"Just take me home," she said, yanking her dress into place around her legs.

He started the engine and put the vehicle into gear. "You got it."

They drove away in silence.

It was five minutes before she spoke up. "You know where you're going?"

"I know where you live." He checked his rearview mirror again, making a mental note of vehicles in the block behind them.

"How do you know that?"

"Mac gave me the address."

"Mac, who was investigating Vern."

"Yes."

Both a blue sedan and a silver sports car stayed with them at the left turn.

"This is creepy, you know that?"

"I don't imagine it's any fun," said Jackson.

"You've destroyed my life."

He gave her a quick glance. "You're blaming me?"

"Of course I'm blaming you."

"Because your fiancé's a jerk?"

"Because you ruined my wedding." She paused for a moment. "It's not your fault my fiancé's a jerk."

Jackson almost smiled as he checked the side mirror.

"I don't know what that was all about," she said.

"Maybe he's not the man you thought he was."

"He's never done that before. He's very even tempered, patient, trusting."

"Is this the first time you've seen him under stress?" Jackson was no expert, but he couldn't help but think it was a bad idea to marry someone before you'd had a few knock-down, drag-out fights. A person needed to know who fought dirty and who fought clean.

"Vern's family is important to him," she said.

"You're defending that behavior?"

"He didn't cheat on me."

"He did. But that's not the point. He didn't trust you. He didn't ask you what happened to you. All he cared about was Mommy and Daddy."

Crista didn't seem to have an answer for that.

"We're being tailed," said Jackson.

"What?"

"Tailed. There's a car following us. What does Gerhard drive?"

She twisted her head to look behind them.

"Three back," said Jackson. "The blue Lexus."

"It could be."

"You're not sure?" Who didn't recognize her own boyfriend's car?

"The Gerhards own a lot of cars. I think they have one like that."

"The tribulations of the rich and famous," Jackson drawled.

"Ha-ha."

"What do you want me to do?"

"I sure don't want to talk to him again."

"Good." Jackson was even more concerned than before. Trent had claimed Gerhard's real interest was a diamond mine. And Gerhard sure hadn't acted like a man afraid for his fiancée's safety. He'd acted like a man with something to lose—maybe money to lose. And now, instead of stewing in his own self-righteousness or giving her a chance to cool down, he was having her followed. This did not strike Jackson as a typical lovers' quarrel.

"Want me to lose the tail?" he asked Crista.

"Can you?"

He smiled to himself. "I can."

"Yes. Do it."

"Seat belt tight?"

"Yes."

"Hang on."

Seeing an intersection coming up, Jackson barged his way across two lanes, moving hard to the left, cutting the yellow way too close and turning onto Crestlake. From there, he took a quick right, drove until they were behind a high-rise and pulled into an underground parking lot.

Crista held on as they bounced over the speed bumps.

He knew the lot had six exits. He took Ray Street, covered

three blocks to the park and pulled onto the scenic drive. It would take them over the bridge to the interstate. After that, they could get as far away as she wanted.

"Did we lose him?" she asked, stretching to look out the rear window.

"We lost him."

They'd probably lost him at the underground, but Jackson had wanted to be certain.

She tugged at the stiff neckline of her dress in obvious frustration, pulling it away from her cleavage. "I need some time to think."

She looked tired and uncomfortable.

"Is there somewhere you want to go?"

"Not to my place, that's for sure."

"You could probably use a change of clothes."

She tugged at the fabric again. "I'm getting a rash."

"We'll take the next exit, find someplace to buy you a pair of blue jeans."

"That would be a relief. I'd also like to throw this thing in a Dumpster."

Jackson liked that idea very much. "I can make that happen."

"Thanks."

"No problem."

"I mean, really. Thanks, Jackson. You didn't have to do any of this."

He shrugged. "I fix problems. You have a problem."

"You don't even know me."

He felt like he did know her, at least a little bit. And what he knew he admired. "I don't have to know you to help you."

"Most people don't think like that."

"Lucky for you, you ran into me."

Her brows rose in skepticism. "Ran into you?"

"I see an exit." He didn't want to get into any of the details of his investigation. He sure didn't want her asking again about who'd sent him.

She watched out the side window. "Looks like a shopping mall down there."

"That'll do. You want to go in and try things on or just tell me your size?"

She looked down at the billow of her skirt. "I'll wait in the car, if you don't mind."

"Worried you might attract attention?"

"The last thing I need is for someone to snap a picture and post it to social media."

He nodded in approval. He was relieved she understood she was being chased by the Gerhards. "Good call. I can see you going viral in that outfit."

She heaved a deep sigh, her cleavage catching his attention so that he nearly swerved off the exit ramp.

"I was supposed to be on a yacht today," she said. "Bobbing around the Mediterranean, sipping chardonnay, reading a celebrity magazine and working on my tan."

Mentally, Jackson added that she would have been under Gerhard's control, at the mercy of his family. His suspicions were pinging in earnest. Gerhard wasn't a worried groom. He was a thwarted con artist.

If everything Trent said was true, the Gerhards were organized and ruthless, and they sure wouldn't want to lose track of Crista. She'd been gone for twenty-four hours. There was every chance Daddy Gerhard had people on her apartment by now. They might even be watching her credit cards and bank account.

Jackson was definitely looking into the diamond mine, its size and location, its ownership, and how it could possibly have made it onto Gerhard's radar.

Crista was going to pay Jackson back for everything just as soon as she had access to her bank account.

For now, explaining that he was invoking his regular precautions, he'd put her up at the Fountain Lake Family Hotel, leaving his own credit card information with the front desk to cover her expenses. The place was full of boisterous vacationers, and it seemed like an easy place for her to blend in with the crowd. Her room was spacious, with a king-size bed, comfy sitting area, a small kitchenette and a furnished balcony overlooking the pool and a minigolf course.

She'd tried right away to call Ellie, her best friend and maid of honor, but she only got through to voice mail. It seemed far too complicated to leave a message, so she'd decided to try again later. Instead, she liberated a soft drink from the minibar and wandered onto the balcony.

The temperature was in the high eighties, but a breeze was blowing across the lake, cooling the air. She was on the third floor, so it was easy to make out the activity below, kids splashing in the pool, teenagers lounging on striped towels. There was a young couple in one of the gazebos. He was slathering suntan lotion on her bare back, playfully untying her bathing suit top.

The woman batted awkwardly at his hand to get him to stop. When he kissed the back of her neck and looped his arms around her, Crista quickly looked away. They were probably on their honeymoon.

She eased onto a rattan lounger, wishing she had a bathing suit herself. She wondered if Jackson's credit card was connected to the hotel shops as well as the restaurants. It would definitely be nice to take a swim, and since her three jewelry stores, Cristal Creations, were doing very well, it would be a simple matter to pay back every dime.

Afterward, she'd order something from the room service menu. She'd get a bottle of wine. Maybe gaze at the moon and the stars out here and get some perspective on life. She toyed with her engagement ring, twisting it around and around as she went over the confrontation with Vern.

He'd been quick to assume she'd run away. She was disappointed, of course, but she wasn't sure she could blame him completely for his reaction. It must have seemed like the most logical conclusion at the time. Though it would have been nice if he'd asked her what happened.

The worst part was that he'd suggested divorce. As if getting married and then quickly divorcing was preferable to ruining a party. He'd worried about the embarrassment to his family. He'd worried about her dress, his mother and the mayor. The only thing he didn't seem to worry about was Crista.

In the thick of the argument, it had seemed clear that it was over. But now other memories were crowding in, good memories. Did one ugly argument obliterate everything they'd shared?

On the other hand, it had been an alarming experience, seeing a side of Vern she'd never known existed. She found herself questioning the photographs, no longer completely convinced they were fake.

She took another swig of the soda. Maybe she should call him. Or maybe she should confront him in person again, flat-out ask him if he was cheating.

Maybe he'd tell her the truth. Or maybe he wouldn't. Or maybe she'd never know.

She came to her feet.

Ellie was her next phone call, not Vern. Ellie would have good advice. She always did.

Crista pulled open the glass door, entering the cool of the air-conditioned room. She was chilled for a moment, but then it felt good. She sat down on the bed and dialed nine for an outside line. Then she punched in Ellie's number.

Before the line connected, there was a knock on the door.

Crista didn't need towels or mints or anything else from a housekeeper. But she also didn't want a hotel employee barging in on her conversation. She quickly replaced the telephone receiver and went to the peephole.

It was Jackson.

Puzzled, she drew open the door. "Did you forget something?"

"Yes." He walked in without an invitation.

"Come on in," she muttered, letting the door swing shut behind him.

"I forget to tell you not to phone anyone from the room."

"Not even Ellie?"

"Who's Ellie?"

"My maid of honor."

"Not even Ellie. The Gerhards have a big security staff. They'll be covering all the angles."

"Their security staff looks after the Gerhard buildings. They don't care about Vern's love life."

"They care about what Manfred Gerhard tells them to care about."

"You're paranoid. And anyway, I thought you'd left."

"I'm not in a hurry."

"You don't have a job to get back to? A life that requires your attention?"

Instead of answering, he sat himself down on the small blue sofa. "What do you know about the Borezone Mine?"

"What's the Borezone Mine?"

"Have you ever heard of it?"

"No. Was it in the news?"

"No."

She waited for him to elaborate, but he didn't. She wondered if he was making small talk, delaying his departure for some reason. She tried to figure out why he might want to hang around.

"I won't go wild with your credit card, if that's what's got you worried," she tried.

"I'm not worried about my credit card."

"Are you worried I'll make a phone call? Because it won't matter if I do."

"Ha. Now I'm definitely worried you'll make a phone call."

"I need to talk to Ellie." What she needed was a girlfriend to listen to her fears about Vern.

"Talk to me instead."

She took the armchair cornerwise from where he sat. "Sure. I'll just sit here and bare my soul to the strange man who kidnapped me from my wedding. I can't see any downside to that."

"Good. Go ahead. Bare away."

"You're not funny."

Surely he could understand that this was traumatic for her.

"You absolutely need to call Ellie?" he asked.

"Yes."

With a shake of his head and an expression that looked like disgust, he pulled out his phone. But instead of handing it over, he dialed a number.

"What's Ellie's last name?"

"Sharpley. Why?"

"It's me," he said into the phone. "Crista needs to make a call. Ellie Sharpley." He paused, sliding an exasperated glance her way. "I know. It's a girl thing."

Crista squared her shoulders. "A girl thing?"

"Let me know when it's done."

"A *girl* thing?" she repeated.

He pocketed his phone. "What would you call it?"

"A conversation. A human thing."

"You'll be able to have one in about an hour. Are you hungry? You must be hungry."

"You must have people you talk things over with. Friends? Relationships?"

"I'm pretty independent."

"No girlfriend?" For some reason, she'd assumed he was single. But there was no reason for that assumption. Well, other than the way he'd kissed her. But he had only kissed her.

"No girlfriend," he said.

She was relieved. No, she wasn't relieved. She didn't care. His love life was nothing to her.

"Hungry?" he repeated.

She was hungry. She'd barely eaten yesterday. She'd been watching calories for weeks now, wanting a svelte silhouette in the formfitting dress. In retrospect, her waist size was the least of her worries. But now there wasn't a reason in the world not to indulge in pizza or pasta, or maybe some chocolate cake.

"I'm starving," she said. "I know it's only lunchtime, but any chance we can get a martini?"

"There's a patio café overlooking the back nine."

"Sold."

A martini wouldn't help her make a better decision, but it would relax her in the short term. Relaxed was good. She could use some relaxing.

She came to her feet. "It feels strange not to take a purse."

He rose with her, and they made their way toward the door. "You want to buy a purse?"

"I've got nothing to put in it."

"We could buy you a comb or some lipstick or something."

She couldn't help but appreciate his offer. She also couldn't help wondering about his motivation. It was strange that he was still here, stranger still that he was putting out an effort to help her.

She exited into the hallway. "Are you feeling guilty?"

He checked to see that the door had locked behind them, then fell into step beside her. "For what?"

"For destroying my life."

"Gerhard was the one trying to destroy your life."

"Jury's still out on that."

Sure, Vern had been a jerk back at the mansion. But to be fair, he'd been under stress. She could only imagine his parents' reaction to the disappearance of the bride. Poor Vern had been alone with them, bearing the brunt of their displeasure for nearly twenty-four hours.

Jackson pressed the elevator button. "The pictures are real, Crista."

"Can you prove it?"

"I'm sure we can. Let me look into the options for that."

They stepped onto the elevator, and it descended.

"We've been together for nearly a year," she said.

It wasn't a whirlwind. And it sure didn't make sense for Vern to marry her if he was involved with someone else.

"People aren't always honest, Crista."

She found herself glancing up at his expression. "Are you honest?"

He met her gaze. "I try to be."

"Well, there's a nonanswer."

"In my profession, I can't always tell everybody everything."

"So you only lie professionally."

There was a trace of amusement in his tone. "Not personally, and not recreationally."

"Interesting moral framework."

The doors slid open.

She started to move, but Jackson's hand shot out to block her, coming to rest on her stomach.

"What?"

He pulled her to one side then stabbed his finger hard on the close door button.

"What are you doing?"

The doors slid shut.

"You must have talked to someone since we've been here."

"No. Well, I tried to phone Ellie. But I got her voice mail. I didn't even leave a message."

Jackson swore as he punched twelve, the top floor.

"What?"

"Vern. He's in the lobby with a couple of guys."

"No way."

"I just saw him."

The elevator rose.

"How is that possible?"

"It's possible because your phone call connected and revealed the hotel number."

"I didn't call Vern." Wasn't Jackson listening? "I called Ellie."

"And Vern knows Ellie's number. They were monitoring her phone."

"That's ridiculous."

"You have a better explanation for him showing up here?"

She didn't. In fact, she was baffled. And she was starting to feel frightened.

"What do we do on the twelfth floor?" she asked as the numbers pinged higher.

"My room," he said.

It seemed every second threw her for another loop. "You have a room? Why would you need a room?"

"To sleep in. You can have a drink there."

"But why would you sleep here?"

"So I can drive you back to the city when you're ready."

"I thought I was going to take a bus back to the city."

"If we'd gone with that plan, Gerhard would already have you."

"Jackson, *what* is going on?"

It took him a moment to answer. He seemed to be weighing his words. "Vern Gerhard wants you back, and he has a lot of money to spend accomplishing that."

"I *was* coming back." She thought about that statement. "I mean, I might go back. I didn't break up with him. I still have his ring."

The doors opened on twelve.

"You should break up with him." Jackson gestured for her to exit first. "Take a right."

"I don't know for sure that he's done anything wrong. Well, except react badly to me wrecking a hundred-thousand-dollar wedding."

"You didn't wreck it."

"You did."

"True enough," he said.

He inserted a key card into a set of double doors at the end of the hallway.

"You don't seem to care."

"I don't care about Gerhard's money, that's for sure."

Crista stepped over the threshold, taken aback by the very well-appointed suite. She gazed around. "Used to traveling in style?"

"I thought I might need a room for a meeting."

"With me?" They needed a meeting?

"With Mac and some of the other guys. They'll be here later."

She digested that statement. "There's something you're not telling me."

"There are hundreds of things I'm not telling you."

The door swung shut behind him and he crossed to a wet bar.

"Those pictures of Vern are fake, aren't they? Is this extortion? Am I still kidnapped? Was this about money all along?"

"We have beer, wine or highballs. And I'm going to order room service. If you're set on a martini, I can have them bring one."

"That's not an answer."

It occurred to her that she might be a whole lot safer with Vern. The suite door was right behind her. She could be out of it before Jackson caught her. Could she make it to the elevator, or would he drag her back kicking and screaming?

"You're not kidnapped," he told her, exasperation clear in his tone. "I left you alone in your room for an hour."

She eased a bit closer to the double doors. "You could have been standing guard outside my door."

"I wasn't. I'm a whole lot more interested in food right now that I am in any of Gerhard's moves. You're free to leave. You've been free to leave since this morning. I took you back to their mansion. You could have stayed there."

He was right about that. She could have walked inside the mansion where the Gerhard family, not to mention a few security guards who would have been waiting. There wouldn't have been a thing Jackson could do to stop her.

She wasn't being held against her will.

"I'll take a glass of merlot," she told him. "And I'd kill for a mushroom and sausage pizza."

He smiled at that. "Coming up."

"We told Vern your name this morning," she felt compelled to point out. "He can probably find your room number."

"What makes you think I'm registered under my own name?" He uncorked a bottle of wine and gestured to a living room furniture grouping. "Probably better to stay off the patio."

"You've got me worried there's a sniper out there," she joked.

He crossed the room with two glasses of wine, setting them on opposite ends of a coffee table. "I'd say a long lens rather than a rifle. But it's healthy to be cautious."

"Of the whole family now?" She took one end of the sofa and lifted her wine.

"The whole family," said Jackson, giving her a mock toast.

She drank, anticipating the hit of alcohol and glad of it. These had been the strangest days of her life. She wished the insanity was over, but it seemed there was more to come.

Five

To Jackson's surprise, Mac wasn't alone.

There was a twentysomething woman in the hotel hallway beside him. She had short, dark hair, blue eyes, a pert nose and set of distracting, full red lips.

In five years working together, Jackson had never seen his security agent behave so unprofessionally. "You brought a *date*?"

"I'm not his date," the woman stated with a sniff of disgust.

"Ellie?" Crista called out from behind him.

"She's not my date," said Mac.

Ellie pushed past Jackson.

"She's the maid of honor," said Mac.

"And you brought her *here*?" Jackson wasn't sure if that made it better or worse.

The two women laughed and embraced.

"I've been frantic," said Ellie, her voice high. "We thought you were hurt or dead."

"She was frantic." Mac's tone was dry as he shut the door behind himself.

"Did anybody see you two come in?" asked Jackson, wondering if Mac had lost his mind. "Gerhard is definitely going to recognize the maid of honor."

"I saw him down there," said Mac. "And I saw his guys. They didn't see us."

"You're positive?"

"I'm positive."

Jackson felt a bit better.

"It's been crazy," said Crista, pulling Ellie toward the sofa. "Jackson hauled me away from the church. Then we were on a boat. I jumped off. When I finally got home, Vern was an absolute jerk about it."

"That doesn't sound like Vern."

"I *know*. He's acting weird. I'm so confused about this whole thing. But tell me what happened after I left."

As Ellie began to talk, Jackson returned his attention to Mac. "I thought you were giving her a burner phone."

"That was my plan."

"Didn't work out for you?"

Hearing Ellie's earnest tone and the pace of her speech, Jackson thought he could understand why.

"Not so much," said Mac.

"Talked you into the ground."

"Something like that."

"Drink?" asked Jackson.

"A beer if you've got it."

The two men moved to the wet bar, and Mac perched himself on one of the stools.

Jackson lowered his voice, glancing to the sofa where Crista and Ellie were engrossed in conversation. "I'm buying Trent's story now. This isn't just about a runaway bride."

Mac nodded. "Those guys in the lobby look way too serious for that."

Jackson twisted the tops off two bottles of beer. "We need to look into the diamond mine."

"Norway's already on it."

Jackson was glad to hear that. "Anything jumping out at him?"

"The Borezone Mine has been around forever. Trent Corday originally bought it twenty years ago at a bargain price. He nearly lost it for noncompliance with the claim. Then he did lose a huge chunk of it, apparently on a gambling debt."

"To who?"

"That's not exactly clear. Shell companies are hiding behind holding companies. But we've confirmed he put his remaining shares in his daughter's name."

"A moment of mental clarity?" Jackson speculated, thinking it was possible Trent recognized his own incompetence with money.

"Or a moment of making amends. It sounds like he was in and out of her life over the years, never provided much in the way of monetary or any other kind of support. He wasn't exactly father of the year. On the other hand, the mine wasn't worth much at the time."

"And now?"

Trent had said there'd been a recent discovery, but that could mean a lot of things.

"Depends on who you talk to," said Mac. "A numbered Cayman Islands company currently owns the majority. We haven't been able to trace the principals behind it, but they hired an exploration company that made the latest discovery. They're hyping it as a hundred million resource, talking about going public with a share offering."

"Could all be a scam—pump the share price and dump the stock on unsuspecting investors."

"Most likely," said Mac. "But we'll keep looking."

Jackson tipped back his beer and took a drink. For Crista's sake, he hoped it was a scam. The last thing she needed was a multimillion-dollar stake in a diamond mine and a group of shady characters out to exploit her.

"Is that how Gerhard found out?" he asked. "Through the exploration company's hype?"

Mac frowned. "That's the strange part. The timing doesn't add up. The hype started six months ago. Gerhard's been with Crista for a year."

"So he found out some other way."

"Or the wedding had nothing to do with the diamond mine."

"I don't believe that for a second," said Jackson. "Those guys in the lobby tell me there's lots of money at stake."

Mac nodded. Jackson's attention switched to Crista. Vern Gerhard had targeted her for the money. Jackson was certain of it. But nothing pointed to how Gerhard found out about the mine. Jackson was missing a piece, maybe more than one. There was definitely something he didn't know, and it seemed likely it was something that could hurt Crista.

"What's next?" asked Mac.

"Norway stays on the mine." Jackson formulated an initial plan in his mind. "You take Gerhard—especially look for any link between his family and that Cayman Islands company. I'll take another look at Trent. There might be more to this story than he's let on."

"Can do," said Mac. "One question."

"What's that?"

"Has someone actually hired us for this job? I mean, besides the two convicts making eight dollars a day?"

"I can't do a favor for my father?" Jackson acknowledged that things had gone beyond the few hours of time he'd planned to spend looking into Gerhard.

"You can, but you don't." Mac looked pointedly at Crista who was smiling at Ellie. "If she wasn't a bona fide ten, would you be dedicating so many resources for free?"

"We'll never know," said Jackson. "She's not going to stop being a ten, and my curiosity's going now."

"Lots of pretty women in the world."

Jackson saw Mac's gaze shift from Crista to Ellie.

"Not a lot of diamond mines."

Mac snorted a laugh. "You don't care about a diamond mine."

"True." But Jackson was finding that he did care about Crista.

It didn't make sense, but he did care. Sure, she was beautiful. And she was in some kind of trouble. And Gerhard didn't deserve to be within a mile of her. But something else was drawing him in.

The closest he could come was that her circumstances were similar to his. She'd lost her mother as a young adult, and her father was in prison. It might be as simple as that.

They were kindred spirits. She wasn't as tough as him. She wasn't as capable of taking care of herself, and he was offended that the Gerhards had targeted her.

Ellie suddenly twisted and spoke up. "Any danger in ordering room service?"

Jackson was reminded that he and Crista were practically starving.

"None at all," he said, straightening away from the bar.

"I was all set for pizza," said Crista, seeming rather cheerful under the circumstances.

"I'm in," said Ellie.

"And chocolate cake," said Crista. "Do you think they'd have chocolate cake?"

Jackson moved to the phone on a side table. "I'll ask."

"It's not like I have to fit into that dress anymore," Crista said to Ellie.

"You can always get something a size bigger," Ellie returned on a laugh.

"I'm not going to eat that much cake."

Jackson paused with the phone in his hand, not liking where she seemed to be going.

"What do you mean?" he asked Crista.

"I mean one piece will be enough."

"I'll take one, too," said Ellie.

"Get a round," said Mac.

"You're talking about getting another wedding dress," Jackson said. "Why would you need another wedding dress?"

Crista looked back at him. "The last one got ruined, remember?"

Both Ellie and Mac disappeared from his vision as it tunneled to Crista. "But you're not getting married anymore."

"Maybe not."

"Maybe?"

"I know he was a jerk back there. But it was a stressful

situation. He had to cope with his parents and all those dignitaries. It had to be incredibly embarrassing."

Jackson took a step toward her, hardly able to believe her words. "You're defending him?"

"It wasn't his finest moment, but—"

"He's messing around on you. He's *been* messing around on you for months."

"We don't know that."

Jackson jabbed his thumb in Mac's direction. "Mac is completely trustworthy."

"I don't know Mac. I never met Mac until today."

"I know Mac."

"Well, *I* don't know you."

"You'd actually give that jerk a second chance?" Did Jackson need to rethink his involvement in all this?

"We can validate the photos," said Mac.

"Why should we do that?" Jackson demanded, annoyance getting the better of him.

"To give Crista peace of mind."

"She doesn't want to believe us, that's her problem. In fact, she can head down to the lobby right now if she thinks Gerhard is so trustworthy."

"Hang on." Ellie came to her feet. "I'm not a Vern fan. But I'd be—"

"What do you mean, you're not a Vern fan?" Crista sat up straight, obviously shocked by the statement.

Ellie seemed to realize what she'd said. Her expression turned guilty.

"Explain," said Crista. "You said you liked him."

"I do. Well, you know, sort of."

"Sort of?"

"There are things about him that I like."

Jackson eased back, waiting to see where the conversation would lead. He was relieved by Ellie's support.

"He's always generous," said Ellie. "And he's always happy."

Jackson couldn't help thinking she hadn't seen his behavior this morning.

"Maybe too happy," she continued. "It's a bit unnatural, don't you think?"

"You're criticizing him for being happy?" Crista was clearly confused by Ellie's attitude.

"There's something about him that's too polished," said Ellie. "My radar sometimes kicks in. Like, he's saying and doing all the right things, but the sincerity's not there in his eyes."

Jackson was beginning to like Ellie.

Crista came to her feet. "Why didn't you say something before now?"

"You seemed so happy," said Ellie in an apologetic tone. "I wanted it to all be true. But now..."

"You've changed your mind because of some pictures? Pictures obtained by a stranger who is obviously willing to break the law, and who has something, some scheme, going on that we don't understand."

"A scheme?" Now Jackson was offended.

Mac stepped in. "I think I'll go ahead and order. Pizza and chocolate cake?"

"All I'm saying," Ellie said, gesturing with both hands as if she was appealing for calm, "is why not verify the photos? What could it hurt?"

Crista didn't seem to have an answer for that.

Quite frankly, neither did Jackson. He knew the photos were authentic. And once Crista knew it, too, she'd start to trust him. He realized he wanted that. He wanted it too much for comfort.

That wasn't good. It wasn't good at all. His instincts with her could lead him into all sorts of trouble.

Crista savored a final bite of the moist chocolate cake decorated with decadent swirls of buttercream icing.

"I bet this was better than the wedding cake," said Ellie, licking her fork.

The two women had moved outside onto the hotel suite balcony. Now that darkness had fallen, Jackson deemed it safe to sit there. He'd pointed out that someone with night-vision binoculars in a neighboring building might still be able to make them out. But he'd admitted the likelihood of that was low.

"I wonder what they did with the wedding cake," Crista mused.

"Not to mention the crab puffs. And what about the ice sculpture?"

"I suppose they could keep it in the freezer."

"For the next wedding with a precious gems theme?"

"It was unique." Crista thought back to the geometric base and the embedded colored stones.

"I thought Mrs. Gerhard was going to have an aneurysm," said Ellie. "She turned all kinds of mottled red. Manfred was bellowing orders. Security guards were rushing all over the building, out on the sidewalk. Man, I wish I'd had my cell phone to take some video."

"Have you checked social media?" Crista hated to think it, but it seemed likely somebody had taken pictures. Vern would be mortified at having the world believe he was left at the altar.

"It'll be all over town by now," said Ellie. "The bachelor-ettes of Chicago will either be laughing at him or hauling out their push-up bras."

Having been with Vern for a year, Crista knew how many women out there were vying for his attention. He'd been de-voted to Crista, but it was clear his ego appreciated the atten-tion from others. He'd hate the thought of becoming a joke.

A clanging sound suddenly blasted through the air.

Both women jumped up, clasping their hands over their ears.

"What on earth?" asked Ellie.

Jackson immediately bolted through the balcony doorway. He grasped Crista and pulled her back into the suite. Mac was there, too, ushering Ellie inside.

"It's the fire alarm," said Jackson.

"Gerhard," said Mac.

"Trying to flush us out."

"He wouldn't do that," said Crista.

Vern was restrained and circumspect, not to mention law-abiding. He'd never pull a false fire alarm.

"He did do that," Jackson said with conviction. "And we're not going anywhere."

"You can't know it was him," she protested.

Sirens sounded in the distance.

"There are at least six fire exits in the building," said Mac.

Jackson was glancing around. "He must have brought in more men to watch them all."

"This is ridiculous," said Crista.

Jackson and Mac exchanged some kind of a knowing look.

"Uh, guys," Ellie broke in as she gaped through the open balcony door. "I see smoke out there."

That got everybody's attention. Crista wrinkled her nose, realizing she could smell it, too.

Ellie pointed. "That's definitely smoke."

Mac was outside like a shot.

"Flames," he called over his shoulder. "Fifth floor." He came back inside. "And the third floor in the other wing."

"He set two fires?" Jackson asked, half to himself.

"What now?" asked Mac.

"We *leave the building*," said Crista. Like there was any question about it.

"You take Ellie," said Jackson. "Leave through the back."

"Will do," said Mac.

"Crista and I will go through the lobby. It'll be easier to hide in the crowd than anything else."

"Good luck," said Mac. He looked to Ellie. "Let's go."

She grabbed her purse from the coffee table and gave Crista a quick hug. "I'll call you."

Crista felt like she'd been swept up in someone else's life. "Vern didn't light the building on fire."

"I hope not," said Ellie, pulling away. But her expression said she thought it was possible.

"But—" Before Crista could finish the sentence, Ellie was out the suite door with Mac.

Jackson grabbed two hand towels and doused them with water. Then he handed her one.

"Hold this over your face and cough. Pretend the smoke is bothering you."

"This is crazy."

Jackson put a hand on her back and propelled her toward the door. "He's determined."

"I was going to call him tomorrow."

"I guess he didn't want to wait."

"This is a coincidence."

"It doesn't matter," said Jackson.

"Of course it matters. You've accused my fiancé of arson." She fell silent as they left the suite.

There were other people in the hall, some quiet, some speculating about the smell of smoke, all making their way toward the staircase.

"You might want to start referring to him as your ex-fiancé," Jackson said in her ear.

"I'm still wearing his ring."

"You can take it off anytime."

He reached over her head to grab the top of the door, holding it open as she walked through then handing it off to the man behind him.

"Protocol says I have to give it back to him," said Crista as they started down.

"So, you *are* giving it back."

"I don't know. I don't know what to do. I don't even know what to think. Do I have to answer this very moment?"

"No. You just have to stick with me. And quit defending him. And put the towel over your face. We're almost there."

The lobby door was held open by successive people exiting. When they cleared the stairwell, Jackson pulled her close beside him.

"See that family?" He pointed to a man, woman and three kids out front of them.

"Yes."

"Go walk with them. Talk to the wife if you can. Gerhard's looking for a couple, so you want to pretend you're with them."

Crista had to admit, it made sense. At least it made as much sense as anything else that was going on today.

"Okay," she agreed.

"Don't look for me. I'll keep you in sight. Just go where they go, and I'll meet you outside."

She nodded.

"Now cough."

She coughed, and he gave her a little shove of encouragement. She quickened her pace and came up beside the woman who was holding the hand of the young girl.

"Did you smell the smoke?" Crista asked her.

"We were on the fifth floor," said the woman, looking stricken. "The fire was right down the hall. We had to leave everything behind."

"Bunny," said the little girl, tears in her eyes.

"Bunny will be fine," the woman whispered, voice breaking.

Crista's heart went out to the frightened girl, and she gave her a squeeze on the shoulder. "The firemen are here. They'll use their hoses to put the fire out."

A dozen firefighters in helmets and gold-colored coveralls strode across the crowded lobby.

"Will Bunny get wet?" asked the girl.

"Bunny might get wet," said Crista. "But it'll be like a bath. Is Bunny a boy or a girl?"

"A girl."

"Does she like baths?"

"I dunno."

"Do you like baths?"

The girl nodded. "Uh-huh. I get bubbles and baby froggy. He hops on the water and spits out his mouth."

"Thank you," the woman whispered in Crista's ear, obviously grateful for the distraction.

They'd come to the front doors, which were wide-open, the night air blowing inside. The drive was a maze of fire trucks, ambulances and police vehicles. Lights flashed and uniformed people rushed past. Some were on radios, some hauling hoses and other gear, and some were aiding people to stretchers or ambulances.

The hotel guests had obviously come out of the building in whatever they were wearing. Few had sweaters, many were barefoot. They looked confused and disoriented.

For a moment, Crista could only stand and stare.

She suddenly felt an arm go firmly around her shoulders. She glanced up, afraid it was Vern. But it was Jackson.

"Let's go," he said, moving her forward.

"This is awful."

"It's under control."

"He didn't do this. He couldn't have done this." The fire had to be an accident.

"I'm not going to argue with you," said Jackson, increasing their pace around the end of a fire truck.

"You don't believe me."

"That's the least of our worries. We need to get out of here. We'll never get my car from the valet, but there's a rental place a couple of blocks away."

"I should just talk to him." The sooner she got it over with, the better.

"No, you shouldn't." Taking her hand, Jackson set an angled course across the front lawn.

She had to struggle to keep up to his pace. "I'll have to talk to him eventually."

"You can phone him."

"I thought I wasn't allowed to phone anyone."

"Don't twist my words."

She came to a halt, yanking her hand from his, annoyed by his high-handed attitude. This was still her life.

"I'm not twisting your words."

He stopped, let his shoulders drop and turned back. "You'll be able to call him, just not tonight, and not on a phone with a GPS."

"I really don't mind talking to him."

She wasn't excited about it. But the prospect of a conversation didn't need to get blown all out of proportion, either. She'd sit Vern down, look him in the eyes and tell him…

She realized she didn't exactly know what she'd tell him. Would she hand him back the ring and break it off completely? Would she ask for an explanation of his behavior? Would she demand to know if he'd been faithful?

"Crista?" Jackson interrupted.

She looked up.

"You need to sleep on this."

She recognized that he was right. That had been her first instinct. She should get a good night's sleep. It would all be clearer in the morning.

She nodded her agreement and started to walk.

To her surprise, he took her hand again. But this time his touch was gentle, and he slowed his pace.

She knew she shouldn't be grateful. He was her kidnapper, not her friend, and there were all kinds of reasons she shouldn't trust him. But she found she did trust him. And at the moment, there was no denying that she also felt gratitude.

"Thank you," she said.

He glanced down as they walked. "For what this time?"

"Rescuing me from a burning building, I guess."

He grinned at that. "Sure. No problem. I had to follow you down quite a few stairs, but that's the kind of guy I am."

"What kind?" she asked, her curiosity piqued.

"What kind what?"

"What kind of guy are you? Tell me. What would you be doing right now if you weren't with me?"

"Probably working another case."

"At ten o'clock on a Sunday night?"

"Mine isn't a nine-to-five job."

She supposed it wasn't. He'd already said he didn't have a girlfriend. "What about family and friends?"

"No family. Friends, sure. But there's not a lot of time in my life for anything serious."

"When was your last girlfriend?"

"It's been a while."

She waited, but he didn't elaborate.

"You know all about my love life," she said.

"That's a professional interest."

"Well, fair's fair. Spill."

"You see that sign?" He pointed down the street.

"The car rental place?" The familiar sign flashed orange and white on the next corner.

"That's where we're going."

"Don't think you can change the subject that easily."

"It was two years ago," he said, increasing their pace. "Her name was Melanie. She's an accountant."

In Crista's mind, it didn't fit. "You dated an accountant?"

"Something wrong with that?"

"Are you making that up?"

"Why would I make it up? You don't think I can get dates?"

The suggestion was preposterous. Jackson was a smart, successful, sexy guy. He could get all the dates he wanted.

"An accountant doesn't sound very exciting," she said as they hustled across a side street to the rental car parking lot.

"Maybe I wasn't looking for exciting."

"Jackson, everything about you says you're looking for exciting."

"How so?"

"Take this weekend. You kidnapped a bride, told one of Chicago's wealthiest men to stuff it, and there's a hotel on fire behind you."

"That doesn't mean I like it." He pulled open the glass door.

"You love it." She grinned over her shoulder as she walked past him and into the small lobby.

There was a single clerk at the counter who was already helping another customer. Crista entered the roped lineup area and followed the pattern to the front, where she stopped to wait.

Jackson came up behind her.

"See that sign on the wall?" he mumbled in her ear. "Behind the counter, with the purple letters."

"That says Weekly Rates?"

"That's the one. Do not turn your head. But look at the reflection in it."

She squinted, seeing a slightly distorted black SUV.

"That's Vern," said Jackson.

She started to look behind her.

"Don't turn," he reminded her sharply.

She held still. "Are you sure?"

"Absolutely. I want you to turn and look at me. Do *not* glance out the front window. Just ask me a question."

She turned. "What question."

"Any question."

"Tell me some more about Melanie the accountant."

"Maybe later. See that hallway at the end of the counter?" He pointed.

She looked. "Yes."

"There's a ladies' room down there. I want you to walk down the hall, go past the ladies' room and out the back door.

You can cut through the alley to Greenway. Hail a cab on Greenway. I'll be out in a minute."

"We're not renting a car?"

"We're not renting a car."

"If I talk to him, it'll stop all this madness."

Before she could move, Jackson blocked her way. "It's not safe."

"I'm going to tell him to back off and that we can have a proper conversation tomorrow. He didn't light any hotel on fire."

"If the fire wasn't a ruse to flush you out, why was he waiting to follow us?"

She opened her mouth. But then she realized it was a reasonable question. Vern had to have been outside in the SUV in order to find her.

"It could have been a coincidence," she ventured. It was possible he just happened to see them leaving the hotel.

"Could have been," said Jackson, surprising her with his lack of argument.

It seemed he'd finally decided to leave it up to her. He was letting her assess the situation and make up her own mind. It was heartening but somehow unsettling.

For some reason, without Jackson's pressure, she found herself looking at both sides. She thought her way through each scenario and decided to play it safe.

"Down the hallway?" she confirmed. "Hail a cab?"

"Good decision. I'll be right behind you."

She resisted the urge to look closer at the SUV. Instead, she sauntered toward the hallway, trying to look like she was visiting the ladies' room. She didn't know how to transmit that message by the way she walked, but she did her best.

As Jackson had said, there was an exit door out the back. It led to a small parking area surrounded on two sides by a cinder-block wall. There was a Dumpster in the corner, and several vehicles in various states of disrepair.

She walked cautiously across the uneven pavement,

coming to an alleyway where she could see a driveway between two buildings that presumably led to Greenway Street.
Avoiding the puddles, she hurried down the dark driveway
to the lights of the busy street.

It took a few minutes to catch a cab. By then Jackson had
appeared, sliding into the seat beside her.

"Anthony's Bar and Grill at Baffin and Pine."

"We're going for a drink?" she asked, surprised he'd suggest something so mundane, though not really knowing what
to expect.

"I'm thirsty, aren't you?" he asked.

She wasn't yet ready to brush past their cloak-and-dagger
escape. "How did you know there was a back entrance to the
rental place? And how did you know where it would lead?"

"I didn't pick the Fountain Lake Hotel by accident."

"You've been here before," she said, glancing back while
the taxi pulled away from the curb, comprehension dawn-
ing. "You've done this before."

"I've eluded a few people in the past." His easy smile
told her he knew what he was doing. He actually seemed to
be enjoying himself.

"You think this is fun." She'd meant it to sound like an
accusation, but it didn't. Truth was, she found his confidence reassuring.

"I think you're fun."

"I'm not having fun. My life is falling apart around my
ears, so I am not having any fun at all."

"You'll like Anthony's," he said.

What she'd like was her life back. And she almost said
so. But just as quickly she realized it wasn't true. She had
no life to get back, at least not a real life, not an honest life.
There was nowhere for her to go but forward.

"I'd like a strong drink," she said instead.

"Coming up," said Jackson as the taxi picked up speed.

"This is the strangest day of my life," she muttered.

"I wouldn't trade mine for the world." His tone was unmistakably intimate, bringing with it a wave of desire that heated her chest.

She wanted to look at him, meet his warm eyes, drink in his tender smile. But she didn't dare. No matter what Vern had said or done, she had no right to feel this way about Jackson.

She fixed her gaze on the traffic, bright headlights whizzing past in a rush. She didn't know Jackson. She didn't like Jackson. By this time tomorrow, he'd be nothing but a fading memory.

Six

Despite the humble name, Jackson knew Anthony's was an upscale restaurant housed in a redbrick colonial mansion. Owned by a close friend of his, its high ceilings, ornate woodwork and sweeping staircase gave an ambience of grandeur and a distinct sensation of class.

Tonight, he hadn't been interested in the restaurant, but in the historic B and B rooms on the third floor of the building. He knew he could count on Anthony not to ask questions or keep a record of their stay. It was the closest thing Jackson had to a safe house.

Their room had a four-poster king-size bed, a stone fireplace and sloped cedarwood ceilings. There was a small dining table in a bay window alcove, and a sofa that the housekeeper had already converted into a second bed.

Crista had opted to take a shower, while Jackson had stretched out on top of the sofa bed, a news station playing on the television and his laptop open to the photos of Vern and Gracie. The resolution on the pictures was high, so it was going to be easy to show they hadn't been altered.

His browsing was interrupted when the bathroom door opened and Crista appeared. She was dressed in a fluffy white robe, drying her auburn hair with a towel.

"That shouldn't be all it takes to make me feel better," she said in a cheerful voice as she padded toward him on bare feet. "But it does." She plunked down on the opposite side of the sofa. "I'm refreshed."

Just her appearance made him feel better. She was easy on the eyes and entertaining for his mind. He realized the only thing he liked better than looking at her was listening to her.

"I don't know if this will make you feel better or worse." It certainly made him feel better.

He slid the laptop across the sofa bed toward her. "I've zoomed way in on the pixels. Stare all you want. The pictures haven't been altered."

She shifted on the bed and moved the computer to her lap.

"The dates and times are registered in the metadata," he said, anticipating that as an argument from Crista, or possibly a defense later from Vern.

"He's hugging her." Crista zoomed the view out.

"And here he's kissing her." Jackson reached over to scroll to the next photo.

"It doesn't look brotherly," she said.

"It's not."

"This is hard to accept."

A female television announcer caught Jackson's attention.

"The Fountain Lake Family Hotel was the scene of a structure fire this evening," she said. "Over three hundred guests were evacuated, while engines and firefighters were deployed from three stations in the area. Fire Chief Brandon Dorsey says that arson has not been ruled out."

The view switched to a reporter at the front of the hotel. He was interviewing a guest against a backdrop of fire engines and police cars.

"Is that code to say that it was arson?" asked Crista, her gaze on the TV screen.

"It means it's early in the investigation," Jackson answered honestly. But it was arson. He knew it was arson.

"Tell me the truth," she said, her gaze not wavering.

"He did it to get us both out of the building. He wants you back. But I'm guessing he also wants you far away from me."

She turned her head, looking surprised. "Why?"

"You have a mirror, right?"

She lifted her hand and self-consciously touched her damp hair. It was tousled and incredibly sexy.

"He thinks I'm your ex-boyfriend," Jackson reminded her.

"I forgot about that."

"He doesn't want the competition. I don't blame him."

If Crista were his, Jackson couldn't honestly say he wouldn't set a building on fire.

Looking unsettled, she turned her attention back to the laptop.

"I'm going to have to end it, aren't I?" Her tone was regretful.

Yes! "That's up to you."

She looked back at Jackson. "I don't think I can marry a man who's been unfaithful."

"I wouldn't."

"Wouldn't marry him, or wouldn't be unfaithful?"

"Neither." He felt himself ease closer to her. It was impossible to keep his true thoughts at bay. "Any man who cheats on you is out of his ever-lovin' mind."

She gave a ghost of a smile. "That's very nice of you to say."

"It's the truth."

Silence descended between them.

He wanted to kiss her now. He desperately wanted to kiss her luscious red lips. The robe's lapels revealed the barest hint of cleavage. Her skin was dewy from the hot shower. And he was all but lost in her jewel-green eyes.

"I guess I'll talk to him tomorrow," she said.

And say what? The question was so loud inside his head that for a moment he was afraid he'd shouted it.

"Unless there's some miraculous explanation," she continued, "I'm handing back his ring and walking out of his life."

"There'll be no miracle."

She nodded, twisting the diamond around her finger.

He gently but firmly took her hands. Then he slipped the ring off her finger, reaching up to place it on the table behind the sofa.

"But—" She looked like she wanted to retrieve it.

"Afraid it might get lost?" He lifted his brows.

"It's valuable."

"It's worthless. You're valuable."

His face was inches from hers. A small lift of his hand, and it was on her hip. Then he slipped it to the base of her spine. He leaned in.

"Jackson." His name was a warning.

"It's a kiss," he said. "It's only a kiss. We've done it before."

He gave her a second to protest.

She didn't.

So he brought his lips to hers.

They were as sweet as he'd remembered, hot and tantalizing. Desire immediately registered in his brain. Passion lit his hormones, while every cell jumped to attention. His hand tightened at the small of her back, drawing her against him.

He stretched his legs out, stretched hers out, and delved into the depths of her mouth. She kissed him in return. Her slight body sank into the soft bed.

Her robe gaped loose, and he knew it would take nothing, nothing at all to untie the sash, spread it wide, feast his gaze on her gorgeous body. But he held back, kissing her neck.

"Jackson," she groaned.

He loved the sound of his name coming from her lips. Her tone breathless.

"We should stop," she said. There was a no-nonsense edge to her voice now and he told himself to pull away.

"I'm sorry," she whispered, sounding as if she was.

"My fault," he readily admitted.

"I keep kissing you back."

"I keep starting it."

"These are extraordinary circumstances."

He summoned the strength and put a few inches between them. His eyes focused on her. "You are so unbelievably beautiful."

That got him a smile, and he felt it resonate through his heart.

"How does he do it?" He had to ask. "How does a man have you and even look at another woman?"

Her smile grew a little wider. "I can ask him."

"You should ask him. Better yet, I'll ask him. No, I'll tell him. I'll tell him he lost you, and I got you, and I'm sure going to keep you."

"While you're still pretending to be my ex-boyfriend?" she joked.

"What?" It took a second for her meaning to register. "Yeah. Right. That's what I meant."

She sobered. "And then this will all be over."

Jackson wasn't ready to say that.

"I should be sad," she said. "I mean, I am sad. But I should be sadder. I should be devastated. This mess is my life."

"You'll be fine," he said.

What he wanted to say was that they'd fix her life. He'd help her fix her life. He was sticking around until everything was settled, until he understood exactly what was going on with the diamond mine and anything else that might hurt her. He was staying until she was completely safe from Vern and all of the Gerhards.

They slept apart. And in the morning, Jackson drove her to the shopping mall parking lot three miles from the Gerhard mansion.

"I'd rather come with you," he said as he passed under the colorful flags that marked the main entrance.

"He's not going to try anything with Ellie there." Crista was nervous, but she wasn't afraid.

Vern would have no choice but to accept her decision. He wasn't going to be happy. But surely at some level he would understand. His relationship with Gracie Stolt might not be a full-blown affair, but they were obviously intimate. Vern needed to do as much thinking about his future as Crista did about her own.

"He lit a hotel on fire." There was a hard edge to Jackson's voice.

"They haven't proven that yet."

"I have all the proof I need. There they are." Jackson angled the SUV across a block of empty parking spots toward a silver sedan.

"Whose car?" she asked, knowing Ellie drove a blue hatchback.

"It's a company car. Mac wouldn't risk taking Ellie back to her apartment for her car."

"They've been together all night."

"It's possible," said Jackson. "I didn't ask."

"So, you didn't assign him to protect her." For the hundredth time, Crista tried to figure out Jackson's motivation for sticking around.

"I didn't need to."

She tried to read his expression.

He seemed to sense her stare and glanced over. "What?"

"Why are you still here?"

He didn't miss a beat. "You've heard of pro bono?"

"That's for lawyers."

"It's for private detectives, too."

She didn't buy it, but let the issue drop for now.

He pulled into the spot close to Mac and Ellie.

"You know you don't have to break it off in person," he said.

"I want to do it in person. I want to see his expression. And it's the only way it'll feel final to me."

"I can come with you."

"Ellie's coming with me. Vern likes Ellie."

Jackson clenched his jaw. After a moment's pause he passed a phone to Crista. "I'm speed dial one. Call me if anything looks suspicious."

"Suspicious how?" She couldn't help but think he was

used to higher stakes and higher drama than this. She was breaking off an engagement, not spying on a foreign government.

"You'll know it if it happens," he said.

She doubted that.

He picked up the phone, waiting for her to take it in her hand. "If I don't hear from you fifteen minutes after you're inside, we're coming in."

"How will you know when we're inside?" She conjured up a silly picture of him on a hillside in camo and green face paint with a set of high-powered binoculars.

"That phone has a very accurate GPS."

"You can't storm the mansion, Jackson. They'll arrest you."

"They can try," he said.

"You're nuts."

"I'm cautious."

She reached for the car door handle. "We're going to be fine."

He put a hand on her shoulder, stopping her from exiting. "*Anything* suspicious."

"Yes. Sure." She would try. "I assume Ellie is getting the same instructions?"

"Mac's cautious, too."

"Okay." Crista took a deep breath and swung open the door.

The butterflies in her stomach had ramped up, and she told herself not to let Jackson rattle her. Yes, Vern was going to be angry. And if Manfred or Delores were there, the conversation would definitely get even more uncomfortable. But it would be over in a matter of minutes, and this would all be behind her.

As she rose to her feet, she wiggled the diamond ring that was back on her finger, checking to make sure it was loose. When she was nervous, her hands tended to swell.

The last thing she needed was to break things off and try to give back the ring only to have it get stuck on her finger.

Mac stepped out of the passenger seat of the silver sedan. He nodded a greeting to Crista and held the door open for her.

"Thanks," she said as she slid onto the seat.

Mac leaned down, looking in the open door, his gaze on Ellie. "Don't forget."

"I won't," said Ellie.

He gave another serious nod then pushed the door firmly shut.

"Don't forget what?" Crista couldn't help but ask.

Ellie gave a sheepish shrug. "I'm not sure. The list was pretty long."

Crista couldn't help but smile. "Do you have a secret agent phone, too?"

Ellie tapped the front pocket of her white shorts. "I'm packin'."

"They've got us hooked up to GPS."

"I heard."

"And Jackson said we have fifteen minutes before they storm the place."

Ellie shifted the car into Drive and glanced back to Jackson's car as she pulled through the parking spot. "Who *are* those guys?"

"I can't figure it out. I keep asking him why he's doing all this, and I keep getting vague answers."

"He's hot," Ellie said with a glance in her rearview mirror.

"Jackson?"

"Mac."

That got Crista's attention. "Really?"

"You didn't notice?"

"To be honest, I wasn't paying much attention to Mac."

"I was." Ellie headed for the traffic light at the parking lot exit. "But forget about me. Do you know what you're going to say?"

"I think so," said Crista. She'd gone over a dozen different versions in her mind. "Did Mac tell you about the pictures?"

"He showed them to me."

"He kept copies." Crista wasn't surprised.

"They weren't fakes," said Ellie.

"I know."

They completed a left turn. Traffic was light, so they'd be at the mansion in about five minutes.

"Vern is pond scum," said Ellie.

"I keep going back and forth between coming out guns a-blazing or calmly asking for an explanation."

"Could there be any reasonable explanation?"

"Not that I can think of."

"I say guns a-blazing."

"Either way, the result will be the same."

"But not as satisfying. He needs to know he hurt you."

"He knows that."

"I doubt he cares."

Crista hoped he cared. The Vern she'd fallen in love with would care.

"Hit him with both barrels," said Ellie. "If you don't, you'll be sorry later."

"I have to at least ask him what happened," Crista countered. As far-fetched as it seemed, Vern might have something to say in his own defense.

"We're here," Ellie stated unnecessarily as they turned in to the long driveway. "Are you sure you're ready?"

"I just want to get it over with."

"Then let's do it." Ellie stepped on the accelerator and took them briskly up the drive.

She wheeled through the turnaround and brought the car to the curb. A security guard immediately came out through the front door, obviously intent on asking their business. But when he saw Crista, he stopped short.

She got out of the car, pausing while Ellie came around the front bumper.

"I'm here to see Vern," she stated, holding her head high.

"Of course, ma'am," said the guard, his expression inscrutable.

For the first time ever, Crista found herself wondering if the guard was armed. Were all of the security staff armed? It seemed likely they would be. She couldn't even imagine what would happen if Jackson and Mac showed up.

"We need to hurry," she said to Ellie, trotting up the stairs. The phone in her purse suddenly felt heavy.

She'd been in the mansion foyer hundreds of times, and she knew it well. It was octagonal with a polished marble floor and ornate pillars. A set of double doors led to a grand hallway and the curving staircase. The hallway was a popular place for guests at the Gerhards' cocktail parties to gather and view the family art collection.

It had never struck her as intimidating before, but rather opulent and grand. It was fit for industrialists, celebrities, even royalty.

She heard footsteps descending the staircase. But she stayed put, not wanting to venture far from the exit. It was Jackson's fault she was feeling so skittish. All his talk of speed-dialing him or him and Mac storming the place had her pointlessly nervous.

Vern appeared in the doorway, coming to an abrupt halt when he spotted Ellie. He frowned, and his nostrils flared.

"I asked Ellie to come," said Crista.

"I would have come anyway," said Ellie.

"She can wait here," said Vern.

"I'm staying here, too," said Crista. "This won't take long."

His brows rose with obvious incredulity. "What do you mean, it won't take long? We have our entire future to discuss."

"I've seen the pictures, Vern."

"What pictures?"

"You and Gracie."

He paled a shade, and she knew all the accusations were true.

But then he regrouped and went on the attack. "Do you mean Gracie Stolt? I told you, she's a client."

"She's your mistress." Then Crista rethought the terminology. "I mean, she would have been your mistress. If we'd gotten married."

Vern moved closer, his tone hardening. "You don't know what you're talking about."

"I've seen—"

"I don't care what you think you've seen. It was obviously a misrepresentation of something. And what about you? Shacked up in a hotel with your ex-boyfriend."

"I wanted to be alone."

"Alone with *him*."

"He was *helping* me."

Ellie reached out to touch her arm. "Crista."

Vern stepped closer still. "You're going to deny you slept with him?"

Crista opened her mouth to say yes. But then she thought better of the impulse. She had no need to defend herself. "I'm here to give you back your ring."

Vern shook his head. "I won't accept it. We can work this out."

"You just accused me of infidelity."

"You accused me first."

Anger rose inside her, and she jabbed her index finger in his direction. "You *did it*." Then she pointed at her own chest. "I *didn't*."

She grasped her ring and pulled. But as she'd feared, her fingers had swollen, and it didn't want to come off. She pulled harder. "But I'm going to," she said defiantly as she tugged. "I'm going out there right now to sleep with Jackson."

The ring suddenly popped off. It slipped from her fingers and bounced across the floor.

They both watched it come to rest on a white tile.

"You're not going to do that," said Vern.

"You can't stop me."

He reached out to grasp her arm, holding her fast.

"Let me go!" She struggled against his grip, but he wouldn't let her go.

In her peripheral vision, she saw Ellie retrieve her phone.

"Don't," she cried out to Ellie.

Jackson and Mac would only make things worse. They could make things a whole lot worse.

"Do I need to call the police?" Ellie asked Vern in a cold voice.

Vern glared daggers at her but then released Crista's arm.

"We need to talk," he said to Crista, schooling his expression, clearing the anger from his face, entreaty coming into his eyes.

"Not today," said Crista. She just wanted to get out of here.

"Not ever," said Ellie.

"You don't understand," said Vern, his expression now projecting hurt and confusion.

He suddenly looked so familiar. Her heart remembered everything they'd had together, and it ached for the loss.

"I have to go," she said, mortified to hear a catch in her own voice. She needed to be stronger than that.

Then Ellie's arm was around her, urging her to the door, picking up the tempo until they were outside. She immediately saw Jackson's SUV pulling up the drive.

"Are fifteen minutes up?" asked Crista, her voice now shaky. It had seemed more like three.

"You're going to sleep with Jackson?" Ellie asked as they hustled down the steps.

"I was bluffing."

"He didn't tell you about the hot mike?"

"The what?"

Mac hopped out of the passenger seat and jumped in to drive the silver sedan.

"Jackson and Mac could hear every word we said. Me threatening to call the police was the secret signal."

"There was a secret signal?"

"Go," said Ellie, pushing her toward the open door of the SUV.

Afraid to look back, Crista hopped inside and slammed the door shut. Jackson peeled away.

Jackson was relieved to have her back. He was stupidly giddy with relief. When Ellie had uttered the distress phrase, his heart had lodged in his throat. A dozen dire scenarios flashed through his mind as they sped up the driveway.

"You're okay?" He felt the need to confirm as they made it to the road.

"Ticked off," she said, fastening her seat belt.

"He didn't hurt you?"

"He grabbed me, but he let me go. His ring's on the floor of the foyer."

"Good," said Jackson with clipped satisfaction.

She shifted in the seat, angling toward him. "You bugged Ellie's phone?"

"We thought it was safest."

"Why didn't you tell me?"

"It would have made you nervous."

"I was already nervous."

"Yes." That had been his point. "It was bad enough for you without knowing you had a bigger audience."

"That was underhanded."

"Maybe."

"It was a personal conversation."

"You mean the part where you announced your intention to sleep with me?"

"That was a bluff."

It was too tempting not to tease her. "I'm very disappointed to hear that."

She moaned in obvious embarrassment. "Mac heard me say it, didn't he?"

"He did."

"Call him. Tell him I was joking."

"He knows you were joking."

"No, he doesn't. He's going to think there's something going on between us."

Jackson glanced her way. "There's not?"

"No, there's not. Well, not that. Not…" She seemed to search for words. "I just broke up with my fiancé. I was minutes from getting married on Saturday." The pitch of her voice rose. "There can't be anything between us."

"Okay," said Jackson. "I'll play along."

"I'm not asking you to *play along*. I'm asking you to accept the reality of the situation."

"Consider it accepted."

She watched him with obvious suspicion. "Tell Mac."

"Are you serious?"

"Yes." She crossed her arms over her chest. "I was illegally recorded, and I want the record set straight."

Jackson struggled not to laugh. "Sure." He fished his phone out of his pocket, pressing the speed dial and putting it on hands-free. He dropped it on the seat between them.

"What's up?" came Mac's answer over the small speaker.

"Crista wants me to set the record straight."

"What record?" asked Mac.

"She's not going to sleep with me."

There was a silence. "Uh, okay." Mac paused. When he spoke again, Jackson detected a trace of laughter. "Why not?"

"Because I barely know him," said Crista.

"He's a great guy," said Mac. "And I hear he's a good lover."

"From who?" asked Crista without missing a beat.

Jackson caught her gaze and mouthed the word *really*?

"Was it Melanie?" she asked, obviously thinking she'd turned the tables on him.

"He told you about Melanie?"

Jackson scooped up the phone and switched it to his ear. "That's enough about me."

Mac chuckled.

"Chicken," said Crista.

"We're not taking her home," Jackson said to Mac.

"Her being me?" asked Crista.

"Where to?" asked Mac.

"The office, for a start."

"Your office?" asked Crista.

"You want to look at the other thing?" asked Mac.

"That's right," Jackson said to Mac. "My office," he said to Crista.

"I should go home," she said. "This is over, and I'm tired of running. I'm pretty sure he got the message."

"He tried to physically restrain you."

"That was for her, right?" asked Mac.

"So did you," Crista pointed out.

Jackson didn't have an argument for that. He could also understand why Crista would think it was perfectly safe for her to go home. As far as she was concerned, she'd just broken up with a cheating fiancé. She didn't know about the diamond mine, so she didn't realize Gerhard and his family might have millions, possibly tens of millions of reasons to drag her back.

"I'm driving," he pointed out.

The car was going wherever he steered it. She could like it or not.

She crossed her arms and gave a huff. "If I'm going to your office, then Ellie's coming, too."

It didn't seem necessary, but he had no particular objection.

"She's my chaperone," Crista continued. "I don't want there to be gossip about you and me."

"You're obsessing," he said.

"Tell them," said Crista.

"Crista wants Ellie to come with us."

Mac's voice went muffled. "You want to stick with us?" He paused. "She's in," he said to Jackson. "I've got a couple stops to make. But we'll meet you there."

It took thirty minutes to arrive at Rush Investigations. The offices were housed in a converted warehouse a few blocks off the river. It wasn't the swankiest address, but the brick building was solid, and it gave them the space they needed to store vehicles and equipment.

They drove into the fenced compound and then accessed the garage area with the automatic door opener, parking the SUV in one of a dozen marked spots along the back wall. There was a customer entrance on the main floor of the attached four-story office tower. It was nicely decorated with comfortable seating, coffee service and a receptionist. But Jackson rarely went through there.

"Wow," said Crista as she stepped out of the vehicle onto the concrete floor. She craned her neck to look up at the open twenty-foot ceiling, where steel beams crossed fluorescent lighting, and her voice echoed in the mostly empty space. "This is huge."

Work benches stretched along two of the walls, while the east end was given over to shelving and a small electronics shop. An orange corrugated-metal staircase led from the shelving area to the second floor of the office tower.

"There are times we need the room," he said. "But most of the vehicles are out right now. This way." He gestured to the staircase.

"Just how big is your company?" she asked as they walked.

"It's grown since I started it."

"Grown from what to what?"

"To somewhere around three hundred people."

"There's that much going on in Chicago that needs investigating?"

He couldn't help a grin. "They're not all investigators. But, yes, there's easily that much going on. We also have offices in Boston, New York and Philly."

She stopped walking and turned to look at him, eyes narrowing, her forehead furrowing. "I know I keep asking this, but what exactly are you doing?"

"A lot of missing-persons cases," he answered. "Security and protection. Infidelity's always a big one. And then there's the corporate—"

"I mean with me. What are you doing with me?"

He knew he had to tell her about the mine eventually. But he didn't want her to bolt. He knew she'd be gone like a shot if she had any inkling her father was involved.

"For the moment," he said, meeting her eyes and telling the truth, "I'm trying to give you some time and distance to consider your options."

"I did. And I just took an option. I broke it off."

"You have other options. Life options. Like what you do next?"

"Why do you care?"

"Because I've spent most of the last three days with you."

She was clearly growing exasperated with his talking in circles. "Which leads me right back to *why*. Who sent you? Why did you even come looking for me in the first place?"

"Somebody asked me a question about Vern. I got curious. And then, I guess, I just kept wading deeper and deeper."

"I'm not your concern."

He found himself moving closer, lowering his voice, increasing the intimacy of the conversation. "I spend quite a lot of time wading around in things that don't concern me."

She shook her head at what she clearly thought was his foolishness. "You normally get paid to do that."

He gave a shrug. "There's getting paid, and there's getting paid."

"One more time, Jackson, I'm not going to sleep with you." She couldn't quite keep a poker face.

He took one of her hands in his and stepped closer still. "You sure?"

She didn't answer.

He brushed his lips gently against hers. "You sure?"

"Not really. I'm not sure of anything anymore."

"You can be sure of this."

He kissed her.

She instantly responded, and he wrapped her tight in his arms, slanting his lips and deepening the kiss.

She molded against him, her softness perfect against the planes of his body. Desire rushed through him, and he gave it free rein.

They'd stop in a moment. Of course they would stop. But for now nothing in the world mattered except the sweetness of Crista's lips, the scent of her hair, and the feel of her hand in his.

Something banged in the reaches of the warehouse.

He silently cursed. Then he ended the kiss, drawing away and smoothing the pad of his thumb over her cheek.

"We have got to get alone at some point," he said.

"I'm so confused." Her green eyes were clouded and slightly unfocused.

"I'm not."

"This isn't simple."

He understood that it wasn't simple for her. It was perfectly simple for him. He desired her, and she definitely seemed attracted to him. It was pretty straightforward and a very nice starting point.

"We don't have to figure it out right away," he said.

She gave her head a small shake. "I'm not about to start dating anyone."

He didn't see why not, but he didn't want to pressure her. "Okay."

"I'm going to work out my life."

"Where do you want to start?" He'd be happy to help.

"Cristal Creations. I need to start with the company."

"How so?" He knew she had three locations around Chicago. From what he understood, they were doing well.

"They're my jewelry designs, and I manage the stores. But I don't actually own them."

Jackson wasn't happy to hear that. "Gerhard owns them," he guessed.

"It's what made sense at the time. The family already owned the shopping malls where we opened."

"So he got his hooks into your business." Jackson shook his head with disgust.

"It was only fair," said Crista. "He paid for it all. I wouldn't even have a business without Vern. He backed my designs when no one else would. Did you see the episode of *Investors Unlimited*?"

"*Investors Unlimited*?"

"It's a TV show. The kind where you pitch an idea and the rich people on the panel can offer to invest. I was on it a year ago."

"You pitched your jewelry designs to Vern?"

"Not to Vern. He wasn't on the show. Nobody there was interested. But after it aired, Vern watched it and contacted me."

"He made you an offer?"

"That's how we met."

The timing was right, and Jackson knew the information could be significant. The show might be a catalyst for the whole scam.

His needed to find out who knew what about Crista and when.

Seven

Crista and Ellie were alone in a big, comfortable room that Jackson had called the lounge. On the fourth floor of the Rush Investigations building, it had banks of windows on two sides, soft chairs and sofa groupings scattered around, along with a kitchen area stocked with snacks and drinks. Easy-listening music filled the background from speakers recessed in the ceiling. It was night and day from the utilitarian warehouse area.

After helping themselves to sodas, they'd settled into a quiet corner with a curved sofa and a low table. Crista had kicked off her sandals and raked her hair into a quick ponytail.

It felt like a long time since she'd been home, and she was struggling for normalcy. Bouncing from place to place with a man she barely knew, desiring him, kissing him, all the while wishing she could tear off his clothes, was not a long-term plan. She needed to get herself organized. She needed to get her life in order and back on track.

"I need to find a lawyer," she said to Ellie, zeroing in on a logical first step.

"At least you don't have to divorce Vern." Ellie fished a throw pillow from behind her back and tossed it to the end of the sofa, wriggling into the deep, soft cushions. "Is there something in your prenup about walking away? Wait, you didn't marry him. The prenup won't count."

"We didn't have a prenup."

The statement obviously took Ellie by surprise. "Seriously?"

Crista took a drink as she nodded. The cola cooled her throat, making her realize she was incredibly thirsty.

"But he's a superwealthy guy," said Ellie.

Crista was acutely aware of Vern's wealth. "I thought it was a show of faith. I was really quite honored."

"That's really quite weird."

"I know. Now, I have to wonder if he wanted to avoid the subject of infidelity."

"He knew your lawyer would advise a big settlement if he messed around on you. If he'd said no, you'd have been suspicious. But if he'd said yes, you'd have made a fortune."

"Assuming he ever got caught," said Crista.

"Maybe you should have married him without a prenup and then divorced him. You could have cleaned up."

"I'm not that devious." Crista wouldn't have even wanted that windfall.

"It would have served him right."

"The thing I'm worried about is Cristal Creations." Crista needed a lawyer to sort out the company. She wanted out from under Gerhard Incorporated as quickly as possible.

"It's yours," said Ellie. "He can't touch it since you never got married. But, hey, if he wants to split it, then he can split his business interests with you, too."

"The jewelry designs are all that I own," said Crista. "The stores are his. Well, his family's, anyway."

"The Gerhards own your stores?"

"They own the shopping malls the stores are inside. I need to get my designs out of there. I'd rather start from scratch than have to work with his family."

"You should definitely call a lawyer."

Crista gave a mock toast of agreement with her soft drink bottle. "Now that it's actually over, I realize how much of my life is wrapped up in Vern. How does that happen in only a year?"

Before Ellie could respond, Crista's mind galloped ahead. "I had six bridesmaids. Only one of them, you, was my friend. Five of them were from Vern's family."

"He does have a very big family."

"And I don't have any family at all. But five out of six? You'd think I'd have more friends."

"You do have more friends."

It was true. Crista did have other friends, some that she'd have loved to have as her bridesmaids. But Vern, and particularly his mother, Delores, had been insistent on including their family in the wedding party. Crista couldn't help but wonder if she'd made a mistake by giving in so easily.

"Good thing you had me," said Ellie.

"Good thing I still have you. All the people I socialize with now seem to be his friends, or his family—mostly his family."

Ellie frowned. "Count me out of that list."

"I know."

"I'm not his friend. I think he's a jerk."

"I wish you'd said something sooner."

"No, you don't."

Crista reconsidered her words. "You're right. I don't. I wouldn't have believed you."

"And I wasn't sure. I could have been wrong. He could have been a perfectly nice guy."

"Not so much." Crista took another drink. She was hungry, too. When was the last time she'd eaten?

She glanced at her watch.

"It's nearly three," said Ellie.

"I'm starving. Are you hungry?"

Ellie's glance went to the kitchen area. "We can probably grab a snack. This is quite the place."

"Isn't it?" Crista took another look around. The room was fresh, clean, with sleek styling and designer touches.

Ellie leaned closer and lowered her voice. "I get more and more curious about those two guys."

"Why are we whispering?"

"I think this place is probably bugged."

"Your secret agent phone?" It suddenly occurred to Crista that they might still be broadcasting.

"It's turned off now, but this is all very cloak-and-dagger."

"Very," Crista agreed, glancing around for surveillance cameras. "They seem frighteningly good at it."

"Do you think we can trust them?"

"Part of me wants to say no, but they've done nothing but help me so far."

"They came out of nowhere."

"True," said Crista. "But whatever this is, Jackson isn't in it for himself. He's been a gentleman. He didn't take advantage, even when I—" Crista stopped herself.

Ellie sat up straight. "Even when you what?"

Crista wasn't sure why she was hesitating. She was an adult, and Vern was now completely out of the picture. "When I kissed him back."

Ellie's brow rose. "Back? So he kissed you first?"

"Yes." It was silly not to have told Ellie. Keeping it a secret made it seem like more than it was. And it was nothing. "Yes, he did."

"When? Where? How?"

"On the boat. And in the hotel. And, well, in the warehouse, too." Crista didn't think she needed to add that it was on the mouth.

"It was mutual?" Ellie seemed rather energized by the news.

"It was very mutual. He's a really sexy guy."

"Good to hear," Jackson drawled from the doorway.

Ellie looked his way, her eyes crinkling with amusement. Crista felt her face heat.

"Don't let that go to your head," she warned him.

"I'll try my best." His footsteps sounded on the floor.

She forcibly shook off her embarrassment and turned to face him. "You shouldn't eavesdrop."

His mocha eyes glowed with amusement. "Occupational hazard."

"That's no excuse."

"I wasn't making an excuse." He sauntered farther into the room, followed closely by Mac.

She refused to stay embarrassed. If Jackson didn't already know she was attracted to him, well, he hadn't been paying attention. And he'd probably long since bragged to Mac about what had happened between them. Crista was going to hold her head high.

"I've got to get home," she said, coming to her feet. "Or to work. I should probably go into work and start figuring out the future."

"You'd planned to be away for three weeks on your honeymoon," said Ellie, rising herself. "Surely you can take a few days off."

"You can't go home," said Jackson.

"Come to my place," said Ellie.

"That's the second place he'll look," said Mac.

"So what if he does?" Crista had no intention of hiding from Vern any longer.

"Take a vacation," said Jackson. "Get out of the city for a few days."

"That's not practical," said Crista. Never mind that she had her business to worry about. She didn't have any extra money to spend on a vacation.

"It's better if you're not here," he said.

"It's better if I figure out what happens with Cristal Creations."

"She needs a lawyer," said Ellie.

"We have lawyers," said Mac.

"Down the hall," Jackson added with a tilt of his head.

"There are lawyers down the hall?" Crista couldn't keep the amazement from her tone.

"Rush Investigations lawyers," said Jackson. "Good ones. I'll introduce you."

She hesitated. The solution seemed too simple. Could she trust Jackson's lawyers? On the other hand, she knew she couldn't trust Vern's lawyers. And she sure didn't have any of her own. It seemed likely that anyone who worked for Jackson would be squarely opposed to Vern.

And it would be fast. Fast seemed like it would be good in this situation.

"They won't mind?" she asked, tempted.

"Why would they mind?"

"Because they have real work to do."

"This is real work."

She made her way toward him, watching his expression closely, trying to gauge what he was thinking. "Are you up to something?"

"Yes."

His easy admission surprised her.

"I knew it," she lied.

"What I'm up to is providing you with legal advice."

"Funny." She leaned closer, keeping her expression serious. "Why are you doing it?"

"Because your ex-fiancé ticked me off."

"And that's what you do when you're angry? Provide strangers with legal advice?"

"No." His jaw tightened. An edge came into his voice. "That's not even close to what I do when I'm angry."

He was intimidating, and it unnerved her. But her attraction to him was also back in full force.

He seemed to realize he'd unsettled her. "I'm not angry at you."

"Maybe not right now."

"Not ever."

But she could picture it. She could easily picture it.

He gave the barest shake of his head. "Don't even think about it. It's never going to happen."

Two days later, Jackson held his temper in check.

He stared across the prison table at Trent Corday. "So I sliced and diced and dissected everyone involved in *Investors Unlimited* looking for a connection to Gerhard."

He stopped speaking and waited, giving Trent a chance to react to the information he'd just tossed out. The more he'd uncovered, the more suspicious he'd become of Trent's involvement. He might not be certain how it had all unfolded, but he was certain Trent was somehow operating behind the scenes.

Trent returned his gaze evenly, his features perfectly neutral. "Why did you expect there to be a connection?"

Jackson mentally awarded the man points for composure. "Because the two events happened suspiciously close together."

"Vern Gerhard must have watched the show," said Trent.

"Seeing the show didn't tell Vern Gerhard about the mine."

"The show could have tweaked his interest in Crista."

"Interest alone wouldn't lead him to the mine."

"I don't see how it matters," said Trent.

"It matters," said Jackson.

For the barest of seconds, Trent's left eye twitched, and Jackson knew he'd found a crack. He could almost hear the wheels turning inside the man's head. Trent desperately wanted to know how much Jackson knew.

Jackson didn't know much. But he pretended he did, putting a smug expression on his face, hoping to draw out something more. "It wasn't somebody inside the show," he said, lacing his voice with confidence and conviction. "It was somebody who already knew about the mine."

"No telling who all knew about the mine."

"No telling," Jackson agreed. "But we both know one person who did."

"Who's that?"

"You." Jackson tossed a copy of a call list on the table in front of Trent.

Trent's gaze narrowed in wariness. "What's this?"

"It's a record of calls incoming to Manfred Gerhard's private line."

Trent didn't respond.

"It's from three days before *Investors Unlimited* aired the episode with Crista."

Jackson hoped Trent would react, but he didn't.

Instead, Trent calmly turned the list to face him. He stared at it for a long moment. Then he sat back and crossed his arms over his chest. "You seem to be making some kind of point."

Jackson indicated a line on the statement. "My point is that call, right there. It's from a prison pay phone, *this* prison's pay phone. You called Gerhard before the show."

Trent pretended to be affronted. "I most certainly did not."

"They record those calls," Jackson reminded him. "I can easily pull the recording."

"The call was made at ten forty-five on a Tuesday," said Trent. "I work in the laundry until noon. I couldn't have made the call."

"This was a year ago."

"I've been working in the laundry for two years. Ask anyone."

Jackson studied the confidence in Trent's expression. He reluctantly concluded Trent hadn't made the call. But he was definitely hiding something.

Jackson leaned forward. "What aren't you telling me?"

"Nothing."

The exchange was getting him nowhere. What Jackson needed was leverage, but he didn't have any.

"You want me to protect Crista?" He played his only card.

He gambled that Trent cared at least a little bit about his daughter. If he didn't, he wouldn't have contacted Jackson in the first place.

"Crista's fine," said Trent. "The wedding's been called off."

"The wedding might be off," said Jackson. "But Gerhard's not dead. He still wants what he wants."

"You don't know anything about it."

"But you do?"

Trent's face twitched a second time.

Jackson pressed his advantage. "I can walk right now, or I can watch her awhile longer. You screw with me, I walk."

Trent stilled, obviously weighing his options.

"Stop trying to play me," said Jackson. "The truth is your only option."

"I didn't call the Gerhards," said Trent.

"Then tell me what you did. Tell me what I need to know, or I'm out of here and Crista's on her own."

To punctuate his threat, Jackson started to rise.

"Fine," Trent snapped. "It was me. I told a guy about the mine. But I had no choice. I had to."

Jackson felt his blood pressure rise, while his tone went cold. "There's always a choice." He couldn't believe Trent would endanger his own daughter.

"They threatened to kill me."

"Why?"

Trent started talking fast. "I owed some guys some money. The deal was to offer her a discount price and pocket the difference. That's all it was. I swear."

"What guys?" Jackson demanded. "Who did you owe?"

Trent hesitated.

Jackson started to stand again.

"It was the Gerhards, okay? It was a land deal a few years back. I guaranteed their city permits. It didn't work out. They lost big-time, and they've been dogging me ever since."

The revelation surprised Jackson. He'd pegged Trent as a small-time criminal. He'd never guessed Trent was involved in this level of corruption.

He wasn't sure he believed it now. "How could you guarantee their permits?"

"I know a guy," said Trent.

"You know a corrupt guy in the permitting office who can be bribed?"

"The Gerhards have men inside the prison. And they *were* going to kill me. It was my only bargaining chip. I didn't think anyone would get hurt, least of all Crista."

"You painted a target on her back."

"And then I came to you when it looked like it would go bad. I came to you for help."

"You lied to me."

"It got the job done," Trent said defensively.

"They didn't get their hands on the mine."

Trent's gaze narrowed, obviously not getting the point.

"What now?" Jackson elaborated. "How are you going to pay them back?"

"I sold them information. About the mine. We're square."

"So, they're not going to kill you?"

"That was the deal," Trent repeated with conviction. He didn't look like a man who feared for his life.

But Jackson knew this wasn't over. If he'd learned anything from his father, it was that criminals didn't give up while there was still a prize to play for.

"It doesn't matter if they kill you or not, they've still got their radar locked on her."

Trent took a beat. "I didn't mean for it to go like this."

"Well, it went like this."

Trent swallowed.

"You're a sorry excuse for a father."

Trent didn't argue the point. He barely seemed to have heard the insult. His cockiness vanished, replaced by apprehension. "You'll look after her?"

"I shouldn't have to." This time, Jackson did come to his feet.

"But you will?"

Trent's emotional reaction had to be fake. But Jackson didn't care enough to lie. "I will."

Trent closed his eyes for a long second. "Thank you," he muttered.

If Jackson didn't know better, he might have thought the

man was grateful. But he did know better. Trent was a self-centered, pathetic loser who didn't deserve any daughter, never mind Crista.

He pivoted to walk away, letting his frustration and determination take him back down the long hallway.

The minute he cleared the prison building, he pulled out his cell phone and dialed his friend Tuck Tucker.

"Hey, Jackson," Tuck answered.

"Got a few minutes to meet?" Jackson asked as he strode toward his car.

"Now?"

"If you can. It's important."

"Sure. Where are you?"

"Riverway prison."

"That can't be good."

Jackson couldn't help but smile. "I'm outside the wall."

"Glad to hear it. The Copper Tavern?"

"Fifteen minutes?"

"Meet you there."

As he started his car, Jackson placed a call to Mac.

"Yo," Mac answered.

"You come across anything on the Gerhards bribing city officials?"

"Bribing them how?"

"Building permits."

Mac went quiet, obviously thinking through the question.

"Did you find something relevant?" Jackson asked as he turned from the parking lot onto the gravel-littered access road.

Poplar trees swayed beyond the ditches, and clouds shadowed the sun as the afternoon moved forward.

"It makes sense," said Mac. "A few committee decisions were overturned in their favor last year. That's not unheard of, but there were more than what might be expected. Let me look into it further."

"Check on Trent Corday while you're at it. He may have

had a hand in something bad at the city. Turns out he was the one who tipped Gerhard off about the mine."

"Why would he do that?" Surprise was clear in Mac's tone.

"He was in debt to the Gerhards and trying to avoid death or bodily harm."

"By using his own daughter?"

"Yeah. Getting the mine into their hands was payback for the debt."

Concern came into Mac's tone. "But they didn't get the mine."

"I know. Trent seems to think they're square anyway."

"That doesn't sound right," said Mac.

"Tell me about it. Did you get Crista and Ellie dropped off?"

"Safe and sound at the Gold Leaf Resort. Ellie's making spa reservations. Crista's arguing, but I think Ellie's going to win."

"I hope Ellie can get her to relax, take her mind off all this."

"If anyone can do it, it's Ellie."

"Good call. I'm meeting Tuck on my way back."

"See you when you get here." Mac signed off.

Jackson followed the expressway to the outskirts of the city, then swung off to cross the bridge and pick up the quieter streets that led to the Copper Tavern. It was a laid-back, comfortable sports-themed bar, with dark wood tables, padded leather chairs and good-humored staff that seemed to stick with the place for years on end.

It was easy to grab a parking spot in the midafternoon. Jackson left the bright sunshine behind and quickly spotted Tuck at a corner table. Tuck gave him a nod of greeting and signaled to the waitress for a couple of beers.

"Wings and ribs are on their way," said Tuck as Jackson sat down.

"Works for me."

"You're buying," Tuck added.

"You bet."

The waitress, Tammy, arrived with two frosty mugs of lager. She gave Jackson a brief, friendly greeting as she set the mugs down on printed cardboard coasters.

"What's going on?" Tuck asked Jackson as Tammy walked away.

"I need a favor." Jackson saw no point in beating about the bush.

"Sure."

"It's a big one."

"How big? Should I have ordered lobster?"

Jackson coughed out a laugh. "It's a whole lot bigger than lobster."

"Lay it on me."

"I need you to buy something for me."

Jackson slid a web address across the table. "Cristal Creations. They have three stores in Chicago. You buy the company now. I'll buy it from you in two years. I'll guarantee whatever return you want to name."

Tuck lifted the folded piece of paper. "Why?"

"I need my name to stay out of it."

"No kidding. I mean, why buy it at all?"

"I know the owner," said Jackson.

"You mean you're sleeping with the owner?"

"It's not about that."

"That wasn't an answer."

"No," said Jackson. "I'm not sleeping with her."

"Yet."

"The person I care about is the jewelry designer, not the company owner. Gerhard Incorporated owns the company. The woman's had a falling-out with them."

Tuck pocketed the paper. "Anything in particular I need to know about that situation?"

"She was set to marry Vern Gerhard. She backed out. He's not happy."

"But you are?"

Jackson didn't bother to hide his smile. "I'm satisfied with the outcome."

"And now you need her to sever all ties."

"I don't trust them. They're dirty, and they've got to be after revenge."

Tuck gave a nod. "We've got a Bahamian holding company that's not doing much of anything right now."

"Can it be traced back to you?"

"It can. But it would take quite a bit of time and a whole lot of lawyers. I don't know why anyone would bother, especially if the price was right."

Jackson tended to agree. It was common knowledge that the wedding had been canceled. And Crista had been on network television last year pitching Cristal Creations. An offer to buy the company from Gerhard should look opportunistic more than anything.

"I really appreciate this," said Jackson.

"Not a problem. My brother's got Tucker Transportation humming like a top. I have to keep myself entertained somehow. So, why'd she do it?"

Jackson didn't understand the question.

"Why'd she leave him?" asked Tuck.

"He was cheating on her."

Tuck's tone went hard. "Nice."

Jackson knew Tuck's brother, Dixon, had been a recent victim of infidelity.

"Anything else I can do to help her out?" Tuck asked.

"Not for the moment."

"You think of anything, you let me know. Dixon will help out, too."

"Thanks for that."

"I'm serious."

"I know."

There was a moment of silence.

"The guy cheated on her *before* the wedding?" Tuck asked.

Jackson pulled out the photo of Crista. He handed it across the table to Tuck. "That's the bride. And, yeah, it was before the wedding."

Tuck whistled low. "Are you kidding me?"

"She's bright, funny…good-hearted. Gerhard's an idiot." For that, Jackson was grateful.

"Or blind."

"His loss."

"Your gain."

"Not yet," said Jackson.

"You want some pointers?"

Jackson turned his attention to his beer. "No, I don't want some pointers."

Tammy arrived with the ribs and wings platter.

"Can I get you anything else?" she asked.

Tuck spoke up. "Jackson needs advice for the lovelorn."

Jackson rolled his eyes at the absurdity of the statement.

Tammy took a single step back and made a show of looking him up and down. She put a good-natured twinkle in her eyes. "Show up."

"Just doubled your tip," said Tuck.

Tammy laughed as she backed away. "Enjoy. Let me know if you need another round."

"I don't need any romantic advice from you," Jackson said to Tuck as he reached for a wing.

"What's your next move?"

"She's less than a week from leaving a man at the altar. I'm not going to crowd her."

Tuck looked skeptical. "You've got to be honest. You've got to be up front. Otherwise women can sometimes conjure up all kinds of wrong ideas."

"Just because you lucked out with Amber, that doesn't make you an expert."

There was a smug smile on Tuck's face at the mention

of his new fiancée. "That wasn't luck, my friend. That was skill, sophistication and—"

"Honesty?" Jackson got the point of the lecture. But the situation with Crista had more than its fair share of complications.

"I was going to say groveling. But let's stick with honesty for a minute. Trust is the hardest part to win and the easiest to lose."

"There are things I can't tell her."

"Like what?"

"Like the fact that her father sold her out to a criminal enterprise over a diamond mine."

Tuck raised his brow in obvious confusion. "You're going to have to throw a few more details into that story."

"Years ago, her father put some diamond mine shares in her name. She doesn't know she owns them, but her father told the Gerhards about them to settle a debt. Vern Gerhard is after the diamonds."

"The Gerhards need money?"

"More like they want money. If they based their behavior on needs, they'd have stopped building their empire a long time ago."

"How many shares does she own?" asked Tuck.

"Four."

"Four," Tuck repeated, obviously looking for confirmation that he'd heard right.

"Yes."

Tuck raised his palms in incredulity. "What can they do with four shares?"

"It's a privately held company. There are only ten shares in the world."

"She owns 40 percent of a diamond mine?"

"Yes."

"Are there diamonds in it?"

"I'm told there are."

"You have to tell her."

Jackson closed his eyes for a long second. "I know."

He'd spent the past few days telling himself there was a way around it. But there wasn't. Jackson wanted Crista, and he wanted her safe. Gerhard might have walked away from a runaway bride. But he wouldn't walk away from millions of dollars in diamonds and an outstanding debt.

Eight

When Jackson's lawyer Reginald Cooper had advised it would take several days to assess Cristal Creations and come up with a plan of action, Mac had suggested a spa getaway. Crista had vetoed the idea of leaving town again. She was tired of running from her problems.

But Ellie had begged her to reconsider. She reminded Crista that they'd been talking about a girls' getaway and how it would give her time to think. Then Jackson had added that the owner of the Gold Leaf Resort was a client of Rush Investigations, making the weekend practically free.

With all three ganging up on her, Crista had finally relented.

Now, lounging with Ellie in the outdoor mineral pool, she couldn't say she was sorry. The breeze was strengthening and clouds were closing up in the sky, but the rock pool was deliciously warm. Lounging on a seat, sculpted into the smooth boulders, with a tall glass of iced tea beside her, Crista closed her eyes and emptied her mind.

She felt more peaceful here than she had in days, and her brain had slowed down enough for her to picture her future. Maybe she'd find herself a new job. She probably would have to find a job, at least in the short term. Crista Creations was about to be dismantled. Without the Gerhards' backing, the company couldn't afford retail space. But without Crista, there'd be no more creations to sell.

She knew her designs were the unique element of the company. Without her, Cristal Creations was just another jewelry retailer. And it was a very competitive market.

She'd keep designing. But she'd pull back, retrench, rent booth space at a few jewelry fairs, work on her website and try to build up brand recognition. She'd make new pieces in the evenings, setting up in her kitchen like she'd done for so many months before Vern came along.

She pictured the work space on the island counter, the dining table covered with supplies, her closets overflowing.

Her eyes popped open. "Oh, no."

"Huh?" Ellie seemed to give herself a shake.

"I can't believe I forgot," said Crista.

"Forgot what?"

"I canceled the lease on my suite. The movers are putting the furniture into storage next week."

"You're homeless?" asked Ellie.

"It's almost impossible to find affordable rent."

"You can stay with me," said Ellie. "The new sofa folds out. It's really quite comfortable."

"That's nice of you. But it's not going to be that simple. I need to work from home again."

"Why not wait and see—" Ellie's eyes widened, focusing on a spot behind her.

"See what?" asked Crista, realizing she'd suddenly lost Ellie's attention. She twisted her neck to look behind.

A cloud partially blocked the sun, and she had to blink to adjust to the light.

Then she saw him. It was Vern. He was pacing along the pathway toward them, and there was a smile on his face.

"How did he find me?" She wasn't exactly afraid, but she was annoyed.

Ellie rose in a whoosh of water.

Crista pushed to her feet, striving for a greater sense of control. She crossed her arms and pinned him with a level stare. "What are you doing here, Vern?"

"I need to talk to you." His tone was smooth, his expression open and friendly.

He was wearing a business suit, but he bent down on one knee on the cobblestones at the edge of the pool. "I hate the way we left things, Crista."

She'd hated it, too, but it was entirely his fault, and there was no going back.

She held her ground. "Go home, Vern."

"Not until you hear me out."

She firmly shook her head. There was nothing he could say to undo infidelity.

"I know you're upset," he said.

"Upset? You think I'm *upset*?" *Try angry. Try incensed.* Everything about their relationship had been a lie.

"I can explain," he said.

"Explain a girlfriend?" Now that she was rolling, she couldn't seem to stop herself. "You can explain having both a girlfriend and a fiancée at the same time? How exactly are you going to do that?"

Ellie touched her arm. "Crista, don't."

Crista struggled to calm down. She knew Ellie was right. She shouldn't be challenging him. She shouldn't be engaging with him at all.

"She's not my girlfriend," he stated emphatically. "It was just a thing. One of those short-term, stupid things. I panicked. I knew I wanted to be with you for the rest of my life, but I panicked. I thought, well, I thought as long as it happened before the wedding—"

"Stop!" Crista all but shouted. "Quit rationalizing. You cheated. And I doubt you regretted it at all. I think you were going to keep doing it."

"That's not true."

"It's entirely true." She was certain of it.

"I love you, Crista. I want to share my life with you."

"You don't love me. You can't love someone and not want what's best for them. You don't want what's best for me. You want what's best for you. And you're willing to sacrifice me to get it."

"That's the thing. I *do* want what's best for you. And I've learned my lesson. I told myself it wouldn't hurt you. If I thought for one minute it would have hurt you—"

"Shut up," Ellie interjected. "Just shut up, Vern. Leave her alone and go away."

Vern's tone cooled as he looked at Ellie. "This is none of your business."

A clipped male voice interrupted. "Maybe not. But this conversation is over."

Jackson had appeared from nowhere.

"How did you…" Crista found herself gaping at him in surprise.

"Well, well, well," said Vern, slowly rising and looking Jackson up and down.

"Goodbye, Gerhard," said Jackson. "Or do I have to call security?"

"So you're here with her," said Vern.

Jackson didn't answer.

"He's not here with me," said Crista. "He wasn't here at all. Not until just now."

Vern shifted his gaze to Crista, clearly trying to decide if she was lying.

She wasn't. Then again, she didn't really care what he thought.

"You don't owe him an explanation," said Jackson. He took a menacing step toward Vern.

"You want to do this?" Vern challenged, widening his stance.

"She wants you gone," said Jackson. "You can walk out or be carried out. It's all the same to me."

Ellie grasped Crista's arm. "Come on." She tugged, urging Crista toward the glass-encased underwater staircase.

Crista realized it was good advice. She had absolutely nothing left to say to Vern, and her presence was only going escalate the situation. She left the pool and walked briskly away, scooping up the towels and robes they'd left draped over a pair of deck chairs.

Jackson caught up to them at the elevator.

"He's gone," he said.

"I'm beginning not to trust that."

The elevator arrived, its doors sliding open for them.

"I don't blame you," said Jackson as they walked inside.

"I'm going to hide in my room now." At least there, people would have to knock.

"You and I need to talk." His expression was too serious for her peace of mind.

"Can it wait?" she asked.

"It's important."

"You can drop me at the smoothie bar," said Ellie, pressing the button for the third floor.

Crista braced her hands on the rail behind her. "You know, I was happy in the mineral pool. All my cares and worries were flowing away."

"Five minutes," he said. "Ten, tops."

"I don't want any more bad news."

Before he could respond, the elevator stopped on three, and the doors slid open.

"Mac's around here somewhere," he said to Ellie.

Ellie's expression brightened. "He is?"

Jackson grinned at her telltale reaction.

"Catch you in a while," said Ellie, and she stepped briskly away.

"She likes Mac," said Crista, happy for her friend despite everything.

"Mac likes her back," said Jackson. "He'll track her down in no time."

"Because he's a skilled investigator," Crista guessed.

"Because she's still got the GPS phone."

"You guys make me paranoid."

"It's healthy to be paranoid."

Their eyes met as the elevator rose toward the presidential suite on the twentieth floor. His gaze was soft, and a rush of awareness heated her skin. She could fight it all she wanted, but he seemed more attractive every time she saw him.

Exiting the elevator, the suite was at the far end of the

hallway. A set of double oak doors led to a spacious set of rooms with a dramatic bay window overlooking the spa.

She extracted the key card from her bag and swiped it through the reader. Jackson reached for the handle and held the door open wide.

"Do you want to change?" he asked as they entered.

She dropped her bag on an armchair and tightened the sash on her robe. "You wanted to talk?"

"I did. I do." He seemed to give himself a mental shake. "I really missed you."

She'd missed him too. And her feelings for him were getting more confused by the moment.

He was an extraordinary man. He was sexy and self-assured in a rugged and dangerous way. But he was also classically handsome. In fact, he could probably be a model. She had a sudden vision of him in a pair of faded jeans, shirtless on a windswept beach. She wanted to tear off his shirt so that reality could mesh with her fantasy.

"Don't look at me like that," his voice rumbled.

"I'm not."

He eased forward. "You are such a liar."

It was true. She was lying to him, and she was lying to herself. She was looking at him exactly like that. She was completely attracted to him and completely turned on, and she couldn't figure out why she was fighting it.

"I'm sorry," she offered.

"For what?"

"For lying."

He seemed to take a breath. Then he squeezed her hands, causing her hormones to surge to life, and she swayed toward him.

He let go of her hands. Then he reached slowly up to cradle her cheek. He canted his head, easing his lips toward her.

"Do you want this?" he asked.

She was tired of lying. "Yes."

"Are you sure?" he persisted. "Because if we shut it down again, it might kill me."

It might kill her, too.

In answer, she reached for the buttons on his shirt, flicking open one, then another and another.

"I'm sure," she whispered and stretched up to meet his lips.

His reaction was immediate. He wrapped his arms around her, kissing her deeply. She molded against him, feeling the strength of his body and the thud of his heart.

He tugged at her sash, releasing the robe.

"I'm soaking wet," she warned. Her bathing suit was going to soak through his clothes.

"I don't care." He stripped the robe from her shoulders and let it fall to the floor.

Then he lifted her into his arms, her flip-flops falling beside her robe. "Which way?" he asked.

She pointed to the bedroom door.

He carried her through then closed the door firmly behind them, setting her bare feet on the thick carpet. The balcony door was partway open, a breeze billowing the sheers. Muted sounds from the pool area below rose into the room. The fan whirred, and dappled sunlight danced on the buttercream walls.

He brushed back her damp hair, raking his fingers through the strands. She tugged free the hem of his shirt. Then she finished with the buttons, removing his shirt to reveal a close-up view of his broad shoulders and tanned muscular chest.

"I was right," she muttered under her breath, then she kissed his smooth pec.

"Right about what?"

She was surprised he'd heard. "About you." She kissed him again, making a damp spot with her tongue.

He gasped in a breath. "In a good way, I hope."

"In a good way," she confirmed.

He slipped off the strap of her bathing suit, kissing the tip of her shoulder. "I was right about you, too." The vibrations of his deep voice penetrated her skin.

It was becoming a struggle for her to talk. "In a good way?"

"In a very good way."

He released the hook of her bathing suit top. It fell, and her cool, damp breasts tumbled free.

He stepped back to look, and his eyes turned the color of dark chocolate. Her nipples beaded and a bolt of arousal spiked through her.

"Gorgeous," he whispered with reverence.

"Not so bad yourself." She ran her fingers from his navel to his chest and across to his shoulders. He was satisfyingly solid over every inch.

His hand closed on her breast, and his smile faded. He caught her lips again and wrapped his free arm around her waist to draw her close, her bare chest coming up against his.

Their kisses seemed to last forever. She wanted them to last forever. The whole world could disappear for all she cared. She wanted this moment, these feelings, this bliss she'd found with Jackson to go on and on.

Her knees began to weaken, and she could feel her muscles relax. He kicked off his shoes and popped the button on his pants.

In a moment, they'd be naked. They'd be on the big bed, and their inevitable lovemaking would finally come to pass.

"Protection?" she asked.

"I have it."

She took a step, the backs of her knees pressing against the mattress. She gave him a sensual smile and hooked her thumbs into her bathing suit bottoms. Feeling sexy and powerful, and loving the molten expression in his eyes, she slowly peeled away the bottoms, stepping from them, standing naked in front of him.

He didn't move. His gaze went from the top of her head to the tips of her toes and back again.

Her confidence faltered.

But then he met her eyes. "I'm in awe."

"In a good way?" she joked.

"You're stunning. I'm afraid to touch you. If you're another dream, I'm going to be bitterly disappointed."

Her confidence came back, and she smiled. "*Another* dream?"

"I've had several dozen." He moved closer, stepping out of his pants.

"That's good," she told him.

"It was terrible," he countered. "They weren't real, and they were wholly unsatisfying."

She wound her arms around his neck, coming up on her toes to kiss his mouth. "I'll try to do better."

"This is better," he said. "So much better." And then he claimed her mouth.

Their naked bodies pressed tight together. She could feel every ripple of his chest, every shift of his thighs. His palms moved down her back, over her rear, smoothing the backs of her thighs.

She moved her feet apart, arching against him, a throbbing insistence growing at her core.

"Oh, Crista," he moaned, burrowing his face in her neck, kissing the tender skin, his hands kneading her fluid muscles.

"I can't wait," she told him.

He produced a condom.

Seconds later he cupped her rear and lifted her up. She twined her legs around his waist, reveling in the friction between them. He kissed her, his tongue teasing her mouth. Her hands tightened around him, gripping hard as he pushed inside, completing them.

She moaned at the instantaneous raw sensations. This wasn't merely pleasant. It wasn't merely nice. It was bril-

liant and intense, breathtakingly wonderful. Ripples of ecstasy radiated through her. He'd barely begun, and she was
flying away, flying off in a million directions. Colors exploded in her mind, and she cried out his name and cata-
pulted over the edge.

He stilled, giving her time to breathe.

"I'm sorry," she managed, embarrassed at her hair trigger.

"For what this time?" he rumbled.

"I didn't mean… I don't know what happened. I'm not…"
She wasn't usually like this.

He stopped her with a kiss. "That was amazing. I'm honored. And we can start all over now." There was a chuckle
in his voice. "Maybe you'll do better next time."

She was about to tell him next time never happened. It
never had. When she was done, she was done. But she'd be
patient with him. He didn't need to—

His thumb brushed her nipple, and her body zinged back
to life. Then he kissed her mouth, and the glow grew inside her.

Curious, she touched her tongue with his.

"Oh, my," she muttered.

He flexed his hips, moving against her.

Arousal teased her stomach, moving along her thighs.

She answered his thrusts, losing track of time all over
again. Their lovemaking went on and on, and he took her to
unimaginable heights, all but shattering her soul.

Afterward, they fell onto the bed together, him on top, her
tangled around him. She couldn't move. She wasn't even sure
she could breathe. She certainly couldn't talk, even though
she wanted to tell him he was fantastic and she'd never had
lovemaking like that.

Minutes slipped past while they both dragged in deep
breaths.

He finally broke the silence.

"That," he said, "was all of my dreams combined."

Crista's chest went tight. Warmth radiated within her.

She didn't know what happened next. She'd worry about that later. For now, all she wanted out of life was to bask in the glow of Jackson.

As Crista nestled against his shoulder, Jackson kept her held tight. All he could think about was how close he'd come to missing this moment. If he'd hesitated outside the church, if he'd let her walk through the door, if he hadn't grabbed her in that split second, she'd be married to Gerhard by now and forever out of his reach.

He'd settled a blanket around them, his instinct to cocoon them together. Faraway shouts from the pool below made their way through the window. He watched as the fan blades whirled slowly above them, dispersing the fresh outside air.

He wanted to order some champagne, maybe some strawberries. He wanted to lounge in her bed for hours, laughing with her, teasing her, asking about her childhood, her friends, her jewelry designs. But he knew he didn't have that luxury. He'd put this conversation off too long already.

She needed to know she was a multimillionaire and that Gerhard was after her money.

"The Borezone Mine," he whispered in her ear.

She tilted her head to glance at him, blinking her gorgeous eyes as her lips curved into a smile. "That wasn't what I expected you to say."

He brushed a lock of hair from her forehead. "You need to hear again that you were fantastic? Because you were fantastic."

She shook her head, her hair brushing his chest and shoulder. It felt good.

"But we have to have this conversation. Have you ever heard of the Borezone Mine?"

"No."

"I'm not surprised. A few years ago, some shares of the Borezone Mine were put into your name."

She didn't answer. Instead, she propped her head up on her elbow, looking curious. "Was it an accident?"

"I doubt it. But that doesn't really matter. The point is you own them."

"How do you know that?" she asked.

"Mac discovered it." Jackson hoped he wouldn't have to mention her father.

"Okay." Her tone was searching. "Should I give them back?"

"No."

"I don't understand your point."

Jackson pulled himself into a sitting position. "Thing is, Gerhard knows about your shares."

Her forehead wrinkled. "How does he know about them?"

"I'm not sure," Jackson answered honestly.

She sat up, tucking the blanket around her. "I think I know what must have happened."

"You do?" Jackson braced himself.

"It had to be my father."

Jackson was surprised at how quickly she'd worked it out.

But instead of angry, her tone turned worried. "Is it an illegal mine?"

"No. It's nothing illegal. The mine is in northern Canada. It's perfectly legitimate."

"If my father is involved in something, it'll be a scam."

"We need to talk about Gerhard."

She was clearly becoming impatient. "Do we have to? Really?" She spread her arms. "Right now?"

"He knows about the mine, Crista."

"So what?"

"So, he wants to get his hands on your shares. That's what this is all about."

She blinked for a moment, clearly parsing through the information. "Are you suggesting Vern was marrying me for a mine?"

"I—"

"Are you saying he felt nothing for me?" She suddenly sounded angry. She bounced from the bed, draping the blanket around herself. "Why would you say that?"

"I want you to be safe."

"It was something, Jackson. I'm not that naive. He wasn't faking our entire relationship."

Jackson realized he'd made a colossal error. He couldn't have picked a worse time to have this conversation.

"Let me start over," he said. "Or better still, forget it for now. We can talk about this later. I am starving."

"Oh, no." She vehemently shook her head. "I want you to finish telling me how my fiancé suckered me and strung me along for a year to get his hands on a few shares in some mine."

"I want you to be safe," said Jackson. "This is all about you staying safe."

"Since the wedding's off—thanks to you, by the way—I don't see how I'm not safe."

"Gerhard is not a nice man."

She lifted her chin but didn't answer.

"And neither is his father. The entire family is shady. We think they tried to bribe city councillors for building permits. Mac is checking into it now. And as long as you have shares in the Borezone diamond mine, you could be a target."

"It's a diamond mine?"

"Yes."

"It has to be a mistake."

"It's not a mistake," said Jackson. "It's easily verifiable."

Her anger seemed to switch back to confusion. "But the Gerhards don't need money. The last thing in the world that family needs is more money."

"I can't say I disagree with that."

"So why would they care about anything I have?"

"They do."

"That's your theory."

"You're right," he said. "It is a theory. But I know I'm

right. They won't go away. They'll try every trick in the book to reacquire you."

"*Reacquire* me?" Her tone was incredulous.

"You have to trust me."

She sat down on the edge of the bed. "Why did you make love to me?"

The question took him by surprise. He wasn't sure what she was driving at, so he didn't know how to answer.

He went with the truth. "Because I couldn't stop myself."

She frowned. "You tried to stop yourself?"

"Not today I didn't." He reached for her hand, but she tugged it away.

"Are you after the diamond mine, Jackson? Is that why you've stuck around all this time?"

"I am not after your mine." He hated that she had to ask. "The mine has nothing to do with you and me."

"Apparently it has everything to do with you and me."

"I'm here to keep you safe, full stop."

"You don't even know me."

"That's not true. I didn't know you. That day at the church, I didn't know you. But now I know you. And I care about you. And I am not about to stand by and let the Gerhards get their hooks into you."

"They can have the stupid mine," she snapped. "I don't want it. I don't care."

"You should. It will help you get your business back."

"How? Why is this so important?"

"They're criminals, Crista. And they have absolutely no right to that mine or—"

"I don't care," she cried.

"Crista." His tone was hard, but he needed to get her attention.

"*What?*"

"That mine is worth a hundred million dollars. And you own 40 percent."

The color drained from her face. Her shoulders dropped. Then her arms wrapped protectively around her stomach.

Silence ticked by, but he was afraid to speak. He didn't know what to say, and he didn't want to make it any worse.

"That's not possible." Her voice was small.

He wrapped a gentle hand over her shoulder. "To Gerhard, you represent forty million dollars."

The words sank in. "He didn't want a prenup." She tipped her chin to look at Jackson. "I thought that meant he trusted me."

Jackson gave in to his urge and pulled her protectively into his arms. "That's what he wanted you to think. You're a kind, trusting person."

She smacked her hand ineffectively against Jackson's chest. "Why didn't you tell me?"

"I just did."

"Why didn't you tell me before?"

"You wouldn't even believe he was cheating on you. I needed you to trust me first."

"I don't trust you now."

"I know, but I couldn't wait any longer. When I saw him out there at the pool, I knew it was time for some hard truths."

"It's been two hours since you saw him at the pool."

"I know that, too." Jackson spoke huskily, tightening his embrace. "But I figured you were safe with me."

"Plus, you wanted to get me naked before you confessed."

"Should I apologize for that?"

"Are you sorry?"

"I'm not remotely sorry for making love with you."

"The mine has to be a scam," she said with conviction. "It's my father. He wants people to believe it has a lot of value, but it will turn out to be worthless."

Jackson knew differently, but he didn't want to fight about it. He could show her copies of the share certificates, but she might think they were faked. It was better to wait and have Reginald take her to an official government office.

"Even if it is a scam," he said. "Gerhard believes it's true. That's the problem."

"He can't steal something I don't have."

"He can hurt you while he tries."

"I'll stay away from him," she said.

"Good decision. Give me the benefit of the doubt, and I'll show you final proof when we get back to Chicago."

"All right. I'll believe it when I see it," she said.

"Fair enough."

Her brow furrowed. "I think that means your job will be done."

"My job will be done," he agreed.

"Will you leave?" She tipped her chin to look up at him, obviously struggling to be brave but seeming vulnerable.

"I'm not leaving."

He was very, very far from leaving. His job might be done, but that didn't mean he was ready to walk away. Not from Crista. Not by a long shot.

Nine

"All I need to do is to find a new normal," Crista said from where she stood on the edge of the green on the resort's par-three golf course. Her life might be in chaos, but with a little effort she could sort it out.

"I'm normal," said Ellie, lining up her long putt. "And you can stay with me as long as you like."

"Concentrate," Mac told Ellie.

They were on the fifth hole. Jackson and Crista were ahead by four strokes. Their lead was thanks to Jackson. Crista could putt fairly well, but her drives were terrible. Conversely, Ellie could send the ball arcing beautifully down the fairway, but her accuracy on the green was abysmal.

"I am concentrating," she said to Mac.

"You're giving Crista life advice."

"I'm multitasking." Ellie hit the ball, sending it wide past the hole to the far side of the green.

Mac groaned.

"Don't know my own strength," said Ellie. "Not sure why you'd be in a rush to find a new place to rent," she said to Crista.

"Why rent?" asked Jackson as he placed his ball. "The market's good right now. You should buy."

"Why is he allowed to give advice and putt?" asked Ellie.

"Because he knows what he's doing," said Mac.

"And he's not your partner," said Ellie with a saucy smirk.

"That's true," said Mac.

Jackson sank the putt.

"But mostly it's because he knows what he's doing," Mac finished.

"And I don't take orders from him," Jackson joked, removing his ball from the fifth hole.

"Neither do I," said Ellie.

"That much is clear," said Mac.

Crista moved to her ball marker, replacing it with her ball. "I'd take orders," she said. "If they were good ones. It's not like I've made great decisions on my own lately."

"Buy a house," said Jackson. "A fixer-upper with good long-term property value. It won't cost much now, and you'll make a nice profit in a few years."

"I don't have a down payment," said Crista, eyeing the line to the hole and the slope of the green.

"She gets to talk while she putts," Ellie stage-whispered to Mac.

"Because Jackson doesn't care if they win."

"You're way too competitive."

"Jackson's a wuss," said Mac.

Crista couldn't help but smile at the exchange. On the golf course or anywhere else, Jackson was anything but a wuss.

She drew back and hit the ball. It bobbled through a hollow but then sank straight into the hole.

"Nice," said Mac.

Ellie elbowed him in the ribs.

He grabbed her, spun her to him and kissed her soundly on the lips. "Keep quiet while I putt."

Her cheeks were flushed, her eyes dazed. "Yes, sir."

"You're killing me." He kissed her again.

"You own a multimillion-dollar mine," Jackson said to Crista as Mac tromped onto the green. "A down payment is not going to be a problem."

"I'm not going anywhere near that mine," she said with a definitive shake of her head.

"You're being ridiculous."

"I'm being smart. Everything my father touches turns to garbage."

"It's legit," Mac called out.

"It might look legit," said Crista. "Trust me, the FBI will be at my door soon enough."

"Reginald can confirm its authenticity," said Jackson.

"Reginald is doing enough for me already. Besides, asking a bunch of questions will only alert the authorities that much sooner. I've got enough to worry about right now without getting involved in one of my father's schemes. I'm ignoring the stupid mine, and I want you to do the same." She stared hard at him, waiting for his confirmation.

His expression stayed perfectly neutral.

"Jackson," she pressed in a warning tone.

"Fine. No Reginald."

"He's in jail."

"Reginald?" asked Jackson.

"Very funny. My father is in jail for fraud and forgery."

"I know. We did our research. Nice shot, Mac."

Mac headed off the green, while Ellie returned.

"It doesn't give you pause," Crista asked Jackson, "that my father's a forger and a con artist?"

"My dad's done time, too," he said, his gaze on Ellie as she lined up.

"Seriously?" Crista had never known anyone else with a criminal parent.

"Embezzlement. He was arrested when I was thirteen. I don't visit him. I don't really like to talk about it."

"Does it bother you?"

"Not on a day-to-day basis."

"Do you worry you might be like him?" Crista worried about that for herself. She had half Trent's genetics. The other half was from her mother, who had married a con man. And now Crista had almost married a con man. That might be the most unnerving part of all.

"Do I seem like a criminal to you?" Jackson asked, an edge to his voice.

"I guess not. I mean, you're on the other side of crime.

You fight it. Then again, that's still a bit of an obsession with the criminal world."

"Your confidence is inspiring."

"I'm only trying to be honest."

"I'm not a criminal, Crista. And neither are you. Our fathers made their own choices—bad choices, obviously. But we're not them."

"My mother married him," she pointed out.

"You didn't marry Gerhard."

Ellie missed the putt but got a little closer to the hole.

"I'm not buying a house," said Crista.

"I hate to see you spend your money on rent, especially since you'll be trying to build your business."

"I'll manage."

"Every penny you spend on rent is a penny you can't plow into Cristal Creations."

"It's still the most practical solution," she said.

"It might be a solution, but it's not practical."

"It's every bit as practical as buying a house."

"Real estate is a capital asset," said Jackson.

Ellie sank her putt. She let out a whoop and hoisted her putter in the air.

Crista grinned at her joy.

"See what happens when you concentrate," Mac called to Ellie, loping toward her.

Crista started for her clubs.

Jackson suddenly grasped her hand and pulled her back. "Hang on."

"What?"

"I have a better idea."

"I don't want to hear about it."

"It's a very good idea."

She turned, letting out a sigh of exasperation. "Can't we just golf?"

"Come live with me," he said.

She blinked at him in astonishment, certain she couldn't have heard him right.

"I've got three bedrooms." His expression turned reflective. "I mean, not that I'm suggesting you'd need your own bedroom. I like sleeping with you. In fact, I love sleeping with you. I'd seriously like to continue sleeping with you, Crista."

She replayed his offer in her head, looking for the punch line.

"It's a great plan," he said, his gaze darting around her expression. "Gerhard would absolutely leave you alone if I was in the picture. And, really…you know…" His eyes lost focus. He had obviously gone deep into thought.

"Jackson?" she prompted.

When he didn't respond, she waved her hand in front of his face.

"I've got the solution," he said. "It's so simple."

"I'm not moving in with you."

They barely knew each other. Jackson had wandered ridiculously far afield in his ramblings.

"Marry me," he said, grasping both of her hands, his expression turning earnest.

She opened her mouth. Then she closed it again. "Uh, earth to Jackson?"

"It's perfect," he said in what looked like complete seriousness.

"Mac," she called out. "Something's gone terribly wrong with Jackson."

"What is it?" asked Mac, immediately starting toward them.

"Vegas," said Jackson, still looking straight into Crista's eyes. "We can take Tuck's jet to Vegas."

"Has he ever done this before?" she asked Mac.

Mac halted next to them. "Done what?"

"I'm proposing to her," said Jackson.

"Then, no," said Mac. "He's never done that before."

Ellie arrived in the circle. "What's going on?"

Mac answered, "Jackson asked Crista to marry him."

Ellie's face broke into a bright smile. "*Really?*"

Crista turned on her. "Be serious."

Ellie schooled her features, lowering her tone. "Really?"

"No, not really," Crista snapped. "He's joking. Or he's gone round the bend. At the moment, my money's on round the bend."

"Are you all done?" asked Jackson, looking normal again.

"Is it over?" asked Crista. "Your fit of insanity or whatever that was?"

"It's a perfect plan," said Jackson. "If you're married to me, then Gerhard is forced to give up and go away."

Neither Ellie nor Mac disputed the logic.

"Perfect plan," Crista drawled sarcastically. "What could possibly go wrong? Oh, wait. I'd be *married* to a man I barely know."

"For a good cause," said Mac.

Crista turned on Mac. "You're actually going to encourage him?"

"You can divorce me if it doesn't work out," said Jackson.

"It's not going to work out," she said, an edge of hysteria coming into her voice. "Because it's never going to happen."

He continued as if she hadn't spoken. "Just like they do in a regular marriage."

It occurred to her that she was being had. She glanced from one man to the other. "Is this a joke? Are you messing with me? Do you guys do this kind of thing all the time?"

They looked at each other.

"No," said Jackson. "I don't make a habit of proposing to women. I'd sure never do it as a joke."

She tugged her hands from his. "Fine. Whatever." She paced away and called back over her shoulder, "I'm going to tee off on six. Anybody coming with me?"

"I'm coming," called Ellie.

In a moment, Ellie was walking beside her.

"What was that?" Ellie asked.

"We were talking about rent and real estate. Next thing I knew, he was off the deep end. I should buy a house. No, I should live with him. No, I should marry him."

Ellie giggled.

"This isn't funny," said Crista.

"It is a little bit funny."

"No…" said Crista. "Okay, sure, it's a little bit funny." And there was some in the idea of marrying Jackson to keep Vern out of her life. "In an ironic way," she allowed.

"He must like you."

"Sure, he likes me. And he likes sleeping with me. Who wouldn't—" Crista stopped herself. She had been about to say the sex between them had been mind-blowing, both last night and again this morning.

"It was that good?" asked Ellie, a thread of laughter in her voice.

"We wouldn't get tired of the sex anytime soon," Crista admitted.

"I wouldn't get tired of Mac, either."

Crista stopped. "You had sex with Mac?"

"Why do you think he was there for breakfast?"

"I thought he came by this morning looking for Jackson."

Crista and Jackson had fallen asleep last night before Ellie had come back to the suite.

"You're not the only hot one, you know."

"I didn't mean—"

But Ellie was laughing. "Mac's pretty great. And he thinks the world of Jackson."

"Jackson seems pretty great, too," Crista said honestly.

"But you're not going to marry him?"

"What sane woman would do that?"

"Will you live with him?"

"No."

"It could be platonic."

"It wouldn't be platonic." Of that, Crista was certain.

"I've only got a sofa for you."

"Your sofa will be fine." They came to the sixth tee box, and Crista stopped. "Your sofa will be perfect. I am putting this crazy week—no, this crazy *year*—behind me. As soon as Reginald works out the details, I'll get to work on rebuilding Cristal Creations, and then I'll find myself a new apartment."

She selected the three wood, pushed a tee into the grass and proceeded to hit the longest drive of her life.

"The marriage proposal was out of left field," Mac observed the next day. They were back in Chicago at Jackson's house. Crista had moved in with Ellie, her belongings going to a storage unit in the morning.

"It wasn't the worst idea in the world," Jackson countered.

"It kind of was."

Maybe. But had Jackson pulled it off, it would have solved a whole lot of problems. And, truth was, the more time he spent with Crista, the more time he wanted to spend with Crista.

"You barely know her," said Mac.

"I know her better than she knew Gerhard."

"I'm not sure I see your point."

"My point is, she agreed to marry him, and he was lying to her from day one."

"That logic borders on the bizarre," said Mac. "You do know you're getting a little too close on this one."

"You think?" Even now as Jackson glanced around his living room, all he could think was how Crista would look good in the leather armchair, or on the sofa, or at the dining room table.

It wasn't clear what happened next between them. He was leaning toward inviting her over for dinner, a simple date. He'd break out the candles and wine, maybe order some flowers, do by stealth what he couldn't do with candor and get her to spend a night, or two or three.

"It may be time to move on," said Mac.

"It's not time to move on."

"She knows the score. She's not going to give the guy the time of day."

Jackson would agree on that front. But he still didn't trust Gerhard. And his gut said they didn't yet have all the pieces.

"It you want to date her, date her," said Mac. "But stop pretending you still need to protect her."

Jackson's phone rang.

He answered. "Hey, Tuck."

"We got it done," said Tuck.

"Cristal Creations?"

"Yes. They drove a hard bargain. Vern Gerhard would have walked, but the old man took double the estimated market value."

"Good."

"I hope she's worth it."

"She is," said Jackson. "Does she know yet?"

"Our Bahamian guy is calling Reginald right now."

"Reginald won't know Tucker Transportation's behind the purchase?"

"He won't. Do you want him to know?"

"No. And Dixon's okay with this?"

"Absolutely. I told him you were in love."

The statement took Jackson by surprise. "I'm not in love."

Across the living room, Mac grinned.

"Sure," Tuck said smoothly. "Keep telling yourself that." He paused. "Until you can't keep telling yourself anymore."

"You're nuts," said Jackson, and he frowned his displeasure at Mac.

"I know the signs," said Tuck.

"I'm hanging up now."

Tuck laughed. "Picturing her in a white dress yet?"

"Picturing her in Vegas." As soon as the words left his mouth, Jackson regretted them. He knew they left the wrong impression. But he also knew that explaining further wouldn't help.

"That'll do it," said Tuck. "I'll bring a jet if you let me be the best man."

"Goodbye, Tuck." Then Jackson remembered the magnitude of the favor. "And thanks. Thanks a lot."

The laughter remained in Tuck's voice. "No problem. This is the most fun I've had in weeks."

Jackson disconnected the call. "Tucker Transportation just secretly bought Cristal Creations."

"You know, you could do it the old-fashioned way," said Mac.

"Do what?"

"Date her. Win her over. And when she loves you back, propose."

Jackson rolled his eyes. "Give me a break."

"The barriers are out of the way. You don't need to be her bodyguard anymore. You're just two ordinary adults."

Jackson didn't know why he took offense to Mac's words. "She's not ordinary."

"And you're not in love."

"Let's talk about you and Ellie."

"I just met Ellie."

"Uh-huh." Jackson exaggerated the skepticism in his tone.

"Me and Ellie, that's me being your wingman."

"That's you falling for a beautiful woman."

"You're forgetting I didn't propose to her," said Mac.

"She's not the one in jeopardy."

Mac's expression turned thoughtful. "See, I can't picture that."

"Picture what?"

"Ellie in jeopardy. She's tough, and she's smart, and she'd take out any guy who tried to mess with her."

"Worried?" asked Jackson, glad to have the topic turned away from himself and Crista.

"Nope."

"Because you're tougher than her?"

"Because I'm not trying to mess with her." Mac's words rang true.

His situation with Ellie was dead simple. While Jackson's situation with Crista was anything but. He knew how she felt about her father. If he told her he'd been working with Trent, she'd never trust him. But if he didn't, their relationship would be built on a lie.

It wasn't a choice. To move forward, he had to come clean and take his chances that she wouldn't walk away.

Crista set down the phone, her brain reeling with the news.

"What?" asked Ellie. She was in the small kitchen of her apartment, tearing spinach into a salad bowl.

"Reginald says somebody bought Cristal Creations."

"What do you mean, bought it? How could they buy it?"

"They bought the company. From Gerhard. Reginald says I still have copyright on the designs."

Ellie frowned. "Is this good?"

"I think so. Reginald says they want me to keep running the company. He seems really excited about the sale."

"Who are they?"

"A group of wealthy anonymous investors."

"Does that strike you as a little hinky?"

"Should it? I do trust Reginald. He says holding companies do this all the time. And it's got to be better than Gerhard Incorporated."

"I suppose." Ellie seemed skeptical, but she went back to tearing the spinach.

Crista told herself to be practical rather than emotional. She fought an urge to call Jackson. She knew the sale had nothing to do with him. He probably wasn't even interested. Still, she found that she wanted to share the news and get his opinion.

"It's not like I have a choice," she said to Ellie instead. "I can't afford to buy it myself."

"How much did they pay?"

"It was confidential."

Ellie shrugged and turned to open a cupboard. "If it's more than fifty bucks, you couldn't have afforded it."

"I'm not that bad off," Crista protested.

"Oh, crap," said Ellie.

"What?"

"I forgot to buy almonds. The salad is going to be boring without them."

"No problem," said Crista, coming to her feet. "I'll pop down to the market. I could use the fresh air."

She could also use a little time to think. Her life felt like a pinball, bouncing off paddles, bonging over points, into traps, some things good and some things bad, but all of them on the edge of control.

"Can you grab a few limes as well?" Ellie called.

"Sure." Crista retrieved her shoulder bag.

The evening was warm, so she tucked her feet into her sandals and swung the purse over her T-shirt and shorts. She looped her hair into a ponytail in case of a breeze. Then she called goodbye and locked the dead bolt behind her.

The sun was setting on the street outside, lights coming on in the apartments above the shops. Ellie lived above a florist, which was next to a funky ladies' boutique and a toy store. There was a bakery on the corner with a compact grocery store opposite.

Traffic was light now that rush hour had passed. Neighbors and shoppers cruised the street, while laughing groups of people from the after-work crowd—or maybe they were tourists—sat drinking at the open-air café on the other side. The buzz of traffic, the aromas of yeast and cinnamon, and the bustle of ordinary Chicagoans on a Thursday night made her feel normal. It felt good.

She stopped at the corner, waiting for the walk signal.

The light was yellow, and a minivan with smoked windows came to a stop at the intersection. A silver sedan came up behind it. The minivan's door slid open and a man hopped out. Crista moved to one side so he could get around the light pole.

Suddenly, she felt a shove from behind. The man stared her straight in the eyes. He moved out of the way, and she was instantly propelled forward.

"Hey!" she shouted, angry at being jostled.

But the next thing she knew, she was inside the van.

The door slammed shut.

"Stop," she shrieked.

A hand clamped over her mouth, and an arm went around her like a steel band. The horn honked, and the van lurched away from the curb, cutting around the corner to a chorus of horns from outside on the street.

A hood was thrown over her head, and sheer terror rocked her.

"Keep quiet," a gravelly voice commanded in her ear. Then he pulled his hand from beneath the hood.

She had no intention of keeping quiet. "What do you think you're—"

A hand immediately came over her mouth, pressing the rough fabric against her teeth.

"Quiet," the voice repeated.

She felt the car slow to a stop, and she screamed at the top of her lungs, hoping someone outside would hear.

The hand stopped her again, and the man swore.

"She pierced my eardrum," he shouted.

"Crista, stop," came another voice.

She froze. She knew the voice. And now she was more frightened than ever.

"Vern?"

"Nobody's going to hurt you," he said.

"What are you doing?"

"We need to talk."

"You're *kidnapping* me."

"You should be used to it by now." His tone was cool.

She kicked the back of the driver's seat. It was out of sheer frustration because her legs were the only thing she could move.

"Hold her still," came a third voice.

"Let me go," she demanded. "This is illegal. You're all going to be arrested."

"Like you had Jackson Rush arrested?"

The question caught her off guard. "He had his reasons."

"And I have mine."

"You can't do this, Vern. Whatever you think you'll accomplish, it's not going to work. You have to let me go."

"Get rid of her cell phone," said Vern.

She felt a hand dip into her purse, rummaging around.

"Hey," she protested.

"Got it," said the voice beside her.

"Toss it," said Vern, his tone cold.

Her sliver of hope faded.

Jackson could have tracked her phone. When she didn't come back to the apartment, Ellie would get worried and she'd call Jackson. At least Crista hoped she'd call Jackson. And Jackson would have known how to access the GPS.

She heard the window roll down and the traffic noise increase, felt a breeze buffet across her, and she knew her phone was in the gutter.

She was at Vern's mercy.

She wished she knew what that meant. But the truth was she didn't know anything about him. The Vern she'd planned to marry never would have kidnapped her. He'd never have cheated on her. He'd never have terrified her like this.

Her throat went dry, and a chill took over her body. She was in the clutches of a stranger, and she had no idea what he might do.

Ten

"She's not picking up," Jackson said to Mac, his frustration turning to worry.

"Maybe she doesn't want to talk to you."

"Why wouldn't she want to talk to me?"

Jackson didn't expect her to call him the minute she finished talking to Reginald. Then again, he didn't see why she wouldn't call to tell him Cristal Creations had been sold and she didn't have to worry about Gerhard owning her company. Did she not think he'd be interested?

"It's only been ten hours since you saw her," said Mac.

"That's not the point. She's had some pretty big news since then."

"Maybe Reginald hasn't called her yet."

"He'd call her right away."

Jackson was sure about that. But he couldn't very well call Reginald to confirm it. As far as Reginald was concerned, the purchase was a completely random act of an arm's-length company. Jackson intended to keep him thinking just that.

"You're obsessing," said Mac.

Jackson tossed his phone onto the coffee table. Was he obsessing? He wanted to talk to her. Was that being obsessive?

"Call Ellie," he said.

"And say *what*?"

"I don't care. Anything. Find out if Crista is with her."

"I'm going to look like a stalker."

Jackson picked up his phone and redialed Crista. It went straight to voice mail.

"Maybe she's talking to someone," said Mac.

"For forty-five minutes?"

"Maybe it's turned off."

"Why would she turn it off?"

"In the shower, taking a nap, in bed with—" Mac cut himself off.

"She's not in bed with some other guy." Though the thought did make Jackson's stomach churn. "You have to call Ellie."

"Fine," Mac said in a clipped voice. He dialed with his thumb. "If I'm going to look stupid, just so you know, you'll owe me."

Jackson nodded.

"Hey, Ellie," Mac said into his phone.

Jackson couldn't help but notice Mac's voice changed when he talked to Ellie, going deeper, smoother, more intimate. He obviously liked Ellie more than he was letting on.

"Really?" Mac's tone turned to alert, causing Jackson to look up. "When?"

"What?" Jackson asked.

Mac's look was intent and focused. "Did you call her?"

Adrenaline rushed into Jackson's system, and he came to his feet.

Mac stood. "We'll come to you."

"What?" Jackson all but shouted.

"Sit tight," said Mac, signing off. "Crista went to the store and didn't come back."

"When?" Jackson asked, his feet already taking him to the door.

"Over an hour. Ellie said she was about to call us."

"What store?" asked Jackson. "Driving, walking?"

"Two blocks from Ellie's apartment. She walked."

Jackson swore as he flung open his front door.

"We don't know anything for sure," said Mac.

"He's got her," said Jackson.

"That's a pretty bold move."

"I shouldn't have left her alone."

"You can't watch her for the rest of her life."

"I could have watched her for the rest of the week." Jackson would have considered the rest of her life. He realized he'd have seriously considered sticking right by her side forever if it would keep her safe.

"You want me to drive?" asked Mac.

"No, I don't want you to drive." The last thing in the world Jackson could do right now was sit idle.

"Jackson, we have to treat this as just another case. Emotion is clouding your judgment."

"My judgment is fine." Jackson wrenched open the door of the SUV. "Call Ellie back," he told Mac as he peeled out of the driveway. "Get whatever details you can."

Jackson pressed on the accelerator, racking his brain. Where would they take her? It wouldn't be the mansion. That was too obvious. Maybe to one of their businesses, one of their construction sites. Would they threaten her? Would she defy them? He was terrified she would.

Then he had an idea. He dialed Rush Investigations, getting the night shift to ping her phone location. It took only moments to learn the phone was southeast of Ellie's.

Jackson disconnected. "Her phone is at Edwards and Ninety-Fifth. It's stationary."

"They ditched it," said Mac.

"Likely."

"They had to know you'd check."

Jackson smacked his hand down on the steering wheel. They could easily have changed directions right after they tossed her phone.

He took an abrupt right turn.

"Where to?" asked Mac.

"The office. Call ahead. I want a list of every known Gerhard vehicle. Give them Ellie's address. Get them to canvass local businesses for security footage. Cross-reference vehicles on Ellie's street at the time to the place where the phone was dumped."

"Roger that," said Mac, disconnecting from Ellie.

At least it was something. If they could find a vehicle

that had been in both places, maybe they could get make and model or even a license plate. If they could, they had a chance of tracking it farther.

"And Gerhard's buildings," said Jackson, his brain clicking along as he drove. "Locate *all* of his buildings. I want it mapped out by the time we get there."

They were going to need intelligence, and they were going to need reinforcements.

"Will do, boss," said Mac. Then he began relaying instructions to the Rush Investigations office.

Jackson sped up.

When they removed the hood, Crista found she was in a warehouse. It was cold and hard, with concrete floors, metal walls and high, open ceilings. The few fluorescent lights that buzzed suspended from the crossbeams did little to dispel the shadows. The cavernous room was full of rusting shelves and aging steel bins, with stacks of old lumber piled helter-skelter along the far wall.

They'd sat her in an old folding chair next to a battered wooden table and three other chairs. They'd tied her hands behind her back. But at least she could see now.

Vern stood in front her, along with his father, Manfred, and a craggy-faced man she didn't recognize. She could see two guards at a nearby door, their backs to her.

"What do you want?" she demanded of Vern.

Part of her was terrified, but another part found the entire situation too absurd to be taken seriously. It was as if Vern and Manfred were both playacting. And for a hysterical moment, she thought she might laugh out loud.

But then the moment passed, and she shivered from the cold and fear. Nobody was playacting. She was in genuine danger.

"I want you to marry me," said Vern in a matter-of-fact voice.

The statement struck her as beyond ridiculous.

"Right here, right now," he continued, glancing at the craggy-faced man. "If you do that, I promise to give you a divorce in a couple of months."

Manfred cleared his throat.

"Six months, tops," said Vern.

"I'm not marrying you," she said. "You cheated on me. You lied to me. You just kidnapped me, and you have me tied up in a warehouse." Her voice rose to an almost hysterical pitch. "I don't know what passes for romance in this dysfunctional family, but I assure you this isn't doing it for me."

Manfred raised his arm as if he was going to backhand her.

She braced herself.

But Vern stepped forward and grabbed Manfred's hand. It was the first time she'd ever seen him stand up to his father. She found herself astonished.

"That's not necessary," said Vern.

"Make her listen," Manfred hissed.

"You need to marry me," said Vern, his tone going earnest.

She kept silent. Tears burned in the corners of her eyes.

"You have two choices," said Manfred, both his voice and his expression more intimidating than she'd ever seen. "Marry my boy now. Sail the Mediterranean just like you planned. Work on your tan, enjoy the food, drink the wine. He'll divorce you soon enough."

"And keep my diamond mine," she dared to say.

"And keep your mine," Manfred agreed, not seeming surprised that she knew.

"You know it's bogus," she said.

Both men looked confused.

"I don't know how you know about it, but my father's a con artist. He will have set this up for some convoluted reason of his own. There is no mine. And if there is, it doesn't have any diamonds."

Manfred gave a chilling smile. "Oh, there's a mine, all right."

Crista shook her head. "This is pointless."

"If there's no mine," Vern added reasonably, "then there's nothing for you to protect."

"I'm not marrying you," she said.

Mine or no mine, she wouldn't promise to love and honor Vern. She'd dodged that bullet when Jackson grabbed her outside the church, and she wasn't about to throw herself back in front of it.

Jackson had shown her the truth about her fiancé. He'd shown her the truth about other things, too, like how amazing and trusting a relationship could be between two people. Despite how it had started, in such a short time, she felt closer to Jackson than she'd ever felt to Vern.

She could be herself with Jackson, her total candid self. He didn't mind if she was opinionated. He didn't mind if she argued. He even knew about her father, and he hadn't pitied her. He'd understood. He understood her embarrassment, her anger, even her denial in a way few other people could.

She suddenly missed him with all her heart. She realized she should have said yes to staying at his place. For a crazy moment, she even wished she'd married him. Maybe they'd be in Vegas right now having an outlandish honeymoon in a garish hotel, playing poker or watching a circus act.

"That brings us to choice number two," said Manfred, making a show of inspecting his manicure as he spoke.

Her thoughts of Jackson vanished, and her fear returned. The ropes were tight around her wrists, chafing her skin. And she was growing colder by the minute. It was clear that Manfred was perfectly willing to have her suffer.

"We sign the papers for you," he said, his expression remorseless.

"What papers?" She couldn't help but ask. She looked from Manfred to Vern.

"Hans over there is a very good forger."

"For the mine?" she asked. Did they want her to sign over ownership of the mine? She'd do it. She was positive there was nothing to lose in that.

Manfred clicked his teeth as he waggled a finger at her. "Oh, no, that would be too suspicious. Hans will sign the marriage license for you."

Crista drew back in the metal chair. Their plan was to forge a marriage license. Exactly how did they expect that to work? She'd only deny it the minute they let her go.

"Then it's off on your honeymoon," said Manfred, sounding like he was enjoying himself. "Only to perish in a very tragic drowning accident off the yacht."

She stilled. Had Manfred just threatened to kill her? Did he expect her to believe him?

She found herself looking to Vern again, searching for the man who'd held her so tenderly. They'd danced. They'd laughed. She'd commiserated with him over his unbending father. He'd proposed on one knee with candlelight and roses.

"You're not throwing me overboard," she said to him. There was no way she'd believe that.

"We don't have a prenup," said Vern, sounding frighteningly practical. "Our wills were drafted weeks ago. It would be tragic, but it would be completely believable."

A sick feeling welled up inside her. "I already told you, the mine's a fake. Take it. It's not about the mine. It's about not wanting to marry you."

"Give me a break," Vern scoffed.

"What about when—" Crista stopped herself. She'd been about to point out that Ellie would go to the authorities. She wouldn't for a second believe Crista had willingly married Vern.

But saying it out loud would only put Ellie in danger. The last thing she wanted to do was hurt Ellie.

As her fear grew to unbearable heights, suddenly a loud crash reverberated through the warehouse. Men shouted over the sound of running feet. Manfred turned, while Vern and the craggy man turned pale. Everything was in motion around her.

Vern grabbed her, pulling her to her feet.

"Let her go!" Jackson shouted.

Crista wanted to whoop and cheer. Mac was there. So were a bunch of other men. The Gerhards' security guards seemed stunned, too.

"Let her go," Jackson repeated and began pacing toward them.

"Don't come any closer," Vern growled, waving a gun.

"Jackson," she cried, both relieved and newly terrified.

"Walk away from this," Manfred commanded.

"Not going to happen," said Jackson.

Crista focused on Jackson, trying to send a message with her eyes. She was grateful he was here. She was so glad to see him. She didn't see a way out, but she hoped he had a plan.

She started to work on the knots, hoping to free her hands from the rope and be ready.

"He's here for the mine himself," said Vern. "Nothing more, nothing less."

"I'm here for Crista," said Jackson.

"You didn't think we'd find out?" asked Vern.

"I don't care what you think you know," Jackson spat.

"He wants the diamonds every bit as much as I want the diamonds," said Vern.

"There *are* no diamonds," Crista shouted. Why wouldn't anyone listen to her?

"Did you ever ask him how he knew?" asked Vern.

Jackson took a step forward.

Vern pulled her tighter, jabbing her with the gun.

"Ask who sent him. Ask him how he knows your daddy's cell mate. Ask him how many times he met with Trent Corday before he dragged you from our wedding."

Jackson's jaw hardened, and his nostrils flared. But he didn't deny the accusations.

Crista tried to make some sense out of it. "You know my father?"

"What was the deal?" Vern asked Jackson. "Were you going to split it fifty-fifty?"

"It's complicated," Jackson said to Crista.

Her heart sank. At the same time, her hands came free of the rope.

"What was the plan?" repeated Vern. "Were you going to marry her instead?"

Crista withered.

Jackson's frown deepened.

Vern laughed out loud. "Oh, that's too rich. You already asked her to marry you? You couldn't even wait, say, a month or so, to let the dust settle?"

"I was protecting her from you."

"You were conning her *yourself*." Vern's tone went lower, speaking to Crista. "His father is your father's cell mate. Colin Rush, the king of the Ponzi scheme. His daddy makes your daddy look like a carnival huckster. He's here for the diamonds. He doesn't give a damn about you."

"Shut up," Jackson shouted, striding forward.

Crista wrenched herself from Vern's arms.

"Crista—" Jackson began.

"You stay away," she warned him. She glanced around the room. "Everybody *stay far away from me*."

She refused to be taken in by anybody. She stopped in front of Mac. "Give me your car keys."

"You sure?"

"I'm sure. And your cash. Give me all of your cash." It was on the tip of her tongue to tell him she'd pay him back. But given the circumstances, it seemed silly to be polite.

Mac gave a small smile. "Smart girl."

"I've learned a few things along the way."

"Let me explain," Jackson pleaded with her.

She dared to look at him. "So you can tell me more lies?" She was heartsick at his deception. Her father had sent him. She'd been such an easy mark. She'd been a laughably easy mark.

"It wasn't lies," said Jackson.

"Do you know my father?"

Jackson's nostrils flared. "Yes."

"He sent you?" She already knew the answer.

"Yes."

"He told you about the diamond mine."

"Yes, but—"

"Joke's on you, Jackson. Trent conned you just like he's conned everybody his whole life. The mine doesn't exist."

"Mac confirmed it," said Jackson.

Crista barked out a laugh. "He thinks he confirmed it. That just says my father is one step ahead of Mac."

She turned her attention to Mac, who was reaching into his pockets. He handed her the keys and a wad of cash.

"What are you doing?" Jackson demanded of Mac.

"Letting her go," Mac said mildly.

"No," Jackson shouted.

Mac gave him a look.

"Right," said Jackson, clenching his jaw. "You're right. She needs to get out of here."

"Norway," he said to the man closest to him, "give her all your money."

The man called Norway didn't hesitate. He pulled a wad of cash out of his pocket and handed it over.

"Dump Mac's car at the bus station," said Jackson, coming close. "You lay low for a while until we clear this up."

"I know what I'm doing," said Crista. She was going to disappear into anonymity. And it was going to be for more than just a while. None of them would find her until she wanted to be found. "You'll keep Vern from coming after me?" she asked Jackson.

"Absolutely," he said.

"Good." Crista stuffed the money into the pocket of her shorts. "Tell Ellie not to worry."

Crista headed for the door.

She located Mac's SUV and started it up. She was doing exactly as Jackson had suggested. She'd ditch the vehicle at the bus station. But then she'd take a taxi to the train station, buy a ticket with cash, switch trains outside the city and find herself a quiet, budget hotel where she could pay cash and hide under a fake name.

She realized she couldn't trust Reginald anymore. But the Yellow Pages were full of lawyers. She'd find her own lawyer. Then she'd work her way through the changes at Cristal Creations all on her own. She was through depending on others for help.

Since calling the police would leave them all with a lot of explaining to do, Jackson assumed the Gerhards would keep the altercation to themselves. And though it chafed to let her go on her own, he'd made sure Crista had a three-hour head start on Vern.

Now, both groups cautiously crossed the parking lot, each watching their backs as the entered their respective vehicles.

Jackson wanted to search for Crista right away. He wanted the Rush Investigations team to head straight back to the office and get started. He knew Gerhard would do exactly that, and it killed him simply sit still and wait for her to come back.

"What if she's right about her father?" Jackson mused out loud as the sun broke the horizon, lighting the world outside the meeting room window.

"That the diamond mine is worthless?" asked Mac.

Jackson wished he could seriously consider that possibility, because no diamond mine meant Crista had no value to Gerhard, so Gerhard would disappear.

"No. Not that," said Jackson. "I'm convinced the diamond mine is legit. But that doesn't mean Trent's not running some other con."

Mac hesitated. "What con would he be running? What are we not seeing?"

Jackson scanned through the facts.

"Problem is you're not seeing anything beyond Crista," said Mac. "You get that you're in love with her, right?"

Jackson wasn't letting his emotions get in the way of solving this. He couldn't afford to do that. He ordered himself to slow down, detach, think harder.

And then it hit him. "Trent's lying."

Trent had initially downplayed his culpability in Crista's engagement. Not that Jackson was sorry about that part. In fact, he was glad Trent had lied to him back then.

"You think he's still lying?" asked Mac.

Jackson was certain of it. "The Gerhards aren't threatening to kill Trent. They're in league with him."

"That would be a cold-blooded move," said Mac. "Voluntarily setting up your own daughter."

Jackson whistled low. It was all coming clear. "Trent told them about the mine, and he told them how to get to Crista. Were they going to split the take?"

"Why wouldn't Trent just split it with Crista?"

"Crista won't even speak to him. She never would have trusted him."

"But why get cold feet at the last minute?" asked Mac. "Why would he call you in and mess it all up?"

"Because they double-crossed him." Jackson stood, absolutely certain he was right. "He didn't call me in to help Crista. He only wanted his leverage back."

Mac seemed to be considering what he'd said. "If that's the case, what's his next move?"

"I don't know." Jackson gripped the back of the chair, tightening his fingers, ordering himself to think carefully. "But she's his bargaining chip. He needs her back in his clutches."

"We better find her first," said Mac.

Jackson started for the door. "And Daddy dearest is going

to help us do that. That creep is going to tell me everything he knows."

"He'll only lie," Mac called.

"Let him try."

It was a two-hour drive to Riverway State. Jackson made it in ninety minutes. For the third time, he found himself sitting across a prison visiting table from Trent Corday.

"What's your new plan?" he barked without preamble.

"My new plan for what?"

"For Crista. Don't bother lying. Nobody's threatening you. You're all the way in Gerhard's pocket."

Trent's fleetingly shocked expression told Jackson he was right.

"You sold out your own daughter," Jackson spat. "It was a setup from minute one."

"If they told you that, they're lying."

Jackson had no interest in debating the past. He was certain Trent had orchestrated the whole thing. "How do you plan to get her back?"

Trent's complexion darkened. "I don't know what you're talking about."

"You think I'm going to let him kidnap her again?"

"What? Kidnap who?"

Jackson was through with the man's games. "Playing dumb gets you nothing."

"I'm not—"

"What is the new plan?" Jackson articulated each word slowly and carefully.

"The new plan to *what*?"

Jackson wanted to take a swing. "Don't you know that once they're married, Gerhard has no reason to keep her alive?"

"I thought the wedding was off." Trent looked confused.

Jackson wasn't buying it. "Your backup plan has a backup plan." He knew how these men worked. "If not a marriage to Gerhard for a kickback from the mine, then what? Who? What do I need to protect her from?"

Guilt flashed across Trent's face. "There was never any reason to hurt her."

"There was always a reason to hurt her. I know you're not burdened with a conscience, but don't lie to yourself. And stop lying to me. *What happens next?*"

"Nothing," Trent shouted. "I mean, I've thought about it. There are tens of millions of dollars at stake. And they're mine."

"They're Crista's."

Trent's tone went sullen. "She never even knew they existed."

"What's the new plan?"

It was clear Trent didn't want to answer.

Jackson waited.

"I haven't had time to come up with one," Trent finally admitted.

Now there was something Jackson could believe.

"Gerhard was my only play," said Trent. "I can't come at her directly. Crista has never trusted me."

"And thanks to you, she'll never trust me, either. Which only makes my job harder."

"What are you planning to do?"

"What you should have done in the first place."

"I don't understand."

"Protect Crista from the lowlifes you put in her path."

"How?"

"None of your business."

"How can it hurt to tell me?"

"You don't deserve to know."

Trent reached out to him. "I'm not as bad as you think. They were never supposed to hurt her."

"Are you saying they planned a divorce all along."

"Yes. There was no prenup to protect the mine, so all he had to do was divorce her."

Jackson couldn't believe Trent would be so stupid. "What about Gerhard's assets? Don't try to tell me he'd give her a settlement."

"It's all in Manfred's name. Vern owns nothing."

"Still, a divorce would mean giving her part of the mine. They wouldn't do that. You put her *life* at risk."

Trent paled a shade. "They said it would be a divorce."

"They lied, and you're a fool."

The two men stared at each other for a long moment.

"What's your plan?" Trent's voice broke. "Tell me how you're going to protect my little girl."

Jackson stepped back, releasing a long breath. "For one thing," he said, "Cristal Creations is out of Gerhard's hands."

"You did that?"

"I had someone do that for me. Tell them, don't tell them. It's too late for them to change anything. Tell them they'll never be able to get to her. She'll be protected 24/7 for a month or a year or forever, whatever it takes."

Jackson wished he didn't have to do all this in secret. He wanted to be honest with her. He wanted to be in her life. He wanted to *be* her life.

He was completely in love with her. It angered him that he was figuring that out in a prison. It angered him more that he was figuring it out while confronting her no-good father. The entire situation was thoroughly wrong and completely unfair.

"Why?" asked Trent, looking genuinely perplexed.

"Because she deserves it. She deserves everything."

Jackson rose from the seat. He was done here. He was done with Trent. He knew the truth now, but it didn't help him. He should have asked way more questions in the beginning. He should have been more suspicious. He might not have purposely conned Crista. But the result was the same. His stupidity had put her in harm's way.

Maybe he didn't deserve her any more than Trent did.

Eleven

It took Crista three days to figure out a solution. But she woke up one morning, and it was fully formed.

"Are you sure?" asked Ellie as they drove east from where they'd met up in Rockford.

Crista had set up an anonymous email account to communicate with Ellie. When she'd sent a message, Ellie had left Chicago, switching from a taxi to a train to a bus, while Crista had made her way from a boutique hotel over the border in Wisconsin.

"It's meaningless," said Crista. "And it's making me a target. Even if the mine is worth some money, I don't want it."

"But him? Are you sure you even want to talk to him?"

"He can't hurt me from behind bars."

"He hurt you by putting a diamond mine in your name."

"And I'm about to undo that. As soon as the mine is out of the picture, Vern walks away—and Jackson walks away." Crista couldn't help the little catch in her voice as she said Jackson's name.

He'd broken her heart. She hadn't realized how badly she'd fallen for him until that night in the warehouse. Anger had carried her for a few hours. But once the anger wore off, his betrayal had devastated her.

He'd seemed so clever, so funny, so compassionate and so incredibly handsome. She'd started to think of him as her soul mate. He'd comforted her. He made her think he genuinely cared about her.

She realized now that her upbringing had left her starved for male attention. It seemed she was willing to take a chance on anyone, including Vern and Jackson. It was entirely understandable, but it was also foolish. And she would never make that mistake again.

"I don't mean the money," said Ellie. "Cristal Creations is going to be wildly successful. I mean, seeing your father in person, talking to him, having him try to manipulate you into…I don't know. But whatever it is, it's going to upset you."

"I'm immune," said Crista.

She'd done nothing for the last three days but be angry with her father, detest Vern and build a wall against her feelings for Jackson. She dared any of the three of them to try to get under her skin.

"I hope so," said Ellie.

"It'll take five minutes," said Crista. "All I need is his signature on the legal papers, and the mine is all his. He can use it in a brand-new scam. He'll like that."

"Mac says it's real," said Ellie.

"Mac is in league with Jackson."

"True," said Ellie. "And I haven't told him a thing. He doesn't know you contacted me or anything."

Crista was surprised. "You've talked to Mac since I left Chicago?"

Ellie hesitated. "He calls me every day. He came by last night."

"You saw Mac last night?"

"Yeah, well…" Ellie turned her head to gaze out the passenger window.

"Please tell me you didn't spend the night with Mac."

"He didn't suspect a thing. I swear. And, anyway, if I didn't let him stay over, he would have been suspicious."

"You're getting serious with Mac?"

"Not exactly serious." Still, Ellie's tone said it was more serious than she wanted to let on.

Crista smiled at the irony.

"I couldn't help myself," Ellie said. "I kept thinking it

would blow over, that one of us would lose interest. And then when you and Jackson broke up—"

"We didn't *break up*. There was no relationship to start with. He was conning me. I was a mark."

"Mac thinks the world of Jackson."

"Mac is Jackson's partner. They were probably going to split the diamonds."

"You said there were no diamonds."

"Everyone seems to think there are. Otherwise…" Crista swallowed. She hated that every memory of being with Jackson made her heart hurt.

Ellie touched her shoulder.

"I'm going to get over it," said Crista. "I'm already over it. Reginald said—not that I can trust Reginald—but my new lawyer says the same thing. They said the Bahamian company is going to give me free rein on Cristal Creations. To them, it's just an investment. And they're very patient, looking for a long-term return. It's going to be great."

"I'm so glad," said Ellie.

"So am I." Crista had so much to be grateful for.

She was out from under Vern. She'd seen Jackson's true colors before it was too late. And she was about to sever the last of her ties with her father. After this, she was a free woman starting a whole new, independent life.

"That's it?" asked Ellie as a chain-link fence topped with razor wire came into view. An imposing dark gray stone building loomed up behind it.

"That's definitely it," Crista said in a hushed tone.

For the first time, she thought about what it must be like to be locked up inside the bleakness of Riverway State prison. She shuddered.

"There's a sign for visitor parking," said Ellie, pointing out the windshield. "Do you want me to come with you?"

"You can't. They needed to have your name in advance." Though the street was empty, Crista signaled right and turned into the parking lot.

She knew she needed to do this alone. Still, part of her wished she could bring Ellie along for moral support.

"It's not too late to back out," said Ellie.

Crista chose a spot and pulled in.

"This won't take long." Crista looped her purse over her shoulder, taking the manila envelope from the seat between them.

"Got a pen?" asked Ellie.

"I do."

"He's going to be surprised by this."

"He's going to be stunned by this."

Crista wasn't sure which would shock him more, that she showed up or that she was calling his bluff. In typical convoluted Trent Corday style, he'd convinced Vern that the mine was worth money. His real objective had obviously been the Gerhard wealth. He clearly thought he could get his hands on some of that if she was married to a Gerhard.

She didn't know how he'd planned to achieve that. But then, she'd never understood the conniving workings of her father's mind.

She reached for the handle and yawned open the driver's door.

"I'll be waiting," said Ellie, worry in her tone.

"I'll be right back," Crista said with determination.

She forced herself to make the long walk to the gate at the fence. There, she gave a guard her name and identification. She let him check her bag. Then a female guard patted her down before they let her in.

A pair of burly, unsmiling guards led her through a doorway and directed her down a long, dank hall. The place smelled of fish and disinfectant. Everything about it seemed hard and cold.

She was determined to feel no sympathy whatsoever for her father. He'd been guilty, no question. But on a human level, she pitied anyone stuck in here. With every step, she fought an increasing urge to turn and run.

Finally, she came to a doorway that led into a brighter room. It had high mesh-covered windows, a checkerboard floor and several small red tables with connected stools.

She scanned the room, easily spotting her father. He'd aged since she'd seen him last, his hair gray, his skin sallow and his shoulders stooped and narrower than she remembered.

When he saw her, his eyes went wide with surprise. His jaw dropped, and he gripped the table in front of him, coming slowly to his feet.

"Crista?" he mouthed.

She squared her shoulders and marched toward him.

"Crista," he repeated, and his lips curved in a smile.

She hoped he didn't reach for her. She inwardly cringed at the thought of giving him a hug.

"I need your signature," she stated up front.

"I can't believe you're here."

"I'm not staying."

"No, no." His head bobbed in a nod. "Of course you can't stay. I understand."

"I know about the mine."

He gestured for her to sit down.

She hesitated but then sat.

"I know about the mine," she repeated.

"Jackson told me."

Her chest tightened at the mention of Jackson's name. She had no intention of pursuing the discussion.

"We both know it's worthless," she said, folding back the envelope flap.

"It's not—"

"But you've obviously convinced people it has some value."

"It's not worthless."

She stared at him. "Right. You forget who I am."

"But—"

"This latest scam of yours has put me in actual danger. Vern threatened to kill me, and I think he was serious."

"He *what*?" Her father put on his shocked face.

"Please, save it."

"I never meant for—"

"Quit trying to fool me. I'm not your mark. I'm your daughter. I need one thing from you, and then I am out of your life for good."

He swallowed. He even teared up a little bit. His acting was impressive.

"What do you need?" he asked in a raspy voice.

She produced the papers. "I had a lawyer draw these up. It transfers my shares in the Borezone Mine to you."

Trent drew back.

"You and I know this is meaningless. But if there's anyone out there who believes there really are diamonds, or if you manage to convince someone in the future that there are diamonds, they'll come after you and not me. That's all I want."

His head was shaking. "It's not worthless."

"There's no point in telling me that."

He lunged for her hand, but she snapped it away.

"Check," he said. "Have a lawyer check. Better still, have a securities regulator check. At today's prices your shares are worth tens of millions."

"Ha," she scoffed, wondering why he kept up the facade. She couldn't figure out what he hoped to gain. Then again, at the beginning of any of his cons, it was never obvious what he hoped to gain.

"Check it," he said with impressive sincerity. "Promise me you'll check it, and then you'll understand what I'm about to do."

Her suspicions rose. "What are you about to do?"

He took the papers from her hands.

"Dad?" The name was out before she could stop herself.

She saw him smile while he looked down. Was he signing?

He flipped through the three pages to the end. There, he made a stroke through his name and printed something else.

"Jackson Rush was here three days ago," he said.

"I bet he was."

Her father looked up. "He said something. Well, he said a lot of things. But he reminded me of something that I'd forgotten a long time ago."

She schooled her features, determined not to react.

"He reminded me that being your father meant something. I owe it to you to take care of you."

She wasn't buying it. "What did you just write?"

"He also showed me what he was, who he was. He's honest, principled and upstanding."

"Stop," she managed. She didn't believe a word of it, but her chest was getting tighter and tighter.

"I'm not going to accept the mine shares. But you're right. You can't keep them, either. They put you in danger. When I put them in your name, I had no idea they'd grow in value."

"They're not—"

"Stop," he said. "You're going to confirm their value beyond a shadow of a doubt. And then you're going to believe that I'll never do anything to hurt you ever again."

She didn't want to believe him. But she couldn't begin to guess his angle. If the shares weren't worth any money, she was going to find out. If they were, why wasn't he grabbing them?

"What did you write on the papers?" she asked again.

"I crossed out my own name. I replaced it with Jackson Rush's."

Her jaw dropped open, and a roar started in her ears.

"You can trust him."

She shook her head. She couldn't. She didn't dare.

"You can," her father insisted. "You know Cristal Creations is out of the Gerhard name."

How had he known that? How was it even relevant?

"Jackson did that for you," he said.

She peered at her father, trying desperately to decide if he was being honest or conning her. But she couldn't tell.

"You're smart," he said. "And you're right. Don't keep the shares. Give them to Jackson. He'll do right by you. He's the only person I'd trust."

"He'll give them back to you," she guessed. "Or he'll split them with you."

Trent smiled. "Then why don't I take them right now?"

She didn't have an answer for that.

"I conned Jackson. I used his father. I blamed the Gerhards. I told him you were in danger and counted on his principles and nothing else to get you out of it. He helped you because he's honest and trustworthy. Trust him, Crista. It's your best and only play. Don't keep these shares a minute longer than you have to."

She searched for the flaw, knowing there had to be something she didn't see. Her father would never willingly give up anything of value.

"It's exactly what it seems," he said softly. Then he tucked the papers back into the envelope. "You don't even have to believe me. You're going to verify every single thing for yourself."

Crista didn't know what to say. She didn't know what to do.

"I'll understand if you never come back," said Trent. "But I hope you will. I hope someday you'll be able to forgive me, and you'll come and see me." His eyes teared up again. "You'll come and tell me how you're doing."

Sympathy welled up inside her, and she knew she was in trouble. Despite her best efforts, he'd gotten to her all over again. She quickly scooped up the papers, jumped up and rushed for the door.

It wasn't until she was through the gate that she felt like she could take a breath. There she stopped, steadying herself.

In the distance, she saw Ellie get out of the car.

"Crista?" she called out.

"I'm coming." Crista's voice was far too dry for Ellie to hear. So she started walking. She gave a wave to show she was all right.

Ellie met her halfway. "What happened?"

"It was weird."

"Weird how? Are you okay?"

"He wouldn't sign." Crista handed Ellie the envelope.

Ellie stared down at it. "What? What do you mean he wouldn't sign?"

They came to the car.

"Take that to Jackson. Tell him to sign it and get Reginald to notarize it. I'm so done with this stupid mine."

"What do you mean, take it to Jackson?" Ellie stopped beside the passenger door, looking over the roof at Crista.

"This is going to sound crazy." It was crazy. "My father says he trusts Jackson. He doesn't want the shares for himself. He agrees I shouldn't keep them. So he wants me to give them to Jackson."

"Mac trusts Jackson," said Ellie. "And I trust Mac."

"Then we're all in agreement, aren't we?"

"Are you mad at me?"

"No."

"For saying I trust Mac?"

Crista let out a deep sigh. "I'm tired. I'm baffled, and I'm too exhausted to figure out the truth. Did you know Jackson was behind the Bahamian company that bought Cristal Creations?"

Ellie's eyes narrowed in obvious puzzlement.

"For some reason, Jackson got Cristal Creations out of Vern's hands. He's somehow set it up so that I can run my own company."

"That was an incredibly nice thing for him to do."

"I don't know why he did it."

"Why don't you ask him?"

"I can't."

"Sure you can."

But Crista knew she couldn't bring herself to face him. "If I was right about him, then I don't ever want to see him again. And if I was wrong about him, well, I doubt he ever wants to see me again."

"That's not true."

"Take him the papers. Let's get this over with."

Crista pulled open the door. By tomorrow, the next day at the latest, she'd be free of the Borezone Mine. She could finally get back to work and push Jackson out of her mind.

Jackson stared at the ownership transfer agreement for the Borezone Mine. "What's the catch?" he asked to no one in particular.

"None that I can see," said Reginald.

"Do you think her old man has really changed?" asked Mac.

"She doesn't believe they're worth anything," said Ellie.

Jackson looked up and took in the three faces. "But they are worth something. We all know they're worth millions. I can't take them." He shoved the papers across the meeting table in his Rush Investigations office.

"That's how you protect her," said Mac.

"She definitely wants you to have them," said Ellie.

"You can still use them to her benefit," said Reginald.

"It's not the same thing," said Jackson. "They belong to her. She has every right to own them, sell them—"

"Or give them away," said Mac.

"Not to me," said Jackson.

"Then who? Give her another solution. What is she supposed to do, sit at home and wait for Gerhard to come back?"

"If only you hadn't lied to her," said Ellie.

"That's not helping," said Mac.

"She's right," said Jackson. "But I didn't think I had a choice," he told Ellie. "If I'd revealed the whole truth up front, she'd have run fast and far from me. Gerhard would have convinced her to come back."

"Maybe," Ellie allowed.

"We should have gone to Vegas," said Jackson. "It was always the best plan."

"Want me to call Tuck?" asked Mac.

Jackson coughed out a laugh. "Right. Great idea. I could kidnap her all over again."

"I wouldn't kidnap her," said Ellie.

"No kidding," said Jackson. Clearly, he had to work on his sarcastic voice.

"But you can probably persuade her."

Jackson huffed. "I can't persuade her. I wouldn't try."

He loved Crista. There was no way he'd do a single thing to cause her more hurt.

"For her own good," said Ellie.

"Not a chance."

"Refuse to sign the papers."

"I already did," said Jackson.

"Offer to marry her instead."

"I already did that, too. She turned me down flat."

"Did you tell her you love her?" asked Ellie.

"I—"

"Don't bother denying it," said Mac.

"I think she knows," said Jackson.

Everyone else had figured it out. He was starting to feel like he was wearing a neon sign. Besides, what other explanation could there be for his behavior?

"She thinks you're angry with her," said Ellie.

"Why would she think that?"

"Because she refused to trust you."

"That's just good sense," said Mac.

Jackson frowned at him.

"I'm serious," said Ellie. "She's afraid you won't forgive her."

"There's nothing to forgive." His brain latched on to the word *afraid*. Why would Crista care about his forgiveness?

Ellie gave him a secretive smile.

"Are you saying…" he asked.

"I don't know anything for sure," said Ellie.

But she suspected. It was clear Ellie suspected. She thought Crista might have feelings for him.

"Where is she?"

"She's in Wisconsin by now. But I can take you to her."

"Wisconsin?"

"Far away from Vern Gerhard."

Okay, that was good.

Mac put his phone to his ear. "I'll get Tuck to warm up the jet."

Jackson was about to protest. Tuck had already done enough. But then he calculated the time savings and decided it was worth asking. Tuck could always say no.

"Good plan," he said to Mac.

"Wisconsin only?" asked Mac. "Or all the way to Vegas?"

Jackson grinned. Persuasion and even kidnapping was starting to sound like a very good idea. "All the way to Vegas."

Crista was in her motel room staring at her email, willing a message to arrive from Ellie. Surely she'd taken the papers to Jackson by now. Surely he'd signed. Crista knew he had to be angry with her, but she also believed he'd been trying to help her. Surely he'd be willing to do this one small thing.

She hit the refresh button, but there were no new messages.

"Come on," she said out loud.

A knock on her door startled her.

Fear immediately contracted her stomach. Her first thought was that it was Vern. Had he followed her from Chicago? Had he staked out the prison? Or maybe he'd threatened Ellie and forced her to reveal Crista's location.

The knock sounded again.

Crista carefully rose to her feet. The chain was on the door, but she had no doubt Gerhard's burly security men would break it down. She could tell them Jackson already owned the shares. But she had no proof. They probably wouldn't believe her.

She started to back away, thinking she'd lock herself in the bathroom and call the police.

"Crista?" came a man's voice.

No...

"Crista, it's me, Jackson."

Relief instantly rushed from her scalp to her toes.

"Open the door," he called.

"Jackson?" She rushed forward. "Jackson?" she called louder.

"Ellie gave me the papers."

"Good. That's good." She gulped a couple of deep breaths, staring at the door.

"Ellie and Mac are in the car."

"Ellie's here?"

"Yes."

That had to be good. It was all good. Vern hadn't found her. She wasn't afraid of Jackson. He must have signed the papers. Maybe he was here to give her a copy.

Her hands trembled as she pulled off the chain. Then she turned the dead bolt and twisted the door handle, opening the door.

Jackson was there, smiling. She was glad to see him. She was ridiculously glad to see him.

"Hi," she managed.

"Hi yourself."

"Ellie brought you?" That much was obvious, but she didn't really know what else to say to him.

"Can I come in?"

"Yes." She stepped back.

She glanced out at the parking lot. "Just you?"

"I need to talk to you alone."

"Okay." She shut the door behind him.

Then she turned to where he was standing, close, looking strong and sexy and not even a little bit angry.

"You signed?" she asked, so happy to have this all behind her.

She wanted to walk into his arms. She could hug him at least, couldn't she?

"I didn't sign," he said.

She stopped herself short. "What?"

"I didn't sign," he repeated.

"Why not?"

"I don't want your diamond mine, Crista."

"But…it's just a formality. You know that. Why would you refuse?"

Had everything he'd said been a lie? Did he not care about her at all? Was he so angry he was willing to let her take her chances with Vern and Manfred?

"Is transferring the shares all about the Gerhards?" he asked.

"Yes. If I don't own the mine, they go away."

"That's true."

She was starting to get annoyed. "So? What's your problem?"

"The problem is, my earlier deal stands," he said.

"You had a deal with my father?" What secret angle had she missed? She braced herself for what he was about to reveal.

"My deal was with you."

She didn't respond. He was talking in riddles.

"Vegas," he continued. "The deal was that I'd keep you safe from Gerhard by marrying you in Vegas."

"Is that a joke?"

"But I don't think I presented it right," he said.

She was growing more confused by the minute. "It was pretty straightforward."

They got married and foiled Vern's plan.

"No." Jackson shook his head, taking a step forward to bring them close together. "It wasn't straightforward at all. What I should have said back then was I love you, Crista Corday. Will you marry me and spend the rest of our lives together? Let's do it in Vegas, because I can't wait another second for you to be my wife."

His face went blurry in front of her and she blinked, realizing her eyes had teared up.

"What did you say?" she rasped. "You're not playing me?"

"I'm not playing you." He cradled her face with his palms. "I've never been more serious in my life."

"Because—" Her voice broke. "Because I couldn't take it if you were. Money I can lose."

"Trust in this, Crista. I love you with all my heart."

He kissed her, and joy sang through her chest. It was long minutes before he broke the kiss.

"I love you," she answered, breathless. "And I'll marry you in Vegas or anywhere else you want."

His arms went around her, and she hung on tight.

"You love me?" he asked.

"More than that. I trust you. I trust you with my heart, my soul and my life."

There was laughter in his voice. "And the diamonds, because the diamonds are very real."

"The diamonds aren't real." How many times did she have to say it?

"Maybe you'll believe it when you start turning them into jewelry designs."

"Maybe." If diamonds showed up in her workshop, she'd concede they were real.

"In the meantime, my friend Tuck is waiting at the airport with his jet."

"Oh, right. Your friend Tuck who has a jet."

"I told him he could be the best man."

"And you brought Ellie for maid of honor?"

"I brought Ellie. Though I don't know what you'll do for dresses and flowers."

"They have stores in Vegas."

"That they do. I'm sure we can find anything our hearts desire in Vegas."

She burrowed against his shoulder, drinking in the solid warmth of his body. "The only thing my heart desires is you."

He rocked her back and forth. "I am so monumentally glad to hear that."

The motel room door opened.

"Are we going to Vegas?" asked Ellie.

Crista grinned. "We're going to Vegas."

"Bachelorette at the Lion Lounge," Ellie sang.

"You'll have maybe an hour before the wedding," said Jackson. "I'd suggest you spend it shopping."

"You will need a dress." Ellie sounded disappointed.

"So will you," said Mac, his arm going around Ellie. "Something slinky. I've always had a thing for bridesmaids."

"Too much information," said Jackson.

Mac just grinned.

"I hope you have a thing for brides," Crista whispered to Jackson.

"I have a thing for one particular bride," he whispered back. "From the first second I saw her, I knew she had to be mine."

"But this time," she said, smiling up at him. "It'll be *my* dress. *My* wedding. But with you, Jackson. Forever."

* * * * *

TO CATCH A CAMDEN

VICTORIA PADE

Chapter One

"This is a wonderful thing you're doing, Gia."

Gia Grant laughed uncomfortably at the compliment from the church pastor. "The Bronsons are wonderful people," she demurred. "I didn't know how tough it could get for the elderly until seeing the way things are for Larry and Marion. And thanks again for letting us use the church basement tonight to organize everything so we can get started."

"Of course. The Bronsons have been church members since my father was pastor here. We want to do all we can."

"That reminds me—thank your mom, too, for the cookies and the brownies and the cupcakes. I was surprised when the Bronsons wanted to come tonight—they just don't go out much—but it's turned into a rare social event for them. Complete with goodies," she added with a nod toward the opposite end of the big room, where the elderly couple who were her next-door neighbors were chatting with other members of the church.

Gia had launched a grassroots effort to help the Bronsons. They were on the verge of losing their house because their fixed income wasn't meeting the cost of living expense increases and the additional medical expenses mounting with their age.

After making several calls and searching the internet for help for them, she'd discovered there weren't a lot of options available to older people in their predicament.

But she couldn't just sit back and watch what was happening to them without doing something. So she'd spread the word in their surrounding neighborhood that help was needed.

Small business owners who knew the Bronsons had put out donation jars at their checkouts. The church had sounded the alarm in their newsletter, and Gia had persuaded a local news station to do a human-interest piece on them. It mentioned both the donation fund Gia had started for them and the need for manpower to do repairs and maintenance on their house.

Gia's highest hope was that she could raise enough money to keep the Bronsons out of foreclosure. If she couldn't do that, then she at least wanted to get the place in order so that it could be sold before that happened.

Tonight, neighbors, friends and church members had gathered to form a plan of action to spruce the place up, and now that the meeting was finished it had become a social hour. Gia was happy to see the eighty-nine-year-old Larry and his eighty-seven-year-old wife, Marion, enjoying themselves.

"I was also wondering if you might have dinner with me some night..." Pastor Brian said, interrupting her thoughts.

Gia had wondered if that was coming. Although she didn't belong to the Bronsons' church, the minister had asked to be part of her efforts to help the older couple, and that had meant seeing him here and there. He'd become more and more friendly over the past few weeks.

At first Gia had thought he was merely trying to entice another sheep into his flock. But then a personal undertone had developed when he talked to her and she'd begun to wonder if he was interested in her.

Thinking that he probably wasn't, she'd still considered what she might do if he asked her out.

At thirty-four, Pastor Brian was only three years older than she was. He was nice looking, with golden-blond hair and hazel eyes. And he certainly came equipped with the attributes she was determined to look for in a man from here on out—he was upstanding and honest. There wasn't so much as a hint of wrongdoing in any aspect of him—he was a minister, for crying out loud.

But the fact that he was the head of his church put a crimp in things. Not only wasn't Gia a member of his religion, his job brought with it obligations and duties that were an uncomfortable reminder of the family ties that had bound her ex-husband and caused her to take a backseat in his life.

Plus, even though it had been nearly a year since her divorce was final, she felt as if she was just beginning to catch her breath, and she wasn't ready to get into the whole dating thing again yet. With anyone.

And then there was the fact that she *was* divorced.

"Thanks for asking, Brian, but no," she answered. "I like you, I do. But right now just the thought of dating gives me the willies. And even if it didn't, I'm *divorced.* And your congregation is old-fashioned. I've overheard

Marion's church-lady friends talking about finding you a wife—"

"I'm surprised they haven't formed a committee. By now I think I've been introduced to every young single female they're even remotely related to."

"You haven't been introduced to the ones who are single through divorce, I can promise you that," Gia said. "Because believe me, when it comes to who they want to see you with, it isn't anyone with that in her background. In their eyes, that's damaged goods and definitely *not* a prospect for their Pastor Brian."

The minister smiled sheepishly. "Yeah, I told my folks I was going to ask you to dinner and they said the same thing," he admitted. "But it would only be dinner and I thought I might risk a little scandal...."

Oh, good, I could go from being a shut-out in-law to a church scandal, Gia thought.

"But I'm really not ready," she repeated honestly. "I'm just barely getting my being-single-again sea legs."

He shrugged. "It's okay. I just thought I'd ask—no harm, no foul. I'm still with you a hundred percent on this project to help Larry and Marion."

"Thank you. I appreciate that." Gia pointed at the restroom sign. "I'm headed to wash my hands—I got into something sticky." And had just avoided getting into something even stickier....

"Yeah, I think I'm ready for another cup of coffee myself," he said, leaving Gia free to go into the bathroom.

Safely behind a closed door, she went straight to the row of three sinks, breathing a sigh of relief now that that was over.

It hadn't been *too* awkward, she decided.

The minister had taken her rejection in stride, so she thought it would all be okay. She hoped it would all be okay. And at least she knew now that she hadn't been imagining things—because even as she'd thought he might be showing her undue interest, she'd also wondered if she was flattering herself.

She washed her hands and took stock of her reflection in the mirror above the sinks. Dark eyes. Decent skin. An okay nose—not too prominent, not misshapen. A mouth she was afraid might be too wide, especially when she smiled. And dark, curly, curly—*really curly*—hair that she had to keep six inches below her shoulders so the weight of it would keep it from bushing out like a fright wig.

A neglectful husband—whose eye had begun to wander at the end of their marriage—and then a divorce had her making more assessments of her looks than she had since she was a teenager. And finding flaws. So even as she'd thought the pastor might have been showing her undue interest, she'd also been skeptical of the possibility that she *could* attract a man's attention.

Of course, there was also the fact that she was only five feet three inches tall—that made her one of the few people the five feet five inch minister was taller than….

That was probably the real reason, she thought suddenly, doubting herself all over again.

Gia's second sigh was a bit demoralized.

Oh, well. At least she could say she'd been asked.

She finished washing her hands and after drying them with a paper towel, she used the towel to brush wrinkles from the black slacks she'd worn to work today with her plain white blouse. Then she tossed the used paper towel in the trash and left the restroom.

Which was when she noticed someone new coming down the steps into the church basement.

A latecomer, was her initial thought.

Before she took a second look and recognized the man.
Unless she was mistaken, that was Derek Camden.

She'd never met him. But not only had the Bronsons'
dislike and resentment of the Camdens brought the well-
known family to her attention whenever they were in the
news or in magazine or newspaper articles, she also had
some small knowledge of this specific Camden. He'd
been involved for a brief time with her best friend Tyson's cousin—a woman Tyson referred to as the family nutcase—and Gia had seen a snapshot of the two
together.

Being reasonably sure that was who he was, she
moved to intercept him before he got out of the stairwell and could be seen by anyone else.

"Can I help you?" she asked in a hurry, hoping not to
draw the attention of the Bronsons.

"Umm…I don't know. I heard through the grapevine
that tonight was the night people were getting together
to talk about helping Larry and Marion Bronson—that's
the group I'm looking for…."

"But you're Derek Camden, aren't you?" Gia said.

"I am. And you are…?"

"Not going to let you in here."

His face erupted into a grin.

The face that she'd already noted was even more striking in person than it had been in the photograph. And
he'd looked incredibly good in the photograph.

His hair was an even darker brown than hers was—
verging on black—with just a touch of wave to the top
that he left slightly longer than the short sides. His nose
was the perfect length and shape—thin and straight. His
mouth was just lush enough. He had the sexiest hint of a
cleft in his chiseled chin. And nothing she'd heard about
the Camden blue eyes had done his justice, because they

were the vibrant blue of the delphiniums she loved to look out at through her kitchen window every morning.

And it all went with six foot two inches of muscular masculinity not at all hidden behind the tan slacks and cream-colored shirt he was wearing with his brown tie loosened at the open collar, and the suit coat he had hooked by a thumb over one impressively broad shoulder.

"You're not going to let me in here?" he repeated, as if her thinking she could stop him amused him no end.

"No, I'm not," Gia asserted. "It would ruin the Bronsons' night."

It only occurred to her as she said it that this man appeared to be about her own age and maybe didn't know what had been done by his family generations before. That maybe he was there purely in response to word getting out, and had genuinely just come to help. Without knowing that his family was at the heart of the Bronsons' hardship.

"I'm sorry, did you know that there's bad blood between the Bronsons and your family?" she asked.

The alarm in her tone only made him laugh. "A lot of people don't like the Camdens," was all he admitted to.

"This is more than just—" she wasn't sure how to put it so she repeated his words "—a lot of people not liking the Camdens on some sort of principal—"

"It's okay. I came to help anyway," he assured as if he didn't view an aversion to his family as an obstacle.

"Yeah…well…it wouldn't be okay with Larry and Marion, and I'm reasonably sure they wouldn't take help from any Camden," Gia said more bluntly because she was concerned that he wasn't getting the picture. "And this may not look like it, but it's a night out for them, they're having a good time talking to people they haven't seen in a while and I don't want it wrecked for them…."

She had no doubt the presence of a Camden would do just that.

"But I do want to help them," Derek Camden said.

He was kind of stubborn. Great looking and amiable and certainly nothing more than tickled by her blockade, but difficult to persuade.

"They lost their hotel years ago to H. J. Camden. So maybe if you give them the Camden store that was built where their hotel was…" Gia suggested to get her point across. And to test his response and possibly learn whether or not he knew the history.

It worked, because he flinched charmingly and Gia had the impression that he knew exactly what she was talking about. "I don't think I can do that. But that doesn't mean that I don't want to do *something*. And by the way, who *are* you?" he asked without any rancor.

"Gia Grant. I live next door to the Bronsons."

"And you've taken them under your wing," he guessed. "The guy who cuts my hair down on University had a donation jar. He said there was some *little lady* behind this. Is this whole thing your doing, Gia Grant?"

"We're friends *and* neighbors. The Bronsons are good, good people and I can't sit by and just watch what's happening to them—"

"Which is what, exactly?"

Gia glanced over her shoulder at the long lunch table where the group that was left was talking. They hadn't yet noticed that she wasn't back from the restroom, but that wasn't going to last forever.

"The longer I stand here, the more likely it is that someone is going to see you and, honestly, I won't let you put a damper on Larry and Marion's night."

"But I *do* want to help," he insisted.

"Donate, then."

He nodded that oh-so-handsome head sagely. "We're interested in more than just stuffing some cash in a donation jar. My grandmother isn't too much younger than the Bronsons, and let's say they've struck a chord with her. She sent me to represent the family and make sure whatever needs the Bronsons have are met."

"Then donate a *lot* of money. Anonymously, or they won't take it."

He inclined his head as if that might be a good solution but he just couldn't accept it. "We don't want to just throw some money at the problem. We want to find out what *all* of the problems are and lend a hand getting them addressed in the best way possible so these people can finish out their lives comfortably, safely and securely."

"You're admitting that what your family did way back when caused the problems, and now you have a responsibility to make things right," Gia surmised.

"We just want to help," he said, firmly holding that line and acknowledging nothing else.

Gia shook her head. "The Bronsons are in trouble. But they're proud people. I've convinced them to accept help from their friends and neighbors, their church, by assuring them that the help is coming from people they've given business to for decades, from the same people they've helped in the past or would help if the need arose even now and they could. I've promised them that it isn't charity, it's people who know and care about them just wanting to do something for them. But they hate you—I'm sorry to be so direct, but that's just a fact. I know them—they'll think that anything you do will have an ulterior motive. If they know you're behind a dime, they won't take it."

"Maybe you can persuade them to," he proposed.

"I don't know how I'd do that."

"I'll bet you can think of a way…" he said pointedly.

"You do owe them," Gia said matter-of-factly because it was true. And even though she knew how the Bronsons would feel about accepting anything from the Camdens, she also knew that they were in need of more help than what her efforts were producing. The Camdens' assistance could go much further in solving the elderly couple's problems.

"Maybe you could introduce me as a friend of yours and leave out the part about me being a Camden."

"They'd recognize you. They might not know exactly which Camden you are, but they follow your family like fans follow celebrities, begrudging you every step of the way. And they might be old, but mentally, they're both sharp as tacks. Nothing gets by them, and you wouldn't, either." With another glance over her shoulder to make sure no one was looking in this direction, Gia added, "And really, I want you to leave before they spot you."

"I'm not giving up," he said then, but he did step one step higher, which made him tower above Gia even more. "So how about I leave it to you to convince them to accept my help?"

He reached into his shirt pocket with his free hand and pulled out a business card. "All my numbers are on that."

Gia accepted the card.

"If I don't hear from you, you'll have me knocking on your door—don't forget you already told me that you live next to the Bronsons."

"I can't make any promises," Gia said, knowing full well that she had to do what she could to convince Larry and Marion, because the Camdens—no matter how despicable—still had the kind of resources the Bronsons needed.

"I'm relying on you anyway," he said, investing her with the responsibility despite her hedging.

"I'll do what I can if you just go!"

He grinned again and took another step up. "I'll tell you one thing," he said as he did, "you're the prettiest bouncer I've ever been ousted by."

"As if a Camden has ever been kicked out of any-place," Gia countered.

"You might be surprised."

"Just go!" she said, trying not to think that he was lingering in order to stare at her—which was how it ap-peared, because his beautiful blue eyes seemed to be taking in every inch of her and his expression said he was enjoying the view.

"Get back to me soon or I'll come for you..." he threatened in a way that didn't sound as if they were still talking about helping the Bronsons.

"No promises," Gia repeated firmly to let him know he wasn't wearing her down.

But he was. Just a tiny bit.

Enough so that, as she turned from the sight of him backing up the rest of the steps so he could go on study-ing her, she felt a smile come to the corners of her mouth.

Because although she had no idea why, just the way Derek Camden looked at her made her feel better about herself than the dinner invitation from the minister had.

Chapter Two

"Georgie! You feisty little beanbag, where are you?" Derek called when he went into his grandmother's house midmorning on Tuesday.

"She's in the greenhouse."

"Oh, hey, Jonah. Hey, Louie. I didn't see you guys up there."

Jonah Morrison—Derek's grandmother's old high school sweetheart and new husband since their wedding in June—seemed to be working on something on the stairs. Louie Haliburton—the male half of the married couple who had worked for the family as live-in staff for decades—was helping him.

"What's going on?" Derek asked the two older men.

"Fixing the banister," Louie answered.

"Or trying to," Jonah added.

"Need help?" Derek offered, even though he was in the midst of his workday and had only stopped by on his way back from a meeting with Camden Incorporated's bankers in his capacity as chief financial officer.

"Nah, we can handle it," Louie assured.

"I'll head for the greenhouse, then. Holler if you change your minds."

Derek went across the wide entryway, down the hallway that led straight to the kitchen. There he found Louie's wife, Margaret.

"Hey, Maggie-May," he greeted the stocky woman, who was old enough for retirement but was still on her hands and knees cleaning one of the ovens.

"Derek! Did we expect you today?"

He leaned over and kissed her rosy cheek. "Nope. Just stopped by to talk to Georgie."

"She's in the greenhouse."

"So I heard. That's where I'm headed."

"Staying for lunch?"

"Can't. Have to get back to the office. I only have a few minutes." He went through the kitchen to the greenhouse, where his grandmother was watering her prize orchids.

"Georgie...don't let me scare you..." he said in a mellow tone once he got there, because his grandmother's back was to him and he didn't want to startle the seventy-five-year-old.

Georgianna Camden was the matriarch of the Camden family, the woman who had raised all ten of her grandchildren after the plane crash that killed their parents and her husband. The rest of the family called her GiGi. Derek had always affectionately called her Georgie.

"As if I didn't hear you shouting from the doorway," his grandmother said, turning off the water.

He crossed the greenhouse to kiss her cheek, too, putting an arm around the shoulders that—like the rest of her—felt as cushy as a beanbag chair.

He gave her a little squeeze before letting her go. "I'm on my way back to the office, but I thought I'd stop for a few minutes to tell you that I went to that church your friend belongs to last night—"

"Jean didn't see you. I talked to her this morning."

"Checking up on me?" he asked with a laugh. "I went but I didn't get in. Some hot little number named Gia Grant caught me at the foot of the steps to the basement and wouldn't let me go any farther."

"I know that name—Jean can't say enough good things about her. She doesn't belong to their church, she's the Bronsons' neighbor and—"

"She's the one behind this deal to help the Bronsons— I know, the guy who cuts my hair told me. But last night she was also the guardian of the gate. Your friend Jean was right about the meeting to organize the work for the Bronsons, but what she didn't say was that the Bronsons themselves would be at the church. Gia Grant spotted me coming, recognized me somehow and wouldn't let me out of the stairwell. She said a Camden would ruin the Bronsons' night."

"Oh, dear…"

"Yeah. We might not have known about what went on between H.J. and those people until you read about it in the journals, but it isn't something they've forgotten."

The man who had started the Camden empire— Derek's great-grandfather H. J. Camden—had kept a journal while he was alive. Only recently rediscovered, it confirmed what H.J., his son, Hank, and his grandsons, Mitchum and Howard, had long been accused of— ruthless, unscrupulous business practices that trampled people and other businesses.

After reading the journals, Georgianna Camden and her grandchildren were determined to make amends for some of the worst of the wrongs done. Including what had been done to the Bronsons.

"Gia Grant says that no matter how much trouble the Bronsons are in," Derek informed his grandmother, "they have too much pride to take anything from us. Her recommendation was that we just donate money anonymously.... And the anonymity wouldn't be so bad for us, because then we'd be avoiding any admission of guilt...."

GiGi shook her head at that suggestion. "I know we need to keep from making any kind of open, public acknowledgment of wrongdoing so we don't have people coming out of the woodwork to sue us for things the Camdens didn't do—"

"Big corporations and money make for easy targets," Derek confirmed. "And you know there are stories out there accusing us of stuff that *didn't* happen—so, yeah, if we say some of the accusations are well founded, there'll be an avalanche of see-I-told-you-so lawsuits for *un*-founded complaints that will tie us up in court until hell freezes over."

"We also don't want to come out and say that H.J. and your grandfather, father and uncle really were involved in underhanded business practices—there's family loyalty at stake here, too," GiGi said under her breath, because this was something that she didn't discuss if Jonah, Margaret or Louie were around.

"So a payout would be a whole lot easier, but it wouldn't protect us," Derek acknowledged.

"And we wouldn't necessarily achieve our goal of making amends with a simple payout," GiGi added. "In this case in particular, just donating some money might not be the best answer for the Bronsons. Jean says they have no family. No one beyond that Gia girl—and she's only a neighbor—to look after them or help them. They're in their eighties, so there are some health problems, and Jean isn't sure they should be living on their own anymore. And what if one of them dies and the other is left all alone—?"

"You want to just move them in here?" Derek joked.

"You know how I feel about this one, Derek. It's going to need some involvement on our part for what remains of the Bronsons' lives," GiGi insisted. "And you know that just donating money doesn't guarantee that the money will get into the right hands or get used in the ways it should be used, especially down the road. We have to know that these people have whatever they need to finish out their lives—financially and otherwise. And their needs can change depending on how their health or situation changes. We have to have some kind of presence in their lives. So you have to make nice with them. Win them over and establish a relationship with them so we can help later on, too, if need be. For their sake."

"I touched on some of that with Gia. But I still couldn't even get in the door...."

"Well, you're going to have to do whatever it takes to accomplish that, honey. Maybe first you'll have to win over the guard at the gate...."

That brought a vivid image of Gia Grant to mind— something that had been happening at the drop of a hat since he'd met her last night.

Maybe because of that hair, he thought.

That hair was just great!

Every time the memory of it popped into his head it made him smile.

Full and thick and shiny and wildly curly...

That was probably why it appealed to him. He liked things that were a little on the wild side.

And he'd loved that hair....

Plus, she had big, beautiful brown eyes the color of espresso sprinkled with gold dust.

And peaches-and-cream skin that didn't show a single flaw.

And a straight nose that turned up almost imperceptibly and just a little impudently at the end.

And a picture-perfect mouth that was exactly the kind he liked to kiss because her lips were slightly full and sumptuous-looking....

All on top of a body that was tight but still soft and curvaceous even if she wasn't particularly tall....

Oh, yeah, he'd done a *lot* of thinking about Gia Grant since last night....

For no reason he could put his finger on.

"I did ask her to intervene on my behalf, but she wasn't too optimistic that she could convince the Bronsons to accept anything from us," he told his grandmother when he'd pulled himself out of his thoughts of Gia.

"Like I said, win her over first, then," GiGi advised. "The better she likes you, the more apt she is to sell you to the Bronsons. And from what I understand from Jean, that shouldn't be too painful for you—Jean says she's never met a nicer, friendlier, more helpful person, and that she's beautiful to boot and doesn't even seem to know it. So she's humble, too. I know Jean has her eye on her for Lucas once his divorce is final, and she and the other ladies in her church committees are all worried that their pastor is very taken with this Gia Grant—"

"So wouldn't that make her perfect for their pastor—a paragon of virtue like that?"

"Shame on you for saying that like it's a bad thing! That's what gets you into trouble."

No truer words were ever spoken, so Derek couldn't deny it. Besides, he didn't dare. Not after his most recent blunder, the one that had really caused him to cross the line.

The one he wanted to kick himself over.

The one that had cost him a bundle and most of his dignity....

"If she's all that your friend says she is, why wouldn't the church ladies *want* her for their pastor?" he asked more respectfully.

"She's divorced."

"And that's an issue?"

"It's only an issue when it comes to their minister— they want someone purer for him, I guess. Plus, like I said, Jean wants Gia for Lucas—"

"Lucas Paulie is a weasel," Derek said, not understanding why it rubbed him wrong to think of the woman he'd spent all of about five minutes with either the church pastor he didn't know or the guy he did know.

"I didn't realize you disliked Lucas Paulie so much," GiGi said.

"I just wouldn't wish him on some poor unsuspecting do-gooder."

"There it is again, Derek James Camden! *Do-gooder*—that is *not* a bad thing. A nice girl is what you need. You'd better start looking for one and stay away from what you've been bringing around here since you were a teenager. Haven't you learned your lesson *yet?*"

"I have, Georgie," he said on a sigh. "I just can't help it if the...*tame* ones don't do it for me. I like a little spice."

"What you've brought around here is not a *little spice*. And this last one—"

"I know. You don't have to tell me—again—how damn stupid that was."

"And yet here you are, barely out from under the mess you were in, looking down your nose at someone doing some good."

"I'm not looking down my nose at Gia Grant."

He was doing anything but that, if the truth be known. He sure as hell hadn't been thinking bad things about her since last night.

It just didn't matter. He knew the way things went for him—regardless of how beautiful the woman, regardless of how much he might respect and admire her or what she was doing, in no time the good girls just couldn't keep his interest. In no time they started to seem ordinary. They started to get predictable. They started to bore him to tears.

But he wasn't a kid anymore. And he had no business letting himself be sucked into situations with the bad girls anymore.

It had been bad enough when he *was* a kid, but now it was inexcusable. Especially when it embarrassed the whole family right along with himself. Like this last time.

Which was why he was lying low. Why he was doing some self-imposed penance by staying away from all women for a while. Why he was putting his energies into work and the Camden Foundation and trying to make things up to the Bronsons the way his grandmother had asked him to. Even if he was reasonably sure that his grandmother's intent was to keep him well-occupied so he wouldn't have time to get involved with anyone else for a while.

Not that he could blame her....

"I gave Gia Grant my card and told her if I didn't

hear from her I'd track her down," Derek said then, ignoring how much he was looking forward to seeing her again. "She apparently lives next door to the Bronsons, so even if I have to knock on the wrong door before I get the right one, I'll find her. Then maybe I can try to go through her to get to the Bronsons. I think she may have seen the benefit of our help over her donation jars and church volunteers, but whether or not she can convince the Bronsons—"

"You'll find a way in," Georgianna said.

"I really will, Georgie. I'm not going to let you—or any of the rest of the family—down again."

"I hope not," GiGi said. "Maybe you should try to let this Grant girl be a good influence on you for a change...."

"You never know," he said, rather than defend himself the way he might have done before the latest fiasco. "But for now I'd better get back to the office."

GiGi nodded. As she reached to turn the water on again, she said, "You're a good boy, Derek. I don't know why you have such a soft spot for bad girls. Maybe you can turn over a new leaf."

"Tryin', Georgie, I'm tryin'."

But even as Gia Grant's oh-so-lovely face came to mind again, he wondered if he could.

"A chicken and steaks and a roast, Gia? You could freeze these, you know," Marion lectured.

"I already froze a bunch. It's cheaper to buy at the bulk warehouse, but I end up with more than I can use. You're helping me out by taking some of it." It was the same thing Gia said every time she brought Larry and Marion groceries. Their budget was so strapped that meat had become a luxury item. But pride wouldn't allow them to let Gia provide that for them unless she made it sound as if they were doing her a favor. So that was the slant she put on it.

"Well, thank you. You're too good to us," Marion said as she put away the groceries that included some other things Gia knew they liked but couldn't afford for themselves.

"Let's open one of those beers right now," Larry suggested.

Marion obliged her husband and opened the cupboard to get glasses. "Will you have some of this, Gia?"

"No, you guys go ahead," she said. She declined their offers every time, too.

"I know you didn't buy *this* for yourself," Marion said as she poured the beer into two glasses.

Gia laughed. "And *I* know how much you and Larry like your little swig of beer before dinner," she said, using the term they used.

They were in the Bronsons' kitchen late Tuesday afternoon. Gia had left work at three o'clock, done some shopping and was now delivering groceries as a pretext for what she really came to talk to the Bronsons about.

The couple had been in such good spirits when they'd left the church the night before that Gia hadn't wanted to dampen them by bringing up Derek Camden. But he'd somehow gotten her cell phone number and left a message this afternoon about the status of persuading Larry and Marion to let him help them.

Gia hadn't returned his call yet, but his invitation to meet her for coffee at seven to talk had inspired this visit.

And given the boring evening she was facing a whole new spin....

Not that she was eager to see Derek Camden again, she told herself. Even if he had shadowed her thoughts since she'd first set eyes on him last night. It was just that she didn't have anything else to do tonight and hopefully the evening would end up benefitting Larry and Marion.

When they were all seated around the Bronsons' aged, scarred kitchen table, Gia said, "There's something I want to talk to you guys about. You didn't know it last night, but a Camden showed up at the church—Derek Camden...."

Marion looked alarmed. Larry was instantly angry.

"What're they doing, coming for the money you've raised to help us?" Larry said.

"Didn't they get enough when they took everything from us? Are those richy-riches even after our pennies now?" Marion said, her tone harsh.

This was the reason Gia hadn't wanted Derek Camden to crash last night's get-together.

"There's no way they could get hold of what's been donated—that's in a secure account at the bank under your names and mine," Gia assured them. Then she added cautiously, "Derek Camden said he came to help... I'm not sure how—"

"Some way that'll put more in his pocket!" Larry again.

"They're probably looking to take our house now!" Marion said, sounding genuinely afraid. "Like with the hotel—right when we were struggling to keep it, they swooped in and made it so we couldn't. Now when the bank wants the house, they're coming for that, too!"

"No, no, no," Gia said quickly, trying to calm the elderly woman's fears. "I'm sure they don't want your house—"

"They probably want the whole block. The whole area for another one of their damn stores!" Larry said, getting more and more worked up. "You'd better watch out, Gia, they could be coming for your place, too!"

"They already have two stores nearby—the one that was built where your hotel was, and the one on Colorado Boulevard. And we're zoned residential—"

"They pay off people to change zoning—don't be fooled by that," Larry contended.

Gia had known this was not going to be easy. "Okay, I know how you both feel about the Camdens—and with good reason—"

"You bet we have reason—they robbed us," Larry ranted.

"I know—"

"Dirty crooks!" This from Marion.

"But what was done to you two was a long time ago, by H. J. Camden. And I'm not defending what he did—" Gia said quickly, because she could see that more comments were coming from the elderly couple "—but H. J. Camden is long gone and maybe—just maybe— the Camdens in charge now want to make up for what H. J. Camden did...."

"Did they say that? Did they admit what he did? Because we couldn't prove anything, but if they confessed, maybe we can sue their pants off now!" Larry sounded excited by the prospect.

"He didn't admit anything," Gia said. "Derek Camden only claimed that he wanted to help."

"How could we ever sue them even if they confessed?" Marion reasoned with her husband. "We'd still be going up against a million of their lawyers. And with what? Where would we even find a lawyer to take them on? Or hire one with no money? They'd crush us like bugs—again!"

"But the three of us know that they still owe you," Gia

said, hoping to ride the wave of Marion's logic. "Derek Camden said they want to help financially, but that they also want to make sure you guys are taken care of all the way around. And we could use help like that...."

"Not from Camdens we couldn't!" Larry proclaimed.

"We could, though," Gia said gently. "We've raised a few thousand dollars and we have people coming over to help clean up the yard and paint the house, but a few thousand dollars isn't going to keep the bank from foreclosing for long—the best it will do is pay some of the back payments and stall so we can sell the house after it's been fixed up."

Gia hated—*hated*—when she had to remind them of the cold, hard facts, because it just deflated them both and made them look as old as they were. Both were white haired—Larry only had a wreath of hair around a mostly bald head, and Marion wore hers in a short style she cut herself. There wasn't an ounce of fat or much muscle left on Larry's five-foot-eight frame, and Marion could easily qualify as frail—she was barely five feet tall and didn't weigh a hundred pounds. They both had blue eyes that still showed a zest for life, and ordinarily they both stood straight and moved fairly spryly. But whenever they discussed their current predicament, it just sucked the life out of them right before Gia's eyes.

"You know I'm with you if that's the best we can do," she added to reassure them. "My basement apartment is yours and I'd love to have you with me. But I know that neither one of you *wants* to do that. You want to stay in this house. And with the kind of money the Camdens have..." She shrugged. "Not that Derek Camden made any promises, but if there's any chance left of coming up with enough to maybe keep you here..."

"I still think they have something up their sleeve," Larry grumbled.

"You can't trust them," Marion concurred.

And they both sounded so beaten that it broke Gia's heart.

But as much as she wanted to side with them and tell them she would throw whatever Derek Camden offered back in his face on their behalf, she had to look out for what was best for them. And if the Camdens followed through on their promise, it could mean better than what she'd been able to accomplish.

"I'll do anything you want. This is completely up to you," she told them, in hopes of making them feel as if they had some control, some power, some choice in the matter. "But if you'll accept help from the Camdens, I'll make sure there are no strings attached to anything they give. That there's nothing up their sleeve. That nothing about this can hurt you—"

"Or you," Marion contributed.

"Or me—in any way. And if you never want to set eyes on Derek Camden or any other Camden—"

"Get him over here to pull weeds and let me turn the hose on him," Larry muttered.

"You can't turn the hose on someone like that," Marion chastised. "He'd probably sue *us!*"

"I can turn my hose on anybody I want to turn my hose on," Larry contended cantankerously.

"We could bring him lemonade while he works and lace it with laxative—then he'd never know what hit him!" Marion suggested, making Gia laugh.

"So you want me to get him over here to help work so you can have a little payback?" Gia asked, reasonably sure that they wouldn't actually do either of the things they were threatening.

"A Camden working for us…" Marion mused.

"That'd serve them right," Larry added.

Gia could tell that they were both finding some fuel in their retribution plots, and she was glad to see them rally.

"So you'll let me talk to Derek Camden about what they're offering? And you aren't opposed to having him come over here and do some of the work?" she said, since she thought she should strike while the iron was hot.

"We don't want anything to do with them," Larry reiterated.

"No, we don't," Marion confirmed. "But you can take whatever they're offering, Gia," she said, as if anything coming from the Camdens through her made it more palatable. "As long as you watch them like a hawk—because they *do* owe us, and whatever helps you help us we'll take."

"But don't say anything that lets them off the hook for anything, those lousy shysters!" Larry added.

Gia marveled at a phenomenon she'd witnessed before—sometimes it was as if they'd communicated with each other and come to a decision without ever having talked about it. Apparently seventy years of marriage put them on the same wavelength somehow. Or maybe they'd always been on the same wavelength and that was why they'd been able to stay married for so long.

But regardless of how they'd come to this particular conclusion, Gia was just glad they had.

"Then I'll tell Derek Camden that we'll take his help."

The scowl on Larry's face and the dour, forlorn creases on Marion's brow told her how unwillingly the offer was being accepted. But Gia thought it was better to get out before they changed their minds. Besides, it would give the Bronsons some time alone to rant and rail about it to their hearts' content while she went off to deal with Derek Camden.

And why she felt as excited as a teenager who had just finagled permission from her parents to see someone forbidden—who she really, really wanted to see again—Gia didn't quite understand.

She was a long way from being a teenager.

Larry and Marion weren't her parents.

And Derek Camden was forbidden because Gia was forbidding herself from him.

Because even if she was ready to date, she wouldn't date a man like Derek Camden. She might not have a grudge against the Camdens the way Larry and Marion did, but her own past experience taught her to avoid men like Derek.

Her ex-husband was also a man with deep-rooted loyalties to a big, corrupt, ruthless, unprincipled clan-like family, and that was a hot-button issue for her.

So Derek Camden was not someone she would even consider getting involved with.

Personally anyway.

For Larry and Marion's sake, she would have contact with him—and she *would* watch him like a hawk, as Marion had ordered—but that was the beginning and end of it.

So any sort of excitement at the thought of seeing him again was something to squash hard and fast.

Which she did as she said goodbye to the Bronsons and left them sitting at the table.

And yet on her way home, a tiny blip of excitement still registered when she started to consider what she was going to wear to see him tonight....

When Gia returned Derek Camden's call, he asked if they could meet at a Cherry Creek bakery rather than the coffee shop he'd suggested in his message.

It didn't matter to Gia where they met, so she agreed. Then she fixed herself a sandwich for dinner and decided she couldn't wear anything different for this meeting than what she had on.

Not that she didn't want to change out of the brown slacks and tan pin-tucked blouse she'd worn to work. She just couldn't let herself. This wasn't a date and she needed not to forget that.

But she told herself that it was purely for her own comfort that she unleashed her hair from the ponytail it had been in all day, brushed it out and let it fall loose and full into its naturally curly mass.

And when it came to refreshing her blush and adding a neutral eye shadow, some eyeliner and more mascara, it was merely to look at the top of her game in order to warn him that he'd better not try to put one over on her.

Arriving at the bakery five minutes early, she spotted Derek Camden through the storefront windows as she pulled her sedan into a parking spot.

He was also still in work clothes, although he'd taken off his tie and suit jacket. He was wearing gray-blue suit pants and a pale blue dress shirt, and Gia's first thought was that no one should look that good after a full day.

But there was just the hint of scruff to his sculpted jawline, and his dark hair was the ideal amount of disheveled; combined with the perfectly tailored shirt and pants, it formed a very sexy contrast.

A split second after the thought occurred to Gia, she reprimanded herself for it.

Handsome and sexy did not make the man. Handsome and sexy could, however, provide camouflage for something very ugly under the surface or behind the scenes.

It was a fact of life that she'd learned well and wouldn't let herself forget.

It would have been easy to, though, because when she went into the bakery and Derek noticed her, he smiled a smile that said he liked what he saw. And it made her heart beat a little faster.

"Hi, thanks for coming," he greeted her.

"Hi," Gia responded simply.

"Excuse me just a minute."

For a moment his attention turned back to the woman behind the counter. "So I can pick up the cake tomorrow at one—that's great, just what I need." Then, with a nod toward Gia, he said, "Let me add what we have now to the tab and I'll settle up with you later?"

When the woman agreed, he said to Gia, "I don't know if you've been here before, but you can't go wrong with anything—"

"Lava cake, Bea," Gia said to the woman, who was already taking one from the case and putting it on a plate.

"Heated with an extra dollop of hot fudge on top," the woman recited her order from memory.

Derek laughed. "Ah, I see I'm not introducing you to anything new."

"She's our favorite chocoholic," the owner of the bakery informed him.

He ordered lemon-meringue pie, and they both asked for iced tea. Then, while the shop owner got everything ready, Derek led Gia to one of the small café tables.

"We order all of our office celebration cakes here," he explained. "Tomorrow I'm surprising my assistant with a little engagement party."

A head-honcho Camden was ordering the cake himself? Her ex-husband and the rest of his family would never have bothered.

"How about you? How do you know this place?" he asked.

"I work around the corner and come at least once a day."

Derek Camden's well-shaped eyebrows rose. "Every day?" he said, taking a quick glance at her body as if wondering where the calories went.

"Sometimes it's the only thing I eat all day," she confessed.

"Chocolate every time?"

Her shrug confirmed it.

He laughed. "You *are* a chocoholic."

Gia didn't deny it.

"What do you do around the corner?"

"I'm a botanist. I work for a company that makes herbal supplements and medicines."

The eyebrows went up again. "Really?"

"My ex said I'm just a glorified gardener."

"Well, I'm just an accountant, so it sounds more impressive than that."

He was being humble. Gia knew he was the chief financial officer of Camden Incorporated. But she preferred humility to arrogance. Elliot had been all arrogance.

Not that she *preferred* Derek Camden, she amended in her thoughts. The only way she wanted to compare him with her ex was in terms of their similarities—like the fact that they both came from big, powerful, rich families willing to do dishonest, shifty, devious and deceitful things.

"How did you get my cell phone number?" she asked then, continuing the vein of small talk while they waited for their desserts.

"My grandmother is friends with Jean Paulie—I believe she was one of the church members at your meeting last night—"

"She was."

"Jean is one of the people who brought the Bronsons to our attention—her and the guy who cuts my hair because he had a donation jar in his shop. Anyway, I asked my grandmother if Jean had your number and she did."

Gia nodded.

"My turn—how did you know who I was last night?" he asked.

"My best friend is Tyson Biggs. You dated his cousin and I saw a picture of you with her." Gia didn't add that the image had stuck with her because he was so terrific looking. Or that now that she'd seen him in person she couldn't shake his image from her mind at all....

He grinned. "Sharon. Dragon nails, always in stilettos, carried a purse that was also a fish tank—complete with her goldfish in it—claimed to be psychic..."

"That would be Sharon," Gia confirmed.

He smiled conspiratorially, in a way that was much too engaging. "Did she ever get a *reading* for you right?"

"I've never had her do one of her actual *readings*. She's offered, but on the two times I've met her she told me out of the blue—"

"To prove her *powers*—she likes to do that," he said as if it amused him.

"Well, the first time she told me I was pregnant and I wasn't. The second time she said to watch out because I was going to lose my job. Luckily, that didn't happen, either."

"Yeah, she's never gotten anything right that I know of. She isn't even good at guessing," he concluded with a laugh that wasn't at all disparaging or unkind. "I haven't seen Sharon in...I'm not even sure how long."

"So long that you've had time to get married and settle down?" she asked because she was curious. She'd heard about Sharon and about her friends that he'd dated later—also all wackjobs, according to Tyson. But Gia didn't know anything about Derek Camden beyond that, and she reasoned that if he'd married and settled down he might be more trustworthy in the Bronsons' eyes.

But the question that shouldn't have been difficult to answer instead seemed to puzzle him.

"Huh…" he said, rubbing the back of his neck and suddenly making a face that conveyed discomfort and confusion. "I was going to jump in and say no, never married. But then I remembered that that isn't exactly true anymore. Is annulled a marital status?"

"Annulled… I don't know, I've never met anyone who was annulled."

"Yeah, me, neither…" he said with a frown.

Their desserts arrived and when the shop owner left them to eat he didn't explain further, leaving Gia curious but not feeling free to ask more than she already had.

Then he changed the subject and she really couldn't indulge her curiosity.

"So did you talk to the Bronsons about accepting some help from us?"

"I did."

He smiled at her tone. "It didn't go well?"

"It went the way I thought it would. But they did come around. They said they would let you help me help them."

He nodded slowly as he ate a bite of his pie. "Okay. A little convoluted but still something. And I'll take what I can get at this point. So what do you have planned?"

Gia had taken a bite of her own dessert as he said that. And when it came to chocolate, there was no rushing her. So she held up a finger in front of her mouth to signify a pause as she savored the warm, rich, dark chocolate of her lava cake.

He smiled. "No hurry, enjoy yourself."

"The lemon pie is good, but next time try one of these," she advised when her mouth wasn't full. "It's just the right blend of chocolates and just melty enough and just…amazing."

His smile stretched into a grin. "Not a big chocolate guy so I'll take your word for it."

If anything could turn her off, it should be that!

But somehow it didn't make him look any less appealing to her, so she just filed the information away and answered his inquiry into what she had planned to help the Bronsons.

"There's a day of yard work and a day of home repairs to get their place in better shape," she said. "And I'm cleaning out their stuff and collecting things to sell at a yard sale that I'm hoping will also raise some money— if you want to bring anything for that, do it. This coming Saturday is the yard work, the Saturday after that will be the home repair day and the Saturday after that is the yard sale."

"So yard work and home repairs—they haven't been able to keep their place up," he deduced.

"They haven't had the money, and they're just getting too old to do most things—"

"Should they be moved into a retirement home or assisted living?"

It was a perfectly reasonably suggestion, one she and Tyson had swatted back and forth, one she'd thrown out to the Bronsons.

And yet hearing it from Derek Camden made her recall Larry and Marion's concern that the Camdens were after their house.

Which still didn't seem at all likely to Gia.

But even though there wasn't anything intimidating about Derek Camden—in fact, he seemed down-to-earth, open and friendly—she'd also heard so much from the Bronsons about the evil Camdens that she felt some concern herself.

"Retirement homes and assisted living are expensive, too, and the Bronsons are really against going somewhere with *old people*—"

He laughed again. "They're how old themselves?"

"Eighty-nine and eighty-seven," Gia said with a hint of humor at the irony of that. "But staying together in their house is a big deal to them."

"Okay. So beyond their home needing some work inside and out, what else is going on with them?"

He'd said the night before that he wanted to get the full picture, not to merely give money but to make sure the Bronsons had what they needed all the way around. So logically, what he was asking was just a way to get that full picture.

But still, Gia was a little uncomfortable giving this man too many details that would let him know exactly how vulnerable the couple was.

"A lot of things are going on with them," she said ambiguously, opting only to give him an overview. "They live on a *very* limited budget. Costs for everything are always rising. They aren't in bad health for their ages but there are some issues—they both have high blood pressure and some heart things, some arthritis, Marion has osteoporosis. And every time they go to a doctor there's another medication added—"

"Not your herbal supplements and medicines?"

"I can't really recommend any of those because they take so many prescription meds I'm afraid of interfering with something or giving them a supplement that reacts badly with a prescription drug—so no. But I help them pay their bills and balance their checkbook—because they both have trouble holding a pen and seeing small print—and there are months when I can't believe the cost of their prescriptions."

"Do they need better insurance? A cheaper place to get their prescriptions filled?"

"I've looked into both of those things and done the best I can for them, but the bottom line is that some things fall outside of their coverage and there's nothing that can be done about it."

"Except to get them more money to pay the expenses they have."

Gia conceded with a shrug and hoped she hadn't said too much.

"So where do I start to help you help them?" he asked as he finished his pie.

Gia couldn't risk telling him too much about the Bronsons' predicament until she was sure his motives really were pure. But the only way she could think to get a better feel for him was to get to know him a little and see if he seemed trustworthy. And she didn't know how else to do that except to enlist him in the manual-labor portions of what was going on and spend some time with him. Talking to him. Watching him.

Even if it meant tempting Larry to turn the hose on him or Marion to lace lemonade with laxatives....

So, in response to his query about where he should start to help, she said, "Like I said, Saturday we're starting with the yard and we can always use two more hands...."

"Okay," he said without skipping a beat. "Are the Bronsons going to throw rocks at me if I show up on their doorstep, though?"

Maybe *he* was psychic....

"I hope not," was the best Gia could promise. "Their bark tends to be worse than their bite—"

"At eighty-seven and eighty-nine their teeth probably aren't their own."

"Every one of Marion's is and she's very proud of them," Gia corrected his joke. "But I'll run with the you-helping-me-to-help-them angle and I think you'll be safe." She didn't add that the Bronsons liked the idea of a Camden working for them, so they were apt to gloat about it—whether to his face or not she couldn't be sure.

"Then just tell me when and where to show up and I'll be there," he said.

Gia gave him the details and finished her lava cake. There didn't seem to be any more to discuss at this juncture, so she offered to pay for her own dessert as a signal that the meeting had come to a conclusion.

"It's going on the tab," he reminded her, refusing to even allow her to leave a tip.

He stood up when she did, and Gia tried not to be bowled over by the pure magnitude of the man as she slipped the strap of her purse over her shoulder, thinking that talking to him so far had not been a hardship, and watching him work on Saturday likely wouldn't be, either....

"Thank you for playing go-between," he said then.

"I'm just looking out for Larry and Marion," she countered.

"They're lucky to have you."

"I'm the lucky one—I don't have any family and they've become that for me."

He nodded as if he understood something about that, although she had no idea what and he didn't offer an explanation.

Instead he said, "I guess I'll see you Saturday, then."

"I'll supply the gloves," she added as they said good-bye and she left him to deal with the bill for their desserts and his office cake.

Then she returned to her car, studying him through the plate-glass windows again as she did and counting how many days would have to pass before Saturday came.

So many...

Oh, no—I don't have any reason to think that! she silently shouted at herself when she realized that was what had actually gone through her mind.

And to punish herself, she spent the short drive home recalling what it had been like to be married to a man who could well be Derek Camden's counterpart.

Chapter Three

"So you don't think there's any way he's going to show up," Gia said to Tyson Biggs on Saturday morning as they had a cup of coffee before going next door to begin the yard work on the Bronsons' property.

Gia's tall, lanky blond friend repeated his prediction, a frown on his hawkish face. "Derek Camden? No way."

Gia and Tyson had been best friends since childhood. His family had lived in the house directly behind her grandparents' house, where she'd grown up.

Gia had received the two-story house where she now lived in the divorce settlement—it was formerly one of her ex-husband's rental properties. Gia lived on the ground floor, but the second floor had been turned into an apartment, where Tyson was living while his own house was being built, and the basement apartment was vacant, so she could potentially use it for Larry and Marion.

"You don't really think Derek Camden is coming here to do yard work, do you?" Tyson asked.

The answer to that was yes, she had thought that. Until now. In fact, Derek Camden was pretty much all she'd thought about since Tuesday night, with the prospect of him coming today the light at the end of the tunnel.

Not that she'd wanted to admit that. But denying it didn't keep Tyson's skepticism from knocking the wind out of her sails just the same.

"What was it your ex liked to say? He could *say* anything, that didn't mean he had to do it," Tyson reminded her.

Gia nodded. "He did like to say that. With that smug smile he had when he felt like he was outsmarting someone by telling them what they wanted to hear when he didn't have any intention of making good on it. But Derek Camden claims he really wants to help."

"People like the Camdens pay people to do *their* yard work, G, they don't turn around and do other people's yard work themselves."

That did make sense.

"You met him, right?" she asked then, wondering if she had been completely mistaken in believing that he truly was determined to help the Bronsons. After all, she'd been totally misled by her ex-husband, so her track record was hardly reliable.

"I only met him that once when he was dating Sharon. But it was in a loud, crowded club—I just ran into them, had one drink and left."

"But you said he was nice to you and you didn't know what a guy like him was doing with Sharon."

"Right, I remember. And it's true—he wasn't her usual type. He seemed normal. But he was with her—so how normal could he be? Plus, Elliot was always nice, too—I'm not sure that means much with these guys. I think they just learn good social graces early to help cover up their darker side. Or maybe as a distraction so you don't see the knife in the back coming."

That had been true of Elliot.

"Well, if Derek Camden only gives a check, that'll still be something," Gia said. "The work is getting done with or without him."

"But why do you sound disappointed—were you really counting on him for some reason today?"

"Me? No! I have you and people from work and a couple of friends from the Botanical Gardens and some neighbors and the pastor and a whole group from the Bronsons' church coming. We'll be able to get it all done."

"Yeah, I can't imagine that a Camden used to living in the lap of luxury would be much help anyway." But then Tyson narrowed his hazel eyes at her. "You don't *like* this guy, do you?"

"I haven't found anything to *dis*like," Gia said with a negligent shrug. "At least not about him personally, if you take away what his family did to Larry and Marion. But no, I don't *like* him, either. I don't even know him."

She really only knew the way he looked. Her ex-husband had been good-looking, too—not as good-looking as Derek Camden, but still, no slouch. As time had gone on and she'd looked deeper, though, she'd begun to think "handsome is as handsome does," and those good looks had meant less and less to her.

"But it's enough to know what Derek Camden comes from," Tyson said, as if he needed to open her eyes. "The Camdens could buy and sell the Grants a thousand times over, and their reputation is even worse—sneakier, but worse. Getting involved with a Camden after just getting away from the Grants would be like going from the frying pan into the fire."

"Oh, I know," Gia agreed wholeheartedly. "Even the hint of shadiness means I don't want anything to do with them."

"Plus, what Sharon didn't like about him was the whole family connection. There's a ton of them and they're all joined at the hip—they work together, they hang out together, there's a family dinner at the grandmother's house every Sunday that none of them ever miss—"

"And believe me, no one knows better than I do that in a family that tight there's no real room for other people. Even spouses are always outsiders." Gia knew that from her own experience; it was something she and Tyson had talked about numerous times before.

"But none of this matters," she said to her friend when she realized they were just rehashing. "I'm not ready to even date right now—I told you I just turned down dinner with the church pastor, and who's more upstanding than him? And even if I was back on the market, people like the Camdens are everything I spent three years fighting tooth and nail to get away from—I would never get into anything like that again."

"And let's also not forget that Derek Camden dated my crazy cousin Sharon," Tyson added in support of Gia. "Plus, she must be the type he goes for because he dated two of her whacko friends after the breakup. I doubt that you're off-the-wall enough for that guy—unless you want to cut your hair into a spiky Mohawk and dye it blue...."

"This hair in a Mohawk?" Gia said with a laugh, pulling a springy curl from her ponytail.

"And I'm good, but I don't think I could face another

divorce from one of those people," Tyson added as if to seal the anti–Derek Camden deal.

Tyson was rated one of Denver's top-five divorce attorneys and had represented Gia when she'd divorced Elliot Grant. But the Grants' dirty fighting and false accusations against Tyson himself had prompted an inquiry from the Bar Association. It had all taken its toll on him and his practice, and wasn't something Gia wanted to put him through again.

"Don't worry, never again, Ty," Gia assured him. "When I'm ready to get back out there, it will only be with nice, average guys from nice, average families."

Gia poured what remained of her coffee down the sink and rinsed her cup, then took Tyson's to do the same so they could get next door to work.

Where Derek Camden probably would *not* show up because Tyson was right.

And where she would throw herself into the job and try not to feel as if she'd wasted almost an entire week fantasizing about Derek Camden flexing muscles to hoist fertilizer bags and paving stones....

Tyson was wrong.

Derek Camden arrived at the Bronsons' small redbrick two-bedroom house along with everyone else enlisted to work on Saturday. He wasn't even a minute late.

His outfit for the occasion—tennis shoes, old jeans and a plain green crewneck T-shirt—let Gia know she hadn't imagined the muscles behind those dress shirts the two times she'd seen him before. The well-worn, unflashy clothes also caused him to fit in seamlessly with the other volunteers.

And when she introduced him to the group, he cut her

off before she said his last name and was simply *Derek* to everyone except her and Tyson.

Derek mentioned how he and Tyson had met the one time, even remembering that Tyson was an attorney and a diehard Miami Hurricanes football fan. He also asked about Tyson's cousin Sharon, wishing her well without any sign of bitterness in regards to their relationship that hadn't panned out.

Then he pitched in. Not only did he have a can-do attitude, he had a surprising amount of knowledge and experience to back it up, especially when he offered to mow the lawn and actually repaired the lawnmower to do it.

But Gia's conversation with Tyson before leaving home served as a warning to her not to be too impressed.

Sure, Derek Camden could fix a lawnmower and mow the lawn.

Sure, he could hoist fertilizer bags and paving stones with the best of them—flexing muscles that made Gia's mouth water in a way that didn't happen at the sight of anyone else's flexing muscles.

Sure, he couldn't have been more pleasant or agreeable or uncomplaining.

Sure, he made friends with everyone there and she even watched Tyson accept more and more of his overtures as the day went on.

But she continued to remind herself that appearances could be deceiving, and that she would not—*could* not—let herself be deceived by them.

Which wasn't always easy to remember as the day went on and she got an eyeful of broad shoulders, thick thighs and a tight, perfectly shaped derriere she knew she had no business looking at.

And yet somehow couldn't help stealing a glimpse of over and over again....

* * *

By six o'clock the Bronsons' front and back yards were in better shape than they'd been in since Gia had known the elderly couple. Weeds were gone, bushes and trees were trimmed and the lawn was a well-manicured green carpet.

The volunteers had added a sandstone path from the front to the back and a second path from the back patio out to the toolshed. Landscapers had built a multitiered rock garden with room for flowers to be planted in the spring, and two of the horticulturists had planted shrubbery to line the fence in back. Gia and another botanist had formed a perennial garden just below the front porch on each side of the steps leading to the house.

The final effect was a vast improvement and upgrade that would require only minimal, easy maintenance either for Gia or for any new owner should the house have to be sold.

Throughout the day Larry had been in the center of things, unable to work but chatting with the people who were, while Marion went in and out of the house with beverages and cookies.

Gia had kept an eye on them both and had seen no indication that they were going to turn the hose on Derek or secretly dose him with laxatives, and she was glad that really had only been a joke.

But after both Larry and Marion had had Gia confirm on the sly that Derek was who they thought he was, neither of the Bronsons ventured too near to him, either. Or made any effort to talk to him the way they did everyone else.

For Derek's part, he gave them the space they so obviously wanted, and the one time there was unavoidable contact he was polite and respectfully pleasant without pushing anything or going overboard trying to win their favor.

It was the best way he could have handled it, but still Gia wasn't exactly sure what was going to happen when the work was finished and everyone—including Tyson—left, and only Derek and Gia remained to roll up hoses and put away tools.

As the elderly couple took a stroll around their newly enhanced yard to see the end results, it was impossible for them not to acknowledge Derek.

Gia was relieved when they spoke to him with guarded courtesy. But it was noticeable how all of their gratitude and praise went to her alone.

Even then, Derek handled the situation with aplomb. He agreed with them that Gia had done a remarkable job and didn't seem in the least offended by their lack of gratitude for the backbreaking work he'd done all day.

When the older couple went inside, Gia said, "Thanks for everything you did today."

"You're welcome." He grinned as if her gratitude was payment enough.

"I'm surprised that you knew your way around this stuff."

"My grandmother raised my brothers, sisters, cousins and me—there are ten of us—and she was originally a farm girl, so she believed in chores for everybody. As a kid, I did yard work—among other things. All the boys in the family did—sexist, I know, but the girls had to do more dusting so I guess it evened out."

"The Bronsons told me that H. J. Camden's son, grandsons and granddaughters-in-law were killed in a plane crash—you were one of the ten great-grandchildren left...."

"I was. Left to GiGi—that's what we call our grandmother—and H.J. and Margaret and Louie Haliburton, who work for GiGi but who are really more like family than anything."

It wasn't how Gia—or the Bronsons—had pictured things. They had imagined the Camdens as growing up like royalty, not as having to do their chores like any other family.

"But even with ten kids around, the Camdens didn't have a troop of gardeners?" she asked.

He laughed. "Sure. A troop of seven able-bodied grandsons. We still trade off going over to help with the yard work even now—you're just lucky that this wasn't my week or I'd have been late getting here this morning."

"Well, I'm glad you weren't since no one else knew how to fix the lawnmower."

"That church minister was making the attempt, though," he reminded her. Then, after a pause, he said, "He wanted to take you to dinner tonight...."

The pastor had given it a second try.

"I didn't know anyone had overheard that," Gia said.

"Is he trying to convert you, or is he interested in more than that?" Derek asked with a hint of teasing to his tone.

Gia laughed. "I've wondered the same thing. I'm not exactly sure either way. But since he knows his congregation doesn't approve of him being with someone who's been divorced, it could be conversion."

"So you said no."

"Because I'm not interested in dating anyone for any reason."

Derek Camden nodded. "Then what would you say to going our separate ways to clean up then meeting for a nondate bite to eat—just because you and I seem to be the only two without plans tonight?" He leaned in so he could add confidentially, "You can tell me how you think I did with the Bronsons today and maybe give me some tips for improvement."

No.

It was a simple answer and the only one she knew she should give him.

But the wheels of Gia's mind instantly began to spin.

It was Saturday night.

She'd put in a long day.

Everyone else *had* gone off on dates like Tyson had, or dinners out with spouses.

Larry and Marion were inside fixing their own dinner, after which they would cozy up on their sofa with popcorn to watch an old movie—their Saturday-night-at-the-movies tradition upheld even though they could no longer afford to go to a theater.

And she was slated for a shower and sitting alone in front of the television, eating whatever leftovers were in her fridge.

Or she could shower and meet Derek Camden for a *bite to eat.* A nondate. Unlike what the minister had invited her to.

She hadn't been at all tempted to accept the minister's offer.

But Derek Camden's?

She just couldn't seem to bring herself to say no....

"Not a date," she clarified firmly, knowing even as she did that she was walking a fine line but really hating the thought of those leftovers in front of the TV....

"Not a date," he confirmed. "We can both wear whatever—shorts, T-shirts, anything comfortable. I won't pick you up. I won't open your car door. We'll just meet at the restaurant. I'll buy you dinner in exchange for tips on how better to win over these guys so they let me really help them," he said with a nod at the Bronsons' house. "And then we'll go our separate ways afterward."

She *did* want to encourage a truce between the Bronsons and this man in order to get the Bronsons as much aid from the Camdens as she could.

That was what put it over the top for her. She was doing this for the Bronsons....

"Okay," she agreed.

"What do you feel like eating—Italian, Mediterranean, Moroccan, Mexican, Chinese, sushi...?"

She closed her eyes to think about it and when she opened them he was grinning at her.

"Did that help you decide?" he asked with a laugh.

"I was just giving my stomach the chance to tell me what it wanted," she said as if it should have been obvious.

"And what did it tell you?" Another question within another laugh.

"Lemon chicken at the Red Lantern on Broadway."

"Your stomach is very specific," he teased. "No dessert?"

"Always dessert—that was actually the deciding vote. The Red Lantern has this really, really dark chocolate pudding—the lemon chicken is just what I have to eat to get to that."

He laughed again but there was something about it—appreciation or delight or something—that didn't make her feel as if he was making fun of her at all. "Of course—really, really dark chocolate pudding. Can you be there in an hour?"

"An hour," she confirmed, knowing that didn't leave her a lot of time.

But that lack of time ensured that she couldn't make this a bigger deal than it needed to be, so that was all she gave herself.

* * *

Gia didn't wear shorts—she wore khaki capris. But she did put on a simple red square-neck T-shirt with a red-and-white-striped tank top peeking from underneath it. Without much time to get ready, she'd washed her hair in a hurry, scrunched it and left it loose in order to spend some of that time applying blush, mascara, eyeliner and a glossy lipstick.

When she got to the Red Lantern she noted that Derek—who was waiting for her by leaning against his black sports car in the parking lot—had also not opted for shorts. Instead he was wearing jeans that were much better than what he'd worn to work in earlier today. But he, too, had gone with a T-shirt—a white V-neck with long sleeves that he'd pushed to his elbows.

He was freshly shaven, his hair was clean and casually perfect, and it didn't matter whether or not he'd put much thought into his attire; he still looked great.

She warned herself not to pay too much attention to that as she parked.

Having spotted her when she'd turned in from the street, he pushed off of his car and followed her all the way back to the only open space at the far end of the lot. As promised, he didn't open her car door for her, but he was waiting right there when she got out of her small hybrid sedan.

She caught him giving her the once-over, which prompted a small smile, as if he liked what he saw. But all he said was that he'd already gone in and put their names on the waiting list, so they should have a table shortly.

Gia wondered if he'd tipped the hostess in advance, because the place was crowded but all it took was him stepping up to the hostess station and giving his name for them to be led right to a table.

They ordered soon after sitting down, and once they'd been served their iced teas, he said, "So, how do you think I did today?"

"You were a lot of help," she assured him.

He laughed. "I don't mean how did I do with the work. I meant how did I do with the Bronsons."

"Oh. Well, no rocks were thrown and the hose wasn't turned on you, so I think that counts as a success at this point."

"You say that as if you half expected it to happen," he said with a laugh.

Gia shrugged. "You were the one who thought rocks might be thrown, so I didn't think that would happen. But the hose part was mentioned...."

His laugh had just a touch of alarm to it. "They talked about turning the hose on me?"

Gia shrugged again. "You know, what your family did to the Bronsons was pretty bad.... Awful, in fact...."

He sobered somewhat and admitted, "Actually, I might not know exactly what went on. It was 1968—my father and my uncle were only teenagers then, so it was my great-grandfather and my grandfather at the helm. But even when my father and my uncle grew up and were on board they all kept things completely separate—business was business, home was home. They *never* brought business home with them—"

"But still the Camdens have a reputation...."

"I know. Over the years we've heard the bad stuff that's been said about us. But H.J. always said it was nothing, not to take it seriously, that he'd never done anything wrong. And to us—" Derek took a turn at shrugging "—H.J. was our great-grandfather. He took care of us. He doted on us. That was all we knew from him. When anyone brought up something that was being said, he'd say that in business, in politics, in sports and in life there were wins and there were losses. And that whoever lost was never happy about it—that that was where the bad-mouthing came from and not to pay any attention to it."

"So you didn't," Gia said as their meal arrived and they began to eat.

"Not really. GiGi's take on it was that success came with a cost, and she guessed that having some negative things—she actually called them lies—said about us was that cost."

"But they aren't lies. I mean, I don't know about anything else, but they aren't lies when it comes to Larry and Marion."

"With the Bronsons, I don't know all the details, to be perfectly honest. I know that they owned a hotel—"

"The Larkspur," Gia supplied.

"It was built in the late 1800s."

"By Larry's great-great-grandfather," she filled in as they ate.

"And it was in the very heart of downtown Denver on a prime piece of real estate."

Again Gia offered information. "A prime piece of real estate that H. J. Camden wanted to build a store on."

"Right," Derek concurred. "But while the real-estate was prime, what was on it had gone downhill…." he said diplomatically.

"The Larkspur needed work," Gia conceded. "Larry and Marion admit that they hadn't had the time or money it needed because of Roddy—"

"Roddy? Who's Roddy?"

"Their son. You didn't know they had a son?"

"I didn't," Derek said.

"So you *don't* know everything," Gia muttered more to herself than to him.

"I don't," he answered. "In fact, I think it's probably safe to say that what I do know is only the tip of the iceberg, and even that I haven't known for long."

Gia wasn't quite sure what that meant but she didn't see a point in trying to figure it out.

Instead she said, "Roddy was born with a lot of congenital problems. Larry says the doctors were actually surprised that he lived, but he thinks that Marion willed him to. He was ill and severely mentally and physically handicapped. He died thirty years ago, long before I knew Larry and Marion—"

"How long have you known them?"

"Three years. As long as I've been in my house— that's when we met, when I moved in. But we got close fast. They were good to me at a time when I needed some—I don't know, some kindness, people who cared about me, some bolstering—and they did all that and... Well, they treated me like *I* was their kid."

But she didn't want to say more about herself so she went on telling him about the Bronsons. "They've talked a lot about Roddy, though, and I've seen a few photographs. He spent his life in a wheelchair—spinal issues made him sort of twisted and he couldn't walk. He couldn't talk or do anything for himself.... But he was their son and they loved him and they were committed to taking care of him themselves, which took a lot."

"I can imagine," Derek said sympathetically. "And that's where their time and money went."

"It was a struggle for them. Roddy's medical expenses were considerable and one of them needed to be with him all the time. And running a hotel is a round-the-clock operation, too, so they were stretched thin—although they never talk about it with any kind of complaint, it just was what it was."

"And what it was was difficult."

"I can't imagine it myself," Gia said. "But *inn keeping*—as they call it sometimes—was all they knew. The Larkspur was all they had. And they also had Roddy. So they did the best they could."

"And the hotel went downhill." His tone suggested that what he was learning didn't sit well with him.

"It had been in Larry's family since it was built. The Larkspur rivaled the Brown Palace and the Oxford, they tell me. And every generation that had managed it had made sure that it was updated and expanded to keep up with the times. Including Larry and Marion—"

"Until they had Roddy."

"For a while they had some family—parents—who helped. But when they lost them, they were on their own with Roddy and with the Larkspur and they just couldn't maintain the standard. So yes, it went downhill. And that was when H. J. Camden swooped in."

"He offered to buy them out."

"In order to tear the Larkspur down and build a Camden store. Of course the Bronsons said no."

"And he increased the offer," Derek said, stating a fact, not being confrontational at all, merely supplying what he *did* know about things.

"It still wasn't a great offer, but it wouldn't have mattered. The Larkspur meant something to the Bronsons. More than the fact that it was their only asset and their only way to make a living. They were going through the process of having it qualified as an historic landmark, which would not only have protected it but would have brought in restoration funds. And they're sure it would have happened if not for H. J. Camden."

The waiter came to remove their plates, and Derek ordered Gia's chocolate pudding and sorbet for himself for dessert.

When the waiter left, Derek didn't comment on her last statement and she had the sense that he didn't know what to say to it. But Gia felt as if she was finally letting the Bronsons be heard, so she continued.

"H. J. Camden had political clout and the money to buy influence. Getting the Larkspur declared an historic landmark was going well until he decided he wanted the property it was on. Then all of a sudden the whole quali- fication process stalled. And at the same time, state in- spectors became overly interested in the Larkspur and cited it with enough health and building code violations to have it condemned—"

"Literally condemned?"

"Literally. Inspectors said it was going to fall down around them and not only couldn't they stay open for business, they couldn't live there themselves anymore, either. And that was absolutely not true—they had an independent contractor look at it and he confirmed that it wasn't in that kind of shape—"

"And the independent contractor's report didn't carry any weight?"

"Not when he was suddenly hired by Hank Camden to build Camden stores out of state and the report dis- appeared."

Derek flinched slightly at that.

"All the hotel really needed was what the Bronsons' house needs now—paint, plumbing and electrical repairs and updating, maybe a new kitchen—but it wasn't fall- ing down around their ears."

Derek's frown caused his brows to twitch together, suggesting he was troubled by what Gia had told him. But he gave no response.

She went on without one. "Larry challenged the rulings, but without the independent contractor's report, without the money to hire another one or to hire a good lawyer, he was no match for what he found himself up against. He lost the challenges, the Bronsons couldn't afford repairs to address the inflated building code violations and they had no choice but to close their doors and take the Camden offer. An offer that was mere pennies on the dollar of the initial offer."

Derek was scowling by the time the waiter served their desserts. But still Gia didn't let up.

"The Bronsons were left with no property, very little money and mounting expenses for Roddy. Not being able to live at the hotel meant they were even homeless. So they used the lion's share of the money from the buyout to get the house they're in now—"

"Over forty years ago—shouldn't that have been paid off years back?" he asked between bites.

"Spoken like a finance guy. Actually, they used the money from the hotel to buy the house outright—it made them feel a little more secure after the rug being pulled out from under them. But without the hotel, they had to go to work for other people, and Roddy went through health crisis after health crisis that would keep them both away from their jobs, so they'd eventually be let go. Over the years the house had to be mortgaged and refinanced and refinanced and second mortgaged—"

"So it isn't paid off."

Again Gia was hesitant to reveal too much of the Bronson's vulnerability, just in case, so she merely shrugged once more in answer and concluded what she was saying.

"No matter how you look at it—and certainly it's the way they look at it—because of what H. J. Camden did to get what he wanted, rather than being the owners of their family legacy and a Denver landmark, the Bronsons saw that legacy and landmark get bulldozed. They ended up having a life of hardship and money problems, and age and no extra retirement funds and trying to make it on a fixed income have only compounded those problems."

Gia watched as Derek rubbed his sculpted jawline in a gesture that conveyed discomfort. "Wow. Most of that is news to me," he said somberly.

Most of it, but not all of it....

Gia noted that he didn't say which parts were *not* news to him.

Never admit to anything—that was legal advice she'd overheard given to the Grants.

That and to put some money into a worthy cause to make themselves look better whenever ugly rumors or accusations surfaced....

"So what you're saying is that the Bronsons took the higher ground today by *not* throwing rocks or turning the hose on me," Derek said then, clearly making a joke to ease some of the tension.

"Kind of," Gia answered.

He nodded as if he understood and didn't necessarily disagree.

"I'm sorry if I got a little carried away," she apologized, taking a deep breath and consciously toning it down because she realized that her own outrage on the Bronsons' behalf might have made her sound heated.

"It's okay. I wanted to hear it from the Bronsons' perspective."

"Oh, they get a whole lot more irate when they tell it...."

He laughed somewhat helplessly. "Better it came from you, then," he joked.

The waiter brought their check at that moment and when he'd left, Derek said, "Well, today we made a little headway—we did the Bronsons' yard. Next Saturday we'll work on the inside of the house. And after that we'll do whatever else needs to be done."

Whatever else needs to be done was not a specific commitment to anything. And yet Gia had the sense that today wasn't the beginning and end of his involvement, that he honestly did intend to follow this through.

But we'll see, she told herself, unwilling and unable to trust him too much.

He paid the bill, refusing to allow Gia to leave even the tip, and they left the restaurant.

Darkness had fallen, and in the parking lot he bypassed his own car to walk her all the way to hers—a date-like courtesy that Gia appreciated only for the safety factor.

Or so she told herself.

"Can I ask a favor?" Derek said as they reached her car and she unlocked the door.

"You can ask...."

"I'm truly sorry for what happened to the Bronsons no matter what caused the life they've had and the position they're in now. And I'll take whatever hit they want to throw—rocks, the hose turned on me... I know that one way or another, the reality for them is that I'm a Camden and a Camden store sits in place of the hotel that—had things gone differently—they could still be benefitting from. The hotel that was their family legacy...."

He paused before he added, "But would *you* try to

keep in mind that I wasn't even a twinkle in anybody's eye at the time this went down? That I didn't have a single thing to do with it, and that now I'm just trying to help these people the same way you are?"

Gia didn't immediately respond.

The parking lot was dimly lit, but they were standing near enough for her to still see his face—which seemed to get better looking the more she saw of it—and to still look into his striking blue eyes. And she openly studied it all, thinking about her ex, about his family, about how good they'd been at making themselves appear innocent when they were anything but.

And yet...

Derek was right. He hadn't had a part in any of what had happened to the Bronsons. He couldn't have had.

Which didn't mean he wasn't responsible for similar things that could be going on now. But it did mean that she couldn't blame him for what went on in the past.

So she conceded to that much. "I'll try to keep in mind that you didn't have anything to do with the lousy deal the Bronsons got."

But she wouldn't completely trust him, either.

She couldn't. Not for the Bronsons' sake, and not for her own.

"Thank you," he said. "Because not only didn't I have anything to do with it, I feel as badly for those people as you do."

Maybe she just wanted to believe that, but it somehow had the ring of truth to it. And the fact that he felt bad for the Bronsons, that he had what appeared to be genuine compassion and empathy for them, was more than she could say she'd ever seen from her ex or his family. So it bought him a slight concession from her.

But only a slight one.

Because feeling bad that his family did something wrong but still managed to get what it was after was not quite the same as that wrong never being done in the first place. At least as far as she was concerned.

It also wasn't the same as openly admitting that a wrong had been committed, renouncing whoever had committed it or relinquishing all the gains that had been made because of it.

"The best we can do now is try to get them out of the position they're in," she concluded.

He nodded and smiled an engaging smile before he said, "And they think the sun rises and sets with you. Every time I was within earshot today, they were talking about how wonderful you are. You're like the daughter they never had. You're a gift from God. They don't know what they'd do without you...." He shook his head as if in amazement at the pure number of accolades he'd overheard. "They *love* you."

"I think of them as a gift to me, too," she said. "It's one of those when-a-door-closes-a-window-opens things."

Derek nodded again, accepting that without questioning exactly what she meant.

Instead, he seemed more intent on studying her the way she'd studied him moments earlier. He seemed to appreciate the sight as much as she had, because another small smile appeared on his handsome face.

A small smile that drew her attention to his mouth. To such supple-looking lips...

And somehow she just knew he would be a good kisser. Though she had no idea why the thought crossed her mind.

Or why she was suddenly wishing—just a little—that he wouldn't be quite as chivalrous as he was being and actually kiss her good-night to let her test her theory....

But he didn't.

And he was true to his word—he also didn't make any move to open her door for her, so Gia finally did it herself, knowing she needed to go home and escape any kind of kissing thoughts whatsoever.

"So next Saturday," she said as she got in, attempting to neutralize the effect he was having on her.

He stepped up to close her door. "I'll be there," he assured her as she rolled down her window. "Text me a time."

"I'll send out a blanket reminder," she said as she started her engine.

"And I'll see you then. Have a nice week…" he said, stepping away from the car after a slap to the roof.

"You, too. And thanks for dinner…and your help today."

He merely raised his chin to that and stayed where he was, watching as she backed out of the parking spot, waving as she drove off.

It was a wave that Gia returned only half-heartedly, but not because of anything to do with him.

She was just aggravated with herself.

For feeling suddenly like a week was a very, very long while to wait to see him again….

Chapter Four

"Hey, Tommy, how's the foot? Jeanine—I like the haircut! Mitch, I owe you a ten spot—you were right about Dallas on Sunday. Tammy, how are you doin' today? I was told our fearless leader was in here somewhere…."

Gia was at the back of one of the Health Now greenhouses on Friday when she heard the greetings to her coworkers. It didn't take her more than a split second to recognize Derek Camden's voice carrying through the greenery, and another split second to recall that he'd met those particular coworkers doing the Bronsons' yard work.

What she hadn't been aware of was how familiar he'd become with them all. And she couldn't help being impressed by what he noticed and remembered, and how friendly he sounded. He'd also impressed her coworkers, if their warm responses to him were any indication because they all greeted him in return as if he was their favorite person, the last of them informing him of her location and that she was planting gingko.

"Hey there!" he said when he finally found her.

"Hey there yourself," Gia answered without masking her surprise to see him, wiping her hands on a damp cloth as she turned from her pots, seeds and soil.

She'd spent the entire week fighting constant thoughts of him, and she could have kicked herself when the very first thing that had popped into her mind when she'd woken up this morning was that there was only another twenty-four hours until she was going to see him again. But having him show up at work was just a shock.

And then an unwarranted disappointment when it occurred to her that he was probably there to make an excuse for why he *wouldn't* be at the Bronsons' tomorrow....

"What are you doing here? Oh, wait, careful! Don't lean against that, you'll get dirt on your suit," she warned before he had the chance to answer.

He glanced down at his suit coat, which was tan but had a mauve cast to it, and brushed away the dirt he'd rubbed against before she'd stopped him.

And in that moment, Gia took in the full image of the tall, broad-shouldered man dressed for *his* work in a suit that couldn't have been better tailored, a dress shirt that was off-white with that same mysterious mauve cast and a brown and mauve tie knotted at his throat.

She registered that he looked jaw-droppingly terrific, and then pushed that thought out of her head.

Which might not have been the best thing, because what replaced it was the sudden awareness of her own appearance.

Today was planting day—a day spent in the heat of the greenhouse. And since it required nothing other than working with soil, seeds and plants, she was dressed in worn-out sandals, jean shorts and a tank top, and her hair was a curly geyser bursting from a rubber band at the top of her head to keep it off her neck. Plus, there wasn't any use applying makeup that would melt in the greenhouse heat, so she hadn't.

It was not how she wanted to be seen by him, and a wave of self-consciousness struck her.

"I came to see if I could take you to lunch."

"I can't go anywhere with you dressed like that and me like this!" she blurted out.

He looked her up and down and grinned. "I don't know about me, but you're kind of adorable. You just look summery—what's wrong with that? We'll go some-place casual, with a patio where we can eat al fresco."

From behind the Echinacea, Jeanine said, "Go, Gia."

She *had* brought a shirt to put on over the tank top to go home....

But that wasn't going to upgrade her look much.

"Come on," Derek urged. "Get me out of this heat—I wanted to talk to you about the Bronsons."

So he hadn't come for her.

Gia knew it was stupid, but that disappointed her, too.

"If you can't make it tomorrow just say it—"

"That's not what I want to talk about—I'll be there tomorrow. But that's part of what I need to go over with you."

"It's time for lunch anyway, you might as well," Jeanine contributed.

Gia knew that Derek had to be more and more uncom-fortable in the greenhouse heat, and since he just wanted to talk about the Bronsons, why should she care what she was wearing? So she gave in. "Okay, but nothing fancy—there's a sandwich place down the street with a few tables outside. Maybe we could just do that."

"Nothing fancy, sandwiches are fine," he agreed.

"I have a shirt I can put on. Let's go out back here," she said, leading him to a rear door and ushering him to the outdoor gardens.

"There's more out here?"

"And more greenhouses, too," Gia told him, pointing to the other two built around the perimeters of the outdoor garden.

"Greenhouses to grow in year-round, this garden to grow in the summer months, huh?"

"Right. We're watching for predictions of the first frost—we'll harvest just before that happens and then close these gardens down for winter. But right now—" She bent down and said to the pale purple flowers, "You're beautiful, aren't you?"

"You talk to your plants...."

"They're living things," she said.

"That smell like—"

"It's thyme. We use it in antiseptic and antifungal creams, and in cough medicine. It's good for bronchial infections. The leaves can be made into a tea, too."

"Also good in food," he supplied.

"Also good in food," she confirmed.

"So you grow all this?" he asked as Gia led him along the path through the plants and into the main building.

"We do. They're our babies, we plant them and nurse them along, then harvest and turn them over to production where some of them are ground and put into capsules or tablets, or pressed for their oils, or whatever can be done with them."

"And this stuff works like medicine?" he asked skeptically.

"This *stuff* has been around longer than contemporary medicine. It's what people used before there were chemicals. Sometimes the effects are more subtle or they take a little while to build up before they work, but rather than take chemicals to get rid of heartburn, give me gum or a peppermint leaf to chew, or an orange to eat, or a pill that doesn't have anything in it but orange oil."

"And those things work?"

"You'll never know until you try them," she challenged as they went into her small office. "Sometimes a spoonful of vinegar works, too."

"So you're anti–contemporary medicine?" he asked.

"No. But I'll always try something natural before I'll go the other route," she said as she took the tailored white blouse draped on her desk chair and put it on, buttoning it over her tank top. "And there are a lot of things that work as preventatives, too. Like the gingko in the greenhouse—that's good for the brain and the memory," she said, pointing to her head. "I take it every day."

He grinned again. "Is that what makes your hair so curly."

"No, that's genetic," she said with a bit of a grimace.

"What? You don't like it?"

"It kind of has a life of its own." She wished she'd worn it some way that tamed it a little more today, but there was nothing she could do about it now.

His grin just got bigger and he reached to gently bounce his palm off the top of the geyser. "A wild life of its own—I think it's great."

Not sure she believed that, Gia just made a face and took her purse from her desk drawer before pointing at the door.

Blouse or no blouse, she still felt woefully underdressed at his side as she guided him to the sandwich shop she'd mentioned.

It was a place everyone from Health Now frequented, so the owner knew her by sight. After placing their orders, Gia slid the donation jar next to the cash register toward herself and said, "I might as well take this with me today, Nick. It's the last jar I have out and I'm going to the bank later. Since we've started to use the money, I'll deposit it. Thanks for letting me leave it here, though."

"For you, anytime. My kids had better take so much care of me when I'm that age. Or maybe I'll have to come get you."

"I'm always right up the block," Gia assured him as they accepted their drinks and meatball sandwiches.

Derek carried the tray with everything on it so Gia could take the gallon-size pickle jar that was three quarters full—mostly with change, but with a few dollar bills in sight, too.

They took everything out to one of the four small tables on the sidewalk in front of the shop. As they sat down, Derek said, "First the dessert shop, now the sandwich shop—do you just make friends wherever you go?"

Gia shrugged. "I'm a creature of habit. I see the same people over and over again. We talk. I get to know them and they get to know me."

"And like you."

She shrugged again. "Maybe. But it takes me going in over and over again. One day with you and everybody I work with seems to think you're great."

He laughed. "Why do you say that as if I did something wrong?"

"Oh, no, I didn't mean that." She'd just been thinking about her ex-husband's surface charm and what it had concealed and wondering if the same was true of

Derek. "I'm only saying that with me it takes some time and repeat business before I get where you got with the people I work with in a single day."

"With everyone but the Bronsons."

Who had cause to be wary because they'd seen beneath the surface of the Camdens.

"What about tomorrow did you want to talk to me about—if you're still coming?" Gia asked, changing the subject as they began eating.

"I wanted to let you know that I've hired a crew of professional plumbers and electricians to check everything out and fix whatever they might find wrong."

"We can't pay for that."

"I'm paying for it. After seeing the age of that house and the shape it's in, I thought it should be inspected—especially the wiring, since it could be a fire hazard. And I know you're trying to get everything done in a hurry, so there will be big enough crews coming in to do just about anything that needs to be done in the one day."

That had to cost a fortune, and while she wanted to believe it was purely an act of generosity, she couldn't help recalling the Bronsons' concerns about his interest in the place and getting slightly suspicious.

"You don't want their house, right?" she asked as he took his first bite of sandwich.

He chuckled and frowned at the same time. "Why would I want their house?" he asked when he'd finished chewing.

"Your family took their hotel. Larry and Marion are a little worried that now—"

"We want their house?" he said in disbelief. "Do they just think we want to persecute them for some reason? That we're targeting them?"

"You aren't, are you?"

"No, of course not. There isn't a reason in the world we would. In fact, after hearing that their house is mortgaged, the other thing I wanted out of this lunch today was to get a better idea of what their financial situation really is. Are they deeply in debt? Are they behind in their mortgage payments? How much is the mortgage as a whole…?"

Gia purposely took a bite of her sandwich so that her mouth was full and she couldn't answer. She wanted to buy herself time to gauge what to do.

She hadn't been forthcoming with him on this subject before out of paranoia that the Bronsons might somehow be right in worrying that there was a self-serving motivation behind the Camdens' help.

But it just didn't seem reasonable that they would want the Bronsons' house for any reason. And since the Bronsons needed a lot more help than the jars of spare change like the one at her feet could provide, she decided to trust him. A little anyway. And just with some information.

So when her mouth was empty she said, "The only debt they have is on their house. But they just can't keep up the payments anymore. They're in arrears and the bank has notified them that if they don't come up with the back payments, foreclosure proceedings are going to start."

"So you decided to mow the lawn and paint the walls?" he said as if he didn't understand her thinking.

"I decided to try to raise money for them. My fantasy was to raise enough to pay the back payments, then maybe get the house refinanced so the payments could be more what they could afford—"

"So shouldn't every penny be going toward the back payments?"

"I waited to see how close I was coming. But unfortunately it wasn't close enough. With what I've raised so far all I can do is make a dent in the back payments—unless the yard sale brings in a *lot,* and I know that isn't likely. So I'm going with the contingency plan—"

"Which is to paint the walls and mow the lawn?" he said, still confused.

"If I can't pay the back payments completely, then the next best thing is to pay enough to stall the foreclosure so the house can be sold—"

"Ah, I see—so you're putting some of the money you've raised into getting the place in better shape in order to sell it."

"Right. And the better shape it's in, the better the chance of getting a higher price, which—I'm hoping—means that the Bronsons would come out with a small amount of cash."

"Then what? If they can't stay in their house, what happens to them?"

She told him about her plan to move them into her basement apartment.

"Really? You'd do that?"

"A couple they knew was in the same situation a few years ago. Social Services ended up involved because they were elderly and didn't have any family. But Social Services put the wife in one nursing home and the husband in a different one—both of them not very nice places—because it was just a matter of available beds. After being married for over fifty years, those people died without ever seeing each other again. And I won't let that happen to Larry and Marion."

"So you'll move them into your basement apartment and be responsible for them, and what? Charge them rent they can afford?"

"I couldn't take money from them. I'll just move them in—"

"And become responsible for them."

"I'll take care of them whether they're next door or in my basement. It's just that they don't *want* to lose their house. They want to stay in it, and I can understand that, so I'm giving it the best shot I can—and who knows, maybe the yard sale *will* put us over the top. But in the meantime I have to be realistic and get the place in selling condition, too. I'm not using much of the money— all the labor and most of the materials are donated—but it has to be done...."

He nodded and seemed to be lost in thought as he finished his sandwich.

Then he said, "Have you told me everything? Because it gets a little bleaker every time I persuade you to talk about it, and I really am trying to see the whole picture so I know what to do for them."

"That's the whole picture," Gia said as she wadded up the paper her own sandwich had been wrapped in, hoping she hadn't put the Bronsons farther out on a limb by revealing it all to him. "They live a simple—and *really* frugal—life. It's just gotten away from them."

"And they honestly don't have any other debt—credit cards, a car?"

Gia shook her head. "Their car is twenty years old and mostly sits in the garage—Larry drives a little if he has to and if it isn't too far, but that's it. They have a credit card for emergencies, but *only* for emergencies. I put them on my cell phone plan with a freebie phone so they could cancel their landline and cut that expense. For Larry's birthday I paid off his dental bill because the payments they were making to the dentist were strapping them, so that's gone. It's just the house, utilities, food and medical stuff—they live hand-to-mouth..."

"And apparently have friends who do, too..." he said, frowning again.

"People who live on a fixed income have trouble making ends meet—it's a fact of life."

"An ugly one."

Gia didn't say anything to that, wondering if it was ugly enough to send him running.

But then his eyes in all their blue glory looked squarely into hers and he vowed, "We're going to take care of this."

Then her ex and his family flashed through her mind and something else occurred to her.

"There's not going to be anything in it for you, right?" she said firmly. "Because the Bronsons would be furious if you used them to make the Camdens look like saints for lending a hand. If that's what's behind this I'll throw rocks at you myself."

He held up both hands, palms outward. "Nothing in it for us, I promise. How would it make us look good to say we're helping out a couple who might not be in the position they're in had a Camden store not gone where their hotel used to be?"

"And I'd stir up that whole story, too," she warned.

"There's not going to be a reason to," he assured her. "This is your deal—we're just trying to give some of the help you've asked for."

Gia decided to take a chance and trust him. While her past experience gave her reason to be wary, so far there was no indication that he had ulterior motives where the Bronsons were concerned.

"Okay," she conceded. Then, because it was true, she said, "I should get back to work."

"What, no chocolate dessert at lunch?" he teased, showing that he hadn't taken offense at her suspicion.

She appreciated that and leaned forward to say under her breath, "Nick only has some Italian cookies that aren't very good."

"I saw them in the case—they're also not chocolate," Derek whispered back. "Could that be the reason you think they're not very good?"

"It's possible," she conceded.

"How about somewhere else? We could go back the way we came and around the corner to the bakery.... Lava cake..."

He thought he was tempting her with chocolate. And while that was always a temptation for her, she discovered that it was equally as tempting to prolong this time with him despite the apprehensions he aroused in her just by being who he was and coming from the family he came from.

There was just some kind of chemistry that got activated in her with this guy that she wished she could deactivate. At least she could try not to indulge it, so she held the line.

"I really can't," she insisted.

"Well, I guess I'll get to see you tomorrow, so I'll let you go today," he said, making her wonder if he was merely being charming or if he actually wanted to spend more time with her.

It doesn't matter! she silently shouted at herself.

Derek took their tray and dumped the lunch remnants in the nearby trash, and then turned to pick up the jar of money.

"This can't be lightweight. Let me carry it." Gia didn't argue because it *was* heavy, and she hadn't been looking forward to toting it herself. But Derek carried it under one arm, against his hip, and didn't seem to exert himself too much.

"So do you grow everything your company needs in the gardens here? Right in the middle of the city?" he asked as they headed back to Health Now, clearly making an effort to put things securely back on more neutral ground.

"No," Gia answered. "This is just where the company started. We expanded about four years ago to an area outside of Broomfield. We produce about a quarter of what's needed here and the rest there."

"Does that mean that you work in Broomfield, too?"

"It does. All the offices are in Denver—Broomfield is just greenhouses and another outdoor garden that's about the size of a football field—but the botanists and horticulturists go back and forth to care for the plants. That's where Peggy and Marshall are today—you met them last Saturday, too."

"Right, I remember—Peggy is the really, really skinny woman and Marshall is—"

"The really, really *not* skinny guy," Gia supplied for him.

"He's a big man," Derek agreed with a laugh. "Knows a lot about music and computers."

"Yes, he does—his two passions outside of work." Again Gia was surprised that Derek had bothered to get so friendly with everyone.

Maybe that was what she was responding to, she told herself. Maybe it was just his general friendliness—the same general friendliness he showed to everyone—and she'd been out of the single world for so long that she somehow read more into it than was there.

The possibility made her feel all the more ridiculous for having thought about him as much as she had for the past week. For having made-up, flirty conversations with him in her head. Flirty conversations that were so much wittier than anything she'd pulled off today....

He insisted on taking the jar all the way inside to her office, where she assured him it was safe to leave it on her desk.

But once he'd done that and she was waiting for him to leave so she could take her blouse off again, he instead turned his focus onto her.

"Thanks for going to lunch with me today," he said.

"Even if I gave you a hard time?"

He grinned. "There does always seem to be a minute or two when we're together when you narrow those big brown eyes and look at me like I'm the enemy. You're just not sure about me yet, are you?" he asked.

Gia shrugged.

And that made him grin. "You're not," he said, as if it amused him. But also with what sounded like affection.

Or maybe she was just imagining it.

She was probably just imagining it.

Along with the sense she kept having that there were small sparks shooting between them as he studied her face.

"You were on my mind a lot this past week," he said then. His mouth eased into a small, thoughtful smile as his gaze rose somewhat and he added, "Must be the hair." His blue eyes returned to hers. "But it made me want to touch base with you on our own just a little before we're in the middle of everything and everybody tomorrow...."

So that was what had prompted the lunch....

Gia nodded because she suddenly couldn't think straight enough to say anything. Instead, her thoughts were drifting to the idea of him kissing her....

Kissing her...

That was something else she'd thought way, way too much about since last Saturday night.

Something that certainly had no place here and now, at work....

And yet he was looking at her so intently that it caused her to actually entertain the notion that he might be thinking about it, too.

That couldn't be...

But he wasn't even making small talk anymore. He was standing there—dashingly handsome in a suit that probably cost as much as her car—just looking into her eyes.

Then down at her mouth....

The outer office had been empty when they'd come in. Everyone was probably in the lunchroom, and her office couldn't be seen from there. Plus, she'd probably be able to hear something if anyone came back....

Her chin went up a fraction of an inch as she looked into those astonishingly blue eyes...and was shocked to find herself ready.

Ready to be kissed by someone other than Elliot.

Ready to be kissed by this man she hadn't been able to get out of her head for two solid weeks now....

And she really, honestly thought he was going to do it as she watched him move forward.

This is crazy!

And yet she didn't back off....

But then Derek did. He caught himself and stood a little straighter.

Without the sound of anyone coming, Gia realized. Without any indication that she would have rejected him. Still, he'd backed off.

He made a sort of confused, mildly troubled face and

smiled a tight-lipped smile before saying, "So I guess I'll see you tomorrow."

"At the Bronsons', bright and early. One of their church friends is taking them out for the day so we can just work. All of us."

Somehow that *we* had had an intimate inflection so she'd felt the need to amend it.

He smiled more openly and she knew he was about to make a joke even before he said, "What was I in danger of this week—a ladder getting kicked out from under me? Being pushed down stairs?"

Gia got hold of herself and said, "No threats this round. You're safe."

He smiled as if he wasn't so sure about that.

Then he took a step toward her office door and said, "I'll let you get back to your plants and saving lives with leaves."

"Saving lives with leaves," she parroted. "Hmm... that could be one of our slogans."

"I don't need credit for that, either," he joked, making her smile.

And like him.

Even though she didn't want to.

"See you tomorrow," he said as he went out.

"See you tomorrow," she answered.

Then she was alone in her office, needing a few minutes to recover before she could go out and see anyone.

Wondering during that time exactly what had just happened between them.

And if not being kissed in a very long time might have robbed her of the ability to read the signs....

Chapter Five

"Oh, hi," Gia said, stopping cold in the doorway of the Bronsons' bedroom on Saturday morning.

When she'd assigned everyone to the work that needed to be done today, it had taken a strong force of will not to team herself up with Derek. Instead, she'd put him with Jeanine to paint the guest room across the hall. So she was surprised to see him in the room she was supposed to be painting with Tyson.

Jeanine was single and actively looking for a mate. Although it had secretly not sat well with Gia, she'd forced herself to put the two together. She'd reasoned that if something got started between them then maybe she could stomp out whatever it was that was going on with her in regards to Derek.

But there he was, managing to look good even in a pair of ragged old jeans and a plain white undershirt-sort-of-T-shirt, taking tarps out of their packaging.

"Hi," he answered her greeting.

"You know the guest room is across the hall…" she informed him.

"Yeah, I did some rearranging—did *you* know that Tyson is dating the blonde bombshell from your marketing department?"

"I introduced them, so yes, I knew that. Minna…"

Minna, who was wearing short shorts and a bandeau top that barely contained her ample chest, while Gia was in throwaway jeans torn at the knee and an equally ratty T-shirt so it wouldn't matter if she got paint splattered.

Minna, whose long blond hair was flowing free, while Gia's had to be pulled back into a twist that hardly contained her geyser of curls.

Minna, who, yes, looked like a blonde bombshell while Gia felt as if she faded into the woodwork in comparison, despite the fact that she'd done her makeup today.

"Plus," she added, "Tyson is not only my best friend, he temporarily lives in the apartment on the upper floor of my house, so there isn't much I *don't* know about him."

"Well, it seemed like they'd want to work together. And last week Jeanine and that Adam Smythe from the Botanical Gardens were getting pretty friendly—I thought Jeanine would rather paint with him than with me. So we made some changes. Is that okay, or did you have your heart set on working with Tyson? He said he didn't think it mattered who worked where as long as everything got done."

Tyson had spent most of the past week with Minna and Gia had hardly seen him. She'd thought a day of painting together would give them a chance to catch up. But more important, she'd counted on him to provide her with a safety net from Derek. She hadn't been able to talk to Tyson, though, and let him know that it felt risky for her to be in close quarters with Derek all day, so he couldn't have known that was her plan.

But she certainly couldn't tell Derek that. Or make a fuss over harmless changes in the roster.

"It doesn't matter," she said, hoping she sounded as indifferent as she was trying to sound.

And at the same time, she wondered if Derek had purposely switched the teams to be with her.

That was unlikely, she told herself.

But it still didn't calm the tiny wave of excitement that it was even remotely possible.

"What's with the bed? It has some...topography..." he said then, pointing his chin at it as he stood at the foot taking the tarps out of their packages and setting them on the floor.

"Oh, I rigged it," Gia said, finally going all the way into the room. "Larry has reflux problems when he lies down flat, so I got him a foam wedge to prop him up a little. Marion has a bad shoulder that doesn't bother her if her arm on that side has something to rest on, and an arthritic hip that hurts less if her knees are bent some when she sleeps. So I put a piece of foam under the mattress pad on the edge of the bed for her arm, and another piece where her knees go. I know it looks weird—they call it the Frankenstein bed—but it works."

He angled his head in the direction she'd just come from. "And the *rigging* on the light switch? I saw that when I moved the dresser away from the wall...."

"If the dresser goes against that wall, they have more space in here, but it covered the light switch. So I fixed it so the light switch is usable with the dresser in front of it."

"Your idea, too?"

"Yeah," she said, taking the wrapping off the roll of tape she was going to use to paint edges.

"Inventive."

"It's just a few pieces of foam and a stick with a hole in one end and knob on the other," Gia said. Then, when he shook out one of the tarps to put over the bed, she added, "Let's take the pictures off the walls and put them on the bed first, then cover it all."

"Good idea."

There was a gallery of framed photographs on one wall, but when Gia met Derek there he was looking at them rather than taking them down.

"These must be their parents," Derek observed of the black-and-white pictures that showed people with Roaring Twenties hairstyles and fashion.

Gia pointed out which was Larry's family and which was Marion's. "And that's Marion with her parents when she was five or six." Then she pointed to another cluster of snapshots. "That's Roddy."

"Oooh, he doesn't look well," Derek said sympathetically.

"Even as a newborn he wasn't just pink and perfect. But they loved him the way he was."

Gia took down the photos and laid them extra carefully on the bed.

"This must be Larry and Marion's wedding picture," Derek said as he brought another black-and-white photograph to set beside those of Roddy.

Gia glanced at it. "I can never get over how young Marion looks in that picture. When I say that to her, she jokes that she was Larry's child bride," Gia said affectionately. "But even Larry was only nineteen."

"How did they meet?" Derek asked as they removed

the remainder of the photos, placed them on the bed and then covered everything with a tarp.

"They met at the Trocadero Ballroom in the old Elitch Gardens," Gia said, referring to one of Denver's original entertainment centers that had included an amusement park and a renowned theater and ballroom.

"Some big band was there," Gia went on. "I've never heard of it, but they actually have an old album of the music—and a record player to play it—and sometimes they put it on and dance to it even now. Anyway, they were there separately with friends and none of them knew each other. But all of Larry's friends had asked Marion to dance and been turned down. Then Larry strolled right across the middle of the dance floor— that's how Marion puts it—and she says he was the one she was waiting for."

"She wasn't afraid that he'd get discouraged by all the other rejections and never ask?"

"Larry says she was giving him the eye from across the room, so he thought he'd have better luck. Marion denies it, but when she does Larry shakes his head to let you know she's lying and she just laughs."

"And they've been married how long?" Derek asked with some amusement in his voice.

"Since a week after Marion graduated from high school when she was seventeen—this year was their seventieth anniversary."

"Wow," Derek said as they draped tarps over the dresser and lined the floor with them.

"I know, hard to imagine, isn't it? And they're still so good together. Even after all they've gone through, one's eyes light up when the other comes into a room, they still flirt with each other and—"

"Sleep in the same lumpy bed."

Gia laughed and hoped she didn't sound like a sappy romantic when she echoed, "They still sleep in the same lumpy bed." Then she said, "And I catch them holding hands just sitting on the couch watching TV sometimes. Marion says Larry has never forgotten a birthday or an anniversary, and I don't know what she does on Valentine's Day, but whatever it is, he always says that she's never forgotten one of those either, and then he wiggles his eyebrows and makes Marion blush."

Derek laughed. "Seriously? Even now, in their eighties, after seventy years of marriage?"

"Seriously. I make sure to give this place a wide berth that whole day and night."

He laughed harder. "Seems like that might be wise."

"And they still kiss…." Gia marveled as they began to put tape around the bedroom window.

"Aren't they supposed to?"

"I don't know," she mused. "Sometimes people who haven't been married anywhere near as long have to force their spouse to kiss them hello or goodbye or… you know, anytime that it isn't going to lead to…sex…. And eventually they just give up trying…"

"Is that the voice of experience?" he asked gently.

It was. But she'd basically been thinking out loud of her own marriage in comparison to Larry and Marion's, and she wasn't willing to let Derek know that, so she merely said, "I just mean that it's still obvious that Larry and Marion really do love each other and enjoy each other's company. They aren't like a lot of people who've been together for a while—they aren't just roommates. They don't bicker. It isn't as if they're only together for convenience or out of habit but don't really like each other—"

"Yeah, I guess I know what you're talking about. I've

seen couples like that, too. The spark is gone, they're bored, there's no excitement or they actually seem to *dis*like each other, and you wonder why they're together at all."

"Larry and Marion still talk. They still laugh together. They still think of each other first. They aren't even impatient with the small things that can get annoying— Larry will say something silly and Marion thinks it's endearing, or Marion will repeat the same story over and over and every time she does Larry will just say that she tells it so well. They're just…happy to have each other, I guess. Even after all this time."

"I envy that," he admitted. "It's how I'd like to end up."

Gia laughed. "Is that what you were thinking when you went out with Tyson's nutty cousin Sharon? That you could find it with her?" she teased as he pried open the paint can and poured some into the tray.

Derek didn't seem to take offense because he laughed, too. "Hey, you never know…Sharon might not have been my Marion, but it beats some of the women I go out with who make me feel like I'm watching paint dry when they talk."

That would probably be me, Gia thought.

But what she said was, "So only psychics and mediums and vampire witches for you!"

He laughed again. "Vampire witches? I don't *think* I've ever dated one of those."

"But you'd probably like the fangs and magic spells, right?"

More laughing. "Now you're starting to sound like my grandmother."

That couldn't be good.…

So Gia opted to change the subject and handed Derek

the roller and the extension pole that went with it. "How about you work on the ceiling while I start the walls?"

He agreed, and as they went to work he said, "So what was the big band that brought Larry and Marion together?"

After telling him the name, they began to talk about what kind of music they each liked. That led to a discussion of favorite television programs and movies, travel destinations, food—besides chocolate—colors, seasons, holidays and on and on.

To subjects Gia only hoped didn't make her sound like his grandmother....

The day flew by for Gia. When it was over, she left Tyson to oversee the finishing work and cleanup so she could run home to do some last-minute preparations for the barbecue she'd invited everyone to afterward.

Seizing the opportunity that afforded her, she quickly changed out of her paint-splattered clothes and into a pair of black capris with a tailored black-and-white flowered blouse.

She also took her hair down and brushed it, letting it fall into its natural curls around her shoulders, and freshened her makeup.

She had pitchers of sangria waiting when, one by one, her workers came over from next door. When she'd emailed everybody about the barbecue, she'd let them know they could change into fresh clothes at her place if they wanted. Those who did were directed to Tyson's bathroom upstairs, her own on the ground floor or the one in the basement apartment.

She tried not to be pleased that Derek was among the barbecue attendees—she'd been wondering if he would skip it—but she was happier than she wanted to be at the sight of him following Tyson in her back door.

She also tried not to notice how good he looked—or smelled—after disappearing upstairs for a while and then reappearing with his hair damp, his face cleanly shaven, wearing a pair of jeans that fit him to sexy perfection and a sunflower-yellow henley T-shirt that accentuated his shoulders, chest and impressively muscled biceps.

"Put me to work here, too," he commanded as Gia tore her eyes away from the sight of him and continued to put sliced pickles on the condiment tray she was preparing.

"What can I do to help?" he persisted. "I'm a great grill man if you want me to cook."

"You're a great grill man?" Gia repeated skeptically.

"Thanks to a burger joint on Colorado Boulevard where I worked when I was seventeen. You can call for references if you want."

A Camden had flipped burgers as a teenager? That was hard to believe, and Gia decided to call his bluff. "The barbecue is lit and the burgers and hot dogs are on a plate in the fridge."

"I'll need this and these—" he said, reaching into the utensil container on the counter for a spatula and tongs, as if he really did know what he was doing. Then he went to the refrigerator.

"There's veggie burgers, too, for anyone who doesn't want meat. They're on the green dish but I'll get that one—you won't be able to carry it all out."

"I think I can manage—don't stop what you're doing," he said, taking the serving platter full of hamburgers and hot dogs in one hand, and the green plate in the one that already held the tongs and spatula.

"You're sure?" Gia asked.

"Sure," he answered, pushing her screen door open with a very, very fine rear end and taking everything outside.

Gia watched him from the window above the sink, finding that he really did seem to know his way around the grill and have it all under control.

He also seemed to be a people magnet because several of her friends and coworkers migrated to the barbecue to talk while he worked.

So it isn't just me, Gia thought when she saw other people drawn to his easy manner, wit and charm.

And yet she was still jealous that other people got to be out there talking to him while she was in the kitchen....

Not only did Derek come to Gia's barbecue and man the grill, he also stayed after everyone had left to help her clean up.

"You really don't have to do this. You've done enough today and tonight," she assured him, even though she was only too happy for his company and the help—in that order.

"Come on, I'll rinse, you load the dishwasher," he answered as they finished with the backyard and headed into the kitchen that was still a mess.

"Yard work, fixing lawnmowers, painting, barbecuing, cleaning up—so much for being born with a silver spoon in your mouth, huh?" she said as he went to the sink and began to rinse the dirty dishes, handing them to her.

"I told you, my grandmother was a farm girl and we had chores. One of the other things she stuck to was that every weeknight GiGi and all ten of us kids had to meet in the kitchen to fix dinner, then eat together, then clean up. We also changed our own sheets once a week, and made our own beds before we left for school every morning. The laundry was done for us and folded, but it was set on the end of our beds for us to put away—and I mean put away, not just toss on the floor. Or else! And as soon as we were of working age and wanted more money than our allowances provided, we got jobs—summer or weekend or after school—as long as we kept our grades up. That's how I learned to be a grill man."

"So you weren't handed a Ferrari for your sixteenth birthday?" Gia said, thinking that Derek had been raised very differently from Elliot, and that while her ex hadn't received a Ferrari when he turned sixteen, he had been gifted with a sports car.

"A Ferrari when I was sixteen? How cool would that have been!" Derek said with a laugh. "Except with a car like that I probably would have been in jail or dead by the time I was sixteen and three days."

"You were not a good boy?" Gia asked as she accepted a platter from him.

"We all had our little scrapes," he answered ambiguously. "But I did run with what my grandmother considered a *fast crowd,* and that got me into some trouble—usually the girls did anyway."

"Uh-oh…" Gia said.

"Did I make it sound ominous? Because I'm not talking teenage pregnancy or anything. Just…you know… kid stuff…."

He didn't seem to want to get into the details. But not only was Gia curious, she was also eager to shut down the growing attraction she was feeling toward him, and finding out he was like Elliot growing up might help.

So she said, "You had a gang of your friends pin down a girl you didn't like in the second grade so you could beat her up? You spray-painted nasty graffiti on some-one's house and framed someone else for it and thought it was great that you got away with it while the other kid got sent to juvenile detention? You tortured some poor scrawny kid in school until the kid had a breakdown and you thought the breakdown was funny?" All things Elliot had done as a boy...which she'd learned after she'd married him.

Derek stopped midrinse to stare at her with a shocked expression. "Geez, no! I'm talking smashing pumpkins in the street on Halloween, or driving too fast, or punch-ing a friend's time card for him when he really left an hour early because *his* girlfriend had just told him she was pregnant. Or a couple of other things I got caught up in that I'm not proud of, but nothing like what you're talking about. Who did all those things? You?"

Did he seem the tiniest bit intrigued by the possibil-ity that she had?

"Me? No. I was never in any trouble."

His expression seemed to say that was what he thought and he went back to rinsing dishes. "If I'd have done even one of those things you were talking about, my grand-mother would have called me a hoodlum and she'd have lowered the boom! We didn't have the kind of perks you think we had because we were Camdens, but we did have it impressed upon us over and over that because we were Camdens we had to set a good example. That we had to step up to the plate if there was a plate that needed step-ping up to. That because we are who we are, we had to be even more above reproach than other kids. 'Eyes are always on you as a Camden,' GiGi would say."

"And she wanted you to live down the bad reputation your family name already had..." Gia said, before it oc-curred to her that maybe she shouldn't have.

But he didn't take offense.

"There was some of that. Like I told you before, GiGi thought the negative things said about us were lies, but just the fact that there were negative things said meant she wanted us to prove they were wrong. None of us would have dared to do anything like what you were talking about. Not to mention that they're really rotten and I don't think that kind of thing was in any of our natures. I don't know who you knew to even hear about stuff like that…"

Elliot Grant. Married him, didn't really know him until it was too late….

But Gia didn't say that. Instead she said, "But you *were* a hell-raiser—with the smashing pumpkins?"

"I suppose smashing Halloween pumpkins is raising hell, but it's pretty normal ornery-boy hell-raising. I went to school, made good grades—"

"And got caught up in a couple of things you aren't proud of, mostly with girls…"

He laughed. "I don't believe I said those two things together. But yes, as a matter of fact, the things I mostly got in trouble for were with girls."

And those things were…?

Gia didn't have the courage to ask that out loud, but she waited silently, hoping he would go on.

But he didn't. Instead, he handed her the last of the dishes, looked around and said, "If you tell me what you use to wash off the counters, I'll do that before I take off."

So she wasn't going to get to hear the dirt from his growing up years, and he was going to leave, too.

There was nothing good in any of that.

Still, she felt obliged to say, "You've done enough.

I'm sure you want to get home. I'll take care of the countertops."

Confirming he was worn out, he rolled his broad
shoulders, arching his spine until she heard it crack,
and she got to see the outline of his pectorals behind
the yellow T-shirt.

Gia felt her jaw drop a fraction of an inch before she
closed her mouth and swallowed. But her eyes remained
glued to him as he relaxed into his normal stance and
said, "Yeah, I'm starting to feel today a little."

Gia just wanted to feel him....

Those shoulders, those biceps, that chest...

She actually had to ball up her fists for a moment to
fight the urge to reach across the open dishwasher door
and touch him.

Then she forced her eyes away and closed the dishwasher, telling herself that she was tired and that it was
bringing out weirdly primitive, primal man-woman stuff.
It didn't mean anything except that he was quite a specimen of masculinity and she was woman enough not to
be immune to it.

"So the yard sale next week..." Her voice wasn't as
steady as it should have been, so she cleared her throat.
"We can use all the donations we can get."

"Yeah, everybody in the family is gathering things
to send. But after seeing this place and the Bronsons',
I'm thinking that it would probably be better if I get
the stuff over here Saturday morning right before your
yard sale starts, because I don't know where you would
store it all."

He was right—space was at a minimum.

"What we've collected so far is at the church," Gia
said. "The pastor is going to bring it over on Friday night
so I can price it all. So far the weather is supposed to be

good, and I'm counting on that because I figure I'll keep everything under our paint tarps in the backyard until Saturday morning, then bring it out front."

"Aah, that's why you wanted to keep the paint tarps. Do you want me to bring everything over on Friday night, too?"

She did. But only so she could see him again a day sooner than she might otherwise.

Which was another urge she was determined to resist, so she said, "No, Saturday morning is fine...." Plus, if they happened to send anything more valuable than the bric-a-brac she had already accumulated, she didn't want to worry about it being outside overnight. "I can price your things then."

"I can help with that, and then I'll stick around to help run the sale with you."

"Okay...that would be nice...."

Better than nice—it suddenly made the yard sale something she was looking forward to for reasons other than the money it would raise for the Bronsons.

"But you don't have to," she added. "It doesn't take the kind of manpower the yard work and the fixes today took. I figured I could just do it myself rather than ask anybody to give up another Saturday."

"You and the minister?"

The church pastor had mentioned that he could help out. "Actually, I told him no, that just bringing the stuff over Friday night was all I needed. I didn't really want it to be just the two of us all day next Saturday—he's being kind of persistent with that going-out-with-him thing...."

And there wasn't a single thought that went through her mind in regards to the minister that even resembled what had just gone through her mind over Derek. So even if she had been willing to start dating again, it wouldn't be Pastor Brian.

Not that it would be Derek Camden, either. But still, she wished the minister would stop asking.

Derek smiled a small, knowing smile. "You sound surprised that he's so determined…."

"I just don't know why he won't give up."

"Really? You don't know why?"

"No. He must have a quota to fill for new recruits."

Derek laughed outright and furrowed his brow at her at the same time. "How long were you married?"

"Seven years."

He nodded as if that explained something. "And losing sight of your own appeal is the result of being married for seven years to a guy who didn't want to kiss you anymore…."

"I was speaking in generalities when I said that—I wasn't talking about myself," she claimed.

But it wasn't true, and she could tell by Derek's expression that he knew it.

He had the good grace not to push it, though.

He jammed his hands into his jean pockets and nodded his oh-so-handsome head in the direction of the front of her house. "I should take off—you've got to be beat, too."

"I'll walk out with you. I just realized I didn't have time to bring in the mail today."

They headed out through the archway that connected the kitchen to the living room and went to the front door.

Gia opened it and Derek held the screen door for her to go out onto the big porch with him.

"Where did you have to park?" she asked.

"A couple of doors down," he said without taking his

blue eyes off her. "But don't worry about walking me out—I think I'll be safe," he joked.

"Thanks for today...and tonight," she said then. "And for bringing in the plumbers and electricians.... You were right to think of that, since there *were* frays in the wiring. And I didn't know the toilet wasn't flushing well—the Bronsons were thrilled when I told them that had been fixed."

The elderly couple had arrived home in the middle of Gia's barbecue and she'd gone over to greet them and show them all that had been done. She'd also invited them to the barbecue, but they'd been tired after their day out and had just sent their thanks for her to convey to everyone. Even to Derek for the extra help of the professionals he'd hired.

"Both crews said things were in pretty good repair otherwise, though."

Gia nodded and once more had the fleeting thought that Derek might have something other than help up his sleeve, something that could ultimately benefit the Camdens.

But it *was* only a fleeting thought, because his gaze was still fixed on her and she wasn't sure why. She couldn't tell anything by the *way* he was looking at her, he just was. Closely. Intently. Smiling slightly.

Then his hands came to her upper arms as he leaned toward her and kissed her cheek—exactly the way a friend would.

But unlike with her friends, afterward he didn't instantly let go of her arms. Instead he went back to looking at her, looking into her eyes this time. A long, lingering look...

Go ahead...kiss me again.... she heard herself say in

her mind. And her chin tipped upward, too, because it wasn't another kiss on the cheek that she wanted.

But then Derek just squeezed her arms a little and let her go, taking the wind completely out of her sails.

"I'll be in touch," he promised as he crossed her porch and went down the four steps to the sidewalk that led out to the curb.

And then he was gone before Gia realized she hadn't said anything at all to bid him good-night.

She was just too busy responding to so many other things.

Like the feel of his big, strong hands on her arms, his fingers pressing into them, kneading them.

And that kiss...

Not the silly one on her cheek, but that other kiss that she'd so desperately wanted on her mouth that the yearning was still there.

In spite of everything...

Chapter Six

Sunday, Monday and Tuesday provided Gia with more than ample time to think about Derek, sternly reprimand herself for thinking about Derek and command herself to stop thinking about Derek. And she certainly needed to stop counting off the days that were taking her closer and closer to seeing him again.

Yet when she got a call from him on Wednesday, everything went out the window the very second she heard his voice on the other end of the line. Her pulse picked up speed and she was so happy she was nearly giddy.

And disgusted with herself for it.

Which had nothing to do with what Derek was saying, and so she also told herself to pay attention!

She realized he was telling her that he had a surprise for the Bronsons and he needed her help paving the way for them to accept it from him.

He wouldn't tell her exactly what the surprise was, he

just asked her if she could meet him at her house right after work.

Gia was disgusted with herself for telling him she would be home an hour later than she really would be in order to buy herself time to change clothes and fix her hair and makeup. But that was what she did.

Then she left work half an hour earlier than she should have in order to shower, too.

She scolded herself through the entire rush of preparations but was pleased with the end result: her hair was curly and clean; she'd applied fresh blush, mascara and lip gloss; and she was wearing her tightest jeans and a navy blue scoop-neck T-shirt over a tank top that she almost never put on because the straps were too long, exposing a hint more cleavage than she ordinarily wanted to show.

Ordinarily, but not today...

When Derek arrived, followed by a large Camden's delivery truck, her curiosity made her forget about herself and her own demons, however, and she went outside to stand on her porch.

The delivery truck parked in front of Larry and Marion's house, and Derek parked his sleek black sports car in front of her place.

She silently reprimanded herself yet again for not being able to take her eyes off him as he got out of the car. But she couldn't help devouring the sight of him. He obviously hadn't had the time to go home and change clothes because he was wearing an amazingly well-tailored tan suit over an off-white dress shirt with a brown tie. And his jaw bore a hint of scruff that was unbelievably sexy and actually made her glad he hadn't spruced up.

Plus, when he came out of his car to stand in the lee

of the open door, she got to watch him loosen the tie and slide it out from behind his collar, then open the collar button with big hands.

Next went the suit coat, which he folded in half before leaning back inside the car to drape it over the passenger seat. Then he straightened up again, unbuttoning his cuff buttons and rolling his sleeves to his elbows.

And the whole scene looked so hot to Gia that she thought he might as well have been on a stage with music playing in the background and women holding their breath waiting for him to take off more....

Well, maybe not *women,* just her....

"Hi." He greeted her with enough enthusiasm in his voice to make her wonder if he was as thrilled to see her as she was to see him.

Not that she was allowing herself to admit to being thrilled to see him....

"Hi," she answered, with some question to her tone as she nodded in the direction of the delivery truck. "*That's* the surprise?"

"What's inside is. Come on down and see," he urged, inclining his head toward the truck.

Gia went down the steps from her front porch and met him at the curb where he was waiting for her. By the time they reached the back of the delivery truck, the driver and another man had opened the rear hatch.

"I saw how old everything the Bronsons own is and I want to update them some," Derek explained. "There's a new TV—"

An enormous state-of-the-art flat screen.

"—a new couch, two recliners to replace the ones with the holes in them, and that—" he pointed to the contents on the right side of the truck "—that's an adjustable bed with a memory-foam mattress. I'm impressed with the way you have their bed rigged, but it just seemed like this might be another solution...."

A better, far more refined one. But Gia appreciated his diplomacy in not saying that.

"Will they take it all? Coming from me?" Derek asked then.

There was no doubt that the Bronsons were desperately in need of what he was offering. The stuffing was coming out of all of their furniture. Their very dated television—the only entertainment they had—was small and the picture was getting dimmer and dimmer, telling Gia that it was going to go out any minute. And the new bed was bound to make sleeping more comfortable and restful for them.

But while Larry and Marion had thawed slightly toward Derek by the time the yard work and home improvements were finished, they'd made it clear since then that their bad feelings toward the Camdens had not dissolved.

"I don't know," Gia answered honestly.

"Will they take it if we say you used some of the money you've raised to buy it all for them at cost?"

Gia couldn't take credit for something she hadn't done. Plus, she'd kept the Bronsons up-to-date on what she'd collected and how she was trying to stretch the money to meet expenses. They would know that she couldn't spend it on this.

"I can't say that, but let me talk to them. Will you wait out here?"

"As long as it takes," he said.

Gia turned and took a deep breath as she went up the Bronsons' sidewalk to their house.

The elderly couple was standing at their picture window surveying what was going on outside, and when she spotted them she smiled and waved. All the while, she was trying to decide the best tack to take on this. She couldn't use the Camdens-helping-her-help-them angle, so she decided as she went in to argue that the Camdens owed them all this.

"What's going on out there?" Larry asked when she went inside.

Gia explained the situation and then listened to their instant objections before she began her attempt to persuade them.

It took a lot, but she finally got them to agree to accept the gifts. They sat on the porch while she went in to take the bedding off their bed while Derek and his men removed the old TV and furniture and replaced them with the new.

The Bronsons' eyes were wide as they watched the men set up the TV and the top-of-the-line furniture, and got even wider as they looked over the pamphlet that told them all the functions of their new bed.

By the time the delivery men left, Larry and Marion were like two awestruck children on Christmas morning—so much so that they even relaxed their attitude toward Derek and thanked him—though not profusely.

But then they took it a step further and insisted that Derek and Gia stay for supper.

"Oh, no, I couldn't do that," Derek said, the invitation clearly taking him by surprise. "Why not let me take us all out?" he suggested, with an imploring glance at Gia that asked for her support.

She could tell just by looking at him that he was concerned about taking food from people who had so little to share. But she also knew the Bronsons, and that if they realized what he was thinking, it would embarrass them.

So she said, "You'd be sorry to miss Marion's soup and salad and homemade bread…."

"All the vegetables are from Gia's garden," Marion added, bragging about Gia. "Every bit of the salad and all but the little bit of meat I use in the broth for the soup came straight from her backyard."

"And Marion makes the noodles," Larry chimed in. "No restaurant soup can compare to that!"

"It does sound delicious…" Derek said, still looking uncertain. "If you're sure…"

"Sure, sure," Larry said.

"We just eat in the kitchen. Nothing fancy," Marion said, leading the way into that part of the house.

The meal was less awkward than Gia had feared. Derek heaped praise on Marion's cooking, which not only delighted the white-haired woman but opened the door to Larry doing some bragging of his own about the other dishes his wife made.

Derek was good about keeping the conversation light and airy, steering clear of anything that might go back too far in history and remind the Bronsons of the past ugliness between them and his family. He didn't try too hard. He just chatted and drew them out and allowed them to get comfortable with having a Camden in their kitchen with them.

"Gia, take some of the soup and a slice of bread for your lunch tomorrow," Marion decreed when they were finished eating.

"I would, but we're going out for lunch tomorrow— three of my coworkers have birthdays this week. So you guys keep it and have it for your lunch. And we're going to the Tuscan Grill—I know you like their salmon, so don't cook tomorrow night, Marion, and I'll bring you takeout from there."

"Oh, that's a treat! And we like the salmon best chilled, so it'll be cooled off by the time you get it home," Marion said.

"We couldn't do without this girl here," Larry confided in Derek. "She's always thinking about us."

"I can see that," Derek said.

Gia was uncomfortable having the attention focused on her all of a sudden, so she said to Marion, "Why don't we get these dishes done and then I'll help you make your new bed?"

"And why don't you let me show you how to operate the television, Mr. Bronson?" Derek suggested.

"Larry—he's Larry," Marion said. Then it seemed as if the words—and her own friendly overtone—surprised her, because she stopped short before she added a bit haltingly, "And I'm just Marion."

Gia waited to see if Larry would go along with the olive branch his wife had just extended. His eyes met Marion's and he smiled an understanding smile, reaching a hand over to pat hers where it rested on the table before he said to Derek, "Yep, you'd better show me what to do—tonight is the start of the new season of Marion's dancing show and she'd hate to miss that if I can't figure out how to turn the thing on."

Daylight was only beginning to wane when Gia and Derek left the Bronsons to enjoy their comfy new furniture and watch their vastly improved television.

It was a beautiful September night, and when they reached the curb in front of the Bronsons' house, rather than turning to the left where Gia's house was and where his car was parked, Derek angled his head to the right and said, "How about a walk down to Bonnie Brae for ice cream?"

Gia smiled at him. "I knew you didn't have a big, late lunch," she said, referring to the excuse he'd used for why he was eating sparingly of the soup, salad and bread. "You're still hungry."

"I felt so guilty taking food from them," he confessed. "I was afraid that whatever I ate meant they had less to eat tomorrow or the next day."

Guilt. That wasn't something she'd ever seen in Elliot.

"But sometimes they have to give a little back," she said. "It makes them feel less…needy. Sometimes you have to take what they offer, the same way you want them to take what you're offering."

"You take what they offer and then make up stories about going out to lunch the next day so you can bring them takeout to replace what you ate tonight?"

"You don't know that I'm not going out for lunch tomorrow," Gia challenged.

But he just looked at her as if he could see right through her, smiling a small smile that said yes, he did know it. "Let me buy you ice cream—you didn't eat any more than I did."

There was no question that she should say no. But when she opened her mouth, "I never turn down ice cream" came out, and they headed toward the creamery walking side by side.

"Do you do as much for your own family as you do for the Bronsons?" Derek asked her then.

"I would if I had a family to do for," she answered.

"Oh, that's right—I think you told me that. That the Bronsons have become family for you, that you don't have any family of your own, right?"

"I might have a father out there somewhere, but he left my mother and me when I was seven and no one ever heard from him again, so I don't really know if he's still living or not."

"He just took off?"

"Just took off," she confirmed. "He'd been telling my mother how he'd made a mistake to get married and have a kid, that it had shown him that he wanted a different life than that. My mother tried to make it work, tried to figure out how he could have what he wanted and us, too, but the truth was that he just didn't want us. One day he went to work and never came home. When she looked for him, she found out he hadn't gone to work at all. He'd used the day to empty their bank account, clear out every other asset they had, cash his last paycheck and leave town—"

"Without so much as saying goodbye?" Derek asked in amazement.

"Without a word."

"And that was it? You never heard from him again? Not a card or a letter or a phone call?"

"Nothing. He'd talked about traveling, about not wanting to live in Colorado anymore, so my mom didn't have a doubt that he'd left the state, but beyond that…" Gia shrugged. It had all happened so long ago that the wounds she'd nursed through childhood had healed. "I have no idea what happened to him."

"Ever thought of looking for him?"

She shook her head. "When I was a kid I had fantasies—he'd come home, say what a mistake he'd made and we'd all live happily ever after. But when I grew out of those… No, I wouldn't look for him. I can understand people who are adopted and hope that they'll find their biological parents and learn that the reason they were given up was just because there was no other way, that it was what was best for them or it wouldn't have been done. But for me... My father spent seven years with me and then..." Okay, maybe there were still some old wounds, because her voice cracked unexpectedly.

She cleared her throat. "He made it pretty clear that he didn't want anything to do with me. It wasn't even a matter of him divorcing my mom, He could have made sure he was still in my life in some way—even long-distance. But he wanted out and he got out. And he didn't leave us a thing, so he obviously didn't care what happened to us—not whether we had a roof over our heads or food to eat or clothes on our backs. That only says bad things about him as a human being, as a man. Why would I go looking for someone like that?"

They'd arrived at the ice cream shop by then and were lucky not to find a line out the door.

As they went up to the display freezers, Derek said, "Chocolate, right? It's just a matter of how dark or what extras might be in it."

"Actually, I like vanilla ice cream."

He laughed. "You're kidding?"

"Really rich, creamy vanilla. With little specks of vanilla bean in it and nothing else. On a wafer cone, not a sugar cone—they're too sweet for me."

"Okay," he said with another laugh, conceding to the unexpected. "When it comes to ice cream, I *do* like chocolate."

"Then there's hope for you yet," Gia teased him.

He laughed once more, as if he hadn't expected that, either. "I'm not sure what that means—was there no hope for me before?" Just then, the girl behind the counter came to take their order, freeing Gia from having to answer that.

VICTORIA PADE   111

When they had their ice cream cones, Gia and Derek sat down at the one unoccupied café table outside.

"So what happened after your father left?" Derek asked when they were sitting contentedly eating ice cream. "Were you and your mom okay? Was there *only* you and your mom, or have you lost siblings along the way, too?"

"I was an only child. And things were rough after my father left. My mom had a lot of health problems— a bad valve in her heart, some immune-system things, bad digestive issues—so she hadn't been working, and the stress of my father leaving made her sicker. We had to move in with my grandparents, who really did more of the parenting than my mom did because she was just too sick. She died when I was eleven, and I just went on with Gramma and Grampa."

"So you were raised by grandparents, too."

"I was. And they were great. They spoiled me rotten, but who's going to complain about that? I loved them dearly."

"But they're not around anymore?" he asked cautiously.

"They were killed in a car accident caused by a drunk driver just before I graduated from college...." Another lump in her throat paused what she was saying and kept her from eating ice cream for a moment. Then she blinked back the tears that came with the memory and went on.

"I didn't go through the graduation ceremony because they weren't there to see it—it felt so bad to finish the education they'd paid for and not have them around for the grand finale." And then she'd leaped into marriage to fill the gap—not only with Elliot and the possibility of a family of her own, but also thinking that the big, close-knit Grant family would embrace her and take the place of her grandparents.

Grief-clouded reasoning…

"Wow, I'm doing a lot of talking about myself tonight," she said in a lighter vein.

But he must not have minded, because he stuck to the topic. "So it seems like the Bronsons are replacement grandparents for you. But you didn't have them until three years ago, when you were going through *another* tough time…."

"Divorce that round. My marriage came out of losing my grandparents and finding myself with no one— except Tyson, but you know, no family—and Larry and Marion came out of the divorce. They're a much better deal," she joked.

Looking perplexed by that, he part smiled, part frowned. "Two eighty-plus-year-olds in hard times are a better deal than your marriage was?"

"Believe it or not," she said with a laugh of her own. But she didn't offer more than that because she really did feel as if she'd been talking about herself for too long.

And since they'd finished their ice cream, she also didn't think she should draw out her time with Derek more than she already had, because it worried her how much she wanted to.

"I should get home," she said then. "I'm harvesting in Broomfield all day tomorrow, so I have to leave here a lot earlier in the morning."

He gave her a slow, victorious smile. "The Tuscan Grill is in Cherry Creek—that's a long way from Broomfield," he said, calling her on her subterfuge.

Gia made a face and laughed at the same time. "Oh, yeah…"

"What are you going to do, order the takeout on your

way back from Broomfield and pick it up before you go home?"

She merely shrugged as they stood and started back toward her house. "Shh...don't give away my secrets."

"Will the salmon be cooled off enough to cover your tracks?"

"I'll come home, put it in my fridge while I shower and then bring it to them."

"So you're a little sneaky," he teased.

"Only when I have to be, and for a good cause."

"I'll bet," he said as if she were predictable that way. And somehow that made her feel a little boring....

"Is there anything I can do for Saturday's yard sale besides bring stuff over in the morning and work it with you?" he asked then. "Do you need help tagging things or setting up or—"

"Thanks, but I have it under control." She wished she could say the same about her responses to him.

Because she'd been overly aware of every tiny detail since watching him get out of his car earlier.

Because each and every time she so much as glanced at him something tingly went off inside her.

Because there was a part of her that kept willing him to take her hand or her arm, to touch her some way, any way.

Because just walking along the sidewalk with him was so nice that she was keeping her pace ultraslow in order to prolong it.

And all of that was out of control....

"Minna left Sunday for Reno to visit her parents and didn't get back until today, so Tyson and I have been going over to the church in the evenings to mark and organize things," she added. "We have almost everything ready, so Friday night I'll just be directing traffic when the church group gets it all here," she explained, sticking to her resolution to resist having him come then.

"You and Tyson..." Derek said then. "You're just friends, huh?"

Even the faintest suspicion that they were more than that made her laugh. "Just friends," she confirmed. "Since we were both seven—"

"When your dad left."

"And when Mom and I moved in with my grandparents. Tyson and his family had just moved into the house behind theirs."

"Did you go to school together?"

"We did."

"But you never hooked up as boyfriend and girlfriend?"

Gia laughed again. "We were *seven* when we met. I've seen him do yucky, disgusting kid things. We had chicken pox together, we've gone through bad skin, braces, the worst of puberty, getting drunk at thirteen on stolen liquor at a wedding and throwing up in matching trash cans. I think we've just never had enough illusions about each other to be anything *but* friends."

"You think people need to have some illusions to be something other than friends?"

Gia shrugged again as they reached her house and she stopped by his car. "I just think people *do* have illusions about the people they get involved with as more than friends. They probably *shouldn't,* but attraction seems to put on blinders and narrow your vision."

"Are we talking about your marriage again?" he asked.

Rather than answer that, Gia said, "Were your eyes wide-open right from the start with Tyson's cousin, Sharon-the-wannabe-psychic?"

He smiled a slow smile, conceding her point. "Attraction makes you overlook anything *except* what you're attracted to. Then, later on, what you overlooked—or missed altogether because of the blinders—is what makes the relationship not work...."

"Exactly," she said.

He nodded toward her house. "Can I walk you up?" he offered.

"No, I'm fine—the porch light is on, you can see no one is lurking in the bushes waiting for me...."

He actually took a glance around to make sure, but he didn't insist.

He also didn't make any move to go around to the driver's side of his car, staying where he was and looking down at her much the way he had when he'd left on Saturday night.

Just before he'd given her that friendly kiss that had been sooo disappointing....

"I guess I have fewer illusions about you after tonight," he joked then, returning to their conversation. "Chocolate everything except ice cream—very strange. Sneaky when it's called for and for a good cause. And you wore braces and got drunk at thirteen...."

"And I talk too much if you let me," she added.

"You only answered my questions. Most of them..." he said, likely referring to what she hadn't said about her marriage.

But the way he was looking at her and the small smile that curved just the corners of his mouth made her think that there wasn't anything about what he'd learned tonight that he didn't like.

And no matter how much she wished she would have discovered something about him that *she* didn't like, she hadn't yet....

Then, just when she was looking up into that handsome face and those shockingly blue eyes and starting to think about kissing again, he must have read her mind, because he said, "How about kissing—did you and Tyson try that out together the first time just for the sake of experimentation or for practice?"

"No," she said as if that was unimaginable. "I wouldn't have kissed a brother if I'd had one, and Tyson is like that to me."

Derek's smile grew. "I don't know why I'm so glad to hear that," he said, his eyes staying on hers.

And staying and staying…

While something seemed to swirl in the air around them, making Gia wonder if they'd been standing that close together the whole time or if they'd somehow moved closer.

Close enough so that he didn't even have to touch her. He just leaned over enough to kiss her—this time not on the cheek like any friend might, but on the lips.

And oh, but that was so, so much better than the kiss on the cheek!

Because he was so, so good at it!

His lips were warm and just right—parted just the right amount, not too dry, not too wet, just a little sweet. And he let the kiss go on long enough for her to kiss him back, all with that indescribable something in the atmosphere around them, making where they were, who they were and everything else feel as if they were somewhere outside of time, protected from it all….

But just when she was drifting away on that kiss, it ended.

Long before she wanted it to….

And he went back to looking down into her eyes for a moment until he said, "I'll see you Saturday morning."

Gia nodded, working to find her voice. "I'll be putting things out by seven and there'll be coffee."

"I'll need a lot of it at seven. See, one less illusion about me—I'm not a morning person."

"Me, neither," she confessed.

"Good," he said, as he turned and went around his car to unlock his door, adding with a second nod at her house, "Go on. If you won't let me walk you up, I at least need to see from here that you're inside."

Following orders, she went up the walkway to her porch, slipping her house key out of her pocket so she could unlock her door when she reached it.

Then she went inside, turned, waved and called, "Safe!"

He smiled, waved back and got behind the wheel.

Leaving Gia to wonder what in the world was going on between them.

And knowing that she shouldn't be letting it....

Chapter Seven

"Thanks for the help," Derek said to Louie Haliburton.

It was late Friday night and Derek and Louie had just finished loading Louie's truck with items for Gia's yard sale on Saturday. They were in the garage of the Camden family home, where the truck would stay until Derek picked it up in the morning.

Louie accepted the open beer Derek had gone into the house for and sat on a stack of boxes to drink it. "Thanks," he said.

Derek sat on the steps that led to the kitchen. "No, thank you for the help," he countered, taking a long pull of his own beer before leaning forward to brace his elbows on his knees, holding the bottle between them.

"This is all for somebody's yard sale?" Louie asked, even though he knew the answer because Derek had told him. "You're helping out some old couple with problems?"

"Yeah. There were donation jars around for the same cause—you probably saw them.... Couple's name is Bronson…"

"Yeah, I did see those. That what got you involved?"

"That and they're members of a church that one of GiGi's friends belongs to, so she wanted us to help out," Derek said, telling a partial truth to cover the real reason.

"And this Gia you've been talking about all night is behind it?"

"Have I been talking about her all night?" Derek was aware of always thinking about her—that had been going on since he'd met her and he couldn't seem to stop it. But he'd mentioned her to Louie, too? Without even realizing it? And a noteworthy amount?

Strange.

"Her name's been about every other word you've said tonight," Louie went on. "Gia this. Gia that. Gia says this, does that, thinks this or that. You'll ask Gia about some natural remedy for Margaret's allergies and for the wart on my finger because she's some kind of plant scientist or something."

Derek chuckled. "A botanist. For a company that makes supplements and natural remedies for things," he clarified, before adding, "Sorry, I didn't realize how much I was talking about her."

"She sounds like a nice girl. I'm surprised you like her."

"Who said I like her?"

Louie merely gave him a look over his beer bottle as the older man took a drink.

"I don't…you know…*like* her like I'm interested in her," Derek protested.

"Sound pretty interested to me…"

Hard to deny when he'd apparently talked about her

all night. When he knew how she was on his mind constantly. When twice he had ignored every warning in his head and kissed her....

"I'm trying to take a breather from women," Derek said.

Trying to...

Before he'd met Gia he'd been *determined* to....

"After Vegas, you know..." he added, not eager to say more than that.

"Turning point," Louie summed up. "Should have been."

A man of few words that still managed to pack a punch.

"Yeah...I know," Derek agreed. And he *did* agree with Louie. And the rest of his family, who all held the same opinion. "I'm just not sure I *can* turn over a new leaf with women," he confided in the man he'd been going to for advice since he was a boy. "You're attracted to who you're attracted to, you know?"

"I know that if you keep doing what you've always done, you're going to keep getting what you've got—"

"Nothing. But trouble." And a whole heaping of embarrassment this time around.

"You're always saying that the regular girls don't keep your interest, but seems to me like the strange ones don't, either..." Louie observed as he raised his bottle to take another drink.

"I never thought of it that way," Derek admitted.

"You haven't ended up with any of them."

"Because either strange gets annoying or *too* strange, or because I'm not weird enough to keep *their* interest."

"Seems like a flawed system."

Derek laughed. "Yeah, so far. But you have to admit,"

he defended himself, "a little wild is fun. It keeps you guessing."

"You just guessed wrong in Vegas?" Louie said before he took another drink of his beer.

Derek flinched.

"Wild is one thing," the older man went on then. "You can put a little wild in anything. Weird is something else. And conniving and devious and scheming that come out of the weird—those are just bad."

"I can't argue with that," Derek muttered. Then he gave the older man a look out of the corner of his eye and an insinuating smile. "So that's the secret of marriages that last—you just add a little wild?"

Louie merely smiled, not taking the bait to tell stories out of school, and finishing his beer instead.

Then he stood and went to the recycle bin. "If you find the right person, it all works out. Everything you need, everything you want is there. But like I said, keep doing what you've been doing, you'll keep getting what you've got."

The challenge came with the clink of the bottle going into the bin, and Derek was reasonably sure that was meant to reinforce the message.

Then Louie headed to where Derek was sitting, patting him on the shoulder to soften the exchange as he climbed the steps past Derek and went into the kitchen, leaving Derek in the garage alone.

And thinking about Gia again.

The way he always seemed to be lately.

Gia was definitely a veer from the norm for him, that was for sure. She was a Girl Scout through and through, someone without any edge at all that he'd been able to find.

But he still liked her. He was still interested in her.

He wasn't sure why, but he was, and after kissing her on Wednesday night it was pretty clear that he was failing at laying low for a while when it came to women.

But since she *was* a Girl Scout and he hadn't yet lost interest in her, maybe he should ride this out and see where it went, he thought. Explore it a little.

Carefully, though.

He didn't want to hurt her.

He wouldn't hurt her for anything in the world. It would be a crime with someone like her.

So he had to be careful in case his attraction to her was only a subconscious overcompensation for the fiasco of Vegas—a sharp recoil from that to someone who was the exact opposite.

Because if that was the case, when the fog had lifted, he might not be so infatuated with Gia. He might return to his old pattern and lose interest.

But the fact was, he *had* found some appeal in Gia, and he couldn't deny it.

Hell, he couldn't resist it.

No matter how hard he tried.

Gia's yard sale was a success. There was virtually nothing left by the end of it.

But after marking and organizing everything until well after midnight on Friday night and then getting out of bed at 5:00 a.m. Saturday morning to set up, when it was finally time to call it a day, Gia was dragging.

Seeing her exhaustion, Derek insisted that she come to his house for a pampering dinner as a reward for all her hard work.

Well, maybe he hadn't *insisted*. He'd invited and coaxed. But as Gia showered and got ready, she told herself that he'd insisted and that she was too worn-out to put up much of a fight. So she'd accepted the offer for those reasons, not because an entire day with him hadn't seemed like enough or because she just couldn't deny herself the chance to see his place and spend a little more time with him.

Besides, she argued with herself after showering, shampooing, scrunching her hair, applying makeup and agonizing over what to wear, today was the last of the fund-raising efforts on the Bronsons' behalf. From here on, she wasn't sure what Derek's involvement might or might not include. A phone call here and there just to check on the Bronsons' evolving situation? An occasional drop by?

One way or another, she was reasonably sure she wouldn't be spending entire days with him the way she had been. And while that thought did not sit well, she didn't want to analyze why, so instead she merely decided that one more evening with him couldn't do any harm.

So, dressed in a pair of black cigarette pants and a flowy white lace top over a tank that fitted her like a second skin, she drove the short distance from her house to his in the heart of one of Cherry Creek's most coveted gated communities.

His house was a sprawling gray-brick ranch built in an L shape around a stone drive that led to a four-car garage.

"Wow! This is *not* what I expected," Gia said as he let her in the oversize front door and she stepped into a traditionally furnished space that was homey despite its size.

"What did you expect?"

"Fraternity house chic? *Playboy* mansion? Snake aquariums—"

"Snake aquariums?"

"You sort of have a reputation.... Tyson says one of Sharon's friends who you dated after her was big on snakes, so I thought maybe—"

"No, no snake aquariums for me. I like snakes, but not when you wake up in the middle of the night and find that one has gotten out and into bed with you—"

"Eww!" Gia said in horror.

He laughed. "Yeah, can't say I was thrilled. So no, no snakes. You can relax."

But as he led her through the expansive entrance to a great room and very impressive kitchen she continued to find the house surprisingly cozy. It had the air of a place that was built for a large family.

"No snakes, but are you sure your wife and half dozen kids aren't coming out any minute?" she said, taking in the sight of the kitchen with its six-burner gas stove and built-in grill, the double ovens, more cupboards than she would know what to do with, the island with its eight bar stools and the dining table not far from it with seats for twelve.

"*Annulled,* remember? So no wife. And no kids anywhere, either," he assured her.

"You just rattle around this big place by yourself?"

"I do. I was looking for a house when it came on the market and it was such a good buy—almost fully furnished, and I even liked the furniture—so I decided to go for it even if it is more house than I need right now. I figure someday I won't be the only one here. And I come from a big family—having poker night or a movie night or a dinner calls for—" he waved a hand negligently in the air "—all this."

Right...

Big family.

Big, close-knit family.

With a history of doing things that weren't nice.

It was a reminder for her.

A warning that she needed to not be distracted by the fact that he looked fabulous freshly showered, wearing jeans that perfectly skimmed a fantastic derriere and thick thighs, and a gray mock-neck T-shirt that caressed every muscle of impressive shoulders, pecs and biceps.

And he smelled good, too....

"It's beautiful," she said about the house, wishing he was less attractive himself.

"Thanks. I thought we'd eat French tonight—there's a new bistro that I heard was good and they deliver. Delivered—about ten minutes ago. I set us up outside. I'm trying to get every last minute I can on the patio before the weather turns and it gets too cold. There's French wine waiting out there for us, too."

He leaned close and confided, "And for dessert they have what I'm told is a remarkably dark chocolate cake with twelve thin layers of cake separated by ganache— I'm not quite sure how that's different from frosting, but I guess it is."

"Frosting has confectioner's sugar. Ganache is just chocolate and cream," she explained.

"And your eyes get a special sparkle just saying it," he observed, laughing. "I also got a crème brûlée—maybe we can share. Although I promise not to eat a full half of your cake, maybe just a bite or two."

"Good, because crème brûlée does nothing for me," she joked.

"The patio is out this way," he directed, ushering her past an entertainment center with a nearly theater-size television at its heart and through sliding doors to his backyard.

Unlike the rest of the house, the yard was not massive. In fact, it was smaller than Gia's and taken up primarily with a stone-paved patio surrounded by a tiered rock garden.

It was equally as beautiful as the house, though, and she told him so. "You just need some greenery and some flowers planted around the rocks for color—all you have is moss."

"Maybe I can be your next project..." he said in a way she didn't take seriously.

There was a waterfall within the rocks, and one of the three patio tables he had was positioned right in front of it. The table was set for two, complete with plates, napkins, silverware, wine and wineglasses. Sitting on another table not far away was a paper bag with the bistro's logo stamped on it.

As he held out a chair for her and she took it, he said, "We have two steaks au poivre, asparagus, baby fingerling parsley-butter potatoes and bread to tear and smear with whipped butter before we can get to dessert—sound okay?"

"It sounds like heaven—I'm starving!"

"You should be," he said, retrieving the bag from the other table once she was seated. "I don't think you took more than two bites of your lunch between customers today."

Customers who had mostly been people Gia and the Bronsons knew, so they'd wanted to chat, too. So no, Gia hadn't had more than a scant taste of lunch.

"The Bronsons seemed to enjoy it all," he said as he poured wine. "I don't think either of them went inside or sat down for five minutes today, they were so busy talking to people. They had to be worn-out."

"They were. By the time I left them they had TV trays set up, and were eating the pizza I talked them into having delivered so Marion wouldn't need to cook. They also had popcorn and their movie ready to watch."

"Good for them," Derek said as he took food from containers and arranged it on each of their plates like a pro.

He sat down then and raised his glass. "To you—for all the work you did for them."

Gia laughed uncomfortably. "Oh, dear. I don't think anyone has ever toasted me before. I'm not exactly sure what to say to that."

"How about you just have a sip of wine and we eat?" he suggested.

She agreed to that and sipped the red wine, which was smooth and dry. "Oh, those French!" she said when she'd also tasted her food. "They know their stuff!"

"We weren't led astray," Derek agreed before he said, "So how did you do—today and on the whole?"

"For the Bronsons?"

He nodded because his mouth was full.

"Today surprised me," she admitted. "I've never had a yard sale or a garage sale where pretty much everything sold. And mostly without any bickering over the price. I think it was just because of where the money was going—everybody wanted to do what they could for Larry and Marion, so they bought something."

"Did it put you over the top for them?"

Gia made a face as she chewed a spear of asparagus. "It helped," she hedged when she could talk. "I should be able to pay a fair share of the past-due payments. Not quite all of it, but I think I have enough to put us in a position to negotiate with the bank—"

"Always negotiate," he advised, listening intently as he ate.

"I'm hoping the bank will take what I have and either

forgive the rest or refinance. *If* I can refinance. And if I can, then there's the new payments—I'm not sure I'll be able to get them low enough for the Bronsons to keep up on them. Then, depending on what comes out of it all, I'll have to talk to Larry and Marion and we'll see…"

"So the house is still in jeopardy," he summed up.

"A little bit less imminent jeopardy, because I should be able to pay the bank enough to stall foreclosure, but yes. And we have to face the fact that rallying everybody, getting donations, fixing everything up, was a one-time thing. If it looks as if Larry and Marion could end up where they are again in a year or two, because even the payments on a refinance are too high, then they're better off selling now while things are shipshape."

"And moving into your basement."

"They'll still have their new furniture and TV and bed…" she pointed out, to let him know that his gifts would not go to waste.

He nodded that handsome head of his but didn't comment. Instead he said, "Well, all I can say is that anybody in trouble should have you in their corner."

Again Gia wasn't comfortable with the praise, so she deflected it. "You brought a lot to the table that I wouldn't have been able to accomplish or give them," Gia said. "I appreciate that."

Which was true.

"So we'll just take it from here," he said.

She wasn't sure what that meant and felt uncomfortable asking because she didn't want to seem avaricious, even on the Bronsons' behalf. So she just let that hang and said, "I also appreciate this food—it's great!"

"It is, isn't it? This place should be around for a while."

"I'm stuffed, though," Gia added, pushing away her plate.

"Too stuffed for dessert?" he challenged, having finished his own meal.

"Oh, I have a special stomach compartment for that," she joked.

He laughed again. "Why don't I doubt that? But how about if we hold off long enough for me to clear, maybe make some coffee to go with the dessert.... I can make espresso if you like your coffee as dark as your chocolate."

"I do, actually. But I never drink it this late or I'll be up all night—"

And why did that get an arch of one eyebrow from him as if that was a tempting idea?

Maybe she was imagining it, because it was gone again a split-second later and all he said was, "So no coffee. More wine, then?"

"Maybe just a quarter of a glass—it might not be far, but I still have to drive home...and I'll help clean up," she said, standing when he did.

"Nooo," he overruled. "This was to pamper and reward you, remember? You sit over there—" he pointed to a built-in, cushioned seating area next to the waterfall "—and I'll clear this stuff and be right back."

Gia tried arguing with him, but he took her by the shoulders, guided her to where he wanted her to sit and pressured her to sit there.

In the few minutes he was gone she caught herself relishing the way it had felt to have those big, strong hands on her shoulders and tried to shake off the pleasure she'd found in it.

The view of the sun setting over the rock garden and the waterfall was spectacular, so Gia focused on that in the hopes of gaining some perspective until Derek reappeared, bringing their desserts.

He sat beside her and poured them both just a little more wine. Then he angled toward her and they tasted both the cake and the crème brûlée.

"Okay, this time I like the chocolate better, too," he admitted.

"I'll share," she offered, but he merely laughed at that, propped an ankle on the opposite knee and settled in to eat the sugar-crusted custard.

Lights automatically turned on around them then, and Gia only hoped she looked as good in soft glow as he did.

"I keep wondering," he said then, "what do I 'sort of have a reputation' for?"

It was what she'd said when she'd first arrived.

Gia shrugged, unsure if she should say.

But despite the fact that she never felt as if she had enough time with him, they *had* been together frequently, for hours and hours on end, and that had established a relaxed air between them. Out of that had come more and more openness, more and more honesty, more and more teasing and giving each other a hard time. And it also allowed her to feel as if she could answer him honestly.

Plus, she *was* curious about his past and this seemed like a route to finding out about it.

So she said, "Well, there was Sharon—the *psychic.* And Tyson heard through Sharon that after her you dated two people you met when you were with her—friends of hers. The one with the snakes and another one who Tyson says was weird, too—something about performance art...."

"When I was with her she was into making herself look like a statue of a Greek goddess and then standing on the street fooling people into thinking she really

was a statue. It was pretty amazing to see, actually—
you couldn't even catch her breathing or blinking. The
trouble was that even when she wasn't all made up and
in costume she liked to spontaneously freeze and go
into the act—walking in the mall, sitting in a restaurant,
with my family... And when she did it, she wouldn't
stop doing it and come back to life until she felt like it."

"How long would that take?"

"I never knew—that was part of the problem. I could
just be walking along, talking to her, and *bam!* I'd look
over and she was gone. Then I'd find her six feet behind
me where she'd stopped in her tracks. And no matter how
inconvenient it was or how much anyone tried to get her
out of it, she wouldn't. She sat through an entire Sunday dinner at my grandmother's in statue mode. It got
to be like dating someone who went catatonic without
warning and I just had to wait until she came to again."

Gia tried to suppress a smile but failed. "So *three* off-
the-wall girlfriends—"

"I don't know that you'd call all of them *girlfriends*—
mostly it was just dating."

But he'd apparently slept with the snake charmer, if
one of her snakes had slithered into bed with him....

"That Sunday dinner was the end for Theresa," he
said, interrupting Gia's wandering thoughts. "And I'd
been seeing her less than a month then."

"Well, that's where your reputation came from. With
Tyson and me. Maybe you just had a brief streak of
strange and out of that we unfairly labeled you."

Wishful thinking?

"Ah, if only I could say it was just a streak of
strange..." he said with a laugh.

"You earned the reputation we gave you with more
than the three?"

"I do tend toward women who are a little different…" he confessed.

"Different…" she repeated.

"Unique…with an edge. Sometimes too much of an edge.…"

"Bad girls?"

"Sometimes… My first crush in second grade was on Molly Ryker—she drew what the teacher called *very naughty* pictures on the back of the girl who sat in front of her. Watching her do it…" He inclined his head. "I was hooked."

"You liked the danger?" Gia asked, knowing that she certainly couldn't be considered dangerous.

"I think what I liked with Molly was the fearlessness. And that's—I don't know—kind of a theme. Bold. Strong. Determined. Dedicated. Women who push boundaries, challenge things. Women with a passion for something. Women who just have an extra element. Who are…let's say, colorful. It's been a pattern with me." He shook his head and laughed as if it had begun to confuse him in some way. "They're just more interesting.…"

"And interesting to you is over-the-top bad girls."

"Over-the-top has, in the past, helped keep me around for a while longer than run-of-the-mill," he confirmed. "But bad girls have gotten me into trouble.…"

"Into trouble…and an annulled marriage?"

"And an annulled marriage," he echoed in a more ominous tone than Gia had said it.

"So there are two categories. There's weird—like Sharon-the-wannabe-psychic and her friends—"

"And there was one who excused herself during Sunday dinner, went into the bathroom and shaved her head just to shock everybody. And there was the one who was heavily tattooed and pierced. And there was a Goth—"

Gia smiled and couldn't resist goading. "You drank blood and slept in a coffin with that one?"

He laughed and took her teasing in stride. "I would never drink blood, and I didn't sleep with her so I don't know if there was a coffin involved. There's also been more than one into extreme diet things—they either drove my grandmother crazy trying to feed us their recipes at Sunday dinner or there was one who wanted to play food police and tell everybody what they could and couldn't eat. And there was one who was into obscure religions—the screechy chanting eventually got to me—"

"Do it," Gia encouraged, again giving him a hard time.

He laughed. "I value my relationship with my neighbors, so no."

"And those were only the weird ones? Those weren't the bad girls who led you to get an annulment?"

He flinched, and she could tell it was a sore enough subject that she needed to be more careful about it.

"Those were the *colorful* ones," he amended. "But no, they weren't the bad girls who got me into real trouble."

"So what did the bad girls do?" she asked, hating herself for wondering so much what it was he found interesting.

His expression made it clear that he wasn't proud of what he was about to say. "I was brought into police custody after my tenth-grade girlfriend took me for a joyride in a car I didn't know was stolen. There was an actual arrest—me and about a hundred other kids got caught trespassing when we went to a party another girlfriend threw at a house she'd broken into that I didn't *know* she'd broken into. And there was an incident with a girl in college who took a picture of me from behind and sold copies of it for fun and profit. That was bad enough, but the picture got into a newspaper article about college campuses gone wild—"

"A *naked* picture?"

"'Fraid so…"

Gia wished she'd seen it….

But she didn't say that. Instead, as they both set their dessert dishes aside and she turned to face him, pulling her legs up underneath her, she said more gingerly, "And then there was the annulment, too…."

Derek took a deep breath, exhaled sharply and said, "*That* came out of a trip to Las Vegas this past spring— so I didn't have the excuse of being young and clueless. I went for a bachelor party and I met a woman—"

"Who you liked because she was either weird or a bad girl."

"She was the bartender at the party and she just seemed like fun."

"Which, for you, means something about her was over-the-top or edgy."

"It didn't seem like that, no. She was just funny, clever, quick, and that made her fun to talk to, so I spent a lot of time standing at the bar talking to her. Unfortunately, that led to getting really, *really* drunk. I know the party went on into the early-morning hours, and then I left with her…." He shook his head. "Things are fuzzy after that…but apparently Krista and I ended up taking a walk through a drive-in wedding chapel, where I guess I got married…."

"You don't remember it at all?"

"Not at all. But there are pictures and a certificate— proof that it happened."

"Was the bartender drunk, too?"

"Oh, I think she was perfectly sober," he said. "I think

Krista basically set a trap when she'd figured out who I was, and I just fell into it. And once I had, she had those pictures and that marriage certificate to hold for ransom...."

"Did she want to stay married to you?" Gia asked, because that didn't seem beyond the realm of possibility to her. This was Derek after all. The man sitting near enough for her to smell the scent of his woodsy cologne, for her to see his strikingly handsome face awash in golden light, for her to know firsthand how appealing he was.

"No, she didn't want to stay married to me," he said wryly. "What she wanted was a boatload of money— that's what it cost three days later to persuade her to agree to the annulment."

"If you didn't pay..."

"She wouldn't let the marriage be annulled. She said she'd wait awhile and then sue me for divorce and breach of promise. The lawyers thought the annulment would be the cheaper route, so—"

"You gave her the boatload of money."

"And got the annulment. Then that wasn't enough. Even though my attorneys had her sign a gag order, her friend—who had witnessed the ceremony and taken the pictures—blogged about it and the whole thing went public anyway—"

"Oh, that's awful. And a rotten thing to do!" Gia said sympathetically.

"Yeah. But...who we are—the Camden name and position—means we have to be especially careful. There are people out there like Krista—and her friend—and if we do something stupid and give them an open door..." He shook his head in what looked like self-disgust. "I haven't paid enough attention to that. But this was the worst yet. The worst embarrassment because it couldn't be written off as teenage stupidity or a college prank. And to have our name thrown around that publicly... I made us a laughingstock. Not a proud moment. Everybody ended up answering for my dumbass mistake...."

It was obvious that he took the blame and was not only embarrassed himself, but ashamed, too, and Gia wasn't sure what to say. She settled on, "It seems like you've learned a lesson."

He laughed humorlessly. "That's what everybody is hoping."

"But you aren't sure?"

"I'm trying to lay low. Change my pattern. Turn over a new leaf. But...I don't know... My family is always trying to find me a *regular* girl—that's what they call them. But somehow the *regular* girls they fix me up with either bore me to tears or...I guess I'm the king of losing interest. And then there I am, back again finding someone more...colorful."

"Tattooed, pierced, chanting, head-shaving, dirt-eating, snake-charming psychics," she concluded.

He laughed and Gia was glad to see that she'd been able to lift his spirits. "Who said anybody ate dirt?"

"Food police, dirt eating—it just seemed possible for you."

He chuckled again, shaking his head at her summary and looking more intently at her.

She had the sense that injecting some humor had helped to draw him out of himself, that he wasn't lost in his own demons any longer, because there was a renewed sparkle to his oh-so-blue eyes as his smile turned slightly wicked.

Which Gia knew meant that he had a comeback for her.

"So I guess somewhere under that good-girl exterior

of yours must be a little evil, since the curse of the *regular* girl never seems to kick in when it comes to you.... What's your secret, Grant? Maybe you're the dirt eater?"

Gia laughed. "It's the real reason I became a botanist—when I'm potting plants I just stuff myself with handfuls of it."

"I knew it!" he said in mock victory. "I knew there had to be something!"

"And there it is—my deepest, darkest secret..." she said, playing along.

He narrowed his gorgeous eyes at her and leaned in slightly closer to look into hers. "You may not eat dirt, but there's still a little evil in there.... You aren't fooling me...I see it," he said suspiciously.

Gia just smiled, terrified by how much she liked him and unable to curb it even when she tried.

Then he closed the gap between them to kiss her.

It didn't take any more than that for her to stop trying completely. To give in to what she seemed to want all the time now. To just be kissed by him. To just kiss him back.

His left hand sluiced under her hair to the back of her head to brace her. When his lips parted, so did hers as she let her head rest in that cradle.

He took her hand in his, holding it, rubbing it with his thumb as she got her first introduction to his tongue.

Inviting and enticing and persuasive, he coaxed her to play and Gia did, volleying and toying and fencing right along with him.

There was just something about him....

Every texture, every taste, every nuance was exactly right. Exactly what she wanted, exactly when she wanted it.

He used her hand to pull her nearer. Then he laid it

to his chest and let go of it so he could wrap his arm around her.

It was almost strange how well she fit there. So well she just wanted to burrow into him as her palm absorbed the heat of his body and the hardness of his pectorals to add to pleasures that seemed to be mounting by the minute.

Pleasures that still centered on their mouths that were locked together, sealed in kissing fueled by more kissing, by tongues that frolicked with each other.

Gia was faintly aware of the sounds of the waterfall nearby, but it only seemed to carry her along, to draw her even more serenely into kissing Derek, into being kissed by him so thoroughly that she felt like it was all she would ever need. Kissing him and kissing him. Being held in his strong arms, against his broad chest now, with her hand the only thing keeping them from coming together seamlessly.

She had no idea how much time passed while they were making out. At some point it occurred to her that it had been a very long time, and that it was late because even through her closed eyes she could tell that the moon had gotten high in the sky to add a brighter, whiter glow to the golden illumination of the patio lights.

She needed to stop this, she told herself. To go home. To talk some sense into herself....

As much as she really, really didn't want to, she knew she had to. So her tongue became a little shy, a little more difficult to catch, and she pushed against the stone wall of Derek's chest and drew back almost imperceptibly.

He didn't want to let her go, because he only held her tighter, kissed her more thoroughly.

But just long enough to convey his reluctance before he conceded to the message she'd given, ending that kiss only to kiss her again—and again and again—with restraint he was clearly having to work for.

Then he stopped altogether and just pulled her to him, wrapped his arms around her and held her with her cheek to his chest while her own arms somehow went around him, too.

"Yeah, no doubt about it—there has to be a wild streak hidden in you somewhere calling to me..." he murmured then, into her hair.

But there wasn't a wild streak in her, and Gia knew it. She just didn't tell him because it felt so fantastic to be held like that by him and she couldn't ruin that one moment with the truth.

Instead, she let herself have a few minutes in his arms, against him, before she gently unnestled herself from the cocoon and said, "I have to go...."

Like with the kiss, he didn't accept that instantly, tightening his grip for a moment before giving in. But when he gave in, Gia stood without hesitation because she knew if she didn't she was too likely to kiss him again.

Derek got to his feet, too, cupping one of those big hands of his around the back of her neck to walk her through the house.

"There won't be dirt on the menu, but what would you say to going to Sunday dinner at my grandmother's house with me tomorrow night?" he asked just as they reached his front door.

A big Camden family dinner.

Like a big Grant family dinner.

Where she'd be an outsider....

"I don't think that's a good idea," she said, her voice a bit gravelly from the kissing.

"My grandmother wants to talk to you about the Bronsons' health needs," he said. "And it just occurred to me that tomorrow would be the perfect time. She has connections with the best hospitals, the best doctors, the best care and management for geriatrics. But it's GiGi who has the inside line on all that stuff, not me, and you know the Bronsons' conditions, so it's really something that's better talked about without me as a go-between."

As much as Gia wanted to see him, she didn't want it to be at dinner with another big, close-knit family. She knew all too well what that was like and she wanted no part of it.

But she could hardly refuse when he put it in terms of helping Larry and Marion.

Still, she had to try....

"Couldn't we meet and talk about it some other time? It doesn't seem like a family dinner is—"

"There's always a ton of people around—not just family, never just family. And everybody mingles and talks—you and I and GiGi can just take a few minutes to chat as part of that, and then we can have a nice meal and I'll take you home.... Come on, you'll like GiGi— she's not too different from Marion—and you'll still have your whole Sunday before that free because hors d'oeuvres and drinks are at five, dinner is at six."

And she'd be with him again.

And she wanted to be.

And she knew she shouldn't want it or give in to it.

But she also wanted Larry and Marion to have the best care they could get.

Then, still standing at his front door, his hand still cupping her nape, he pulled her toward him as he leaned down and kissed her again.

As if *that* would help her decide!

And yet it did. Because when he stopped kissing her she said, "Okay. I guess…"

"Not enthusiastic, but I'll take it."

He kissed her again—the play of his tongue reminding her of their kisses on the patio—before he finally ended it and took his hand away.

"I'll pick you up a little before five. Comfortable, casual, but no jeans," he warned.

Gia nodded, trying to recover from the effects of that last kiss.

"Thanks for dinner," she said, remembering her manners belatedly as he walked her out to her car and she opened the driver's door, looking up at him again then.

His handsome face slid into a slow grin and he kissed her one more time before he said, "Drive safe."

"I will," she assured him, getting behind the wheel.

But that assurance was false, because as she put the key in the ignition and started the engine she realized that while she might have been careful about the wine, she hadn't realized that the kissing was even more heady, and she could only hope to focus enough to get herself home.

Where she didn't have a doubt that she'd relive the feel of him holding her, kissing her, right up until the minute she fell asleep.

Chapter Eight

"I can't believe I have to do this tonight," Gia said to Tyson on Sunday morning.

Tyson and Minna had broken up and he'd invited Gia upstairs for pancakes to tell her the news. The relationship had burned hot and fast, then fizzled, and he was taking it in stride. He'd just wanted Gia to know since she'd introduced them and there was the potential of her running into Minna at work. He'd also wanted her to be aware that there were no hard feelings on either his or Minna's part.

"It was just, you know, a good time," he'd concluded before asking what he'd missed while he was preoccupied. That was when Gia had told him that she'd agreed to go to the Camden Sunday dinner this evening with Derek.

"I'm kicking myself because I know it's bound to be just like the Grants' family dinners," she went on. "I'll walk in and get the squint-eye like I'm a geek who's wandered into cool-kid territory. Most of them won't bother to talk to me. The ones who do will be rude or nasty or will grill me like a captured spy. No matter what, I won't be good enough for them and I'll just want to be anywhere but there."

Tyson didn't refute any of that. Instead, he said, "At least you know going in that there's one thing different—you won't be *trying* to fit in or be accepted. You *are* an outsider with them. The Grants still treated you that way even after you'd been one of them for seven years."

"Still, I'm dreading it...." Except for the fact that she'd be with Derek, and she was worried about that for other reasons.

"Sharon went to a couple of the Camden Sunday dinners," Tyson told her. "She loved them—"

"I thought she complained about them."

"She did. But it was the fact that there *was* a mandatory Sunday dinner every week that she didn't like. She said the dinners themselves were good—fantastic food, booze, a big party. And you know Sharon—a lot of people means an audience, and she goes in like a lounge act and loves that. She just didn't like the Sunday after Sunday routine."

"Apparently she wasn't the only one of Derek's old girlfriends to use the Sunday dinners as a forum or to make a spectacle," Gia said, going on to tell him about the head shaving and the food policing.

"So it wasn't just nutcase Sharon and the two weirdos after her, this guy *does* go for—"

"He calls them unique, colorful or edgy." Gia supplied the terminology for her friend. "But your cousin and her friends were not his only venture into—"

"Wackjobs?"

"And bad girls who have led him astray," Gia added. But she decided suddenly that she wasn't going to tell Tyson about Derek's Las Vegas wedding and the subsequent disaster. Which was a little odd, because she'd always told Tyson everything and it made her feel slightly disloyal that she didn't.

But seeing how the event had affected Derek also made her feel protective of him and of what he'd confided in her, and that feeling won out.

Which only compounded what worried her in regards to Derek....

Tyson passed her the syrup as he said, "I'm betting that it won't be like the get-togethers with the Grants anyway. When you walked into any social situation involving Elliot's family, he forgot you were alive the minute he hit the door, but I don't think that's going to happen with this guy."

"Don't be too sure," Gia said, because it was actually what she expected.

"I don't know. Derek doesn't seem to want you out of his sight no matter where you are."

"What do you mean he doesn't want me out of his sight?" And why did the mere suggestion please her?

"He keeps an eye on you every minute—don't tell me you haven't noticed."

She hadn't. She'd thought she was the one always trying to catch glimpses of him. "I don't think so," she said, voicing her doubt again.

"Oh, yeah," Tyson insisted. "When we painted Larry and Marion's house, the minute he found out he wouldn't be working with you, he did some fast maneuvering to make sure he would. And every time you moved two steps away at the barbecue, he looked around till he spotted you again. The same at the yard sale. Plus, he hangs around after we're done doing whatever we're doing for Larry and Marion—he's always the last one to go. Unless I miss my guess, he's got it bad for you, G. He probably just wants you at this dinner so he can have you there himself."

"He said it was so I could talk to his grandmother about Larry and Marion's health care."

Tyson snickered. "I'm sure he did," he said knowingly.

"I'm not his type, Ty," she contended, even more convinced of that after hearing what Derek had said the night before.

"You're not a wackjob or a nutcase or completely loony tunes, no. And you're a long way from a bad girl," he added. "But there's a lot more to you and it's all great and unless I'm mistaken, ol' Derek Camden has taken notice."

"It doesn't matter," Gia claimed, emphasizing to herself that it *needed* not to matter.

"Yeah, he's probably still more like Elliot than *not* like Elliot," Tyson agreed.

"You don't like him…."

"Nah, I like him fine. But one-on-one I liked Elliot, too. I just didn't like him as your husband. He was lousy at it and his family treated you like dirt."

"Plus, Derek isn't the kind of guy who settles down with someone like me to have a normal life and a couple of normal kids. He goes for the thrill ride, and that's not me."

"Wow! Why do you sound so sad about that?"

"I don't!"

"Yes, you do! You were all perky when I said he keeps his eye on you, but that stuff about how wrong the two of you are for each other? It's like you just burst your own bubble."

Maybe she had.

But it was a bubble that needed to be burst.

"You *do* like him," Tyson said more carefully, repeating what he'd accused her of the very first time they'd talked about Derek. Only now it wasn't merely a question; there was some conviction in it.

"I do," she broke down and confessed. "Maybe I have a thing for bad boys."

"Maybe you do…" Tyson said ominously, under his breath.

"I know better, though," she swore. "I'm not going to let it go any further…."

Tyson's eyebrows shot up. "How far have you let it go?"

Gia made a face. "You know…just some kissing…." An understatement when the kissing was so fabulous that merely recalling it made her toes curl.

"God, be careful, G…" Tyson said with a voice full of concern.

"You're supposed to say, 'Sure you know better, Gia, and of course you won't let it go any further.'"

Tyson nodded, but he didn't say the lines she'd given him. Instead, he said, "Hey, I know how it is—you meet somebody and things click and even if you know better, that doesn't make them unclick. Just be careful," he repeated. "Maybe mess around with him, but don't get into more than that. A little fun, a little…release…. Just enough to boost your ego and remind you how you are much more than Elliot Grant deserved. But other than that—"

"I know."

"Can you do just that?" Tyson asked as if he didn't think she could.

She shrugged. "You can," she said as if that meant she could, too.

"Yeah, I just did with Minna. She just did with me. But you... I don't know, G.... You haven't had anybody since Elliot. It could be a rebound thing—and I don't want to see you just close your eyes and fall...."

"My eyes are open," she said.

"And how clearly are they seeing?"

"Clearly enough to see that Derek has close ties with a big family that's done really lousy things to other people. Clearly enough to see that Derek could very well be like Elliot and be more surface than substance. Clearly enough to see that he's been through a lot of women and the only ones who keep his interest for any amount of time are nothing like me. Clearly enough to see that I'm a babe in the woods when it comes to dating again and am not ready to do anything serious."

Just not clearly enough to see her way past how terrific looking Derek was. Or how sexy. Or how good it felt to be with him. Or how wonderful it was to have him hold her and kiss her. Or how much she just wanted to be with him again the minute they were apart....

And even though she didn't say all that, she knew that Tyson could tell, because his expression was concerned and helpless.

"Just be careful," he said a third time. "Just get in, hook up, get out—can you do that to get it out of your system?"

Gia laughed, thinking about how much more than kissing she'd wanted the night before.

"Maybe," she said. "I can tell you that it isn't white dresses and wedding chapels and picket fences and bouncing babies that are on my mind when I'm with him, that's for sure."

"Oh, geez, you do want him," Tyson said somewhat forlornly. "Then go for it, I guess. But if you start picturing white dresses and wedding chapels and picket fences and bouncing babies, run for the hills!"

"I promise."

For Gia, the Camden family Sunday dinner was a combination of good and bad.

Derek *did* stay by her side through the entire thing. That was a vast improvement over how Elliot had treated her at similar gatherings.

But merely being faced with the big, obviously close-knit family was intimidating to her.

She gave the Camdens credit for going out of their way to be friendly and welcoming, because they were. Unfailingly. But there were so many of them. And after being introduced, after chatting warmly, when talk would turn even for brief moments to things between Derek and other members of his family that she couldn't participate in, Gia flashed back to Grant family gatherings in which she'd been excluded and felt invisible.

She also gave the Camdens credit, because not a single pocket of conversation had stopped when she came within hearing range. There weren't any withering, disapproving looks cast her way. There was no indication that there was anything secretive going on.

But Gia was still very aware of the fact that she was not a part of things when the family fussed over the pregnant Jani, or everyone teased the newly married matriarch, Georgianna, or focused on the antics of Lang's three-year-old son, Carter, or bantered about when weddings should be held for the engaged couples among them.

So while the whole affair lacked the ugly overtones

that had come with the Grants, still—despite every effort by Derek and the rest of his family to put her at ease—Gia just couldn't relax or enjoy herself. And she was never as relieved as when it was finally over with and she and Derek were walking to his car.

"Okay, now breathe…" he joked, sounding like a birthing coach.

"Haven't I been?"

"*Have* you been?" he challenged. "I don't think I've ever had anybody at Sunday dinner who was more tense. The whole time. And I haven't seen you like that before. Are we that scary?"

They hadn't been scary at all. It was just her. And her own baggage. So she said, "No. Did I seem scared?"

He opened the passenger door of his sports car for her to get in, frowning rather than answering her.

Once he went around and got behind the wheel, Gia veered from the topic by saying, "It was really nice of your grandmother to offer to get Larry and Marion in to her primary-care physician even though he isn't ordinarily accepting new patients. I'd like it if they saw someone new. The doctor they've been using acts like she doesn't want to be bothered with them."

"Will they switch doctors? Especially to a doctor a Camden arranges for them?"

"I think they'll be glad for better care no matter how it comes about."

"Good. I'm glad."

"And the food was great!" she continued, trying to distract him when he looked at her out of the corner of his eye and she knew he was still thinking about how uncomfortable she'd been. "You're grandmother's home-made biscuits were better than any I've ever had."

"She loves it when anyone likes her cooking—"

"It was nice of her to send some home. I was kind of surprised that she cooks, though."

"She does everything. Farm girl, remember?"

"I just wouldn't think that someone in her position would—"

"Her position?" he repeated with some humor in his tone. "That would make her laugh—she'd be the first one to say that she isn't the queen of England."

When they pulled into her driveway, Gia was relieved that she'd effectively filled the short drive to her house with small talk.

Derek stopped the engine and got out, and so did Gia, not waiting for him to come around to her side.

As they went up to her house, he nodded toward her porch swing. Her porch formed an L around the front and one side of her house, and the swing hung from chains hooked into the porch's roof. It faced the street at the rear-most portion of the L, between the side of her house and the Bronsons' garage. It was so far back from street lights and in such deep shadow without her porch light on that it was almost completely hidden in darkness. But he'd been there when it wasn't dark and seen it.

"It's a nice night and it's early yet," he said. "How about we sit out here for a little while? Or did you have something you needed to get done tonight for work tomorrow?"

"No, nothing. That sounds good," she said, realizing only in that moment that she hadn't thought beyond the dinner and so hadn't considered whether or not to ask him in. Had he not made the suggestion she might have been at risk of having him say good-night at the door and leave.

And she wouldn't have liked that.

"Can I make coffee or pour some iced tea? Or I have

soda," she offered, beginning to come back to herself now that she was on home turf.

"No, thanks. Just go in and put your biscuits away. I'll wait out here for you."

"I'll be right back," she answered as she unlocked and opened her front door.

Inside, out of his sight, she finally did take a few of those deep breaths he'd recommended.

Then she popped into her guest bathroom for a quick check in the mirror. No mascara smudges. Blush still adding color to her cheekbones. Left to fall loose, her crazy curly hair was still as tamed as it ever got. And the khaki slacks, white tank top and tailored red shirt she wore open all remained wrinkle-free.

The only thing she did was reapply a little lip gloss, and then she went back outside.

She still didn't turn on the porch light because it attracted bugs. In the dark, the swing was in such deep shadow that had she not known Derek was there she wouldn't have noticed him.

But he was there. Sitting in the center of the swing, angled to his left, with an ankle propped on the opposite knee and his arm across the top slat, waiting for her.

Once her eyes had adjusted and she could see him, she was struck all over again by how ruggedly handsome he was. And after not having any time alone with him through the dinner, it felt as if this was only the beginning of her time with him today.

He'd left her no option but to sit in the lee of his arm and that was just what she did.

When she was fully settled, he said, "Now tell me why the hell you were so stressed out tonight. Did I do something?"

"No," she assured him without hesitation. "I really appreciated that you never left my side. It was just me...."

"It can't be that you don't like crowds—there weren't any more people there tonight than at your barbecue and you were just fine. Was it us? All of us? Too many of us? Was somebody there an old lover?" he added with some levity.

Gia managed to laugh. "No, it was just me.... My ex-husband came from a family like yours...sort of...."

"A family like mine? In what way?"

"Big. Close. In business together," she said, sanitizing it. "I was married to Elliot Grant—of Grant Moving and Storage."

"I know the company. We used them when we moved our offices from three different buildings into the one we're in now. They do commercial moving and storage, not residential, right? They move businesses, corporations, things like that."

"Right. I'm not surprised you've used them, they make sure to keep their competition to a minimum, especially in Colorado."

"I guess I didn't know it was owned by one big family the way Camden Superstores is."

"Uh-huh. Elliot is one of eight kids and he has thirteen cousins who all—along with his parents, aunts and uncles—own and operate the company."

"Those numbers beat ours—they *are* a big family."

"Uh-huh."

"Okay, come on, stop holding out on me. I told you last night about the worst mess I've made. So what gives with the ex and the ex's family that triggered you looking like you wanted to hide under a table all night tonight?"

She'd already learned that Derek was insightful and perceptive and observant, that there wasn't much he missed. It was part of what she liked about him. Except maybe now.

"Grant family dinners were not fun," she said, knowing he wouldn't be satisfied until she was honest with him.

"Were they bigger than tonight's?"

"No, about the same—some of the cousins and one brother live out of state, where they keep an iron-fisted presence in a couple of other places. But the Grants weren't very welcoming to people who married into the family—"

She was close enough to Derek to see his confused expression. "They weren't?"

"Oh, no. *Grants are born Grants or they aren't really Grants,*" she said, adopting the imperious tone that they had used. "Elliot's mother and the other wives of the older generation aren't even considered *real* Grants. Long marriages have given them more insider status and made them as bad as the real Grants when it comes to those of us who were new. But their sisters-in-law—the two women born into that generation of Grants—never let them forget that they weren't *real* Grants and if they got divorced, that would be it for them."

"That would be *it* for them…." he repeated melodramatically and with a slight chuckle. "Now, *that* sounds scary. Would they be hunted down? Shot like dogs? What?"

"No, but…" Gia shrugged. "Anyone who isn't a Grant is an outsider. Divorce makes you not only an outsider but an enemy. And outsiders are treated bad enough. Enemies… Well, I think that can actually get dangerous…."

He frowned again. "Okay, explain—dangerous how, and you only *think* that, you don't know for sure?"

"I didn't know a lot about the Grants *for sure.* I wasn't

privy to inside information, and when it came to the business, Elliot would say that it was nothing I needed to know—"

"Ooh, that sounds familiar," Derek admitted. "That's what my great-grandfather used to say."

"But I was married to Elliot for seven years and there were things I overheard here and there. Sometimes I'd pieced it together with what I heard elsewhere...."

"Like what?"

"Like something I'd hear on the news later about vandalism to another moving company's trucks or a competitor's storage facility catching fire. Once I heard something about being underbid, then later they were all laughing about how that guy's rubber wouldn't ever be hitting the road again...." She shrugged once more. "You kind of get an idea for what happened. And then I saw what went on when a sister-in-law divorced one of Elliot's brothers—"

"They weren't just thugs in business?"

"I don't know that the Grants are thugs," she said. "I know that they pay to have anything done that they don't want to do themselves, and I can't see any of them actually getting their hands dirty—"

"So you figure they hire out the dirty work."

"I only know that they aren't upstanding people. They have power and money and feel entitled to do whatever they want—or as they see it, *need*—to make money and succeed and get their way. They aren't ethical—they make sure they're friends with and big contributors to other people in power, and that's helped them buy their way out of anything."

"Why does it feel like somewhere in your head you said *like the Camdens?*"

So he *was* a mind reader....

But when she didn't confirm or deny it, he didn't push it. "What went on when your sister-in-law wanted out?" he asked instead.

"She was welcome to go. Empty-handed and without her little boy."

"Who had Grant blood so he *was* a real Grant."

"That's how it works. And like I said, they have lots of money and power and really good lawyers and friends who are judges. First they did a horrible smear campaign against Linda that made her look like the most unfit parent on the planet—which she wasn't at all! But by the time they were finished, the best she got was three hours of visitation every other weekend, under court-ordered supervision by the Grants. Then they made even those three hours impossible for her to actually ever arrange and no matter how hard she tried, there just wasn't anything she could do. By the time I left Elliot, Linda had only seen Bobby twice in six months."

"For three hours, with an in-law watching."

"I felt awful for her. She just lost that little boy to them and there was nothing she could do."

"And you couldn't risk backing her up?"

"I offered...behind Elliot's back," she said in a quieter voice, knowing it wasn't rational but still somewhat leery of bringing down any of the Grants' wrath. "But her lawyer said it wouldn't help. It was just my word against what looked like proof that she was unfit, and that anything I said would just get shot down. I was still willing, but Linda said no. She said she didn't want to be responsible for what my life would be like with the Grants—or even with Elliot—if I did."

Derek took a deep breath and exhaled. "Why did you marry this guy—and into all of this?"

"I honestly, honestly have no idea. He seemed like the

nicest guy. He's very personable—you can ask Tyson. Even he liked Elliot until I was years into the marriage. Elliot is smart. Good-looking. Charming... I knew he was close to his family, that they all worked for the family business and that it was very successful, but I had no idea of anything beyond that. And to tell you the truth, I had fantasies of belonging to a big, close family—"

"You'd only had your grandparents and you'd lost them just before," he recalled.

"Right. Plus, while we were dating I only met his parents and a few of his brothers and sisters—I never went to a big family dinner or saw the dynamics of it all. His family was kind of standoffish, but Elliot wasn't. As I told Tyson at the time that I was going out with Elliot, not his family...."

"But when you got engaged...still no inkling?"

"No. They warmed up a little and I thought that was just the beginning, that it would get better from there. They threw a big wedding shower for us, but at that point Elliot was all about being with me and we were the guests of honor, so everything was revolving around us—like with the wedding, too. It was only afterward that I started to see the way things really were...."

"With his family. But what about him? Did the marriage go instantly south, too, or did you keep on the blinders awhile longer?"

The blinders...

He was referring to what she'd said the night they'd walked home after having ice cream.

"No, the marriage didn't *immediately* go south," she said, finding it more difficult to talk about this than about the entire Grant family. "For the first year or so we were like any married couple—happy, settling in, getting to know each other, in love—"

"How long did you date before you got married?"

"We met at a benefit for the Botanical Gardens and there was six months of dating, another six engaged and planning the wedding."

"And after the first year of marriage?"

"It was a case of a relationship going bad by inches," she said, again with some difficulty. "The marriage suffered at the expense of how close he was to his family. They came first—and I mean that literally. A phone call from any one of them and he went running day or night for even the smallest things. It didn't matter if I was miserably sick, if I needed him for something, if we were on a vacation—everything stopped, he went to his family and I was just out of luck. Little by little it wore on me."

"But you were *his* family—*you* should have come before anything except maybe an emergency somewhere else," Derek said, as if what she was describing was unfathomable to him.

"That's how I thought it should be, but that's not how it was. Once, about five years in, I was in the emergency room with a broken wrist and his brother got a flat tire—"

"And he left a wife with a broken bone to fix a flat?"

"He did. And he didn't come back. I had to call Tyson to pick me up when my wrist was set. I was really getting the picture by then that I would never be even a close second to his family."

"Is that when you left him?"

"No. I was having doubts about him, about us, about the future—"

"About the fact that the kissing had stopped?"

Oh, more of her words haunting her—from when she'd marveled that Larry and Marion still kissed without either of them having to force it....

But she was in this far, she decided she might as well not try to sugarcoat anything.

"Yeah, the kissing had stopped. By then I was like..." This just wasn't easy—not to talk about and relive, and not to explain. "When Elliot and I first met, I was something he really wanted—the way a kid wants a Christmas present. So he was great. He couldn't have shown more interest, he couldn't see enough of me, he wanted to please me any way he could. He swept me off my feet—"

"Then it wasn't Christmas morning anymore."

"At first it was still good, except for his family, but I just thought...you know, *in-laws...*" she said with exasperation. "I blamed them for calling him away all the time, not him for running to them, and I hadn't started to get an idea of their other...practices...so I just thought they were a pain in the neck."

"Then the newness of the favorite Christmas toy wore off?"

Gia shrugged. "Yes," she said because there was no better way to describe it. "He barely knew I was alive or cared if I was," she admitted. "*Whatever*—that got to be a word I hated! Everything I tried to talk to him about, everything I asked of him, he wouldn't so much as look away from watching TV or playing a video game or texting or doing something else on his phone, and he'd just say, 'Whatever.' Which meant that he hadn't heard a word that I'd said. It just got to be like I didn't exist. Or if I did, it was only on the very edges of his life. I guess I was the Christmas gift on display on a shelf in the living room rather than a totally forgotten one hidden on a shelf in a closet. But I was still just stuck on a shelf."

"And you stayed for seven years?"

"We were married," she said, "and I kept hoping

that things would change, that the spark would come back...."

The spark she'd tried putting back only to be rejected....

"What made you finally leave—especially given that these people were not kind to anybody who did?"

"I'd been thinking about it for a while when Elliot decided we should start having kids—which was just after what I'd watched happen to Linda."

"So faced with a token marriage to a husband who neglected you and pressure to have kids you would lose to the clan if you ever left after that—"

"And the fact that by then I had some idea of the Grants' seedy side and I was not proud to be part of it even by association—"

"You decided to get out."

"I did. Which became a nightmare of a battle for both me and for Tyson—he was my lawyer against the Grants' *team* of lawyers through a process that they dragged out for three years."

"Even without kids and a custody fight?"

"I'd inherited my grandparents' place when they died, and Elliot said he knew more about those kinds of things than I did, so he should take care of it. He decided the best thing to do was to sell it. But I never saw any of the money from it—he said it was safe and sound for the future—"

"But without a future with him, that money was rightfully yours."

"It was. And Tyson went after it—"

"Which set off a three-year battle?"

"We fought over that for two and a half of the three years. That was when Tyson and I finally gave up the idea of seeing any of that money. Instead, Elliot offered me this place—only because his last tenants had been college kids and it was completely trashed. But by then, I just wanted it all over with, so I agreed."

"And that was when you met the Bronsons...."

"When I got the house, yes."

"How long have you actually been divorced?"

"A year."

"And since then? Have this guy and his family left you alone? Or are we at risk of a drive-by shooting sitting out here like this?"

"It's pretty dark back in this corner, so I think we're safe," she joked. "No, once it was over, I stopped existing for the Grants. I saw my former mother-in-law with one of Elliot's sisters and two of his brothers at a restaurant not long ago and they all looked right through me, as if we'd never met."

"I'm sorry," Derek said sympathetically.

"It's no big deal."

"Not only for you getting snubbed by your former in-laws, but for all of it."

Gia laughed. "Well, that's more than Elliot ever said."

Derek bent the elbow of the arm resting on the slat behind her so he could bring one hand forward and move her hair from the front of her shoulder to the back of it. Once he had, his fingers returned again to brush a few strokes against the side of her neck as he peered into her face, studying her. His feather-light touch eased her tension and replaced it with something tingly and titillating that scattered through her like glitter.

After a few minutes of studying her as if he was searching for something, he shook his head and said, "How that guy could watch TV or text or play video games rather than look at you, talk to you, *kiss* you... I'm finding it hard to understand."

"You? The king of losing interest?" she teased.

"Me. Yeah..."

Just saying the word *kiss* had triggered the need in Gia, so when he leaned forward then to do just that, she met him halfway.

And while it hadn't been on her mind for more than a few seconds in advance, the first meeting of mouths really was what she needed in so many ways. Not only had she been longing to have him kiss her again since she'd stopped him the night before, but it helped her to believe that she hadn't completely lost her appeal—the way just recalling the end of her marriage had made her feel.

Gia was instantly lost in kissing him. Her hand went to his chest without his encouragement this time, and when his other arm came around to enclose her in that splendid circle of biceps, she sank into him.

Lips parted and tongues reconvened with giddiness at the reunion, and everything else faded into oblivion— the hours that had passed without him, the family dinner, even her own past. There was just Derek and kissing him and being held against him again in those arms.

But her hand was like a brick wall between them, and she didn't want that.

So she snaked it around his shoulder, moving her other arm, too, so she could have both hands pressed to his strong back. And her front to his....

She hadn't realized how much her body had been craving that until she got there—to have her own arms around him, to absorb the feel of his back through her palms, to have her breasts in contact with his well-muscled chest.

She felt her nipples turn into tiny pebbles and wondered if he could feel it, too, since the tank top's built-in bra wasn't much of a barrier.

And yet, at the same time, it was enough to blunt sensations that she suddenly didn't want blunted....

Oh, that was a dangerous thought!

But it was true. Her body was craving things she'd made it stop craving a long time ago. Things she'd stopped thinking about so she wouldn't miss them. Things she'd thought might seem strange to do again with someone else.

Only that wasn't the case. Not with Derek. Instead, wanting him, wanting his hands on her, came naturally and it was all she could think about.

She deepened their kiss as a new drive came to life in her. And she upped the sexiness quotient of their tongues at play, entreating and tempting him as she expanded her chest into his and kneaded the taut muscles of his back through the sport shirt he was wearing with slacks that fit him so well that during his grandmother's dinner she'd stolen every opportunity to catch a glimpse of his great rear end in them.

Merely recalling that caused her to draw one hand down and forward to his thigh, wanting also to know if it was as thick and hard as those slacks seemed to hint at. And when she found that it was, her nipples got tighter still, nearly aching for his hand on them.

She sometimes liked to sit on her porch swing in the dark and just look out unseen at passing cars or neighbors walking by, but never had she been as grateful for those deep shadows as she was when Derek intensified the kiss himself and one of his hands trailed down to the hem of her outer shirt and then from there under her tank top.

Something that was more than a sigh but less than a moan rumbled in her throat at that first moment of his big, warm hand meeting skin.

The feel of a man's touch...

It had been a long time.

But more than that, this was the feel of Derek's touch, and there was something electrifying in that contact not only of skin on skin, but of his skin on hers.

She didn't know if he knew how much she needed more of that contact or if he needed it, too, but after only a moment of resting his hand on her bare back he brought it around to her front and upward.

Her breath caught when he enclosed her breast in his grasp. When his fingers pressed into her flesh and her nipple turned harder still, nestling into the center of his palm.

Gentle then less gentle, firm then less firm—he caressed and kneaded and pulled and pushed her just so, just right, just enough to arouse and inspire her to thoughts of more. More of him. More of his touch. More of his mouth on more parts of her....

She wanted that.

She wanted every bit of it. Every bit of him. She wanted to know every inch of him with her own hands, her own mouth, and she wanted him to know every inch of her.

I could take him inside....

Her breast swelled even more boldly into his hand with that thought, and her own hand went up a few inches on his thigh.

But only a few.

Just short of reaching that part of him that she really wanted to touch.

But despite her talk with Tyson that morning, despite how much she wanted Derek—and she wanted him so much she was almost ashamed of herself—she just wasn't sure.

Could she merely mess around with this man, have

only a little fun—enough to boost her own ego—and then go on about her business without a blip?

It wasn't something she'd ever done before. And she just wasn't sure if she could now....

Be careful— Tyson had said it three times and the warning pinballed through her mind, rejected by pangs of desire only to warn her again, be rejected again, then warn her once more.

Once more was enough.

Damn it all anyway....

She groaned softly, covered Derek's hand at her breast to press him tightly to her as if that would help engrave the feeling into her skin forever, and then she let go of his hand and ended the kiss by increments.

"I don't know if we should be doing this...." she said. "I don't know if *I* should be doing this...."

His fingers pushed into her flesh once more as if he was doing the same thing she had—memorizing the sensation to take with him—before he let go of her and took his hand out from under her shirt.

He didn't say anything as he dropped his forehead to the top of hers, stayed there a moment, then kissed her again—so sweetly she had second thoughts about why anything she did with him could be anything other than right.

But she couldn't let herself get carried away, and when that kiss ended, too, she bit back the words that would have invited him inside after all.

She heard him exhale and knew that he was working at regaining some control before he said, "Work tomorrow... Monday," as if trying to put order to things. "You're meeting with bankers for the Bronsons...."

"I am."

He nodded. "Okay. I'll call you after. You can tell me what happened."

But what about this? What about us?

That was what went through her mind before she told herself there wasn't any *us* and *this* probably shouldn't be anything, either.

And just the fact that she'd had these thoughts warned her that she might not be able to take anything she did with him as lightly as she needed to, so she was right not to go any further.

He stood then, keeping hold of her hand to bring her to her feet, too, and walked her to her door.

"Oh, what you do to me…" he said when they got there and his glance went through the screen, as if he'd also been thinking about taking things inside.

Gia wasn't sure whether to apologize for not asking him in, so she didn't say anything but "Drive home safe."

"Always," he said, pulling her toward him again by the hand he was still holding. He wrapped his other arm around her and kissed her once more so thoroughly, so intensely, so temptingly, that she melted all over again and very nearly threw reason out and dragged him inside anyway.

But then that kiss ended and he smiled down at her and said, "Night, Gia."

There was enough finality to that for her to find some acceptance, too, and she said, "Good night."

But when he kissed her yet again, when the tip of his tongue teased hers, when his hand just barely brushed her breast before he said another ragged-voiced goodnight and left her to watch him go down her porch steps to his car, she wasn't sure she'd made the right choice.

Because her body was screaming at her for it.

And the pure and simple truth was that she was sorry she'd sent him away....

Chapter Nine

"Tonight. Dressed up—heels, hose, hair, the whole works. I'll be at your house at seven. I have some things to tell you that have to do with the Bronsons and then something else to tell you, too. Then I'll take you out to the best dinner money can buy—even though you've earned much more than that for what you've done for your neighbors and for a whole lot of other people."

That was what Derek had said to Gia when he'd called her at work on Tuesday morning.

Mysterious, intriguing, a little flattering.

How could she say no?

Especially when she wanted to see him so badly she might have gone running if he'd just snapped his fingers.

Plus, she had a dress....

So she left work early Tuesday afternoon and went home to shower and shampoo and condition her hair.

As it was drying she scrunched it to actually add more curl so it was even fuller, with extra flair for fanciness.

Tonight's makeup routine included eye shadow and liner, as well as a bit more blush and a second layer of mascara.

After that, she put on her thigh-high black nylons with her matching lace bikinis and strapless bra. Then the dress.

Slinky and black, it fit like a second skin. It had an off-the-shoulder neckline that went straight across, and didn't miss a curve all the way to a few inches above her knees.

She'd loved the dress when she'd bought it four years ago but she'd never had the chance to wear it, and was glad to find that she still could.

Since Derek was so tall, the height of her heels didn't matter, so she went with the strappy black four-inch sandals.

She was just applying a pale mauve lipstick rather than simple lip gloss when her doorbell rang at seven sharp.

"Wowza!" Derek said, his expression reflecting how much he liked what he saw when she opened the door.

Right back at you, Gia thought as she thanked him.

She'd seen him in work suits and had no idea what made this suit different. But was it ever! He could have been inaugurated president in it.

It was midnight blue with a grayish cast and it accentuated to perfection his broad shoulders and divinely shaped torso. Under it he wore a dove-gray shirt with a matching tie, and she'd never seen anyone outside of a fashion magazine look as dynamic as he did.

"You clean up pretty well yourself," she said as she let him in, fighting not to close her eyes and just breath in the clean woodsy scent of his cologne when he stepped in front of her.

Then she closed the door and turned to find him ogling her from the center of her living room.

"I wanted you dressed up, but you've blown me away, lady," he said. "Look at you... Positively sultry."

Me, sultry?

But the way he was looking at her confirmed that he liked what he saw as his gaze went from top to bottom to top again. With those gorgeous blue eyes wide.

"Turn and give me the whole thing."

"No," she demurred, beginning to feel self-conscious. Pleased, but self-conscious.

But he was determined because when she got farther into the room to join him he walked around her, making a full circle.

"Wowza from all angles" was his conclusion. "And here I am, just wanting to take it apart...." he mused under his breath before he surprised her by catching her hand in his to pull her to him so he could kiss her.

Wowza...

Then, just when he'd kissed her so thoroughly her knees were weak, he let go of her, and it took Gia a minute to regroup.

When she had, she found him smiling at her as he seemed to start over. "Hi."

Gia laughed at him. "Hi," she parroted.

"How was your day?" he asked mundanely.

"Good. How was yours?"

"Productive. I bought the Bronsons' house."

Screeching halt.

Gia froze and she could actually feel the color drain from her face. "You bought the Bronsons' house?"

"I did."

"Out from under them?" she said, her voice louder as panic began to hit. "Why would you do that? That's just what they were afraid of from you! Do you hate those poor people or what? What did they ever do to the Camdens? You're no better than the ones who ran them out of their hotel—"

"Whoa! Whoa! Whoa! After the time we've spent together, that's still where you go? Come on—"

"You bought their house out from under them!" she repeated, louder still.

"Think about that, Gia.... How would I do that?"

"They're behind in their payments. The bank has threatened foreclosure. You're the *Camdens*—you could own the bank for all I know. You have more money than God and probably more power. You strolled in and got the bank to sell it to you right out from under Larry and Marion!"

He shook his head. "Take a breath."

She couldn't. Her mind was racing. Her heart was pounding. Even her breathing felt restricted.

Derek took her by the shoulders—bare shoulders that responded to the feel of his hands on them even as she was whirling with shock—and guided her to the sofa. "Sit down and hear me out," he commanded.

Her knees were weak all over again so she did sit, terrified that she'd pushed Larry and Marion right into the lion's den when they'd warned her not to let the Camdens be involved.

Once she was sitting, she kept her eyes on Derek. Only now it wasn't because he looked fantastic, it was because she was right back to wondering if she had to.

He sat down beside her, angled toward her, his brow furrowed. "Think a little better of me, would you?"

"First the Camdens who came before you ran the

Bronsons out of their hotel and now you've taken their house! What do you want me to think?"

His lips went tight and thin before he seemed to give in to something. Then he said, "I'm trusting you by saying this...."

He paused, obviously still weighing whether or not to say it.

Then he said, "The Bronsons got a raw deal at the hands of H.J. and my grandfather—"

An admission of guilt.

The Grants would never—ever—have made one.

But rather than that seeming like a good thing, all Gia could think was that she might have to use it in court, testifying that he'd said it in order to try to fix this for her neighbors.

"But I...my family now...had nothing to do with that," he went on. "And not one of us would ever do something like that to anyone. Or stand for it being done in our name. No one is more sorry than I am that it was ever done. So what we're trying to do now is make it up to them. I did *not* buy their house out from under them! What I did was pay off their loan. The title is free and clear *in their name*—that's the first thing I wanted to talk to you about," he said. "You told me yesterday what happened at the bank—"

The bank would agree to refinance only if there was a co-signer, and even if Gia did that, the payments were still higher than the Bronsons could comfortably afford. Gia knew it was better for them to sell and move into her basement. But she couldn't make that decision for them, so she'd left it up to them to think about and decide. Then Derek had called and she'd told him.

"I know you'd be fine having them move in here," he was saying. "But I also know—because you told me—

that they'd rather stay in their house. So I made it so they can. They own it free and clear—*they* own it, not me, not any Camden. The title will come to them, in the name of Larry and Marion Bronson, without another soul attached to it. If they wanted, they could sell it next week and come away with every penny of the money in *their* pockets, and if they haven't done that when both of them pass away, it's theirs to leave to whomever they choose."

Gia studied him, searching for a sign that he wasn't telling the truth, mentally scanning for a hole in what he was telling her. But she didn't find any sign, any hole, and she calmed down. But only slightly.

"There's also an account opened for them," Derek continued. "I'll make sure it's funded to pay the taxes and insurance, any upkeep and utilities—everything that has to do with the house for as long as it's theirs. The account is in their names and yours so you can access it for them. It only needs you and them to sign the signature cards and it's ready to go. And again, we'll deposit into it but we have no access once the money is there—like the donation account you set up for them before. No access to the money and no claim on the house *whatsoever*—not now, not later, *never*."

"That's very generous...." she said. But only tentatively, because he'd raised all her red flags again and it wasn't easy for her to lower them.

"I'm not finished," he said patiently. "We want to pay for someone to come in and help with the cleaning and look after whatever they might need—it can be live-in, round-the-clock care or whatever they'll be comfortable with. And as their needs change, so can the help that comes in—I'll leave it to you to talk to them about what they want now and we'll reassess whenever things change."

"Okay…" she said quietly, still afraid this was all too good to be true.

"I know they're just barely warming up to me, but I want to build on that so I can keep in contact to make whatever alterations need to be made as time goes by. GiGi called her doctor and told him that any bills not covered by the Bronsons' insurance are to be sent to us—that includes anything they need healthwise, now or later."

Gia nodded and she knew that it was her eyes that were wide now because all he was explaining stunned her.

He smiled slightly. "Relax, will you? I came in to assess how much damage was done by them losing their hotel years ago. I watched and listened so I could learn what they need, and I waited to see what you could accomplish for them. But now that I have the whole picture, I can see that the damage was extensive and the needs are far reaching, and even your best efforts aren't going to save them. So let me. We owe them that."

Another admission of guilt.

"We're going to make sure that they have *anything* they need from here on out," he assured. "We're going to make sure they're comfortable, that they're well taken care of and that for what's left of their lives, they're unburdened. But if they're still opposed to accepting it all from us, until I can build on the crack I've made in the ice, I'm going to count on you to keep running interference. And I'm definitely going to count on you to let us know if something happens suddenly that changes their needs or calls for more help—"

"And what's in it for you?" she heard herself ask, thinking about her ex-husband and his family again, concern overcoming her.

"Nothing. This is straight restitution, nothing else. If you think it's better for them not to even know it's all coming from us, even that's okay. If it will make them happier, you can say the house was paid off by an anonymous donor. Or I even have something else you can tell them—it won't be true, but it might make them feel better. That's the second part...."

"There's more?" she said, unsure how there could be.

"You and the Bronsons opened our eyes to the needs of the elderly in general, so the Camden Foundation is developing a program to provide this type of assistance to whoever needs it. What we do for the Bronsons is separate, but I'm assuming that they have friends and know other people in their own age bracket who can benefit from this kind of program, and if you think they'd feel better believing that what's coming to them is no more than any of their friends can access, let them think that."

"Seems like what you're talking about for them is more than anyone is going to get through a foundation, so they'd see through that. Plus, I think they'd like to know that you're admitting what was done to them was wrong—"

She could tell that was a sticky subject by the arch of his eyebrows and the resignation in his expression. "We don't need any credit, but we don't need the negative attention stirred up either, if that could be kept to a minimum."

Gia could understand that they were trying to live down a reputation that this generation might not deserve and that bringing up old wrongs wouldn't help. But she couldn't vouch for what Larry and Marion might do, so she could only say, "I'll do what I can."

Then, as more of what he'd told her sank in, she said, "So you set up a program that can help any elderly people who need it, and you did that with just the wave of a wand?"

He shrugged and she saw humility in the acknowledgment that yes, he had that ability. But what he said was, "The criteria are being hashed out now and put in place. By the first of the month, people can apply for help and if they qualify, it'll be there for them."

"For just any older people in need? No one in particular who might have some history with you the way Larry and Marion do?"

"For any elderly people in need. Before this, we just weren't really seeing that there *is* a need. But my grandmother is seventy-five—I told you, the thought of her being in the position the Bronsons are in…" He shook his head a second time. "We wouldn't want that. The Bronsons' situation got us all thinking, so we wanted to do what we can to help. I know what you think of us, but we really are trying to do better than what was done before.…"

Gia was still looking for an ulterior motive. The Grants would have had one, because they weren't about actually doing good, they were just about cover-ups to make themselves *look* good.

But there just didn't seem to be an ulterior motive here. Derek had even admitted that he and his family bore some guilt. He'd been open with her, honest. And the scope of what he was giving to the Bronsons, what he was going to provide for other people, was impressive.

She thought that she might just have to concede that the Camdens—at least the current Camdens—were different than the Grants. That they acted with ethics and integrity, that they genuinely wanted to atone for whatever was done before them and give back. That they really were a different ilk than her former in-laws.

"This is all for real? You're serious," she said then, the shadow of disbelief hovering.

"About it all," he confirmed. "But you don't have to believe me—tomorrow you can confirm with the bank and see for yourself."

The fact that he wasn't going to any other lengths to prove himself, that he was willing to have his actions speak louder than his words was what put it over the top for her and she finally believed him.

"I don't think just saying thanks is enough...." she muttered as it began to genuinely register with her.

Derek put his hand on her knee then, and she instantly flashed back to having that hand on her breasts Sunday night. And to how much she'd wanted that again ever since.

But this time his touch wasn't sexual—except in what it roused in her. It was comforting and imploring at the same time as he looked into her eyes and said, "I was also serious about how amazingly beautiful you are if you'd just stop looking at me like I pulled the rug out from under you."

"I was afraid you had," she said. "Out from under me and the Bronsons."

"Nope. But I also don't want to minimize your part in all of this—you did so much for your neighbors and you're really responsible for showing us the overall problems. So we thought we might like to call the fund the Gia Grant Fund...."

Oh.

"The Gia Grant Fund..." she repeated.

"Within the Camden Foundation. Would that be okay?"

"I don't know.... It seems so weird to have something named after me. This wasn't that big of a deal—I was just trying to help Larry and Marion. Shouldn't I be dead or something before my name gets put on anything?"

"No!" he said with a laugh. "It's just recognition for what you've done. And we'd also like to invite you to be on the committee that will go through the applications so you'll have a vote on who gets what. It doesn't pay anything, though—to us or to anyone else who sits on our committees. We want all the money within the foundation to go toward the causes we support, so we run it, and we recruit and badger people to help out."

"I'd...be willing to do that...." Gia said, suddenly finding herself a little misty at the thought of it all. And very impressed with this man. And with his family.

It was a turnaround for her, and Gia looked at Derek through new eyes.

Not that he looked any better to her than he had, because that wasn't possible—he was just as drop-dead gorgeous as she'd registered the very first time she'd seen him. But she suddenly saw more substance to him than she'd given him credit for before, and that just made him all the more appealing.

"Dinner..." she said then, realizing that she needed something to get her to her feet and out of there. Because admiring him, appreciating him in new ways, only compounded feelings that had been set in motion Sunday night. And all she really wanted to do at that moment was what he'd said he wanted to do to her earlier—take his clothes off.

"Dinner..." he echoed, though in a quiet tone that lacked conviction while his eyes held hers and he began to massage her knee, sending little shards of light from that spot all through her. "Are you starving?" he asked then.

She was.

But for him....

That thought caused her to laugh a little, to smile at him, all of it infused with unintentional innuendo that he read because he mirrored that smile and a knowing look came into his blue eyes.

"The reservation isn't for a while...." he informed her, a question in his statement.

"No?" she answered buoyantly.

"But you said no the other night...." he reminded her, making it clear they *were* on the same wavelength.

"I did," she confirmed.

"The thought of committee work goes right to your head?" he joked, his smile going crooked and so, so sexy.

"I think it does." She played along rather than say that it was him who'd gone to her head.

Which meant that she really was getting carried away, and she knew it.

But not indefinitely.

She'd thought a lot about this since Sunday. She hadn't been able *not* to think about it most of the time. And the truth was that she wanted him so much that she just had to have him.

But only for right now. A little surrender without looking for tomorrows.

As long as she wasn't expecting anything more—no white dresses or wedding chapels or picket fences or bouncing babies—why couldn't she indulge the way Tyson did? The way Tyson had suggested she do in order to try to get it out of her system?

Because she just didn't know any other way she was going to get it out of her system.

That was what she'd concluded. Even before she'd accepted Derek's dinner invitation tonight.

The dinner invitation that had provided her with this chance.

And now here he was, and she had even less reason to resist, and even with the reasons that remained, she just didn't care. She still wanted him.

He moved a little closer on the couch, squeezing her knee and smiling devilishly. "If it helps cancel out that no, I can put you on the scholarship committee. And the arts committee. And the committee for animal rights.... You name it and there's probably a committee for it and I can put you on it."

"Oh, yeah—committees and committees and more committees—that gets me going," she joked in return, putting her hand on his thigh—about where it had been before she'd shied away on Sunday night. Or maybe an inch higher...

He was more serious when he said in a voice that was suddenly deeper, raspier, "You look sooo good, it's a shame to wreck it...."

"I kind of hate to ruin this, too...." she said, reaching with her other hand for the tie that was knotted meticulously at his throat and tugging on it.

"Go ahead, ruin it," he urged as his free hand went to the side of her neck and glided around to the back.

He pulled her forward to meet him as he leaned in and gave her a kiss that was so much hotter than the kiss he'd given her when he'd first come in. Hot enough to let her know that Sunday night had maintained its impact on him, too.

Gia did some multitasking, kissing him back as she untied his tie, slid it free of his shirt collar and kicked off her shoes.

When his tongue came to greet hers, she took off his suit coat and felt him unfasten his collar button to aid the cause of that kiss, their mouths going wider as the hunger that was only for each other ran rampant.

His free hand came to her breast, but only on the outside of her dress and bra, and that wasn't enough. It was something—something nice and arousing—but not enough. Not after she'd already learned the glory of having his hand on her without the filter of clothing between them.

She did some quick work undoing the rest of his shirt buttons so she could demonstrate, reaching inside once she could to lay her own hands on his chest.

Which was when she realized that that was the first time it had been bare to her....

And that it felt as glorious as it looked. Warm, smooth, sleek skin over muscles as solid as a brick wall. She couldn't resist going from the cut and carved pectorals down to the sharp six-pack of abs that led right to his waistband....

She just unhooked his belt and the button on his pants while she was there and then sluiced her hands around his waist to his back and up again.

That back that was oh, so nice....

His shoulders were big and broad and powerful and she filled her hands with the muscles there, massaging and mimicking what he was doing to her breasts, which were still locked in her bra and dress, her nipples trying their best to nudge their way out.

In spite of the fact that his shirt was beautiful, it was just in Gia's way, so she finessed it off him as her tongue parried playfully with his in a game that was growing ever more sexy.

And that was when he took his hand from her breast, his other hand from her nape and found the dress's zipper.

His mouth was wide over hers as the zipper went

down, as he spread the back of the dress and unhooked her strapless bra, too.

But as his hands went to her shoulders to take the dress off, it occurred to her somewhat belatedly that they were in her living room, it was still daylight so the drapes were open, and that they might be visible through the picture window.

Which meant that this needed to be taken to the bedroom.

And if she did that, it also meant that there was no turning back....

But that only gave her a split-second's pause before she plied the tip of his tongue with the tip of hers in one parting tease and ended the kiss to take his hand in hers and tug him to his feet.

He smiled when she did, apparently knowing what she was doing, going along willingly into her bedroom, where she'd already pulled the curtains in order to dress for tonight.

Still, bright September sunlight shone through, and Gia knew how much she wanted this when the fact that she was about to be undressed with Derek without the cloak of darkness didn't daunt her. Instead, she was just glad for the opportunity to see him when she took him to the foot of her double bed and turned to have a look at that torso, those shoulders, those biceps, that flat belly and the dark line of hair that went from navel down behind the waistband she'd left unbuttoned.

And as fantastic as he'd looked in the suit, what was underneath it was even better....

He used the hand she held to yank her to him, catching her mouth with his again in a wildly abandoned kiss that made everything that had happened in the living room seem tame. He continued what he'd begun there as he took off her dress, leaving it and her bra to drift down around her ankles.

Lace bikinis and thigh-high nylons—that was all she had on when he deserted her mouth for a look.

A look that adored and relished and came with a groan of approval as he took both breasts into both hands and recaptured her mouth with his.

Again her knees really did go weak in that first grip of big, gentle hands, of fingers that tenderly dug into her soft flesh, of palms where her nipples nestled impudently.

As if he knew he'd taken the starch out of her legs, one hand left her breast so he could wrap that arm around her and brace her as he went on kissing her into oblivion.

But not so far into oblivion that she didn't realize he was still partially dressed. And that she didn't want him that way.

So she did some unzipping of her own and let everything he had on from the waist down join her dress on the floor.

And then she wanted a look....

So she coyly escaped his kiss and took one.

Wow all over again....

Clothed, the man was something.

Naked, he was something else....

Hard and honed everywhere, he was the image of masculine perfection.

But he only let her have a brief glimpse before he swept her off her feet and tossed her good-naturedly onto the bed.

He joined her there, sitting on the edge and reaching for his slacks to take his wallet out and get protection— giving her a prime view of his divinely brawny back—

before he turned toward her, set the condom aside and put his full attention on her again.

His mouth took hers once more, his hand reclaimed her breasts and the other curved over her head to play with her hair as one thick thigh rested atop hers.

Gia let her hands go exploring. Exploring the expanse of those shoulders she just couldn't get enough of. The dip of his spine. Muscles and tendons that fanned from there. Tight derriere. The back of that thigh that pinned hers. The front of that same thigh. Then higher still than she'd gone before until she found that part of him that she'd only gotten a brief glimpse of.

The moan that rumbled in his throat let her know how much he liked it when she circled him with her hand. When she learned all he had to offer and teased him just a bit.

Just enough to put things into another gear.

He tugged with careful teeth on her lower lip. He kissed her chin, the hollow of her neck, and then he replaced his hand at her breast with his mouth and drove her just a bit crazy, too, sucking and nipping and running the tip of his tongue around the oh-so-sensitive outer circle of her nipple. Flicking at the eager nipple itself. Drawing her well into that hot, moist mouth that seemed to have the power to perform miracles. Miracles that awakened sleeping needs that had never been quite that demanding before.

And then he shifted up another gear when he slid his free hand down her stomach and inside her bikinis....

Her neck arched, pulling her shoulders right off the mattress when he first found her, his long, thick fingers easing into her. Slowly. Tenderly. Just asking permission for more to come later....

Her grip around him tightened in response, and that

brought a sound that was part laugh, part groan from him just before he withdrew his fingers and made her panties disappear.

Then his mouth returned to hers as his hands worked the condom, and more than his thigh rose over her.

Gia opened her legs to him as he came between them, his hands on either side of her shoulders, bracing his weight, his mouth finding her breasts again—one, then the other, flicking her nipples with his tongue and tormenting her with ever-increasing need—as he rediscovered that spot he'd made friends with moments before, slipping into her gradually, carefully, tenaciously.

Sound escaped them both when he reached his destination and she could feel him fully inside of her—long and thick and hard—where he stayed embedded and motionless, as if he was relishing it, too.

But only for a moment before desire took rein and he began that primal, fantastic trip. Slowly out and in again. And again. Each time with more speed. Each time diving deeper. Each time bringing more and more awake in Gia to make her blood rush, her heart race.

Her arms were around him, her hands splayed on that back that seemed like it could bear the world, as she matched his pace, meeting him with her hips, tightening around him then releasing as they found their rhythm and harmony.

Faster he went, and so did she. Working together in finely tuned unison. Bodies asking and answering instinctively until everything inside Gia grew and gathered and then couldn't be contained no matter how hard she tried.

Bursting wide-open, ecstasy thrust her into a space where she had no control and could only be carried away with it, by it. Carried away into an exquisite paradise where he waited for her. Where he exploded, too, holding her to cushion the blow and meld them together so tightly she didn't know where she began and he ended and the only thing she knew for sure was that she wanted it to go on and on and on....

And it did. Blessedly on and on until it spent itself. Then ebbed. Easing them down a little at a time, as they clung to each other in a meshing of more than bodies....

"Leave it to you to do dessert first," Derek joked after a time of just lying there atop her, catching his breath, kissing the side of her head.

Gia could only smile at his jest, too exhausted for a retort.

"Are you okay? I didn't break you, did I?" he asked then.

Gia laughed and realized she was going to have to find some strength to assure him. "Not broken, no. Are you?"

He flexed inside of her again. "Parts seem to still be in working order."

"Thank goodness!"

"You're telling me."

He didn't move, though. He stayed where he was, at home in her, it seemed.

At some point in the aftermath, Gia's arms had fallen away from him to the mattress, and now she wrapped them around him again, rubbing his back and absorbing all the sensations she could.

"I think we missed our reservation," he said then.

"You had some reservations? It didn't seem like it...." she teased him, playing with the words.

He laughed and nuzzled her ear, then sighed and whispered, "It was too good to be true."

Which was what she'd thought earlier.

What she still thought of him....

"It was," she whispered in return.

"I think we'd better give it a second test to be sure."

Gia took a turn at laughing. "Is that what you think?"

"It is. After a rest...."

He came out of her then and rolled to his side, his big body still half covering hers, one arm canopied over her head on the mattress again, the other across her chest much the way his thigh was across hers.

"What do you say?" he asked then. "The sun is going down.... We can try it in the dark now that we know the way...."

"I'll think about it," she said.

"Good," he answered, pulsing against her hip temptingly. But his voice had drifted and after another kiss to her temple, she could tell he'd gone to sleep.

Which beckoned to her, too.

But she fought it for a moment.

She just wanted to lie there with Derek as her blanket, enjoying the afterglow.

And all too happy with the thought that he would still be there when she woke and they could do this all again....

Chapter Ten

"Why did we only take half the day off?" Derek moaned when he came up behind Gia. He slid his arms around her waist to pull her back against him and nuzzle her neck.

They'd both called in to work and said they were taking Thursday morning off. It had seemed like a necessity after being up all night making love. Although part of the morning had been spent that way as well, rather than catching up on sleep.

"Maybe we should just take the afternoon, too," he suggested.

It was almost eleven. When Gia had finally gotten out of bed she'd put on the first thing she could reach—his shirt. That was all she was wearing to make coffee.

Derek had followed her into the kitchen after pulling on what had remained of his clothes on the bedroom floor. His chest was bare and even though Gia was facing the counter, she could see his reflection in the side of the toaster. And that was enough.

She melted against him, tipping her head to one side to allow him free access to her neck, closing her eyes and wanting to go back to bed with him so much it was as if they hadn't made love at all yet.

"I have a meeting with the owner of the company," she reminded. "He's coming in from Fort Collins just for that. I have to be there." But there was nothing she wanted more than to climb back into bed with Derek.

Which was beginning to worry her all on its own....

Making love hadn't had the effect she'd thought it would. It hadn't taken wanting him out of her system the way it was supposed to. It hadn't been the kind of freeing release Tyson had claimed it would be.

Instead, every minute with Derek had just made her want him even more.

And more. And more. And more than before....

And now not only was she facing that, she was facing the fact that his car had been parked out front all night, so Tyson would have seen it. And so would Larry and Marion.

Plus, the cold light of day was forcing her to face some other things, too....

"How 'bout I buy the company and then I'll be your boss, and we'll hold all of our meetings in bed," he joked.

"Harry Cooley would never sell out."

Derek grumbled and nibbled on her earlobe. "Okay, okay, okay..." he sighed. "We'll work this afternoon. Then maybe we can actually get to dinner tonight. Before we start all over again...."

Gia wanted to do that, too. But that was the problem.

If she didn't stop this now, what was she in for? That was what she'd started to ask herself as she'd made coffee.

Being with Derek all night long, making love, sleeping with him on and off had already gotten her in deeper emotionally than she had been. If she kept this up, she knew she'd get in even deeper. She'd be all the way in.

And then what?

Where would—where *could*—this go for her? she asked herself.

And the answer to that was *nowhere.*

Which, she realized, was the worst of what she had to face.

So she took a steeling breath and forced herself to wiggle out of his hold, moving away from him to the opposite side of the kitchen.

"I…" With the second steadying breath she wondered how she was going to do this. "We…"

"Yeah, I know—we have to go to work," he complained. "But my head is *not* going to be in it—I'll just be watching the clock and counting how many more hours have to pass before I can get back here."

"No," she finally managed. "That isn't what I was going to say. I was going to say that we…*this*…" She made a waving motion with her hand that included them both and what was between them. "We can't do *this*…."

Derek frowned in confusion and fell back against the counter. "This?"

"Everything. Seeing each other again. Dinner. What we did last night…and this morning…. We can't do any of it after this." And why did her gaze drop to his naked chest and make her yearn just then to start all over right this minute and make a liar out of her?

"I'm confused…." he said, as if she'd told a joke he didn't get.

Gia forced her eyes to his face—that face that looked

impossibly good even scruffed up with morning beard—
and thought that this was all hard for her to believe, too.

But it had to be done.

"I have to look at the big picture," she told him.

"The big picture," he repeated.

The big picture. That it was only a matter of time before she woke up and found herself head over heels in
love with a man who also woke up and realized that she
wasn't colorful or outrageous or wild or unique enough
to keep his interest.

That it was only a matter of time before she woke up
and found herself head over heels in love with another
man whose enormous family came first. Another man
whose strongest attachments and loyalties were to that
enormous family. Another man whose enormous family might not have the same kind of skewed practices
and principles as they once had had, as the Grants had,
but who no doubt could and would close rank against an
outsider like her if things didn't work out.

Or that it was only a matter of time before she woke
up and found herself head over heels in love with a man
who was with her for the wrong reasons. Who had met
her at a time when he was trying to please and appease
that enormous family that was so important to him by
denying his penchant for the kind of colorful women
who had so recently caused them all embarrassment.

But she couldn't say all of that so she said, "I'm fresh
out of a marriage…." Which was also true. "And so are
you—"

"There's nothing even remotely alike in the end of
your marriage and canceling out what I did in a drunken
stupor in Vegas."

"There is a little," she insisted. "I came out of my
marriage knowing what I do and don't want. You came

out of yours thinking you want to break old habits and turn over a new leaf."

"Okay, I guess those aren't too different," he conceded.

"But there are things that come along with you that are like what I just got out of and I don't want to get wrapped up in those things again. And I don't think I can be that new leaf that you may or may not be able to stick with…."

"And you're not willing to give it a little while to find out?"

"A little while and…it would just make it harder," she said softly, unwilling to reveal too much of how she already felt about him. "You said yourself that *regular* girls always end up boring you. And you know that because your family keeps throwing them at you and you try to like them to please your family, but eventually you just lose interest—"

"Yeah, I said that."

"Well, there's nothing unique or weird or colorful about me, Derek. So it stands to reason that given a little while, you'll want a rule breaker or a line crosser or…"

She stalled and shook her head. "I'm not any of the things you look for—that's the reality. I'm an ordinary, everyday person, and that isn't what you've *ever* wanted. But your family is as important to you as Elliot's was to him, and that carries weight—nobody knows that more than me. You want to please them, to be in their good graces, and instead the Las Vegas wedding shook the foundations. You're rebounding from it—I get it. You need to compensate for it. Atone for it. You want to prove you can clean up your act…. But I can't risk—"

"That I could be using you to make myself look good?"

Gia flinched. "I didn't say that. I don't think that's something you'd do consciously.... Is it?"

"No, it isn't."

"But I know how things work in a family like yours—if Elliot had done something that his whole family came down on him for, the way yours disapproved of the Las Vegas wedding, Elliot would have stopped at nothing to make it up to them. To redeem himself—"

"So you think my being here now, with you—liking you—is just me proving to my family that I can be a good boy?"

"Like I said, not consciously. But yes, I think it's possible." *Likely*...

"And you figure that once the dust settles I'll look up and it'll just be ordinary, everyday you who I brought in because it made my family happy, and what, Gia? I'll put you on a display shelf like your ex did and forget about you?"

Yes.

But she didn't want to say it like that, so she chose to be more diplomatic. "I don't want to risk it. And I also don't want this to get to the point where things have gone so far that we can't come back from them. That *I* can't come back from them. You said you still need some help from me with Larry and Marion, and they have too much at stake. I need to be able to call you or see you without it being awkward or ugly or... I need it not to hurt...."

"Because there isn't a doubt in your mind that that's where it'll end up—me hurting you? And what else? Are you thinking that I'm a Camden, and if things between you and I end I'll pull out of helping the Bronsons? Or do worse to them, like your former in-laws would?"

"No, I hope not. I'm just thinking that if this goes on—"

"It doesn't have a chance in hell of working—that's

what you're thinking. And that when it bombs, the Bronsons could end up collateral damage."

And me, too....

"I'm thinking that if things end later rather than sooner, it would make it hard for us to work together."

Because it would be impossible for her to be anywhere near him or even hear his voice without breaking down.

Which she was oddly close to doing already, just saying what she was saying.

"So you want to get out while the getting is good," he summed up.

What she wanted was him.

But only if *she* was what *he* wanted—ordinary, everyday her.

Only if she could be sure he would go on wanting ordinary, everyday her forever.

Only if she could be sure that he didn't merely want her *because* she was ordinary and everyday, as a path to redemption. A path that would be a dead end for her.

And since she couldn't be sure of any of that on top of everything else, she knew she had to shut this down. And she had to shut it down now or she wasn't going to be able to shut it down at all.

"I just think that to be safe, we need to take this back to it only being about Larry and Marion," she said, wondering how she was going to actually do that.

"After last night?" he demanded with more disbelief.

"Especially after last night," she said so quietly it was almost inaudible. "Even one more night like last night and...it'll get out of hand and complicated and that's not good for anybody, and it isn't what I'm ready for."

"So we'll keep it *un*complicated. We'll make sure—"

"I can't do that," she insisted, sounding slightly panicky. "I thought maybe I could—that's what got me into last night. But now I know…it's complicated for me no matter what…. So no. No more now. Last night was a one-time thing. We go back to me just being the go-between with Larry and Marion, the person who lets you know when their needs change down the road."

Her voice had risen an octave and was forceful enough to leave no question that she meant what she said. But still she felt compelled to add, "I mean it!"

For a moment Derek stared at her, frowned at her, stunned. Then he said, "I don't know what to say. There's no way I saw this coming, not after last night."

"Say we can go back to this just being about Larry and Marion," she repeated.

"I want to say that Larry and Marion, and *this*—" he mimicked her earlier gesture "—are two completely damn different things."

"But they're intertwined."

Even if they weren't, she just felt as if she had to protect herself. From Derek. From her own feelings for him. She felt as if she'd gone too far out of the safety zone she'd built around herself after her marriage and she needed to scurry back into it before it was too late.

"So this is it?" he asked, sounding dumbfounded. Then he shook his head in hard denial. "No, it can't be—things were too good…. I know you weren't faking it."

"No, I wasn't faking it," she said, trying madly not to cry and not understanding why she was on the verge. "It was…amazing."

Too amazing. Too good. It hadn't freed her, it had pulled her in the way Tyson had worried it would, and now she knew she had to get out while she still could.

"It was amazing," he parroted. "So you want to leave me wanting more? Is that it?"

She didn't want to leave him at all.

But being left wanting more herself was part of what she was afraid of. Which could happen if this wasn't real for him. If it was just something temporary, if it was just his attempt to prove to his family that he was sorry.

"I'm not playing a game," she told him. "I'm not trying to leave you wanting more. I just think it's better if it doesn't go any further."

"For the Bronsons' sake?" he said dubiously.

"And for mine...." she admitted quietly.

"So that's it?" he asked, disbelief still in his voice.

"I think it just has to be," she said, holding her ground.

"Fun while it lasted?"

Get in, hook up, get out—that was what Tyson had said.

Gia shrugged in answer to Derek's question, feeling at a loss and knowing suddenly that she'd been wrong when she'd told her friend she could do this.

"You didn't think it was going to be white dresses and wedding chapels and picket fences and bouncing babies, did you?" she said, trying to sound glib and hating that she heard an undertone of hope in her own voice.

"I hadn't thought that far."

"I can't let it get to where I do."

She looked at him again—the sight stabbing her through the heart because he looked so excruciatingly good to her—and said, "So let's turn back the clock."

"Twenty-four hours?"

"At least...."

"And we're just two people with one goal—to keep two other people together to the end?"

"Yes."

"I hate this, Gia. I don't know if I can do it...."

"You can," she assured him. "You wouldn't go back on your word, would you?"

"I wasn't talking about the Bronsons," he said. "I will do everything I said I would for them—that's not and never will be at issue."

"And that's all there can be to it," she said with finality. "This—" she waved her hand between them again "—was just…one of those things—something that happened along the way. And now needs to end."

Then she pushed away from the cupboard she was leaning against. "I'll change into something else and give you back your shirt."

His brow was a mass of lines—he looked as if he didn't know what had hit him, and didn't seem to have any idea what else to say to her as Gia left him standing in the kitchen and went to her bedroom.

But seeing that rumpled bed where everything had been so, so good all of last night and this morning cost her. Tears came flooding.

And she couldn't let him see that.

So she opened her bedroom door slightly, took off his shirt, hooked it on the outer knob and closed the door again.

Then she pressed her back to the wall beside the door and closed her eyes, just listening to him go.

I've lost my freaking mind….

That was what Derek told himself as he parked across the street and four houses up from Gia's place on Sunday night. He was positioned with a view of her house and the Bronsons', just hoping to catch a glimpse of her.

I'm worse than a crazy teenager. I've turned into her stalker.

And yet he didn't drive away. He shut off his engine and stayed where he was, staring at Gia's house and thinking the worst of himself.

It was just after dark. He'd left his grandmother's dinner and it was as if his car had driven itself to University Boulevard rather than home.

He hadn't heard from Gia since Friday when she'd called to tell him she'd convinced the Bronsons to accept all he and his family wanted to give them, that she'd spoken to the bank and taken the Bronsons there afterward, that the title papers on the house had been signed and so had the signature cards on the account he'd set up.

Her voice had been a little soft, a little shaky, but otherwise just businesslike. Until he'd asked if they could talk. Then she'd said a clipped "not about anything but Larry and Marion," and hung up.

And he was a damn mess.

He hadn't slept in the three nights since he'd left her.

He couldn't concentrate on work.

Television couldn't keep him from thinking about her.

He'd eaten very little because no food he could think of sounded good.

The one night he'd tried booze to get himself to sleep he'd just ended up drunk and morose and then had a hangover the next day.

And today, after not even being able to focus on a Bronco football game, he'd gone to GiGi's for Sunday dinner, where he'd been through-the-roof miserable.

How could he have been anything else when so many of his siblings and cousins had turned into such ridiculously happy couples! And remembering the past Sunday dinner when Gia had been there with him, he'd wished so damn bad that she was with him tonight that he couldn't wait to get out of there.

He'd begged off dessert, and since he'd been so quiet and withdrawn all through the evening, his grandmother had decided he must be coming down with something and encouraged him to go home to bed.

But bed was his torture chamber now, and instead here he was, parked a few houses away from Gia's, wondering what he was going to tell everybody if he got arrested for loitering or stalking or something.

What the hell is going on with me?

He hadn't ever gone through anything like this.

He'd been dumped a few times before, but it had never affected him this way. He'd always taken it in stride. In fact, he'd always seen it coming and actually been on the verge of doing the dumping himself, so it had saved him the trouble.

But this? This was something else. Something different. This was extreme....

As he watched Gia's house, the porch light at the Bronsons' place came on and caught his eye. He trained his gaze there, hoping Gia might have been visiting the elderly couple and was leaving.

He could feel his pulse gain speed at just the thought, and he began instantly to consider whether or not to intercept her if she did. To try to get her to talk to him now....

But it wasn't Gia who came out of the house next door to hers. It was Larry and Marion. Dressed in sweat suits—Larry's a plain heather-gray but Marion's a more flashy silver and purple—they were each carrying a bowl they took with them to sit on the chairs on their porch.

Ice cream. Derek thought they were probably having a bowl of ice cream before they went to bed. Enjoying the end of summer warmth of a September night.

They hadn't had an easy life, those two, he thought, feeling bad about his family's part in that on top of how bad he felt in general. But they had each other, he reminded himself. They still had each other.

And Gia was right; more than merely having each other, they did seem to still care for each other and enjoy each other's company, because there they were, talking and laughing when Larry stole a bite of whatever it was in Marion's bowl, then held out his own to offer her a taste of his as consolation when she put up a fuss.

God, he really did need some sleep when just the sight of that made his eyes sting.

And all he could think was that he'd give anything to be sitting on the porch next door to the Bronsons with Gia, just like that.

Just like that....

His own thought surprised him a little.

All that the Bronsons were doing was sitting on their porch, eating something, keeping each other company the way they had for seventy years. And that was what he wanted?

No boundary pushing? No line crossing? No rule breaking? No novelty in any way? Just sitting on the porch? Talking? Playing around like they must have a million times before? *That* was what he wanted?

But yeah, it was, he acknowledged with surprise. And a little skepticism.

Was he really envying something that plain and simple?

Pre-Gia, he certainly wouldn't have been. He'd have thought that it was nice for the Bronsons, but that it would be mind-numbing for him.

So why was he not only *not* thinking that, but wishing it was what he had?

It struck him as very weird.

And what made it even weirder was that if he imagined himself in that situation with anyone he'd ever met other than Gia, it didn't appeal to him at all.

A lifetime of Sharon the psychic? Of Celeste the head shaver? Of Carol the food police? Of Lila the statue?

Not a chance.

Not any more of a chance than with Brittany or Reagan or Nancy—the *regular* women who hadn't kept his interest as long as Sharon, Celeste, Carol or Lila.

But plug Gia into the picture and everything lit up like a neon sign for him.

Maybe Louie knew what he was talking about....

Because it had been the Camdens' handyman who had suggested that the strange women didn't keep his interest any more than the normal ones did. But that the *right* woman would....

He hadn't been sure *any* woman ever would. But all of a sudden here he was, realizing that he hadn't lost a drop of interest in Gia no matter how much time they were together. That it was the opposite, in fact—the more he got to know her, spend time with her, learn about her, the more he wanted to know. The more interested he was.

The more interested and enthralled and captivated and fascinated. The more charmed...

And yet she wasn't unusual at all.

But still he'd found even the small workings of her mind intriguing—her inventiveness, how she decided what to eat, her innovations for helping the Bronsons. It was nothing big, but it had left him with half a dozen instances since he'd met her when he'd wondered what she might think of something, how she might look at it differently than he did, what she might see in it that he didn't, how she might think to improve on it.

He just liked the way her brain worked. Somehow he'd discovered excitement in that. More excitement than he'd found in all the edginess and strange stuff with other women.

She surprised him in small ways—nothing elaborate or showy, nothing with any kind of shock value. Silly things like a simple comeback remark. The fact that she was obsessed with chocolate but ate vanilla ice cream. Nothing wild or bizarre, just things that were the tiniest bit out of the ordinary that made him feel like he could never be too sure what might come next....

He didn't know what Larry had said to Marion as he went on watching the two of them, but the elderly woman gave her husband a teasing little kick.

Moving with surprising speed, the geriatric Larry caught her ankle, bent over and kissed it, making both of them laugh.

There was still a spark there—Derek could even see it from where he was. And it helped him understand why Gia felt so strongly about not letting anything separate them.

Which made him think that there was also something so appealing—and even sexy—about that understated fierceness Gia had shown for her cause, about the energy she'd put into saving them, about how much she cared.

Again, it wasn't banner carrying or picketing or loud protesting—it had just been donation jars and a savings account and her yard sale and hard work getting the word out, and yet he admired her methods more than anything that had come before her.

He admired her....

And the longer he sat there thinking about her, watching the Bronsons and feeling the way he did, the more he knew that he just wanted to be part of a couple like they were, as long as the other person could be Gia.

Gia, who he suddenly knew was that *right person* Louie had talked about.

Gia, whose passion and sexiness were understated, too, until they were unleashed in the bedroom.

But Gia had shown him the door....

With good reason, he admitted then.

Because even he had thought she might be a subconscious overcompensation for the Vegas debacle. A sharp recoil from that to someone who was the exact opposite.

Even he had thought that when that recoil subsided he probably wouldn't be so infatuated with her. That he might revert to his old pattern and lose interest in her....

"God, you're an idiot," he said to himself as he realized that what he felt for Gia wasn't just infatuation. It wasn't about what had happened in Vegas.

He'd fallen in love with her.

That was why it was the way it was—the way she'd said it was between Larry and Marion. That was why it didn't take anything big or flashy or freaky for her to light up a room for him. All she had to do was walk into it.

That was why he thought every tiny detail about her was so special and intriguing and brilliant.

That was why it didn't matter to him that the wildest thing about her was her hair.

That was why he was going out of his mind without her.

And that was all why he had to get her back.

If he could....

The thought that he might not be able to sent him into a tailspin.

She'd stopped everything cold.

She hadn't given him even a hope for things to go on.

She wouldn't even talk to him on the phone about anything except the Bronsons.

The Bronsons...

Who were sitting on their porch at that moment.

Who she just might listen to if he could get them on his side....

Had he found enough favor with them to get *them* to play go-between with Gia?

He was afraid he hadn't.

But at that point he was willing to try anything.

Anything!

He had to.

Because suddenly he knew that the rest of his life was at stake. That Gia was the only one for him. And that if he couldn't convince her of that, he was never going to have what the Bronsons had.

So he restarted his engine, waited for a break in traffic and moved from his watching spot to park at the curb partially in front of the Bronsons' house and partially in front of Gia's.

Hoping *this* didn't get the hose turned on him....

Chapter Eleven

"You're having Larry and Marion get you in my door?"

When Gia's doorbell rang Sunday evening, she was surprised to peer through her peephole and see her elderly neighbors on her front porch.

And that was all she'd been able to see through her peephole.

Of course, she'd opened her door to them instantly.

Which was when she saw Derek standing at the bottom of the porch steps behind them.

"I figured if I could convince them, maybe they'd help me convince you," he said, coming up to join the Bronsons.

"Convince me of what?"

"We think you should hear him out, sweetheart," Marion said before he could answer her question.

"We saw his car out here the other morning," Larry contributed.

Gia had been grateful that they hadn't mentioned that before. Tyson had. But not the Bronsons.

"We know you, Gia," Marion continued. "We knew when we saw that that we were right about you—you're taken with this man. And we know you've been putting on a cheery face for us, but we can see you've been sad since he hasn't been around—"

"We blamed him—" Larry added, still easily falling into his old familiar criticism of the Camdens.

"But he says it was you who kicked him to the curb—is that right?" Marion asked.

"I didn't… I just thought that for all our sakes… Yes, it was me…." Gia stammered her admission under her breath because she was embarrassed to have to be talking even in a roundabout way about the night she'd spent with Derek. The night that had unleashed too many things in her and caused her to suffer horribly without him ever since….

"Well, we've heard him out and we think you should, too," Marion concluded.

"But if you need us we're right next door. And you know I can come running if I have to," Larry said with a still-not-completely-trusting glance out of the corner of his eye at Derek.

"Just talk to him," Marion encouraged. "Then, if you still want to hand him his walking papers, go ahead. But hear him out first."

The elderly woman took her husband by the arm then and turned him away from the door, tugging him toward the stairs.

"Right next door," Larry said over his shoulder, but Gia wasn't sure whether it was a reminder to her or a warning to Derek, who was now standing in front of her looking as tired as she felt. Though not as puffy eyed as she was from crying instead of sleeping since she'd sent him away....

"There's nothing to say," she told him when the Bronsons were headed next door again.

"I have a lot to say," he insisted firmly. "A lot to say that I just figured out—and if it helps, part of it is that you were right."

"Then why do we need to talk?" she asked. She didn't think she was strong enough to listen to him confirm that it wouldn't have worked out between them. It was bad enough having to go through what she was already going through without adding to it by hearing it from his own lips.

Lips she wanted to be kissing, in spite of everything, and was suffering with the knowledge that that would never happen again....

"You need to hear me out because you *were* right—past tense—to think what you were thinking. But now that I've had some time to come to grips with myself and what's really going on with me, to open my eyes... you aren't right anymore."

About which part? He still had a huge family to appease, a huge family he was intensely loyal to, and he still had a pattern for the kind of woman he wanted.

So Gia remained standing on her threshold, blocking his way, staring at him and wishing things were different but reminding herself of the realities that had caused her to send him away in the first place.

"Do I have to bring Larry and Marion over here again to get me in the door?" he threatened.

"I can't believe you talked them into getting you this far," Gia said, because while she'd persuaded the Bronsons to accept all the Camdens were doing for them, they still had hard feelings about the past. They wouldn't have conceded had she not convinced them all over again that what they were getting was nothing more than the Camdens owed them. That it was restitution they were rightfully due, and that Derek had admitted as much to her.

"They brought me here because they believed me when I told them what I just want the chance to say to you."

Gia continued to study him and keep him cooling his heels on her porch as she argued with herself.

She trusted the Bronsons, so if they'd brought him to her, they had to have felt that what he had to say was worth hearing.

And even though she didn't want to feel it, there was also hope—however fruitless it might be. Hope that there was something—anything—he could tell her that could fix things....

She sighed and swiveled so that her back was to the inside door, her arm outstretched to keep the screen door open, freeing a path for him to pass in front of her and come in.

He did, the scent of his cologne wafting to her along the way and making her wilt and pray for the strength not to give in to just anything that might mean she could be with him again....

Once he was inside, she closed the door and stood with her back against it, watching him again as he moved several feet into the living room before he turned to face her.

Why did he have to look like that? she bemoaned silently. Because even appearing as if he hadn't slept any more than she had since Wednesday night, he was still a sight for her very sore eyes in gray slacks and a black sport shirt that made him look dark and dashing.

And here she was in a pair of old jeans and a double layer of tank tops—gray over white—with her hair haphazardly pulled up into a ponytail to get the unruly curls out of her face.

"I just came from GiGi's Sunday dinner," he began. "I couldn't get past hating that you weren't there with me. And I also couldn't help thinking that if you said to them what you said to me on Thursday about being with you just to please them, it would have made them all laugh and scoff. It would have caused an uproar. Because I'm the last one in the family who'd do anything just for that reason. And I'm sure—especially after Vegas—that they wish I would."

"Maybe subconsciously you are," she suggested.

"Not subconsciously, not unconsciously, not consciously. When it comes to you, I might as well be an orphan, because nothing to do with you has *anything* to do with them. So take that off the table right now!" he commanded.

Gia didn't say anything to that.

"And you need to get something else straight about my family," he continued. "Yes, I'm loyal to them. But when any one of us partners up or starts a family, *none* of us expects to take priority over the relationship—"

"In an emergency—"

"A flat tire is not an emergency," he said, referring to the story she'd told him about her ex-husband. "And even in an emergency there are lots of us—whoever is available would show up. But if you didn't need me and I was the one running to help them, I'd drag you along so I could have you with me—because I'd *want* to have you with me, I wouldn't want to do it alone."

That carried weight for her. Leaving her behind was something Elliot had done whenever he'd answered any call from his family, emergency or not. Nothing would have pleased her more than if he'd actually wanted to have her by his side. He just never had.

"And when any one of us *chooses* someone," Derek went on, "that someone becomes family. So completely that I'm willing to bet you that of all the people you met last Sunday there's at least one or two you think were born Camdens who weren't...."

He was wrong. She knew exactly who the Camdens were and who among them weren't.

But she also knew what he was getting at because the more she'd thought about that dinner a week ago, the more she'd acknowledged to herself that spouses and fiancés of the Camdens were not treated the way spouses and fiancés of the Grants had been. That even she hadn't felt as much like an outsider with them as she had among the Grants right to the end of her marriage to Elliot.

"I know that your family *now* is different than the Grants," was all she said to that.

"But even though you were dead wrong about the family stuff," he went on in a more peacemaking tone, "it was reasonable for you to look at my history and figure there was some cause for concern about where my taste in women has led me before. To worry that it might lead me there again...."

If the Bronsons had gotten him in her front door so he could tell her she was right to stop things from going any further between them because she wasn't his type, she wasn't sure she'd be able to forgive them. Because she wasn't sure she could bear to hear him say it.

"There's just one really, really big factor that you couldn't have known about," Derek continued. "You couldn't have known about it because I just realized it myself...."

Gia raised her chin in question, steeling herself for the worst.

"I never actually had a weakness or proclivity for bad girls or rule breakers or psychics or zealots or weirdos in general. It's that their…colorfulness…offered enough of an extra to cover up the fact that I didn't actually feel much for them. A little attraction, sure. But that's all. So what their oddity or fervor about things did was fill a gap. They provided a few thrills and chills—entertainment—that distracted from the fact that I could take the women themselves or leave them. And with the few normal women… Well, there was nothing to cover up the fact that I could take them or leave them, so I—"

"Left them," Gia concluded fatalistically, still afraid he was acknowledging that she was in that category.

"That makes it sound worse than it was. My interest in them just ran out quicker," he amended. "But tonight—after being so down since Thursday morning that I've been pathetic, when I was actually parked down the street just hoping to be able to see you through your window or on your porch or in your yard—it came to me…."

He shook his head as if he couldn't believe he'd been so dumb.

"It came to me when I compared how I feel about you with how I felt about each and every one of the women I've dated or been involved with. It came to me that I've just never had strong feelings for any one of them. There was just more of a charge if there was something else going on with them."

Gia wasn't sure she'd heard him correctly. For all she knew, hope was skewing her understanding.

"How you feel about me?" she said softly.

And then he told her.

He told her about watching the Bronsons on their

front porch. About seeing for himself what was between them. About wanting that for himself. Wanting it with her and only with her. About how and why every little thing about her gave him chills and thrills. About how she fascinated and interested him. Endlessly…

"And it isn't even just what I already know about you," he went on. "It's that I can't wait to see what will come next—what you might do, what you might say, the way you might look on the beach at sunset or bundled in ski gear on top of a mountain. I can't wait to see you pregnant. I can't wait to see how you'll be as a wife, as a mom, as a grandma and a little old lady…."

Just the thought of that made him laugh and take a step closer to her before he said, "I love you, Gia. You're my Marion…."

But could he be her Larry?

"I have to think…." she said.

"Think. All you want. I'll wait. But I'm not getting out of here," he said, planting one hip on the arm of her couch to prove it. "It was too hard to get back in. Larry and Marion weren't easy to convince."

Because of what they thought of the Camdens in general, Gia surmised.

But in thinking that, she could honestly say that she believed the current Camdens weren't unscrupulous or unethical the way the Grants were, the way previous generations of Camdens had been.

She'd watched all Derek had done for the Bronsons, she'd tested and followed up to check out everything he'd claimed and promised and arranged, and she hadn't found that a single thing he'd said or done was anything but what it appeared to be.

Regardless of who or what had come before him, he was trustworthy. He was a man of his word.

And if he was a man of his word, then maybe she could believe him when he said that her appeal for him did *not* lie in the fact that she might be more acceptable to his family. That he wasn't trying to please them or make it up to them for having embarrassed them.

Which also meant that maybe she could believe him when he said that he would never put his family before her, too.

But what about the rest? The most important part of it all? Could his feelings for her keep him interested?

She didn't know. How did anyone ever know if someone they loved would go on loving them and finding them interesting?

That was the leap of faith that had to be taken, but she'd already taken it once and failed. And Elliot hadn't seemed like a risk at all....

Because Elliot had only shown her what he wanted her to see, she thought. About himself. About his family. About everything.

But when she thought about it, she realized that that wasn't true of Derek. Despite the fact that she'd worried about it, feared it, been suspicious, there hadn't been any subterfuge from Derek. And not merely when it came to the Bronsons.

He hadn't hidden anything about his past from her, including his history with unusual women and the trouble it had gotten him into.

He hadn't even hidden what he was most ashamed and embarrassed about—the Las Vegas wedding.

Instead, he'd been open with her. Honest with her even at his own expense. As open and honest with her as Larry and Marion were with each other.

No, there hadn't been any subterfuge, nothing superficial from him at all. Not the way there had been with Elliot.

So maybe she could trust that what was between them was real....

More real than what she'd had with Elliot.

But real enough to take a second leap of faith?

Somewhere along the way she'd dropped her head and stared at the floor, but now she raised her gaze to Derek, wondering...

But one look at him made her doubts begin to dwindle.

Because there he was, not only incredibly handsome and so hot she wanted to fling herself at him, but looking as if he'd been through the same kind of agony she'd gone through since they'd parted.

That wouldn't have been the case with Elliot—he'd have glided in making sure he looked his best to bowl her over. So it was actually preferable to see that Derek had suffered. It brought home to her that he really did have feelings for her. Feelings as intense as she had for him.

Because there he was, the man she'd come to see the merits of with her own two eyes, strong and powerful, promising to put her first—something Elliot would never agree to even when she'd pressed for it.

Because there he was, the man who had watched and listened and made sure that every little thing the Bronsons would ever need would be provided for them, the man who had started a foundation to help other people in their situation, because he was a caring, compassionate human being, not just to make himself and his family look good.

Because there he was, the man she loved.

She'd tried to deny it. To fool herself. But that was

the reason that sleeping with him had only gotten her in deeper.

She loved him. With all her heart.

And he was the one who made her want to become a wife again.

To become a mother.

He was the one she wanted to grow old with the way Larry and Marion had grown old together....

She took a breath, and he lifted his eyes to her face. His expression was full of hope, too. But also full of vulnerability—something else that only won her over all the more.

Then she pushed away from the door and went to him as he stood up as if to face sentencing.

"You're sure?" she whispered.

He smiled a smile that went straight to her heart. "More sure than I've ever been about anything. You *are* my Marion. If you'll just let me be your Larry..."

That brought tears to her eyes as she reached a hand to the side of his face, desperate just to drink in the warmth of his skin again.

"Marry me, Gia," he said then. "Say you'll marry me and I promise you I'll never stop kissing you until the day we die...."

She laughed and blinked back even more tears. "I'll hold you to that," she warned.

"You won't have to," he said, clasping his arms around her waist to pull her closer.

Then he did kiss her. Profoundly, before he stopped and repeated, "Say you'll marry me...."

It was all there in his eyes, in his voice—he wanted it from her as much as she wanted everything from him. He needed to hear her say it. Needed to know he could have what truly was his heart's desire....

"I will," she said without any hesitation now.

"And say that when I'm old and decrepit you'll rig my bed to fix whatever ails me," he joked.

"And when you're old and decrepit I'll rig your bed to fix whatever ails you," she pledged.

The small smile was replaced by a sober expression as his blue eyes delved into hers with pure sincerity. "I love you," he said quietly. "I love you more than any words can say."

"I love you, too. It's why I had to send you away Thursday—I loved you too much to pretend I didn't."

He nodded. "But don't do it again. I won't live through it."

"Never again," she vowed.

He kissed her then, and as Gia kissed him back her arms went around him and she let her whole body melt into his.

And just like that she knew.

She knew that there in his arms, their bodies fitted together flawlessly, was where she was meant to be.

Through good and bad.

From now until time stopped.

* * * * *

RESISTING HER
REBEL HERO

LUCY RYDER

I couldn't have done this without my wonderful supportive family, especially my beautiful daughters, Caitlin and Ashleigh. I love you to infinity and beyond. A special thanks to Dr Jenni Irvine who started it all and to Flo Nicoll for seeing something in my writing you liked.

And lastly to my colleagues—Ladies, it's amazing how people bond through complaining.

CHAPTER ONE

THE LAST PLACE Dr. Cassidy Mahoney expected to find herself when she fled the city for a wilderness town deep in the Cascades Mountains was the county jail. She could honestly say it was the first time she'd ever been in one, and with the smell of stale alcohol and something more basically human permeating the air, she hoped it was the last.

And absolutely nothing could have prepared her for *him*—all six feet four inches of broad shoulders and hard muscles, oozing enough testosterone to choke a roomful of hardened feminists.

Draped languorously over a narrow bunk that clearly couldn't contain his wide shoulders and long legs, the man lustily sang about a pretty *señorita* with dark flashing eyes and lips like wine. The old man in the neighboring cell cheerfully sang along, sounding like a rusty engine chugging up a mountain pass while his cellmate snored loudly enough to rattle the small windows set high in the outside wall.

Pausing in the outer doorway, Cassidy felt her eyes widen and wondered if she'd stepped onto a movie set without a script. The entire town of Crescent Lake had turned out to be like something from a movie set and she was still having a hard time believing she wasn't dreaming.

Quite frankly, even her wildest dreams couldn't have conjured up being escorted to the sheriff's office in a police cruiser like a seasoned offender—even to supply medical care to a prisoner.

From somewhere near the back of the holding area a loud voice cursed loudly and yelled at them to "shut the hell up." Hazel Porter, the tiny woman currently leading Cassidy into the unknown, pushed the door open all the way and gestured for her to follow.

"Full house tonight," Hazel rasped in her thirty-a-day voice, sounding like she'd been sucking on smokes since the cradle. "Must be full moon." She nodded to the cell holding the old-timers. "Don't mind them, honey: long-standing weekend reservations." Her bunch of keys jangled Cassidy's already ragged nerves.

"And ignore the guy in the back," Hazel advised. "Been snarlin' and snipin' since he was hauled in a couple hours ago. I was tempted to call in animal control, but the sheriff said to let him sleep it off."

"I'd be sleeping too, you old crow, if it wasn't for the caterwauling, stripping paint off the walls."

Hazel shook her head. "Mean as a cornered badger, that one," she snorted, closing the outer door behind them. "Even when he ain't drunk."

Cassidy sent the woman a wary look, a bit nervous at the thought of being closed in with a bunch of offenders—one of whom was apparently violent—and a pint-sized deputy who could be anything between sixty and a hundred and sixty.

"So…the patient?" she prompted uncertainly, hoping it wasn't the fun guy in back. Hippocratic oath aside, she drew the line at entering his cell without the sheriff, a couple of burly deputies and a fully charged stun gun as backup.

"That'll be Crescent Lake's very own superhero." Hazel headed for the baritone's cell and Cassidy couldn't help the relief that left her knees a bit shaky. "He's a recent addition and a wild one, so watch yerself," wasn't exactly something Cassidy wanted to hear.

The deputy slid a key into the lock and continued as though she'd known Cassidy for years. "Wasn't a bit surprising when he up 'n left med school to join the Navy." Her chuckle sounded like a raspy snort. "Heck, 'Born to be wild' shoulda been tattooed on that boy's hide at birth."

Cassidy blinked, unsure if she was meant to respond and uncertain what she would say if she did. She'd learnt over the past fortnight that mountain folk were for the most part polite and taciturn with strangers, but treated everyone's business like public property. She'd even overheard bets being placed on how long *she'd* last before she "hightailed it back to the city."

The sound of the key turning was unnaturally loud and Cassidy bit her lip nervously when the cell door slid open and clanged against the bars. Drawing in a shaky breath, she smoothed damp palms down her thighs and eyed the "born to be wild" man warily.

One long leg was bent at the knee; the other hung over the side of the bunk, large booted foot planted on the bare concrete floor. Although a bent arm blocked most of his face from view, Cassidy realized she was the object of intense scrutiny. Her first thought was, *God, he's huge,* followed almost immediately by, *And there's only a garden gnome's granny between me and Goliath's drunk younger brother.*

"Is that why he's in here?"

"Heck, no," Hazel rasped with a snort. "Was the only way Sheriff could be sure he stayed put till you arrived. Boy thinks he's too tough for a few stitches and a couple of sticking plasters."

Cassidy hovered outside the cell, aware that her heart was banging against her ribs like she was the one who'd committed a felony and was facing jail time. Besides, she'd heard all about people going missing in wilderness towns and had the oddest feeling the instant she stepped over the threshold her life would never be the same.

Turning, she caught the older woman watching her and gave a self-conscious shrug. "Is it safe? Shouldn't we wait for the sheriff? A couple of deputies?" A shock stick?

Small brown eyes twinkled. "Safe?" Hazel cackled as though the idea tickled her funny bone when Cassidy had been as serious as a tax audit. In Boston, violent offenders were always accompanied by several burly cops, even when they were restrained.

"Well, now," the deputy said, wiping the mirth from her eyes. "I don't know as the boy's ever been called 'safe' before, but if you're wondering if he'll get violent, don't you worry about a thing, hon. He's gentle as a lamb."

Cassidy's gaze slid to the "boy," who seemed to be all shoulders and legs, and thought, *Yeah, right.* Nothing about him looked gentle and "boy" wasn't something he'd been for a good long time. Not with that long, hard body or the toxic cloud of testosterone and pheromones filling the small space and snaking primitive warnings up her spine.

Even sprawled across the narrow bunk, he exuded enough masculine sexuality to have a cautious woman taking a hasty step in retreat.

Hazel Porter must have correctly interpreted the move for she cackled gleefully even as she planted a bony hand in the small of Cassidy's back and gave her a not-so-gentle shove into the cell.

Her pulse gave an alarmed little blip and Cassidy found herself swallowing a distressed yelp, which was ridiculous, considering he'd done nothing more dangerous than sing in that rich, smooth bedroom baritone.

"Whatcha got for me, sweetheart?" the deep voice drawled, sending a shiver of fear down Cassidy's spine. At least she thought the belly-clenching, free-falling sensation was fear as goose bumps rushed over her skin beneath the baby-pink scrubs top she hadn't had time to change out of. The baby-pink top that was covered in little bear doctors and nurses and an assortment of smears and stains from a day spent with babies and toddlers.

Not exactly the kind of outfit that gave a woman much-needed confidence when facing a large alpha male.

"You get the rare steak and fries I ordered?"

Hazel snorted. "We're not running some five-star establishment here, sonny," she rebuked mildly, eyeing him over her spectacles. "You wanted steak and fries you shoulda thought about that *before* you decided to pound on Wes."

A battered lip curved into a loopy grin. "Aw, c'mon, Hazel." He chuckled, sounding a little rusty, as though he hadn't had much to laugh about lately—or had awakened from a deep sleep. "He was drunker than a sailor on shore leave. The coeds he was hassling were terrified. 'Sides, *someone* had to stop him trashing Hannah's bar. He threw a *stool* at her when she tried to intervene, for God's sake."

"Your sister can handle herself," Hazel pointed out reasonably, to which the hunk sleepily replied, "Sure she can. We taught her some great moves." He yawned until his jaw cracked. "Jus' doin' my brotherly duty, 'sall."

"And look where that got you."

The man lifted a hand wrapped in a bloodied bar towel and peered down at his side. "Bonehead took me by surprise," he growled in disgust, wincing as he lowered his arm. "Was on me before I could convince them to leave." He grunted. "Better my hide than her pretty face, huh?"

"You're a good brother," Hazel said dryly.

A wide shoulder hitched. "Didn't you teach me to stand up to the bullies of this world, ma'am?"

"*Ri-ight*." Hazel snorted, beaming at him with affectionate pride. "Blame the helpless old lady."

The deep chuckle filling the tiny cell did odd things to Cassidy's insides and spread prickling warmth throughout her body. Her face heated and the backs of her knees tingled.

She uttered a tiny gasp.

Tingled? Really? Alarmed by her body's response, she backed up a step until she realized what she was doing and froze. Feeling her face heat, Cassidy drew in a shaky breath and took a determined step forward. She dropped her medical bag between his long hard thighs since he took up the rest of the bunk.

So what if she was dressed like a kindergarten teacher? She was a mature, professional woman who'd spent an entire day with babies and toddlers—not some silly naïve schoolgirl dazzled by a pair of wide shoulders, long legs and a deep bedroom voice.

Well…not usually. Besides, she'd already done that and was not going there again. *Tingling* of any sort. Was out.

"Nothin' helpless about you, darlin'," the bedroom voice drawled with another flash of even white teeth as Cassidy pulled out a pair of surgical gloves. She couldn't see his eyes but knew by the stillness of his body that he was tracking her every move.

"Save the sweet talk, sonny," Hazel sniffed, amused yet clearly not taken in by the charm. "And play nice. Miz Mahoney doesn't have time to waste on idiots."

Cassidy snapped on a latex glove and opened her mouth to correct the deputy's use of "Miz" but he shifted at that moment and every thought fled, leaving her numb with shock as she realized exactly who she was in a jail cell with.

Ohmigosh. Her eyes widened. *He really was a superhero.* Or rather Major Samuel J. Kellan, Crescent Lake's infamous Navy SEAL and all-round bad boy. She stared at him and wondered if she was hallucinating. Wasn't he supposed to be a local hero or something? Heck, a *national* hero?

What was he doing in the county jail?

Besides, he'd been injured protecting his sister and saving a couple of young women from harm. And according to local gossip, everyone adored him. Women swooned at the mention of his name and men tended to recount his exploits like he was some kind of legendary superhero. And *really.* There wasn't a man alive who could do *half* the things Major Kellan was rumored to have done and survived. Well…*not* outside Hollywood.

Yet, even battered and bruised, it was clear the man deserved his reputation as big, bad and dangerous to know. Looking into his battered face, it was just as clear that one thing *hadn't* been exaggerated. With his thick dark hair, fierce gold eyes, strong shadowed jaw and surprisingly sensual mouth, the man *was* as hot as women claimed. She could only be grateful she'd been immunized against fallen angels masquerading as wounded bad boys.

Frankly, the *last* thing she needed in her life was another man with more sex appeal than conscience. Heck, the last thing she needed, *period*, was a man—especially one who tended to suck the air right out of a room and make the backs of her knees sweat.

Hazel cleared her throat loudly, jolting Cassidy from her bizarre thoughts. "Anything you need before you sew up his pretty face, hon?"

"He really should be taken to the hospital," Cassidy said briskly, ignoring the strong smell of hops and thickly lashed eyes watching her every move. "I'll need a lot more supplies than I have with me. Supplies I can only get at the hospital." Especially if the hand wound was serious. Nerve damage was notoriously tricky to repair.

"Not to worry," Hazel rasped cheerfully. "Sheriff keeps all kinds of stuff ready for when the doc's called in unexpectedly. I'll pull Larry off front desk and send him in. You'll have your ER in a jiffy." And before Cassidy could tell the woman a jail cell was hardly a sterile environment, the desk sergeant disappeared, leaving her standing there gaping at empty space and wondering if she'd taken a left turn somewhere into an alternate universe where pint-sized deputies left unsuspecting young doctors alone in jail cells with a violent offender and…and *him*.

Her heart jerked hard against her ribs and a prickle of alarm eased up her spine. The closest thing she had to a weapon was a syringe and, frankly, even tanked, her patient looked like he could disarm her with a flick of one long-fingered hand.

Frowning, she slid a cautious look over her shoulder, trying to decide if she should make a break for it, when his voice enfolded her like rich, sinful chocolate. It took her a moment to realize that she had bigger problems.

"Hey, darlin'," he drawled, "wha's a nice girl like you doin' in a place like this?"

You have got to be kidding me.

Ignoring the lazy smile full of lethal charm, Cassidy sent him a sharp assessing look and wondered if his head injury was worse than it appeared. According to gossip, Major Hotstuff—her staff's name for him, not hers—was smooth as hundred-year-old bourbon and just as potent. *That* line had been about as smooth as a nerd in a room full of cheerleaders.

Opening her mouth to tell him that she'd heard more original pickup lines from paralytic drunks and whacked-out druggies, Cassidy's gaze locked with his and she was abruptly sucked into molten eyes filled with humor and sharp intelligence. Whether it was a trick of the light or the leashed power in his big, hard body, she was left with the weirdest impression that he wasn't nearly as drunk as he seemed, which was darned confusing, since he smelled like a brewery on a hot day.

This close she could clearly make out the dark ring encircling those unusual irises, and with the light striking his eyes from the overhead fixture, the tiny amber flecks scattered in the topaz made them appear almost gold. Like a sleek, silent jaguar.

A frisson of primitive awareness raced over her skin

and she tore her gaze from his, thinking, *Get a grip, Cassidy. He's the pied piper of female hormones. He seduces women to pass the time, for heaven's sake. And we are so done with that, remember?* Unfortunately, the appalling truth was that *her* hormones, frozen for far too long, had chosen the worst possible moment to awaken.

Annoyed and a little spooked, she drew her brows together and reached for his hand, abruptly all business. She was here to do a job, she reminded herself sharply, not get her hormones overhauled.

But the instant their skin touched, a jolt of electricity zinged up her arm to her elbow.

She yanked at her hand and stumbled back a step. Her head went light, her knees wobbled and she felt like she'd just been zapped by a thousand volts of live current. He must have felt it too because he grunted and looked startled, leaving Cassidy struggling with the urge to check if her hair was on fire.

Realizing her mouth was hanging open, she snapped it closed and reminded herself this was just another example of static electricity. *Big deal. Absolutely nothing to get excited about. Happens all the time.*

However, one look out the corner of her eye made her question whether the thin mountain air was killing off brain cells because Crescent Lake's hotshot hero could hardly be termed "just another" *anything*. With his thick, nearly black hair mussed around his head like a dark halo, glowing gold eyes and fallen-angel looks, he was about as ordinary as a tiger shark in a goldfish bowl.

Giving her head a shake, Cassidy realized she was getting a little hysterical and probably looked like an idiot standing there gaping at him like he'd grown horns and a tail.

Exhaling in a rush, she looked around for the missing glove. And spied it on the bunk.

Right between his hard jeans-clad thighs.

Her body went hot and her mouth went dry because, *holy Toledo*, those jeans fit him like they'd been molded to…well, *everything*.

Tearing her gaze away from checking out places she had no business checking out, she reached for the latex glove and gasped when their hands collided. He picked up the glove and held it out, tightening his grip when she reached for it. Her automatic "Thank you" froze in her throat when she looked up and caught his sleepy gaze locked on her… mouth. After a long moment his eyes rose.

Cassidy's pulse took off like a sprinter off the starting blocks and all she could think was… *No! Oh, no. Not happening, Cassidy. Get your mind on the job.*

Her brow wrinkling with irritation, she tugged and told herself she was probably just light-headed from all the fresh mountain air. Dr. Mahoney did *not* flutter just because some bad boy looked at her with his sexy eyes or talked in a rough baritone that she felt all the way to her belly.

"Excuse me?" she said in a tone that was cool and barely polite.

"I don't bite," he slurred with a loopy grin. "Unless you ask real nice."

Narrowing her gaze, she yanked the glove free and considered smacking him with it. She was not there to play games with some hotshot Navy SEAL, thank you very much.

Setting her jaw, she wrestled with the glove a moment then reached for his hand when she was suitably protected.

"So…" he drawled after a long silence, during which she removed the blood-soaked bar towels to examine his injury, "where's the cute white outfit?"

She looked up to catch him frowning at her pink scrubs top and jeans. "White outfit?"

"Yeah. You know…white, short, lots of little buttons?" He leaned sideways to scan the empty cell. "And where's the box?"

"Box?" *What the heck was he talking about?*

"The boom box," he said, as though she was missing a few IQ points. "Can't dance without music."

What?

"I am not a stripper, Major Kellan," she said coolly, barely resisting the urge to grind her teeth. "And nurses don't wear those any more." She was accustomed to being mistaken for a nurse and on occasion an angel. But a stripper was a new one and she didn't know whether to laugh or stab him with her syringe. Instead, she lifted a hand to brush a thick lock of dark hair off his forehead to check his head wound. He had to be hemorrhaging in there somewhere to have mistaken her for a stripper. Her hair was pulled back in a messy ponytail and her makeup had worn off hours ago.

So not stripper material.

"You're not?" He sounded disappointed. She ignored him. The wound only needed a few butterfly strips and he'd probably have a whopping headache on top of a hangover. *Hmph. That's what you get for making a woman flutter without her permission, hotshot.*

His left eye was almost swollen shut and a bruise had already turned the skin around it a dark mottled red. She gently probed the area and found no shifting under the skin. No cracked bones, but he'd have a beaut of a shiner and his split lip looked painful enough to put a crimp in his social life.

No kissing in his *immediate future.*

Wondering where that thought had come from, Cassidy reached into the bag for packaged alcohol swabs. "He did a good job on your face," she murmured, dabbing at the wound.

Something lethal came and went in his expression, too quickly for Cassidy to interpret. But when he smirked and said, "You should see the other guys," she decided she must have been mistaken and finally gave in to the mental eye roll that had been threatening. Other *guys*?

Maybe he'd been listening to too many stories about his own exploits.

"And I guess the knife wasn't clean either?"

He grunted, but as she wasn't fluent in manspeak, she was unsure if he was agreeing with her or in pain. "Broken beer bottle. Talk about a cliché," he snorted roughly. "And forget the tetanus shot. Had one a few months ago… so I'm good."

Good? It was her turn to snort—silently, of course.

Her obvious skepticism prompted an exasperated grimace. "I'm not drunk."

She eyed him suspiciously. "You're not?"

He shook his head and yawned again. "Just tired. An' it's Friday," he reminded her as though she should know what he was talking about.

"Been carousing it up with the boys, have you?"

His look was reproachful. "Fridays are busy and Hannah's usual bartender has food poisoning."

"So, you were what?" Cassidy inquired dryly. "Keeping the peace as you served up whiskey and bar nuts?"

His gold eyes gleamed with appreciation and his battered lip curved in a lopsided smile. "If you're worried, you could always stay the night. Just to be sure I'm not suffering from anything…fatal."

Flicking on a penlight, Cassidy leaned closer. "I'm sure that won't be necessary, Major," she responded dryly, checking his pupil reaction. The only fatal thing *he* was suffering from was testosterone overload.

She stepped back to pick up another alcohol swab, before returning to press it to the bloodied cut above his eye. His hissed reaction had her gentling her touch as she cleaned it. "How much did you have to drink?"

"A couple," he murmured, then responded to her narrow-eyed survey with a cocky smile that looked far too

harmless for a man with his reputation. "Of sodas," he
added innocently, and her assessing look turned specu-
lative. For a man who slurred like a drunk and smelled
as though he'd bathed in beer, his gaze was surprisingly
sharp and clear.

"I don't drink on the job," he said, hooking a finger in
the hem of her top, and giving a little tug. His knuckles
brushed against bare skin and sent goose bumps chasing
across her skin. "Beer and stupidity don't mix well."

"Mmm," she hummed, straight-faced, turning away to
hide her body's reaction to that casual touch. "Do you need
help removing your shirt?" she asked over her shoulder
as she cleared away the soiled swabs. "I want to see your
torso."

He was silent for a few beats and when the air thickened,
she lifted her gaze and her breath caught. "Your…um…
torso wound, I mean." It was no wonder he had women
swooning all over the county.

As though reading her thoughts, his lips curled, drawing her reluctant gaze. The poet's mouth and long inky
lashes should have looked ridiculously feminine on a man
so blatantly male but they only made him appear harder,
more masculine somehow.

"Isn't that supposed to be my line?"

Cursing the fair complexion that heated beneath his
wicked gaze, Cassidy injected a little more frost into her
tone. "Excuse me?"

His grin widened and he let out a rusty chuckle. "I like
the way you say that. All cool and snooty and just a little
bit superior."

Leveling him with a look one generally reserved for ill-
mannered adolescents, Cassidy queried mildly, "Are you
flirting with me, Major Kellan?"

"Me?" Then he chuckled. "If you have to ask," he
drawled, leaning so close that she found herself retreating

in an attempt to evade his potent masculine scent, "then I guess I'm out of practice."

She said, "Uh huh," and reached for the hem of his torn, bloodied T-shirt, pulling it from his waistband. The soft cotton was warm from his body and reeked of beer and something intrinsically male. She hastily drew it over his head and dropped it onto the bunk, ignoring his finely sculpted warrior's body. It had been a long time since she'd found herself this close to a man who made her want to bury her nose in his throat and breathe in warm manly skin.

But medical professionals didn't go around sniffing people's necks or drooling over every set of spectacular biceps, triceps or awesome abs that ended up in their ER. And they certainly didn't get the urge to follow that silky-looking happy trail that disappeared into a low-riding waistband with their lips either.

Or they shouldn't, she lectured herself sternly, considering the last one had left her with a deep sense of betrayal and a determination not to get sucked in again by a set of hard abs and a wicked smile.

Relieved to focus on something other than silky hair and warm manly skin, she leaned closer to probe the wound, murmuring an apology when he gave a sharp hiss. Over three inches long, it angled upwards towards his pec and the surrounding area was already darkening into what looked like the shape of a fist. Wincing, she ran the tips of her fingers over the bruised area just as the outer door banged opened, slamming against the wall.

The sound was as loud and unexpected as a gunshot. In a blur of eerily silent movement, Major Kellan surged off the bunk, shoving her roughly aside as he dropped into a crouch. Deadly menace slashed the air, sending Cassidy stumbling backwards.

She gave a shocked gasp and gaped at a wide, perfectly proportioned, perfectly tanned, muscular back bare inches from her face.

CHAPTER TWO

INSTANTLY ALERT AND battle-ready, Sam barely felt the burn of his injured palm or the line of fire streaking across his belly. Adrenaline and blood stormed his system and in some distant corner of his brain he realized it was happening. Again. *Dammit.*

Not now. Please, not now.

But he was helpless to stop it—helpless against the firestorm of images that tended to explode in his brain—instantly warping his sense of reality and triggering an instinct to protect. With deadly force.

From somewhere behind him he heard a gasp, and the young deputy entering the holding area abruptly stopped in his tracks.

One look at Sam and the kid's eyes widened to dinner plates. He went sheet-white and dropped the fold-up steel table. It teetered a moment then toppled over with loud clatter. The deputy jerked back as though he'd been prodded with a shock stick.

"M-Major K-Kellan?" he squeaked, his wide-eyed look of terrified embarrassment reaching Sam as though from a distance.

"It's just m-me, M-Major Kellan. L-Larry?"

Pain lanced through Sam's skull and he staggered, clutching his head. Sweat broke out along his spine so abruptly he felt dizzy. His strength drained, along with the surge of adrenaline that had fired his synapses and instinctively turned him into a lethal weapon. It had also turned him into something he didn't recognize any more. Something he didn't like.

Sam forced back the bile that came with particularly bad flashbacks—triggered no doubt by the violence of the evening and the sudden unexpected noise. *Dammit*. He wanted to smash his fist into the wall and roar with anger and despair.

But he couldn't…*couldn't* lose control now. Not with an audience.

The blood drained abruptly from his head, leaving him clammy and light-headed. "Dammit, Larry," he growled, and sagged as though someone had cut him off at the knees.

Squeezing his eyes closed to block out the wildly spinning cell, he staggered and hoped he wouldn't embarrass himself by passing out—or tossing his cookies. He could just imagine what the sexy nurse would think about the hotshot SEAL then.

"I'm s-sorry, M-Major…it's just that I had b-both hands f-full."

He felt her an instant before her arms wrapped around him, easing him backwards, soft and silky and smelling like cool mountain air. Mortified, Sam pulled away and collapsed wearily onto the narrow bunk, slinging an arm across his face.

"Don' sweat it, kid," he slurred, and prayed for oblivion. Unfortunately, sleep always came with a heavy price and he wasn't ready to go there. The nightmares were still too real, the memories too raw, the latest flashback still too recent. So vivid he could taste the fear, hear the furious pounding of his pulse in his head.

The Navy shrinks had warned that they'd get worse before they got better. They'd also warned that they'd last for years.

Well, hell. Just what he was looking forward to. A constant reminder of his greatest failure.

"Major Kellan?"

In the meantime he had to face Nurse…what's-her-name.

Swiping his good hand over his face, he eased open his eyes and focused on the statuesque blonde watching him warily and with more than a hint of concern.

He didn't want her pity—or anything else she had to offer. He wanted to be left alone. *Needed* to be left alone. "I'm fine," he snapped, furious with himself and embarrassed that she'd witnessed an episode. Hoping to distract his brain from the endless loop of horrifying images, Sam focused his attention on her.

Yeah, much better to focus on the nurse.

With her thick silvery blond hair haphazardly pulled off a stunning face dominated by deep green eyes and a lush wide mouth, she looked like a sexy angel and smelled like a wood sprite—all fresh and clean and earthy like the mountains in spring. Raindrops glistened in her hair like diamonds, giving her an ethereal quality that made him wonder if he *was* drunk or just plain losing it.

"No, you're not," she contradicted softly. "But you will be."

For one confused moment Sam wondered if he'd spoken his thoughts out loud before he remembered he'd said he was fine.

"Sure," he growled, clenching his teeth on a wave of grief and anger. I *will. But my friends are still dead. And the woman patching me up thinks Crescent Lake's hero is a whacked-out crazy with a drinking problem.*

Yeah, right. Hero. What a joke.

Heroes didn't let their teams down. They didn't return home with their buddies in body bags no matter what the Navy shrinks said. But his week of detention in a small, dark hole, deep in mountainous enemy territory wasn't something he talked about. He could barely *think* about it let alone talk about the hours of interrogation and torture that had left half his team dead.

The only reason *he'd* survived long enough to escape had been because they'd found out he was a medic and wanted him to treat some sick kid. He'd tried to bargain until they let his team go but they'd dragged in the team rookie and held a gun to his head. Afterwards they'd—

No. Don't go there. Not when the horror was still so fresh in his mind that every time he closed his eyes, he was back in that hellhole.

"Major Kellan?"

Jolted from his unpleasant thoughts, Sam saw the syringe and shot out his hand to wrap hard fingers around her wrist. Other than a slight widening of her eyes, the nurse held her ground without flinching. After a couple of tense beats she arched her brow, the move managing to convey a boatload of indulgent concern. Like he was a cranky toddler up past his bedtime. He groaned silently. *Just great.*

His face heated and he narrowed his eyes but she silently held his gaze, like he wasn't almost a foot taller, a hundred pounds heavier, and a whole hell of a lot meaner.

Clearly the woman was missing a few IQ points, he decided with a mix of admiration and annoyance, or she wasn't as soft and silky as she looked. He closed his eyes on a surge of self-disgust. All he needed to complete his humiliation was for her to ruffle his hair and kiss his "owie" better.

Way to go, hotshot.

"Do I need to wave a white flag or are you a friendly?" she asked with a hint of amusement, and when his lashes rose, she indicated the hand wrapped around her wrist.

He grimaced and released her. *Jeez, could this get any worse?* Embarrassment had him muttering, "I don't hit women." He jerked his chin at the syringe. "Unless they're armed."

She followed his gaze. "Oh, this?" Her mouth curved

sweetly into a smile that instantly made him suspicious *and* want to take a greedy bite of that lush lower lip. "Surely you're not afraid of a little needle, Major?" Her smile grew as though she'd just learnt his deepest, darkest secret. *Not even close, lady.* "A big tough SEAL like you?" She made a soothing sound in the back of her throat. "It won't hurt a bit. Trust me."

Sam grunted out a laugh and hauled himself into a sitting position, hissing through clenched teeth when the move sent pain radiating through his chest and burning across his belly. "That's what they all say," he growled. "Right before they stab you in the heart."

"Not to worry," she said, moving closer and wrapping him in clean mountain air. "I have no interest in your heart, Major. I'm aiming a little lower than that."

And then, as though suddenly realizing what she'd said, her cheeks turned pink and she sucked in a sharp breath while Sam choked out a stunned "*Huh?*" and dropped his uninjured hand to protect his crotch.

"Not th-that low," she stuttered with a strangled snicker. "Although I'd probably be doing the rest of the female population a favor."

He choked for the second time in as many seconds but before he could demand what she meant, the outer door banged open again and she froze, eyes jerking to his, all wide and apprehensive as though she expected him to go all psycho GI Joe on her.

Dammit. He did not go around terrorizing women. Well…not unless they were holding a machine gun on him. Then all bets were off.

Scowling, he opened his mouth to tell her to knock it off, but his brother strode into the holding cells looking all officious and in charge, and Sam turned his irritation on someone more deserving.

Unfortunately, one look at Ruben's face had Sam's annoyance abruptly fading. He knew that look. Had seen it a thousand times on his CO's face. Something was up. Something bad.

"I hope you haven't used that on him yet." Ruben tossed an armful of clothing onto the bunk. "Get dressed," he told Sam. "We're heading out."

Blondie gasped and stepped between them. "What—? No!" she hissed. "Are you insane?"

Sam ignored her outburst and rose, pain abruptly receding as his SEAL training took over. "What happened?"

"A group of hikers didn't check in after closing," Ruben said, his wary gaze flicking to the syringe, "and the weather's turned bad. Park rangers just found their vehicle up near Pike's Pass. Lake route turned up empty and they think the group took the trail leading up into the mountains."

"Elk Ridge," Sam guessed, fatigue instantly forgotten as adrenaline surged through his veins. Here was the opportunity he hadn't even realized he'd been waiting for, to get out there and do something more useful than working the taps at his sister's bar. Frankly, after months of "recuperation" he was thoroughly sick of his own company and damn tired of sitting around feeling sorry for himself.

Ruben nodded and backed away, keeping a wary eye on Cassidy, as though expecting her to use the syringe on *him*. "Can't you just wrap him up or something? My usual tracker had a family emergency and we're in a hurry."

Her eyes widened. "Wrap—? He's not a cheeseburger," she snapped, sending Ruben's eyebrows into his hairline. "And in case it escaped your notice, Sheriff, the major is bleeding, *and* he's been drinking. It would be suicidal to go climbing mountains in his condition. I'm going to insist you leave him here. Or, better yet, let me take him to the hospital."

Sam brushed past her to where Larry had set out the medical supplies. "I'm fine," he said brusquely, reaching for a wound dressing. "I told you I wasn't drunk."

Before he could open the packet she snatched it from him and shoved her shoulder into his side as though she'd physically keep him from leaving.

As if.

He would have snickered at the absurdity if he hadn't been sucking in a painful breath. Turning a scowl on her that usually had people backing off in a hurry, she surprised him with a snapped "Back it up, Major," clearly not intimidated by his big bad Navy SEAL attitude.

He gave an annoyed grunt and tried to snatch it back.

"I mean it," she warned, jabbing her finger into his chest. "Or I'll use the syringe and the sheriff will have no choice but to go without you." She narrowed her eyes at him when he continued to glare at her while contemplating letting her try.

Heck, he might even enjoy it.

"And FYI, *buddy*, I nearly got intoxicated on the alcoholic haze surrounding you when I arrived, and not five minutes ago you almost fell on your face. You are *not* in any condition to go anywhere, least of all into the mountains on S&R. Besides," she reasoned sweetly, "you're bleeding all over the sheriff's nice clean jail cell. You need stitches." She paused and dropped her eyes meaningfully to his hand and then his abdomen. "Lots of them."

Staring down at her, Sam felt his lips twitch. She was like an enraged kitten—all fierce green eyes and ruffled silver fur. For just an instant he was tempted to reach out and smooth his hands over all that soft skin and silky silvery blond hair until she purred. One look into her narrowed eyes, however, and Sam knew she would probably bite his hand off at the wrist if he tried.

He made a scoffing sound filled with masculine impatience and amusement, which only served to narrow her eyes even further. "I've had mosquito bites worse than this," he assured her, feeling unaccountably cheered by her concern. "And if you're worried about blood alcohol levels, I'm sure the sheriff can organize a breathalyzer."

For long tense moments they engaged in a silent battle of wills until she finally uttered a soft "*Aargh*" followed by "Fine" in a tone that clearly meant it wasn't, and Sam had to clench his teeth to keep from grinning. He had a feeling grinning would be bad for his health.

"Oh…and FYI, *sweetheart*," he continued, while she sorted through the supplies with barely leashed temper, "I wasn't drinking. The weasel tried to break a bottle over my head. When I ducked, it shattered against the bar and soaked into my shirt. That was *before* he tried to gut me with it."

She turned towards him with a derisive sound and raised a brow that clearly conveyed her opinion of his explanation. "I said fine, didn't I?"

"You most certainly did," Ruben said dryly, shoving his face between them. "But I'm still not seeing anything happening here, people." He waited a couple of beats as his gaze ping-ponged between them. "So if you kids could save the lovers' spat for another time, I'd like my chief tracker."

Feeling her face catch fire, Cassidy broke eye contact with the Navy SEAL to send the sheriff a long, silent, narrow-eyed look that had him backing away with his hands up.

She turned back to snap, "Lift your arm." When he did she swiped disinfectant across the angry gash, completely ignoring the hissed response to her cavalier treatment.

After a long murmured conversation during which she cleaned and applied a few adhesive cross-strips to keep the edges of the wound together, the sheriff left. Cassidy knew the instant the SEAL's attention shifted back to her because the tiny hairs on the back of her neck prickled.

With unsteady hands she dressed his wound then cleaned and tightly wrapped his hand in a waterproof dressing, before turning away to gather the debris.

The length of her back heated an instant before a long tanned arm reached over her shoulder to snag a bandage. Cursing the way her skin prickled and her body tightened with some kind of weird anticipation, she sent a dark look over her shoulder and watched in silence as he awkwardly attempted to wrap it around his torso. After a moment she sighed and put out her hand, saying wearily, "I'll do it."

Clearly surprised by her offer, Samuel held her gaze for a long tension-filled moment. His laugh was a husky rasp in the tense silence and did annoying things to her breathing. "You're not going to strangle me with it, are you?"

Cassidy knew the taping would help him move—and breathe—more comfortably as he leapt tall mountains in a single bound. She rolled her eyes and waited while he gingerly raised his arms to link both hands behind his head.

Hard muscles shifted beneath his taut, tanned skin and she had to bite her lip to keep from sighing like a stupid female drunk on manly pheromones. She swallowed the urge to lean forward and swipe her tongue across his strong, tanned throat. As though he'd read her mind, he sucked in a sharp breath and she froze, watching in awed fascination as flesh rippled and goose bumps broke out across his skin an inch from her nose.

Heat snapped in the air between them and her mind went numb. *Good grief,* she thought with horror, *I'm attracted to him?* Appalled and more than a little rattled, she lifted her gaze, only to find him watching her, the expression in his gold eyes sending her blood pressure shooting into the stratosphere. She didn't have to wonder if he was as affected by their proximity as she was.

Tearing her gaze from his, she muttered, "You're an idiot," unsure if she was addressing him or herself. In case it was him, she continued with, "And so is the sheriff for expecting you to go out like this."

"Hikers are missing," he reminded her impatiently.

She rolled her eyes. She'd treated people suffering from

trauma and knew enough about PTSD to be worried about the battle-alert episodes that culminated in dizziness, muscle tremors, sweating and confusion.

"You almost fainted," she pointed out.

"Don't be ridiculous," he snapped, as though she'd suggested something indecent. "SEALs don't faint. I was just a bit dizzy, that's all. I suffer from low blood pressure."

Cassidy looked up at the outrageous lie and shut her mouth on a sigh. Clearly he was in denial. *Fine*. She was just doing her job.

Besides, he was a Navy SEAL. She reminded herself that he did this kind of thing all the time. A shiver slinked up her spine as she pictured him sneaking into hostile territory, wiping everything out before ghosting out again as silently as he'd arrived. She could even picture him—

"What?"

Yeah, Cassidy. What?

Shaking her head, she went back to binding his torso, reminding herself that she didn't need rescuing. She wasn't a damsel in distress and those gold eyes couldn't see into her mind or know what was happening to her.

Except—*darn him*—he probably did. He was no doubt an expert at making women lose their brain cells just by flexing those awesome biceps—or staring at them with that brooding gold gaze. It was no wonder she felt like she was running a fever. It was no wonder her blood was humming through her veins. Her hormone levels were probably shooting through the stratosphere along with her blood pressure.

Finally she fastened the bandage and took a hasty step back, nearly knocking over the table and its contents in her haste to escape. A large hand on her arm kept her upright and when it tightened as she turned away, she looked up. With his gaze on hers, he gently swiped a line of fire across her bottom lip. She gasped and her heart gave a shocked little blip at the unexpected contact.

"Thank you," he said, leaning towards her. And just

when she thought he meant to kiss her, he snagged a plastic container of pain meds behind her. Grinning at the expression on her face, he popped the top, shook a couple into his palm.

He gave a mocking little salute and tossed the container back in the box. "Gotta go," he said, scooping up his clothing in his good hand. With one last heated look in her direction he sauntered from the cell, all long loose-limbed masculine grace, leaving Cassidy staring at the wide expanse of his muscular back and the very interesting way he filled out his faded jeans.

Fortunately, before the outer door could close behind him, Cassidy pulled herself together enough to croak, "You need stitches, Major. I suggest coming to the hospital before you get septicemia and die a horrible death."

Grinning at her over one broad shoulder, he drawled, "It's a date, darlin'," and disappeared, leaving Cassidy with the impression that he had absolutely no intention of following through with his promise.

At least, not for sutures.

CHAPTER THREE

THE SMALL TOWN of Crescent Lake had been established when traders heading north had come over the mountains and found a large crescent-shaped lake nestled in a thickly wooded area. According to Mrs. Krenson at the Lakeside Inn, it had started out as a rough fur-trading town that had gradually grown into the popular tourist town it was today.

The inn, once the local house of pleasure, had been re-modeled and modernized over the years. Rising out of a picturesque forest, with mountains at its back and the lake at its feet like a small sparkling sea, it now resembled a gracious, well-preserved old lady, appearing both elegant and mysterious. At least, that's what it said in the brochure and what Cassidy had thought when she'd arrived a few weeks before.

Now, with dark clouds hanging over the valley, the lake was nothing like the crystal-clear mirror it resembled in the pictures and Cassidy had to wish for "sturdy" rather than mysterious.

The day had dawned gray and wet and, standing at her bedroom window, Cassidy couldn't help shivering as she looked up at the mountains shrouded in swirling fog, eerily beautiful and threatening. She wondered if the hikers had been found.

And if she was thinking of a certain someone, it was only because he had no business being out there in the first place. He might be an all-weather hero, but he'd been exhausted, injured and on an edge only he could see. All it would take was one wrong move, one misstep and... And then nothing, she told herself irritably as she spun away from the window. Samuel Kellan was a big boy, a highly trained Navy SEAL. If he wanted to scour the mountains for the next week, it was what he'd been trained for. Heck, he could probably live off the land and heal himself using plants and tree bark.

Whatever effect he'd had on her, Cassidy mused as she closed her bedroom door and headed for the bathroom at the end of the hall, it was over. She'd had the entire night to think about her reaction to him and in the early hours had come to the conclusion that she'd been suffering from low blood sugar...and maybe been a little freaked at finding herself in a jail cell. Maybe even a little awed at meeting a national hero. All perfectly logical explanations for her behavior.

Fortunately she'd recovered, and if she saw him again she'd be the cool, level-headed professional she had a reputation for being. Besides, Samuel J. Kellan was just a man. Like any other.

After a quick shower, she brushed her teeth and headed back to her room to dress. It was her day off and she intended playing tourist. She might have come to the Cascades to escape the mess she'd made of things in Boston, but that didn't mean she had to bury herself in work. Crescent Lake was a beautiful town filled with friendly, curious people who'd brought her baked goodies just to welcome her to town.

She'd read that the Lakefront Boardwalk housed a host of stores that included a few antiques shops, an art gallery selling local artwork, a quaint bookshop and, among others, a cozy coffee shop with a spectacular view of the lake and mountains.

She hadn't had a decent latte since leaving Boston,

and according to the nurses, Just Java served a delicious Caribbean mocha latte, and the triple chocolate muffins were better than sex.

Just what she needed, a double dose of sin.

A soft knock on her door startled her out of her chocolate fantasy and sent her pulse skittering.

"Dr. Mahoney?" a muffled voice called from the hallway. "Cassidy, dear? Are you awake?"

Shrugging into her wrap, Cassidy fastened the tie and shoved damp hair off her forehead. She pulled open the door as a ball of dread settled in her belly. Her landlady wouldn't disturb her unless there was an emergency.

Val Krenson's brows were pinched together over her faded blue eyes and one hand was poised to knock again. "I'm sorry to wake you, dear," she apologized quickly. "That was the hospital. They found the hikers. How soon can you get there?"

"Ten minutes," Cassidy said, already morphing into emergency mode. "Fifteen at the most." She stepped back into the room and would have shut the door but Val held out a hand to detain her.

"John Randal is downstairs, dear. Shall I ask him to wait?"

"That's okay, Val," Cassidy said with a quick shake of her head. "I'll need my car later and I don't want to inconvenience anyone." The last time the deputy had driven her anywhere she'd landed up at the jail. So not going there.

"Planning a little down time?" Val asked with a warm smile.

"It'll have to wait." Cassidy sighed. "They didn't say how serious, did they?"

"I'm afraid not, dear. Just that you get there as soon as possible." She leaned forward. "I'm glad you're here to help Monty out, dear. He tires easily these days." She shook her head. "That man should have retired years ago but not many people want to bury themselves in the mountains."

In some ways Cassidy could understand why. They were a couple of hours from the nearest large town and there wasn't much in the way of nightlife that didn't include a few bars, steakhouses and the local bar and grill, Fahrenheit's.

She might feel like a fish out of water, but she'd been surprised to discover she liked the close-knit community where people knew each other and exchanged gossip with their favorite recipes.

At least here people stopped to chat when they saw you, she thought with a smile, instead of staring right through you as though you didn't exist, or scuttling away like you were an escaped crazy. Surprisingly she was enjoying the slower pace. It was a nice change to be able to connect with the people she was treating. But long term? She didn't know.

"It's a beautiful town, Val, but I've only got a short-term contract."

Val laughed and patted Cassidy's arm. "Don't worry, dear," she said over her shoulder, a twinkle lighting her blue eyes. "I have a feeling you're going to be around a long time."

Cassidy uttered a noncommittal "Hmm" and shut the door behind her landlady. She hunted in the closet for a clean pair of jeans, underwear, socks and a soft green long-sleeved T-shirt. Dressing quickly, she shoved her feet into the nearest pair of boots and grabbed a brush that she hurriedly pulled through her wet hair before piling it on top of her head in a loose style that would dry quickly. Foregoing makeup, she grabbed her medical bag and jacket and headed for the door.

Fifteen minutes after closing the door behind the innkeeper, Cassidy pulled up beside the hospital's staff entrance. Locking her car—which everyone said was unnecessary—she hurried into the waiting room, which was already bustling with chaos and reminded her of a busy city ER.

Her eyes widened. There were people everywhere—sprawled in chairs with their heads tilted back in exhaustion, while even more hovered near the entrance, propping up the walls, slugging back steaming coffee and wolfing down fat sandwiches handed out by a group of women.

Sandwiches? Coffee? And where had all these people come from? It looked like a temporary ops center—or a tea party for big hulking men.

"Good, you're here." A voice at her elbow distracted her from the chaos and Cassidy turned to see the head nurse holding out a clipboard.

She accepted the board, feeling a little shell-shocked. "What on earth's going on?"

Fran Gilbert followed her gaze. "The town's disaster committee in action," she explained with a shrug, as though it happened every day.

Disaster—? Oh, no. Cassidy gulped down a sudden sick feeling. *Please don't tell me...!* Shaking off her pessimistic thoughts, she frowned at the older woman. "Disaster? How bad?"

Fran frowned in confusion. "Bad?" Then realizing what Cassidy was thinking, she said, *"No!* God, no. Cassidy, I'm sorry. I didn't mean to scare you." She gave Cassidy a quick hug. "I just meant that the disaster committee responds whenever the rescue teams go out. The junior league ladies take turns providing hot food and drinks. To practice they set up basic first-aid stations for minor injuries. When news came through that the hikers were being brought down, they moved operations here."

"Oh." Cassidy let out a whoosh of relief, a little awed at the way the community mobilized when the need arose. Any disaster in a big city was met with looting and rioting.

"They say it's to practice for a real disaster but I think it's just an excuse to get out and socialize."

Cassidy nodded. "Okay, no disaster. What *do* we have?" she asked, as Fran led her towards the ER cubicles.

"Mostly minor but too many for poor Monty to cope with," the older woman said, before launching into a rapid-fire report worthy of a busy city ER nurse.

Rebecca Thornton, she told Cassidy, had slipped and fallen off the trail. She'd broken her leg and her husband had climbed down the steep embankment to get to her. He'd slipped near the bottom in the treacherous conditions and knocked himself out. Several others had then climbed down to carry the injured couple out but had found their way blocked by huge boulders. With the gully rapidly filling with water, the group still on the trail had elected to return and alert the authorities. They hadn't made it back yet and a team was still out, looking for them.

Dr. Montgomery looked up briefly from checking a young man's bruised and lacerated arm. "Glad they found you," he said with an absent smile, before turning to give the attending nurse instructions.

Soon Cassidy was swamped, treating a broken leg and collarbone, a fractured wrist and a concussion. There was a bruised and swollen knee that she suspected might be cartilage damage, a host of cuts and scrapes, and hypothermia along with exhaustion and dehydration.

And that was just the hiking party.

Once they'd been examined, treated and transferred to the wards for fluids and observation, Cassidy turned her attention to the rescue crew. Among the expected lacerations and contusions, she diagnosed torn ankle ligaments, a dislocated shoulder and a broken finger. Pretty mild considering the awful night they'd endured, she mused, sending one nurse to the suture room and another to X-rays.

She'd just left Hank Henderson propped up with an ice pack on his foot when the elderly doctor called to ask her opinion about the shoulder injury.

After examining Andy Littleton, Cassidy decided there didn't seem to be any serious ligament damage that would require surgery. She told Andy to take a deep breath and quickly pulled his shoulder back into place. He went white and swayed alarmingly before throwing up in the kidney dish she shoved at him.

Listing drunkenly while she strapped his shoulder and arm, he made Cassidy swear a blood oath that she wouldn't tell anyone he'd cried like a girl. Biting back a grin of sympathy, she squeezed his hand, and turned to find Harry Montgomery beaming at her like a proud teacher whose pupil had surpassed his expectations.

"Looks like old Howie's loss is our gain, eh?" The big man chuckled, his age-spotted hand patting her shoulder awkwardly. "He said you were a bright young thing. What he didn't say was that you have an easy way with people along with that sharp diagnostic mind." He studied her shrewdly. "I guess the old buzzard didn't want to lose you, eh?"

With heat rising to her cheeks, Cassidy looped her stethoscope around her neck. She felt like a new resident under scrutiny. Besides, one didn't have to be Einstein to pick up the question behind the compliment. The question of why she was treating runny noses and middle-ear infections in a small mountain hospital instead of running her own ER—which was what she'd originally intended.

"He's a wonderful man," she replied with a warm smile. "And I loved the daily challenges in ER." Thrusting her hands into her lab-coat pockets, she chose her words carefully. "But big city ERs are like operating in a war zone, and when you lose count of the number of ODs, stabbings and rapes you treat..." She sighed. "I realized I needed a change—to get back to basics. Howie mentioned Crescent Lake and I thought it might be the perfect place to try out something more community-oriented."

She didn't say that hearing it was deep in the Cascades and a continent away from Boston had sounded appealing. She'd been desperate to get away and work on forgetting the career-damaging fallout of treating a real-life hero injured in the line of duty. A "hero" who'd turned out to be anything but.

She shuddered at the memory. *God*, she'd been stupidly naïve and had paid a very high price. Then again, how could anyone have known the handsome vice cop wasn't one of the good guys?

The charming wounded-hero act had been just that—an act. He'd used it to lull people—*her*—into a false sense of security. He'd pursued her with flowers, gifts and romantic dinners then stolen her hospital security card, giving him access to the ER dispensary as well as a stack of prescription pads, which he'd used by forging her signature. In the end there'd been a full-scale police investigation—with her as the prime suspect.

In truth, all she'd really been guilty of had been bad judgment. She'd trusted someone who'd proved to be anything *but* trustworthy. In hindsight he'd been too good to be true: too romantic and too sensitive for it not to have been a very clever performance from a man who knew exactly what women wanted.

By the time she'd realized something was wrong, the media frenzy had crucified her, calling her professional competence into question. It had been a nightmare.

Fortunately for her, Lance Turnbull had been under internal investigation. One that had involved a dozen other women doctors around the city. Cassidy had eventually been cleared of all charges but the damage had been done. She'd suffered through snide comments and cruel jokes from her colleagues until she'd finally buckled under the stress.

"GP work is pretty boring compared to the excitement of ER," the old doctor warned, wrenching her from her disturbing thoughts. "Especially here in the boondocks."

Relieved to focus on something other than her past failures, Cassidy looked around at the controlled chaos and sent him a small smile. "I wouldn't exactly call it boring," she said, her smile turning into a grin when his deep chuckle filled the hallway.

"No, it isn't," he agreed, "especially during tourist season. But off season gets pretty quiet."

"I can do quiet. And I'm impressed with the way everyone bands together. It's wonderful knowing that there are still places where people are willing to step in and help their neighbors without expecting something in return."

"That's what's kept me here for sixty years," he said, moving to the door. "The warm community spirit. You don't find that in the city." He turned and studied her intently. "I've watched you over the past two weeks, Cassidy, and you're a very perceptive diagnostician. We could use someone like you heading up the hospital." And when Cassidy opened her mouth to remind him that she was only there for three months, he beat her to it with his parting shot, "Think about it," before disappearing down the hallway.

Cassidy watched him leave. Admittedly she was enjoying the opportunity to practice family medicine in a town where people cared about each other, but Boston was her home. And that kind of decision couldn't be made lightly.

It wasn't until late afternoon that she finally realized she'd been hanging around waiting for something to happen. It didn't take a genius to realize that *something* was a certain Navy SEAL and that she'd been waiting for him to come in to have his injuries treated.

Irritated with herself, she'd collected her purse and jacket and was on her way out when the door banged open and there he was, looking like he'd just blown in from a big, bad superheroes convention with his big, bad SEAL attitude.

When her knees wobbled and her head went light, Cassidy assured herself it was simply because she hadn't eaten anything all day. It certainly didn't have anything to do

with the way his gold eyes latched onto her like a trac-
tor beam.

Gesturing to an empty suture room, Cassidy wordlessly
handed her jacket and purse to the receptionist and ignored the jitters in her belly as the sheriff half-dragged,
half-carried him down the corridor and through the doorway to heave him onto the narrow bed. And just like that,
every delusional thought she'd had in the early hours blew
up right in her face.

"You may now stick him with as many needles as you
like," the sheriff announced, shoving his hands on his hips
and glaring at his brother. "In fact, that's an official order.
Maybe it will improve his attitude and I won't have to toss
him in jail again for disobeying a direct order."

"I said I was fine," the SEAL snarled as Greg, the young
deputy who'd helped drag him into the examination room,
ducked his head and made a beeline for the door.

Wise move, she thought when a string of muttered
threats turned the air blue. She might be relieved he'd made
it back in one piece but it had been a long day and an even
longer night, obsessing about whether or not she had been
imagining things. The good news was that she was sane
and not hallucinating. The bad news was, Cassidy thought
with a sinking sensation, he was even more dangerously
attractive in the cold light of day.

And that was bad. Very bad. Because Cassidy Mahoney
was done with dangerous bad boys who made women
swoon. She really was too busy getting her life back to
deal with two hundred and forty pounds of belligerent male.

It seemed the sheriff was too since he folded his arms
across his chest and glared at his brother, clearly not intimidated by the show of aggression. "And if he gives you
any trouble, make him wear a pretty pink hospital gown,"
he barked, ignoring the way Sam's lip drew back over his
teeth in a silent snarl. "He deserves to have everyone laugh
at his ugly butt after the stunt he pulled."

Cassidy watched the silent clash of wills and her first thought was that nothing about Major Kellan was ugly. She was pretty sure her staff wouldn't be laughing either. More like swooning from the thick cloud of testosterone and bad attitude that surrounded him.

A fierce golden gaze caught and held hers as though he knew what she was thinking, and Cassidy felt a flush creep up her neck into her cheeks. Besides being grossly unprofessional, picturing him naked wouldn't do a thing to convince her she'd imagined her earlier reaction to him.

The sheriff raked his hand through his wet hair, looking tired and exasperated. "Listen up, man," he growled, "I know you're a big, mean SEAL and everything, but just let the doc check you out, okay? I don't have time to babysit you or keep you from bleeding to death. You wouldn't believe the paperwork. It's a nightmare. Elections are coming up and I can't afford to have you die and make me look bad."

"I keep telling you I'm fine," Sam snarled. "Quit hovering like a girl. There's nothing Old Monty can do that I can't do for myself, so get the hell out of my face before I break your ugly mug."

"Oh, please." Ruben snickered rudely. "You can't even break a sweat without help. Now suck it up and let the doc check you out. You look like hell."

Samuel said something that Cassidy was pretty sure was anatomically impossible but before her eyes could do more than widen, Ruben turned to her with a grim smile. "Doc, he's all yours, just as I promised. He's a bit more battered and bloodied but I refuse to take credit for that. He's a hard-headed pain in the ass so you might consider sedating him." He sent his brother a meaningful glare. "In fact, unconscious would be a real improvement."

Ignoring the derisive suggestion, Sam turned narrowed eyes her way. "Doc?" he demanded. "You're the *doctor*?" His tone suggested she'd deliberately misled him. "I thought you were the nurse."

"No," she corrected smoothly. "You thought I was a stripper."

"And with that," Ruben drawled mockingly, "I rest my case." He slapped his hat on his head and adjusted the brim. "Cassidy, ignore the inscrutable death stares. Underneath all that macho SEAL *hoo-yah* attitude he's really quite sweet."

The SEAL snarled something impolite and with a deep laugh the sheriff sketched a salute and disappeared down the hallway, leaving Cassidy with two hundred pounds of seething testosterone. Sweet wasn't a word she'd associate with Major Hotstuff, she mused, moving to the supply cabinet for a towel. Just the idea of it made her want to smile. So she frowned instead.

"So," he said, taking the towel and fixing her with his mesmerizing stare, "you're a doctor."

She sent him a cool look then turned to remove disinfectant and a package of swabs from the overhead cabinet. "Is that a problem, Major, or an apology?"

His amused gaze drifted over her face and breasts to the neat row of supplies she'd begun setting out and he drawled, "Only if you're plotting revenge."

"Fortunately for you I'm not the vengeful type, Major."

His mouth curled at one corner and he said, "Uh-huh" into the towel. Cassidy ignored the impulse to bang her head against the wall. She had a feeling it would be a lot less painful than getting caught up in the man's web.

Fortunately, her little chat with the elderly doctor had reminded her of why she was off men in anything but the professional sense. Flicking him an assessing glance, she decided the sheriff was right. He did look like hell.

"There's no one to save you from the needle this time, Major." She opened another cabinet and removed a suture kit and syringes. "In fact—" her voice was brisk as she moved closer "—I can foresee more than one in your immediate future."

Ignoring the dark eyebrow hiking up his forehead, she stepped close and pushed the soaked parka over his wide shoulders and down his arms. He shrugged and sucked in a sharp breath, before drawling, "Not just beautiful and smart, but psychic too?"

Cassidy bit back a snort and tossed the garment onto the floor, before turning to wash her hands at the small basin. "It doesn't take a clairvoyant to see that you're an action junkie looking for trouble," she replied smoothly, pulling a strip off the paper towel dispenser.

He shrugged. "Goes with the job."

"For which the free world is eternally grateful." She dried her hands and dropped the paper into the bin as she turned. She caught his eyes crinkling at the corners as though he didn't take himself half as seriously as other people did, which…surprised her. She was accustomed to being surrounded by alpha males who thought they sat at God's right hand. Discovering he could poke fun at himself had something warm and light sliding into her belly. Something that felt very much like admiration.

Telling herself that certainly didn't mean she *liked* him, Cassidy focused on his once white T-shirt, now covered in mud and blood. Shaking her head, she pulled it out of his damp waistband and grabbed a pair of scissors off the counter.

With a few snips, his shirt fell away and she quickly unwound the soiled bandage. When the move exposed fresh blood oozing from the loosened dressing, she bit back a curse.

"You're an idiot," she muttered, knowing exactly who she was addressing this time. Lifting a loose edge, she pressed her hand gently against his hard belly and ripped it off in one smooth move.

Sam hissed audibly in surprise and pain. "*Holy…!* Hell

and damnation, woman, what the *hell* was that?" His fingers whitened around the edge of the bed and he looked like he wanted to wrap them around her throat.

"Sorry," she said, and meaning it. It would have been worse if she'd taken her time removing it. "It's better coming off fast."

"For you maybe… *Jeez*…does the CIA know about you?"

"The CIA?" she asked, sending him a narrow-eyed look out the corner of her eye, fairly certain he wasn't being complimentary.

"Yeah. Hear they're looking for interrogators." Definitely not complimentary. "My CO would recruit you on the spot to torture the tadpoles in BUD/S."

"Tadpoles? Buds?" she asked, pouring disinfectant into a stainless-steel bowl and filling it with warm water.

"Wannabe SEALs in Basic Underwater Demolition SEALs," he told her. "Have to knock the cra…I mean stuffing out of them during hell week to sort out the men from the boys. You'd be perfect for the job."

Apparently *he'd* managed to survive without having the stuffing knocked out of him. She wondered how he'd managed it. Sheer stubbornness most likely.

She pulled on a pair of latex gloves then ripped off a large section of cotton wool. "I'm good, but thanks anyway." She pressed a hand to the smooth ball of his shoulder. "Lie flat and lift your arm over your head."

His scowl turned into a grimace when he realized he was too big and had to scoot down the bed, ending up with half his long legs draped over the end. Growling irritably about "damn midget beds", he raised his arm and bent it behind his head. With lids lowered over his unusual eyes, he sent her a sleepy look.

"Although if you continue ripping off my clothes and making me lie down," he drawled softly, "I'll start thinking you have ulterior motives, Miz Honey."

"That's *Dr.* Mahoney to you," she said absently, carefully cleaning the area around the wound before selecting another wad of gauze to clean the wound itself. It would take about a dozen stitches to close.

"Yes, *ma'am*." His voice was polite and subdued but a quick look caught the irreverent smirk curling his mouth. Cassidy swallowed the impulse to return that impudent grin. Or worse—kiss his battered mouth better. From all accounts he was the kind of man who wouldn't stop at kissing. From all accounts he was only interested in quick tumbles with the nearest available woman. Probably because being a SEAL precluded any kind of stable or long-term relationship.

She shivered. If she knew what was good for her, she'd shove her libido back into hibernation and stop getting all excited every time he invaded her space.

Dr. Mahoney was back in charge, she reminded herself, and there would be no mixing her chemistry with his. On *any* level. She was going to patch him up, send him on his way, and hope like hell she never saw him again.

CHAPTER FOUR

SAM WATCHED DOC BOSTON work on his torso and wondered why he was so drawn to a woman who made it abundantly clear she wasn't interested. He tried reminding himself that he'd be heading back to Coronado soon and anything more than harmless flirting was impossible. It didn't help. Not even when he observed the competent way she wielded sharp objects.

Sure, she was beautiful but then, so were a million other women, and he'd had little problem leaving them behind. Except there was something compelling about her that told Sam she wouldn't be easy to forget or walk away from. She was smart and mouthy and didn't take his reputation as a badass seriously or treat him differently from other patients. And *that* more than anything made him like her.

Okay, he *really* liked the look of her—he was a guy, so sue him—but lately all the feminine adulation had begun to irritate him. All a lot of women saw was a SEAL with hard muscles and weird eyes. A guy they could brag about being with to their friends. He'd enjoyed that in his twenties, but in the decade since he'd seen and done things no one should see or do.

Cassidy Mahoney, on the other hand, did more of the squinty-eye thing that for some strange reason made him want to smile when he hadn't felt the urge in a long, long time. It made him want to push her up against the nearest wall and taste all that soft, smooth skin.

He thought of how she'd react if he acted on the impulse, and had to suppress a grin when her suspicion-filled look said she knew what he was thinking. His what-have-I-done-now eyebrow-lift had her eyes narrowing, as if she suspected he was up to no good. A flush rose from the lapels of her lab coat and climbed her neck into her cheeks.

If she only knew.

"I promise not to wrestle you to the ground and stab you in the throat with that," he assured her, then decided to qualify it with, "Well…maybe wrestle you to the ground…" His gaze smoothed over her breasts and up her long throat to her lush mouth. "Okay, *definitely* wrestle you to the ground. But the stabbing thing? You're safe. SEAL's honor."

She didn't disappoint him. Thrusting out a plump lower lip that he yearned to take a greedy bite out of, she huffed out an annoyed breath that disturbed the long tendrils of fine silvery hair escaping her tousled topknot. She appeared at once exasperated, embarrassed and incredibly appealing.

"Give it a rest, Major." She huffed again, shoving the needle into a vial of local anesthetic like she was probably imagining it was his hide. He covered a wince by scratching his chin. "It must be exhausting trying to keep that up."

"Keep what up?" he asked innocently, wanting her to keep talking. Even rife with irritation, he liked the sound of her voice—smooth and silky, like hundred-year-old bourbon. It intoxicated his senses and kept him from thinking about gut-wrenching guilt and things he couldn't change.

She removed the needle and flicked the syringe a couple of times before gently depressing the plunger. A tiny spurt fountained from the tip. "The seduction routine," she said, wiping an area close to his wound with an alcohol swab. "Heaven knows, just trying to keep up with it is exhausting."

"It's really no trouble," he assured her, except lately

it *had* become exhausting. Most likely he was just out of practice. Life-and-death situations didn't leave much time for fun and games. "I can do it in my sleep."

She gently slid the needle into his flesh. There was a tiny pinch and almost instantly cold numbness began to spread along his side. He sighed with relief as she removed the needle and pressed a small swab over the puncture wound.

"That's the problem, isn't it?" she murmured, tossing the syringe into the nearby medical waste container. She opened the suture kit onto a strip of newly torn paper toweling. "It's meaningless."

He shrugged and this time couldn't prevent a wince from escaping. Last night he'd wrenched his shoulder hauling an injured man up a slippery cliff face. "Women seem to like it," he said on a yawn, deciding he really liked the way her wide green eyes went all squinty and irritated when he piled on the charm. It made him want to lay it on extra-thick just to see her scowl at him.

She made a noise that sounded like a snort and he had to clench his jaw to keep from grinning with satisfaction. "They probably don't want to hurt your feelings," she pointed out.

"You think so?" He tried the wounded look but he suspected she wasn't fooled.

"This is not the eighties," she informed him with a *get-real* lift of an eyebrow. "Not all women appreciate being charmed out of their panties with lines from a bad movie script."

He looked skeptical and she shook her head as though he was beyond help. Sam waited until she turned back with a suture needle and monofilament thread, before handing her needle scissors. He watched surprise flit across her face and knew what she was thinking. *What did a macho idiot know about needle scissors?* He grimaced. *Other than having first-hand experience?*

"I went to med school," he reminded her, when she made

no move to take them. He was annoyed for caring about her opinion—which had been pretty obvious from the outset, thanks to the sheriff locking him in a jail cell for no good reason.

"The way I hear it," she said, accepting the instrument as well as the implied reproach with a nod, "you cut med school to play pirates." He watched her get a firm grip on the needle and press the edges of his skin together with her left hand. She pushed the needle through, released it and gripped it with the flat edge of the scissors, before carefully pulling it free.

"You shouldn't believe everything you hear," he advised darkly, talking about more than embellished stories of his SEAL exploits. He had a feeling someone had been filling her head with his youthful indiscretions—*most* of which were gross exaggerations, the rest outright lies.

Her open skepticism confirmed his suspicions. "You mean you don't wear a cape and fly around the world in your underwear, saving humanity?" Her movements were quick and confident and a neat row of stitches began closing the three-inch slash on his belly.

Sam chuckled and thanked God for BDUs. It was kind of nice having a conversation with a woman who didn't treat him like he walked on water or was there to scratch her itch. It was even better watching her full pink mouth when she talked. It made him think of long dark nights, crisp cool sheets and hot wet kisses when he hadn't thought about them in a while. It was a relief to discover he was still normal in one important area.

"You don't believe that, do you?"

She deftly tied off and started on a fourth suture. "I stopped believing in superheroes a long time ago, Major," she said absently. She looked up and caught his gaze. "So why *did* you?"

"Why did I what?"

"Join the Navy instead of finishing med school."

"I did finish," he told her, "courtesy of Uncle Sam."

"But why the armed forces when you were already doing something that would save lives?"

He fought a knee-jerk reaction to come up with some stupid macho excuse that would confirm her not so flattering opinion of him. But something held him back. Something deep inside wanted very much for her to think of him as more than a battered sailor with big muscles.

"I was in New York when the Towers fell," he said, wincing as the words emerged. He'd never shared his true reasons with anyone but for some reason found himself spilling his guts to her.

He remembered exactly what he'd been doing when his safe world had fallen apart. He'd been living the life of a typical student, concerned only with enjoying the hell out of being young, healthy and surrounded by girls and parties.

"You...you were *there*?"

Sam looked up, almost surprised to find he wasn't alone. Cassidy's green eyes were huge and filled with a compassion he knew he didn't deserve.

"A few blocks away," he said impassively. "I'd cut class and was staying in Brooklyn with a friend for a few days. We were sitting at a sidewalk café, having coffee and bagels, when...when the first plane flew into the towers." He fell silent for a couple beats before continuing. "We tried getting through but the cops stopped us. Never felt so helpless in my life. There I was, a fourth-year med student thinking I had it all."

His lips twisted self-deprecatingly. "Thinking I *knew* it all." He speared her with a haunted look. "I saw many draw their last breaths. I don't ever want to feel that helpless again. The next day Jack and I enlisted. We were determined to take a more active role in protecting our country."

"Healing the sick and saving people *is* taking an active

role, Major," she reminded him, but he was already shaking his head.

"Not active enough, Doc. Besides, there are thousands of civilian doctors Stateside," he pointed out. "What about the men and women protecting our country? Protecting the free world? Who saves them?"

"I…"

"My friend's father was one of the firefighters killed that day," he continued, as though she hadn't interrupted. "I'll never forget the look on Jack's face when he heard his dad was never coming home." Sam closed his eyes on remembered devastation—of that day as well as events more recent than 9/11. "You never forget that kind of pain."

You never forget, Sam admitted silently. *And the guilt eats at you that you are alive and they aren't.*

Cassidy watched as fierce emotions moved across his features, through his beautiful eyes. She felt a little pinch in the region of her heart. Crescent Lake's hero was hurting, and the discovery that he was more than just a pretty face and a hot body terrified her in ways that she didn't want to analyze.

She'd rather think of him as a shallow womanizer who'd enlisted because men in uniform got more girls. Although, in or out of uniform, the man would attract more than his share of women.

Using her wrist to push away the tendrils of hair that kept obscuring her vision, Cassidy studied him closely. The events of 9/11 may have changed the course of his life, but she had a feeling something more recent had put that *haunted* look in his eyes. And suddenly, more than anything, she wanted them glinting wickedly at her again.

Whoa, she warned herself silently when the notion seemed more appealing than it should. *Way too intense for someone you can't wait to get away from.*

In silence, she completed another suture before asking casually, "So you didn't?"

His muscles bunched beneath her fingers and he went strangely still for a couple of beats before asking, "Didn't what?"

There was a sudden shift in the air and she felt the hair at her nape rise. Primitive warning whooshed up her spine and she sucked in a sharp breath. Lifting her head, she found his attention locked on her—laser bright and strangely intent. It was odd, feeling as though they were communicating on different levels, only one of which was verbal. And even more disturbing to realize that she didn't have a clue what it was all about.

"Cut med school to play pirates on the high seas," she reminded him, and watched, mesmerized, as his big body relaxed. His gaze lost that fierce glitter and his mouth its tight, forbidding line, even going so far as to kick up at one corner. The air surrounding them shifted again and she was left dizzied by the sudden shifts in mood.

His teeth flashed white in his dark face. "Well…technically…I suppose I did."

Cassidy sighed and concentrated on the last suture. "You're an idiot." Sam snorted, apparently as relieved as she was to lighten the tension. The band of pressure around her skull eased a little more. She really, *really*, didn't want to like him. At least, not any more than she already did. That would be so utterly irresponsible—not to mention stupid.

"That's the third time you've said that," he accused plaintively.

"I meant it before too."

His eyes crinkled at the corners. "Why? Because I like to jump out of airplanes?"

"No," she said, unlacing his mud-caked boot and dropping it on the floor, along with his wet sock. "Because you blow people up instead of healing them." She retrieved a stool from the corner and slid it under his hard calf, reaching for a pair of scissors. There was no way she was going to wrestle him out of his wet jeans to get to the thigh injury. Just the thought of him lying there in his underwear—*God, did he even wear them?*—gave her a hot flash.

"I do heal people," he said mildly as she began cutting the wet denim. "All spec ops teams need medics."

She paused and frowned at him. "Well, why aren't you doing *this*…" she gestured to the room around them "… instead of wreaking havoc and blowing things up?"

His expression clearly questioned her intelligence. "I just told you. Besides, I like blowing things up," he said as though she was a particularly dense blonde, and she wanted to smack him. She had a sneaky suspicion that had been his intention. It seemed he was as eager as she was to move away from intensely personal subjects. "And I'm good at wreaking havoc."

Cassidy rolled her eyes and said, "You are such a guy," with such feminine disgust that Sam laughed.

"And that's bad, how?"

He was so delusional that she stared silently at him for a couple of beats as though she couldn't believe what she was hearing.

Besides, the man's blood was probably ninety-nine percent testosterone and she'd been lucky to escape unscathed the first time around. Well, not completely unscathed, she admitted reluctantly, but she had a feeling if she allowed Samuel Kellan to matter, she wouldn't be so lucky. "It's bad when you won't talk about what's bothering you."

He snorted and sent her a look that said she was delusional. "Talking's for politicians…and girls," he scoffed, and she huffed out an exasperated breath, suspecting that he was being insulting on purpose. *Sneaky.* "SEALs are doers," he continued. "They don't do a lot of standing around, talking. If they did, nothing would get done." His eyes crinkled and his grin turned wicked. "But if you want to know what I was thinking last night, I'd be happy—"

"I *know* what you were thinking," Cassidy quickly interrupted, slicing through tough, wet denim towards his knee. "Clearly your seduction techniques need adjusting."

He grinned and said, "Oh, yeah?" before waggling his eyebrows in a comical way that had her rolling her eyes. When she stopped checking out the state of her brain she found him studying her with an intensity that had her pulse hitching then picking up its pace. The man's mercurial mood changes made her dizzy.

"I'm talking about whatever it is that has you brooding when you think no one's looking," she said casually, as though she was just making conversation to take his mind off what she was about to do. "I'm talking about reacting to sharp stimuli like you're expecting a ninja attack." Something dark and haunted flickered in his gaze before his expression hardened. "Plenty of people suffer from PTSD, Major," she continued casually, as she hacked through the denim to his knee. "It's nothing to be ashamed of."

He made a rude sound. "You're a shrink now?" he drawled, and Cassidy continued as though he hadn't spoken. "I specialized in trauma medicine. People who survive traumatic experiences come through ER on a daily basis. It's very common."

"Just being a SEAL exposes you to stressful situations," Sam interrupted impatiently. "It's the job. If you can't deal, you have no business being a SEAL. So you deal. End of story." He was silent a moment and she felt the air shift again. "Besides, I like blowing things up, remember."

He clearly didn't intend to say anything more, but that was okay, Cassidy reflected. At least next time—*if* there was a next time—she could bring it up when he was in a better frame of mind. For now she'd respect his need to avoid the subject.

Lifting the denim at his knee to make the final cuts, she acknowledged quietly, "Yes, I remember."

She'd barely exposed his mid-thigh when he flinched and grabbed her hand with an alarmed "*Whoa.*" He'd clamped his free hand over his crotch and was eyeing the scissors like she was holding a live grenade.

Cassidy rolled her eyes and gently peeled away the blood-soaked denim, grimacing at the jagged gash on his hard thigh. "This is going to hurt," she said, reaching for disinfectant and cotton wool. After liberally dousing the area, she probed the wound gently, before injecting a pain-killer into his thigh.

"So," he murmured when she'd tied off the first suture and was starting on the second, "what's a big-city ER girl doing in a place like this?"

Cassidy flashed him an exasperated look and deftly maneuvered the needle scissors as she completed another suture. "We've already had this conversation, remember?"

Sam scratched his chin and the rasp of his stubble sent a shiver of awareness down her spine. It reminded her of how virile and dangerous he was to her peace of mind. "I was a little tired last night."

"Uh-huh," Cassidy said dryly, and tied off the next suture.

"You never did answer the question, though," Sam pressed, before she could ask about his sleeping habits. He looked more exhausted and drawn than a single night without sleep warranted. And with his other symptoms, he was most likely having nightmares as well.

She studied him intently. "What question?"

"You. Here in the boondocks."

Cassidy turned away from his keen gaze and sorted through a box of dressings. She needed a few moments to gather her composure. After selecting what she needed, she turned with a shrug. "Big-city burn-out. I just needed a change."

"Ahhh," Sam drawled, as she tore open the packaging with more force than was necessary.

"What's that supposed to mean?" she demanded, stripping off the backing and gently pressing it over the sutures on his belly.

He grimaced. "Romance gone bad."

Cassidy gave a shocked laugh, staggered by his perception, and dropped her gaze to his thigh. She knew what he was doing. And, boy, was his diversion effective. "Believe me, romance is *way* off base."

"Then…?"

Rattled, Cassidy sucked in a steadying breath then answered, "Let's just say I needed to find some perspective."

"Yeah," he said softly, his eyes taking on a bleak expression that had her own problems vanishing in the sudden urge to wrap her arms around him. His mouth twisted in a sad, bitter smile. "God knows, I'm acquainted with perspective."

Unsure how to respond in a way that wouldn't have her coming across as an emotional wreck, Cassidy silently went back to work. Besides, what was there to say? Fortunately, he didn't seem to have any clue either. By the time she'd finished he seemed to have slipped into sleep but when she eased away, he groaned and sat up.

A quick glance over her shoulder caught his grimace of pain. His jaw bunched and he grabbed the side tattooed with bruises as he swung his legs over the side. Having finally come off his adrenaline high, he was pale, exhausted and hurting.

"I'll get you some pain meds," she said quietly, turning away to reach into the overhead cabinet. She heard a faint sound and felt the air shift at her back an instant before heat spread along her shoulders and down to the backs of her thighs. Her pulse leapt, her chest went tight and it was all she could do to keep from turning into his big, hard body. To lean on him and let him lean on her.

A long tanned arm reached over her shoulder and he snagged a bottle of pain meds. "This'll do," he said, his voice gravel-rough and sexy. She felt his gaze and turned her head, slowly lifting her gaze up his tanned throat to the hard line of his shadowed jaw, past his poet's mouth and strong straight nose.

He was close. Too close. His gold eyes darkened and something vibrated and snapped between them. Something deep and primal. Something so incendiary she was surprised her clothes didn't catch fire.

Cassidy opened her mouth to say—*God, she didn't have a clue*—then snapped it shut when nothing emerged. The air around them abruptly heated and to her horror his eyes went all hot and sleepy. He felt it too, she realized, and all she had to do was shift a couple of inches closer...and their mouths would—

No sooner had the thought formed than Sam was moving, and before she could do more than squeak out a protest, he'd spun her around and pushed her up against the wall and the heat became a liquid fire in her blood.

She saw his lips moving but heard nothing past the rush of blood filling her ears. Her palms tingled, her body tensed in anticipation and time slowed as his head dipped. Then his mouth was closing over hers and everything...*everything*...sound, heat, sensation...was rushing at her like she'd entered a time warp and was speeding towards something destructive...and wildly exhilarating.

Shock was her first reaction, her second was "*Hmmf...*" When she realized her palms were flat against his hard belly, she tried to shove him away. She didn't want this. It was too much, too little and...*God*...too *everything*. Instinctively she knew that if she let him continue, he'd suck her into his force-field and she'd burn up in the impact. But then he lifted his head and his battered lips brushed across hers, soothingly and so sweetly, and her resistance crumbled.

With a low growl she felt in the pit of her belly, his mouth descended, opening over hers to consume every thought in her head and pull the oxygen from her lungs, leaving her senses spinning.

She heard a low, husky moan and realized with a sense of alarm that it had come from her. *God*…she never moaned. *Ever*. But, then, she'd never been kissed like her soul was being sucked from her body.

She clutched at him to keep from sliding to the floor and an answering groan filled the air, cocooning them in heated silence. This time she was certain it wasn't her.

Tunneling long fingers into her hair, Samuel wrapped them around her skull to tip her head so he could change the angle of the kiss. Instantly his tongue slid past her lips to tangle with hers. Cassidy's breath hitched, her mouth softened and her eyes drifted closed. As if she welcomed the all-encompassing heat.

And, God, how could she not? She'd never felt anything like it. It was like being suspended in a thick, heated silence with nothing but the taste of him in her mouth, the hard feel of him against her, the sound of her pounding pulse filling her head, while heat and wildness rushed through her veins.

And just when her body flowed against his and she thought she would pass out from lack of oxygen, he broke the kiss and murmured a stunned *"What the hell...?"* between dragging desperate breaths into his lungs.

Confused by the sudden retreat, a small frown creased the smooth skin of her forehead and her eyes fluttered open to see his gaze burning into hers with a fierce intensity—as though he blamed her for the tilting of the earth.

For long stunned moments he stared at her like he'd never seen her before. Then, so abruptly her knees buckled, he shoved away from the wall and retreated, leaving her feeling like he'd drawn back his fist and slugged her in the head.

"Wh-what…? Why…?" Great, now she was stuttering. She gulped and tried again. "What the hell was that?"

Angling his body, Sam folded his arms across his chest and propped his shoulder against the wall where not seconds ago he'd had her pinned. Abruptly inscrutable, his arched brow questioned her sanity.

After a long moment his gaze dropped to her mouth again. "I had to see if you taste as delicious as you look," he drawled, as though it was perfectly normal to push someone up against a wall and suck the air from their lungs.

Infuriated with the quiver in her belly and the urge to slide back against the wall with him, Cassidy shoved at the hair that had been disturbed by his marauding fingers and glared back at him. "Look," she snapped, "I'm not some brainless Navy bunny desperate to trade passable kisses with a hot Navy SEAL. I haven't the time or the inclination and this is certainly *not* the place."

His eyes narrowed in challenge and for a second she thought he'd get mad, but finally his mouth slid into a slow, sexy grin. "*Hot?*" His eyebrows waggled. "You think I'm *hot*?"

And she wanted to slug him.

Deciding to escape before she did or said something she would regret, Cassidy headed for the door on shaky legs. She paused with a cool look over her shoulder, as if she hadn't just had her tongue in his mouth. *Not going to think about that.*

"If you feel feverish or the area surrounding your injuries becomes inflamed and swollen," she said curtly in parting, "phone in for a prescription. Otherwise make an appointment to have those stitches removed in a week."

CHAPTER FIVE

SAM STOOD BEHIND the solid oak bar and mixed cocktails for a table of women in the corner near the dance floor. It was their second set of drinks for what looked like some kind of ritual girls' night out. Gifts were piled in the corners of the booth, leading him to surmise it was either someone's birthday or a bachelorette party.

He just hoped they didn't get out of hand and start dancing on the tables and shedding their clothes or he'd be forced to throw them out. Some of the male customers tended to get a little upset when he broke up impromptu floor shows, but even in Crescent Lake the sheriff's department frowned on that kind of behavior. The last time it had happened he'd ended up in a jail cell at the mercy of an evil blonde.

Shifting to ease the pressure on his injured thigh, Sam nodded to a few old acquaintances and poured a cosmopolitan into a martini glass.

He'd never understood how any self-respecting adult could order cocktails called orgasms or pink panthers, let alone drink them. He was a strictly beer and malt kind of guy and the thought of slugging back sickly-sweet concoctions the color of candy floss was enough to make him gag. Of course he'd also been known to toss back the occasional tequila with his buddies—but only as a matter of pride.

An off-duty deputy called out, "Hey, Sam," as he pushed

his way through the crowd, arm slung across the shoulders of a hot babe in tight jeans and even tighter tank top. Sam responded with an eye-waggle in the woman's direction and Hank grinned, calling out, "She's got a friend. Interested?"

Sam laughed and shook his head. His sister wasn't due in till ten, but until then he was in charge. It was only a little after eight and Fahrenheit's was already packed. He could hardly hear himself think over the sound of music pouring from the jukebox. The band was busy setting up but wasn't due to start until nine and the kitchen was pushing out huge platters of buffalo wings, fries and chili hot enough to singe the varnish off the bar.

He'd spent the entire week rescuing stray cattle, hauling in joyriders and dodging buckshot from old man Jeevers, who thought the deputies were aliens beamed down from the mother ship. And when he wasn't playing cop he'd worked the taps behind the bar, listening to Jerry Farnell recount his experiences in Desert Storm.

His brother had talked him into "helping out" at the sheriff's office, but Sam wasn't fooled. Ruben wanted some fraternal bonding time so he could casually talk about why Sam was home, acting like a moody bastard instead of parachuting into hostile territory and sneaking up on bad guys.

He suspected his family had formed a tag team to work on him, hoping he'd crack and spill his guts. They were clearly as tired of his bad attitude as his CO had become. Heck, *he* was tired of his bad attitude. He wanted to get back to the teams, doing what he'd been trained for.

What they didn't understand was that SEALs didn't crack under pressure or talk about their missions. What they did was mostly classified so they *couldn't* talk. Besides, he'd seen and done some pretty bad things that he didn't want to think too hard about. *Ever.* If he did he'd go crazy and end up like Jerry, propping up a bar somewhere, getting drunk while reliving his glory days.

Finally, the bozos taking up one side of the bar got tired of trying to provoke him and turned their attention to speculating about the fancy Boston babe helping out at the hospital.

He eventually stopped listening to their inventive illnesses just to have "five minutes alone with her so I can drop my shorts and show the little lady what a *real* man looks like."

Sam snorted. Doc Boston might have come to town to "get some perspective" but he suspected her *perspective* didn't include checking out the local talent. She was a beautiful, classy woman who'd probably seen countless men drop their shorts, and an idiot like Buddy Holliday would hardly impress her. Besides, her reaction to *his* kiss had told him he'd been right. Some guy had worked her over and she was taking it out on him.

Except in his experience a woman didn't always need a reason to act like a man was a pervert for pushing her up against the wall and sucking the air from her lungs. They often behaved irrationally for no apparent reason—which was why he enjoyed being a SEAL. Guys didn't mind if you scratched yourself in public, and burping was an accepted form of male bonding.

Furthermore, before she'd stormed off, bristling, with insult, she'd had her beautiful body pressed against his, her hands in his hair and her tongue in his mouth—and had enjoyed every hot minute of it, no matter what she'd said.

The good news was people suffering from PTSD didn't dream or fantasize about kissing a woman until her muscles went fluid and her breath hitched in her throat. They didn't obsess about running their hands through long, silky hair or down smooth, sleek thighs and they sure as hell didn't have erotic dreams about someone who treated them like she wanted to slide her lush curvy body up against you one minute then scrape you off the bottom of her shoe the next.

He'd be insane to even consider pursuing someone who

ripped off a dozen layers of skin along with an adhesive
dressing. And, contrary to popular opinion, Sam Kellan
wasn't insane.

Fortunately someone called his name and Sam turned,
grateful for the distraction. He'd spent way too much time
thinking about her as it was.

Over the next hour he kept the drinks coming and tried
to work up some enthusiasm for the trio of woman bellied
up to the bar, heavily made-up eyes currently stripping him
naked and acting like he should feel flattered.

He didn't. He'd learned early that women liked Navy
SEALs. They liked their big muscles and hard bodies and
they liked their stamina. He mostly liked women too, but
tonight he wasn't in the mood to oblige them.

By the time his sister arrived for her shift, he was ready
to head off into the wilderness to get away from people for
a while. "Where the hell have you been?" he demanded,
in a tone that had her welcoming smile morph into a confused frown.

"What are you talking about?"

"You're late."

Hannah flicked her attention to the wall clock. "Fifteen minutes. Big deal. And quit scowling like that, you're
scaring away my customers." She looked over the happy
crowd and noticed the group of men cozied up to the bar,
scarfing down buffalo wings, and grimaced when she recognized them. "What did Buddy say to upset you?" she
demanded, eyeing him cautiously, like she expected him
to morph into a psycho.

"I'm not upset." *Yeesh*, what was with women lately?
"Women get upset, guys get mad."

She rolled her eyes. "Fine, what are you *mad* about
now?"

"I'm not mad. Listening to them yap about the length
of their johns and betting on who's going to score first is
giving me a brain bleed."

"So? They do that every week. Last week it was with that group of coeds from Olympia. You thought it was pretty damn funny then and told me to chill when I wanted to throw them out."

He grimaced. "It gets old real fast. You'd think they'd move on from the high-school locker room talk."

She looked skeptical. "You're talking about Buddy Holliday, right? The guy who calls himself Buddy Holly and plays air guitar against his fly?" Sam couldn't prevent a grunt of disgust. Hannah cocked her head and asked casually, "Or is it because they've been betting on a certain doctor over at the hospital?"

Sam folded his arms over his chest and flattened his brows across his forehead. "What are you yapping about now?" Except Hannah wasn't fazed by his intimidating SEAL scowl—in fact, she moved closer, as though anticipating some juicy gossip and didn't want to miss any salacious details. Sam didn't know why she bothered. They could stand at opposite ends of the bar and bellow at each other and no one would hear them over the band.

"Don't worry, Sammy. That lot are big on talk and small on action. Emphasis on small."

"And I need to know this, why?"

Hannah ignored the question. She was like a Rottweiler with a chew toy when she was on the track of something. "Ruben says she could be in Hollywood, playing a classy playboy doctor." She snickered. "I think he's in love."

And suddenly Sam felt like he was suffocating. He tore off his apron and threw it onto the counter behind the bar, barely resisting the urge to rip the bottle of gin out of his sister's hand and smash it into the mirror behind the bar—after emptying the contents down his throat. But he drew the line at sissy drinks and knew his sister would be mad if he broke up the place.

Shoving his fingers through his hair, he bit back an extremely explicit curse. He needed air. He needed to get a grip. He needed to get away from people for a while.

"I'm out of here," he snarled, pushing past his sister. "You're on your own."

Stunned by the leashed violence tightening his face, Hannah turned to gape at him. "Wha—? What did I say? What did I do?"

Sam's snarled expletive over his shoulder died at the baffled hurt in her huge eyes. Guilt slapped at him and he let go with an angry hiss of frustration.

"Nothing," he said, wearily pressing his thumb and forefinger into his eyes to ease the headache threatening to explode his brain, along with his temper. He really needed to get a grip. Hannah didn't deserve his filthy mood. "I'm just tired and I have a headache."

"Again?" She looked concerned. "Do you need to see a doctor?" And all Sam's irritation returned in a rush.

"*No.* I *don't* need to see a damn doctor," he said wearily. "I *am* a doctor, remember?" Her expression turned skeptic and he knew what she was thinking. That he needed a shrink, not an MD.

"You never used to let Buddy bug you, so what's your problem?" she demanded, and before he could remind her he was a SEAL without a team, her eyes got big and a startled laugh escaped. "It's her, isn't it? The fancy Boston doc the guys are always talking about." Her eyes gleamed with fiendish delight, like when she was ten and she'd found him reading the *Playboy* magazine he'd found clearing out Mr. Henderson's garage. He almost expected her to burst out with, "I'm gonna tell Mom." What came out was worse.

"It *is*." She cackled gleefully and before he could ask what the hell she was talking about, she snickered. "*You're* the one with a thing for Doc Boston. Oh, boy, this is great. It's like the time you and Ruben fought over Missy Hawkins, and came home sporting black eyes and split lips. So what's it gonna be, huh? Pistols at dawn or down-'n-dirty street fighting? Can I watch?"

Sam bit back a curse and felt the back of his skull tighten. "And they think *I'm* the family nut job." He squinted at her. "So, what are you, thirteen? I'm a Navy SEAL, for God's sake. We don't get *things* for women or fight over them. People get killed that way."

Hannah's eyes widened, she looked intrigued. "Has that ever happened?"

"*No.*" Yeesh. "I don't fight over women. It's juvenile." Not to mention stupidly dangerous.

She stuck her tongue in her cheek. "*R-i-i-ight,*" she said, like he was acting so mature.

"Yeah, short stuff. Just remember I know a hundred different ways to kill a man—or a kid sister—that'll look like they died of natural causes. Besides, I'm not interested in some fancy Boston debutante playing wilderness doctor."

Hannah looked disgusted and sent him a *yeah, right* look as she gave his shoulder a patronizing pat. She muttered something that sounded like, "Keep telling yourself that, you poor clueless moron," which he took exception to. But when he demanded she repeat it, she smirked and said, "I've got this, big guy. You go off and crawl into your man cave with your denials and delusions. I'm sure the Navy shrinks will be interested to hear you've finally gone over the edge."

Sam snarled something nasty about Navy shrinks, before turning on his heel and heading down the passage towards the back exit. He yanked open the door and slammed it on the sound of her laughter.

Hannah was wrong, he told himself, firing up the engine and shoving the vehicle into first gear. He *didn't* care if his brother had a "thing" for the fancy doctor. He'd be gone soon and didn't do relationships that lasted more than a week, tops. He was never around long enough for more. And if the voice in his head told him he was deluding himself, he ignored it since it sounded a lot like his sister. He was just tired.

Yeah, he thought with a snort of disgust. He was tired all right. Tired of sitting on his ass, waiting for his CO to call. And he was damn sick and tired of trying to convince people he was fine.

Sam had every intention of heading for the Crash Landing, a rough bar on the other side of town that catered to truckers, loggers and general badasses, but found himself pulling into the hospital parking lot instead.

When he realized where he was, he swore and scowled at the light spilling from the small ER, worried that maybe he *was* as crazy as everyone claimed. Only a crazy man would be sitting outside a hospital, staring at the glowing emergency sign and thinking of a woman whose bedside manner rivaled that of a BUD/S training instructor.

He was also a doctor, for goodness' sake. He could remove his own damn stitches. Nevertheless, he found himself killing the engine and climbing from the cab.

So he was here. Might as well get them removed. They were starting to itch like crazy anyway.

Sam entered the building, surprised to find the reception deserted. He headed for the emergency treatment rooms but found them empty as well. A little alarmed, he retraced his steps just as a door opened somewhere behind him and before he could turn, a voice called out.

"Be right with you… Oh, Samuel, what a surprise," Fran Gilbert, a friend of his mother's, said when she saw him. "Is there a problem?" She was pushing a medicine trolley and looked a little preoccupied. Sam held up his bandaged hand and watched her face clear. "Cassidy will handle that, dear. I'm doing the rounds."

"Busy?"

"Just the usual. In addition to the usual, a dozen pre-schoolers with high fevers came in earlier. We're waiting for spots to appear but in the meantime we've got our hands full with cranky little people demanding attention every second. Through that door," she said, gesturing behind him. "I made her take a break. Who knows what will happen during the night with a bunch of miserable little people." And then she was gone.

Sam stared after her for a moment, wondering if his mouth was hanging open. He hadn't had an opportunity to utter so much as a grunt. Shaking his head, he turned and headed for the privacy door she'd indicated. He pushed it open and immediately heard talking.

So much for resting up for a rough night, he thought darkly. Ignoring the fact that she was free to entertain whomever she pleased, he let the door shut silently behind him and headed down the corridor. What he found wiped all dark thoughts from his head.

Shoving a shoulder against the doorframe, Sam folded his arms across his chest and let his eyes take a slow journey up long denim-clad legs perched halfway up a ladder. Doc Boston was alone and muttering to herself about something that sounded like bedpans and floor polish as she consulted the clipboard in her hand.

She turned a page to skim it from top to bottom and then back again, before huffing out a breath and turning another page, oblivious to his presence.

"You have *got* to be kidding," she muttered with a sound of disgust. "Who puts bedpans with surgical scrubs? This system sucks." She froze as though she'd said something indecent then shook her head with a laugh. "Yes, Cassidy, you can use the word 'sucks' without the world imploding." She exhaled as she studied the clipboard, her breath disturbing silvery blonde curls near her face. "Besides, if someone can walk around with a T-shirt saying '*Eat the Worm*' or '*Loggers do it with big poles*' in public, you can certainly say 'sucks' in private without it being followed by lightning bolts."

Sam grinned. "You sure about that, Doc?" he drawled, making her shriek and jump about a mile into the air. She grabbed for the shelf with one hand and the ladder with the other. The clipboard and pen went flying, her boot slipped and with a panicked shriek she went flying as well.

Without thinking, Sam leapt towards her. She landed against his chest with a thud, knocking the breath from them both. He staggered back against the wall and wrapped one arm securely around her back. The other he clamped around her thighs.

Planting his feet wide to accommodate his curvy armful, he grinned into shocked green eyes, conscious of lush pink lips forming a perfectly round O—which for some reason made him think of hot, wet kisses in the dark—an inch from his.

"I… You… Oh…*God*," she wheezed out, fisting her hand in his T-shirt and sounding about as coherent as Cindy Dawson in the third-grade spelling bee when Frankie Ferguson had let go with a loud burp right there on stage.

She sucked in a shaky breath and uttered one word. "*You!*" Making him wonder if she was relieved to see him or cursing him. He suspected the latter.

"Expecting someone else?" The idea did not appeal.

"I…uh… You…" She shut her mouth with an audible snap and swiped her tongue across her lips. Then, realizing how provocative her action might appear—especially as his gaze had dropped to her mouth—she rolled her eyes and shoved against his chest. "Put me down."

"'I…uh… You'?" Sam lifted his brow, ignoring her order. "You've developed a stutter since I last saw you?"

"*Dammit*, you scared the hell out of me," she snapped, and shoved at his shoulders again.

Both brows hiked up his forehead. "*Hell*?" He was enjoying the feel of her in his arms and the light fruity scent of her hair. He was enjoying seeing her flustered when she was normally so poised. "Doc, Doc, *Doc*," he tutted, shaking his head. "First 'suck' and now 'Dammit' and 'Hell'? What's next? The *b* word?"

Cassidy froze and stared open-mouthed for a couple of beats before a faint flush rose up her neck into her cheeks. "You *heard* all that?" And when his eyes crinkled and his mouth lifted at one corner, she groaned.

"Oh, God, just shoot me."

Sam laughed. "I only shoot bad guys," he assured her, slipping his arm out from under her shapely bottom to let her slide down the length of his body while he enjoyed the friction of soft curves against hard angles. Her face flamed when she felt a certain hard angle and he bit back a groan, suddenly realizing why he'd come.

He wasn't cool with his brother putting the moves on her and he sure as hell didn't like the idea of Buddy or Jake dropping their shorts in her presence either.

Ignoring what that might mean, Sam inhaled the flowery, fresh scent of her hair and enjoyed the soft press of full breasts against his chest. Suddenly nothing mattered but putting his mouth on hers again and finding out if she tasted as good as he remembered.

As if sensing his intent, she made a sound of protest and scrambled out of reach, her eyes huge and dark with suspicion and…was that arousal?

"What are you doing here, Major?" she demanded a little breathlessly. For a long moment he watched from beneath heavy lids before taking a step towards her, enjoying the flash of annoyance that replaced the mild panic when she found herself backed against the wall.

Blocking her escape with a palm to the wall, he tunneled his free hand beneath the soft, fragrant cloud surrounding her flushed face. He wrapped his fingers around the back of her neck and gently pressed his thumb into the soft hollow at the base of her throat. The rapid flutter beneath his touch had him lifting her face to his.

The scent of peaches drifted to him and his gut clenched.

Damn, he thought, *she makes me hungry.* Dropping his gaze to her mouth, he feathered a knuckle across her jaw to the corner of her lips and when her breath hitched in her throat, his blood went hot.

"I had no intention of coming here," he accused in a voice rough and deep with need. "But you…make me crazy. I couldn't stay away."

With a sharply indrawn breath Cassidy fisted her hands in his shirt as though she couldn't make up her mind whether to push him away or pull him close. Sam took advantage of her indecision to open his mouth over hers in a soft kiss that stole her breath and sent his head reeling.

"Samuel," she protested tightly against his mouth.

With a deep "Hmm?" he slid his tongue along her lower lip before dipping inside where she was warm and delicious. He hummed again, this time with growing need.

God, he thought, he hadn't exaggerated the memory of her taste, or the feel of her mouth moving beneath his.

"S-Samuel," she stuttered, "this…this is a bad idea." *You're telling me.* But she didn't pull away, which told Sam he wasn't the only crazy person here. In fact, she tilted her head to give him better access and her breath hitched in her throat.

It was the sign he'd unconsciously been waiting for.

"I like the way you say my name," he growled against her lips, before rocking his mouth over hers, his control rapidly slipping. "I like the way your breath hitches in your throat when you're aroused." He pressed his hips against hers. "It makes me…hard."

"*I'm not!*" she protested. "I…don't…" Then flattened her palm over his heart, drew in a shaky breath and tried again. "You're *not*." But her words emerged on a moan when she felt exactly how hard he was, ruining her denial.

"I beg to differ," he drawled, and chuckled when she blushed and huffed out an embarrassed giggle.

"No, I'm s-serious," she stuttered, squirming away,

only to find herself backed into a corner. Huffing with annoyance, she narrowed her eyes, stuck out her chin and clenched her hands as though she was contemplating taking a swing at him.

He smiled. He wouldn't mind letting her try.

"Look," she said, shoving the hair off her forehead, "I have bigger problems than your…um, ego, okay?"

Sam folded his arms and propped a shoulder against the wall, taking in the tousled, appealingly flustered picture she made. She looked about sixteen, and there was absolutely nothing cool or distant about Dr. Mahoney from Boston now.

His brow rose. "Yeah, like?" He grinned into her flushed face. "Like why bedpans are listed with surgical scrubs?"

CHAPTER SIX

CASSIDY LAUGHED. "DON'T be ridiculous," she said, rolling her eyes. Her voice had emerged all breathy and excited, like she was a teenager again, for heaven's sake. She'd been muttering about bedpans, of all things, while trying not to think about a certain Navy SEAL. Then suddenly there he was—looking like hot sin, bad attitude and way better than she remembered. And if, when she'd been pressed up against all that hard heat, she'd been tempted to get reacquainted with that awesome body, she wasn't about to admit it out loud. She'd been a little startled, that's all. She was over her attraction to him. Well, mostly.

Looking into his darkly handsome face, Cassidy admitted to herself that he was a very dangerous man. He made her forget about good sense, heartbreak and painful lessons. He made her yearn to toss good sense out with her inhibitions. Fortunately she'd come to her senses in time.

Nibbling nervously on her bottom lip, she kept a wary eye on him and focused on getting her heart rate down from stroke level, only to have it kicking into high gear again when he pushed away from the doorframe.

"Look, Major," she said quickly, throwing up a hand when he moved closer and looked like he wanted to nibble on her lip too. "I'm…busy." His chest connected with her out-flung palm and didn't stop. "*Really* busy." She squeaked and retreated, annoyed that just a minute in his presence and she was acting all girly and flustered. "Stop. *Dammit*, I don't have time for your…um…warped idea of…of foreplay. Samuel, *stop*!"

A dark brow hiked into his hairline and his mouth curled up at one corner. Great, now he was laughing at her. She huffed out a breath. Could this get any more embarrassing?

"Foreplay?"

Ignoring his question and figuring it was rhetorical anyway, Cassidy scuttled sideways and headed for the door, turning when she reached the relative safety of the hallway. *Ready to make a run for it if he made any sudden moves.*

"So what *are* you doing here, Major?" *Besides making my knees wobble and my pulse race.*

He turned, his gaze leisurely moving over her face until his hooded glance met hers, and add making her head spin to his sins. After a long moment, during which Cassidy thought she'd hyperventilate, he finally held up his bandaged hand.

"Oh." Her breath whooshed out and a small frown wrinkled her brow. For heaven's sake, she wasn't disappointed that he hadn't come to push her up against any walls. In fact, she was relieved. She was really very busy and didn't have time for games.

"Why didn't you just say so?" she gritted through clenched teeth, before spinning on her heel to head down the corridor at a sharp clip. She led the way through Reception and into the suture room, reaching for a lab coat on a nearby hook, figuring she needed the added protection against that penetrating gaze if she wanted to appear professional. Heck, if she wanted to *think*.

She fumbled for a button and was horrified to find that her hands were trembling too much to perform a task she'd mastered at five. Biting back a growl of disgust, Cassidy huffed out a breath, smoothed out her expression and turned to find him leaning against the bed, watching her thoughtfully as he slowly unwound the bandage covering his hand.

Crossing her arms beneath her breasts, she made herself focus on medical issues and not on how good he looked. "Frankly, I'm surprised to see you," she remarked, as coolly as if her pulse wasn't skipping all over the place like she was on an adrenaline rush. "I expected you to just rip them out with your teeth."

His raised brow suggested she was missing a few IQ points. "And what?" he demanded. "Use them as lethal spitballs?"

Her lips curled without her permission. "You're exaggerating."

Sam snorted. "Have you ever had nylon thread holding your flesh together?"

"No," she said, taking his hand and feeling the jolt clear to her elbow. *Whoa. Not this again.* Firming her lips, she resolutely ignored the sensation of his warm calloused skin against hers by inspecting the healing wound. After a few moments she reached for needle scissors and gently lifted each suture before snipping and tugging it free. "As a rule I avoid bar fights," she continued, looking up briefly to find his mouth tilted in an ironic half-smile.

Her chest went tight. *Yikes.* The man was living, breathing sin. *And she had a dangerous urge to...well, lick him up one side and down the other.* She frowned at her unprofessional thoughts. "And throwing myself out of moving aircraft."

The chuckle vibrating deep in his chest filled the small room and created an odd sensation in her belly. "You don't know what you're missing."

"Yes, I do," she corrected mildly, as she wiped disinfectant along the tender scar before spraying the area with a thin layer of synthetic skin. "I'm missing broken bones and you're clearly missing your mind." She covered his hand with a waterproof adhesive dressing. "Be careful with that for another few days and keep it clean and dry."

He caught her wrist before she could turn away and her startled gaze rose to his.

"Don't you want to know what it's like…hurtling towards earth at a hundred feet per second?" he murmured deeply, softly.

Cassidy swallowed hard at the expression in his gold eyes. *Holy cow.* "No, I…" *If it's anything like I'm currently feeling…terrifying.*

Without waiting for her brain to clear, Sam reeled her in until the warm male scent of him enveloped her and her common sense scattered, along with her reasons for keeping him at arm's length. In fact, she suddenly couldn't recall why she'd thought this was a bad idea. Without the slightest effort on his part he was rendering her speechless.

"Major…" She thought maybe a token protest was necessary, even though she couldn't remember what she should be protesting against.

"It's like that moment during sex," he rasped, closing the gap to her mouth as she watched, frozen with fascination, "when you realize…" his lips brushed hers and he flattened her captive hand against his chest "…there's no going back."

"Major…" she croaked again, terrified that he would feel the way she trembled. His mouth smiled against hers, as though he knew what he was doing to her. His tongue emerged to sweep across the seam of her mouth. His heart pounded like a jackhammer beneath her palm. *Or was that hers?* "And then, like a heated rush…" he murmured silkily, sending blood thundering in her ears. A breathy whimper escaped and before she could stop it her palm slid up his warm chest to his neck. "It hits you…*wham!*"

She jolted the instant his teeth closed over her bottom lip to tug on the sensitive flesh. Hot shivers scattered from the base of her spine into every cell and Cassidy thought, *Oh, God,* as her knees wobbled.

Before she could protest again, Sam's mouth opened

over hers in a kiss that instantly spiraled out of control. It turned the moisture in her body to steam and sucked air from as far down as her toes.

It felt like she'd been tossed into the center of a tornado. She told herself that if he hadn't been holding her captive she would have pulled away. Broken free. Run for her life.

At least she would have if she'd been able to formulate a single thought. Then she was being yanked up against all his hard heat, his arm an iron band across her back while he fed her hungry kisses that were all tongue and greed and stole her breath along with her mind.

Cassidy's breasts tightened and her blood caught fire. Just when she felt that insidious slide into insanity, he froze and pulled back.

Wha—?

Stunned by the force of emotions storming through her, Cassidy sucked in a desperate breath and stared back at him, wondering a little hysterically if the pounding in her head was a sign that her brain was about to explode. The man literally sucked up everything around him like a level-five twister.

His hands tightened and his eyes looked a little wild— *kind of like she was feeling*—and it took a few moments to realize the pounding wasn't in her head.

A loud *bang* was abruptly followed by yelling that had Sam shifting from sexy and sleepy to sexy and…*lethal*. Without a sound he shoved her roughly aside to move on silent, deadly feet towards the hallway, his hand reaching for…a weapon?

Awareness returned in a rush and Cassidy flung herself after him before he could launch a silent attack on some poor unsuspecting person. She grabbed for his shirt to hold him back and he rounded on her, eyes deadly and cold. It was clearly his attack SEAL face, Cassidy thought with a shudder. She could easily imagine the enemy quailing with terror. Heck, *she* was trembling.

"It's all right, Major, it's just…it's just a medical emergency." At least she hoped it was and not an invasion by paramilitary groups that gossip said hid in the mountains. Then all bets were off. And when he gave no indication that he'd heard, she shook him. "Stand down, Major, I've got this."

For long scary beats he stared at her, his expression cold and flat. Just when she thought he meant to swat her like a pesky fly, he blinked, slowly, like he was coming back from…*a flashback*?

Cassidy gulped, but then his face abruptly lost color and before she could move, he staggered. She reached for him but he threw out a hand to steady himself against the wall.

"Go," he rasped, giving her the sharp edge of his shoulder. She hesitated, watching his forehead drop against the bulge of his biceps. The muscles in his wide back bunched and turned hard. After a couple of hesitant beats she turned and took off down the hallway.

One look at the couple in ER had all thoughts of Sam's flashbacks flying from her head. The woman being propped up by a clearly freaked-out man was as white as a sheet and covered in sweat. She clutched her heavily pregnant belly, and Cassidy noticed blood and fluid staining the front of her maternity dress.

"*Help her*," the man yelled wildly when he saw Cassidy. "Help her. *Oh, God,* help her. She's bleeding. It won't stop," he croaked pleadingly. "It just won't stop and the baby…" He swallowed. "I think the baby's stuck."

Cassidy grabbed a nearby gurney and met them halfway, swallowing the urge to yell at them for waiting so long. This had all the signs of a home delivery gone wrong. So dreadfully wrong. She just hoped it wasn't too late.

"What happened?" she demanded. "Why didn't you come in earlier?"

"She wanted a home birth, but the midwife's not answering her phone," the man babbled through bloodless lips, his

eyes wide and wild. "I didn't know what to do. What the
hell do I know about babies? Nothing. I know *nothing...
Oh, God,* what have I done?" As white as parchment, he
swayed and Cassidy put out a hand to steady him. That's
all they needed. Another casualty.

Before she could snap out an order for him to get a grip,
the woman gave a low moan and her legs buckled. Yelling
out a code blue and hoping someone would hear, Cassidy
lurched forward just as the woman fell, her weight taking
them both to the floor.

Vaguely aware that the man was screaming and crying
hysterically, Cassidy opened her mouth to rap out an order,
but the breath had been knocked from her and all she could
manage was a strangled gasp.

Sam's face appeared overhead and before she could
blink at his abrupt appearance he'd bent and lifted the
woman off her with easy strength. Sucking in air, Cassidy
scrambled to her feet.

"You okay?" he demanded in a low tone as he gently
placed the woman on the gurney.

She should be the one asking but even as she opened her
mouth to voice her concerns, she noted that other than a
faint pallor and a hard, closed expression, Sam seemed to
have recovered. His eyes were clear and sharply focused.

"Cassidy?"

She shook her head to dispel her misgivings and noticed
he'd pulled on a lab coat that strained the shoulder seams
and rode up his strong wrists. He'd also slung a stethoscope
around his neck. He met her pointed look with a raised
brow, silently telling her she had more important things to
worry about. Things like their distressed patient.

"I'm fine," she rapped out. "Get her details." And took
off down the hallway with the gurney, hitting the emergency button as she streaked past.

The next few minutes were a blur as she wheeled the
gurney into the OR, where she checked the woman's vitals.

Her concern ratcheted up a notch at the patient's labored breathing and erratic pulse.

"Dammit, dammit, *dammit*," she muttered, grabbing a pair of scissors to cut away the blood-soaked dress. She needed another experienced professional. Preferably someone who had done this before. She needed Dr. Montgomery.

By the time the night nurse burst into the OR, Cassidy had finished intubating the mother. With swift, competent movements she hooked up a saline drip and rapped out orders for drugs.

Ripping open a syringe package with her teeth, she fitted the needle and shoved it into the first vial the nurse handed to her. "Prep her for a C-section," she told the nurse briskly, injecting the contents into the port. "And then call Dr. Montgomery. I'm going to need help on this one."

"You've got help," a deep voice informed her from the doorway and Cassidy looked over her shoulder to see Sam striding into the OR.

Cassidy's eyes widened. "Major—"

"Her name is Gail Sanders," he interrupted in a voice as deep and calm as though he did this every day. "She's a kindergarten teacher. This is her first pregnancy—no history of problems." His eyes were calm and steady on hers. The silent message was clear. They didn't have time to wait for the elderly doctor or discuss *his* mental issues. "Moving her when you're ready."

Cassidy frowned and held his gaze for a couple of beats, conscious of the look of wide-eyed apprehension the nurse flashed between them.

"Dr. Mahoney…?" Heather prompted, breaking the tension filling the room.

"Major Kellan will need the ultrasound,' Cassidy said briskly with a curt nod in Sam's direction, before moving to Gail's feet. They transferred her to the operating table as Heather rolled the ultrasound into position. Cassidy took the proffered tube of gel and squirted a thick line over the apex of the patient's distended belly.

Sam lifted the probe. "Go suit up," he said quietly, eyes on the screen as he rolled the probe through the gel. "I'll handle this."

"Major—" she began, breaking off when his golden eyes lifted. "This is…" She bit her lip and ran her fingers through her hair in agitation. "Are you…?" *Damn*. How did you ask someone if they were sane enough to handle a delicate procedure like this one was going to be?

His face darkened with impatience, and Cassidy knew he wasn't going to discuss what had happened in the hallway. Watching the expert way he wielded the probe, she was forced to admit he looked fine. More than fine. As though he hadn't had a flashback—or whatever had happened—just minutes earlier.

"I'm fine, Doctor," he snapped, returning his attention to the patient. "But *they* aren't and unless you get your ass into gear, they won't be for much longer."

Cassidy hesitated another couple of beats. "I hope you know what you're doing," she said quietly, unsure whom she was addressing.

It took her less than a minute to throw off her clothes, pull on clean scrubs and scrape her hair off her face. By the time she'd finished scrubbing Sam was behind her, holding out a surgical gown that she slipped over her arms after a searching look up into his dark face.

He must have correctly interpreted her probing look because his mouth pulled into a tight line. "This is a job for two people who know what they're doing."

"Monty—"

"Isn't here," he interrupted smoothly. His eyes caught and held hers. "We can't wait, Cassidy. And you know it."

Knowing he was right, Cassidy ground her back molars together. "You're right," she admitted briskly, moving towards the OR doors, "but *you* assist."

Heather Murray had already positioned the colored electrode pads and was fitting a saturation probe over the patient's forefinger when Cassidy hit the doors with her shoulder. Tying the surgical cap at the back of her head, she slipped her hands into surgical gloves the nurse held out.

She watched as Heather hooked Gail up to the heart monitor, a wrinkle of concern marring her brow when a rapid beeping filled the silence. Stepping closer to the ultrasound screen, Cassidy studied the strip of images Sam had printed out, before gently palpating the woman's belly. A quick examination revealed the baby lying breech, with its spine facing upward.

She felt rather than saw Sam come up behind her. "I've delivered babies in worse positions than this," he said at her shoulder.

"So have I," Cassidy agreed, "but not without an OB/GYN on standby. The bleeding is also a major concern." When he remained silent, Cassidy lifted her head to find him studying her intently. Her heart gave a little lurch. "What?"

His eyes lit with a warm smile. "You can do it, Doc. Have a little faith. Besides, I'm right here."

She was about to ask if he'd done *this* before but the monitor beeped and Heather called out, "Heart rate increasing, Doctor," and Cassidy realized they didn't have time to hang around debating his experience.

Sam shoved his hands into latex gloves while the nurse tied his gown and mask. Cassidy moved to the patient's side and hoped she wasn't making a terrible mistake. As the doctor on duty, she was about to trust a man who thought parachuting into hostile territory armed to the teeth was like making love. "Major—" Cassidy began, only to have him cut her off.

"I think we've had this conversation before, *Cassidy*," he drawled, putting her firmly in her place as a colleague now. He looked big and tough and impatient—and most of all competent. After flicking a pointed look at Heather, he returned Cassidy's gaze meaningfully. "We're good."

Biting back a sigh, she opened her mouth and said, "Let's do this."

Heather called anxiously, "Blood pressure dropping, Doctor."

Cassidy's gaze snapped to the monitor. "Keep an eye on the baby's vitals and let me know if Mom's BP drops below fifty." Sam expertly swabbed the woman's belly with iodine as Cassidy waited, scalpel in hand. The instant he was finished she felt for the correct place with her left hand and then made a clean incision with her right. The scalpel sliced through layers of skin, muscle and uterine wall. Sam gently coaxed the baby into position while she slid her hands into the exposed uterus. Within seconds the infant's head and shoulders emerged and Cassidy could see why the baby had been lying breech—and why the mother was bleeding.

The placenta had detached from the uterine wall and the umbilical cord was looped around the baby's neck and under her arm. The infant was blue and flaccid.

Cassidy's heart gave a blip of alarm. *Dammit, dammit, dammit,* she chanted mentally, getting a firm hold on the infant while Sam gently unwound the cord. He accepted the heated towel the nurse offered as Cassidy slid the infant free and handed her over. Deftly cutting the cord, she applied the clip and looked up briefly to catch Sam's intense gaze over the top of his face mask. His gold eyes were dark and solemn on hers. "She's yours," Cassidy said simply, and turned back to save the mother. Gail Sanders's time was running out.

"I've got this," he said, but Cassidy had already tuned out everything, instinct telling her that Sam really *did* have it. She didn't have to make a choice or leave the endangered infant to the nurse.

Besides, there was nothing she could do for the baby now that Sam couldn't do just as well.

Over the next half-hour she communicated with the nurse in terse bursts until she finally managed to get the bleeding under control. Heaving a relieved sigh, she wiped her burning eyes against her shoulder and ordered additional units of blood. Then she set about closing the uterus, the layer of muscle and finally the incision wound.

Lastly, she inserted a drain and stepped back to check the patient's vitals. Finding her still critical but edging toward stable, Cassidy stepped back, wondering for the first time in more than an hour if Sam had managed to save the infant.

She caught sight of him waiting just beyond the lights. For long moments their gazes held, his eyes so intensely gold and solemn her pulse gave a painful little jolt. Had she…? *Oh, God, had she imagined that feeble little cry?* Then his eyes crinkled at the corners in a rare moment of shared accord and gestured to the pink bundle in his arms.

Suddenly tears burned the backs of her eyes and she sucked in a quick breath at the blaze of emotion blocking her throat. *They'd done it,* she thought on a burst of elation that she attributed to their accomplishment and not… well, anything else.

She sent Sam a wobbly smile, rapidly blinking away her emotional tears as she turned back to recheck the patient's vitals to give herself a minute. She clamped off the anesthetic, leaving the shunt in place. "We'll keep her sedated while we wait for the chopper," she told Heather, conscious of Sam's silent scrutiny as they transferred the patient to the gurney.

"You're not keeping her here?" he asked, as they covered Gail with a cotton spread and then a thick woolen blanket. Cassidy shook her head and went to the OR refrigerator, withdrawing a couple of vials of antibiotics.

"The hospital doesn't have the facilities for such a critical patient," she explained, hooking up another saline bag. "Besides, mother and child both need proper neonatal care.

I want them in a large center with access to hi-tech facilities and equipment if anything goes wrong."

Pulling down her face mask, she took a new syringe, slid the needle into first one vial and then the other, finally injecting the cocktail into the new saline bag.

"I'll go speak to her husband," she said, when she finally ran out of things to do, her emotions suddenly as fragile as the lives they'd just saved.

Disposing of needle, syringe and surgical gloves, she quickly wrote down the details of the procedure and the drugs she'd used. With a sigh of relief she turned to leave, stiffening in surprise when long fingers closed over her shoulder.

Looking up into Sam's shadowed face, Cassidy sucked in a startled breath. Illumination from the surgical lights slid across the bottom half of his face, leaving the rest in deep shadow. It made him appear bigger and darker and… *hell*, more dangerous than ever.

Unbidden, images of what had happened in the suture room flashed through her head and she winced. *Darn*. One look into his dark gold eyes brought on a flashback of his mouth closing over hers in a hot, greedy kiss. She'd hoped to escape before he remembered that she'd almost climbed into his lap and rubbed her body against his. She licked dry lips.

"What?" she asked huskily, her throat tight with awkwardness and a sudden baffling anxiety.

"You want to see her?"

Sam watched confusion chase wariness across Cassidy's face until he gently handed over his precious bundle. She'd been instrumental in saving the infant and deserved to share the joy of that new life.

Drawn by the subtle scent of her, easily discernible even over the antiseptic smells of the OR, Sam moved closer. He'd been immensely impressed with her ability and the efficient way she'd handled the crisis. She'd never once hesitated or panicked. Hell, he'd seen seasoned soldiers panic in less dire situations and had to admire how she'd kept a cool head.

It had been touch and go there for a while, but the new-born was finally pink and glowing with life. Tiny hands were tucked against a petal-soft cheek and the infant looked, Sam thought, like a cherub praying. Huge dark eyes stared up into Cassidy's face with such mesmerizing intensity that the hair on his arms and the back of his neck rose. It was as though she knew she was being held by someone...special.

Her expression both delighted and enthralled, Cassidy gently touched a pink cheek and the tiny folded hands. "Look, Sam," she breathed, "she looks like a little angel. Like she's praying. Isn't she the most beautiful thing you've ever seen?"

For long silent moments Sam found his gaze locked on Cassidy's face, unable to utter a sound. Her expression was one he'd never thought to see on her beautiful face—soft and sweet and glowing with uncomplicated delight.

God, he thought painfully, *she really is beautiful.* And so much more than he'd thought. Swallowing the lump blocking his vocal cords, he finally managed a raspy, "Yeah. Beautiful."

Oblivious to his chaotic emotions, she continued to murmur softly to the infant, laughing when the little rosebud mouth opened in a wide yawn.

Feeling like he'd been shot in the chest with a high-powered rifle, Sam forced his emotions under control and moved to untie her gown. He finally gave in to the urge to brush his lips against the long elegant line of her throat as he leaned forward to murmur, "You did great, Doc."

Goose bumps broke out across her skin and a shiver moved through her as she jerked away, her face flushing as she aimed an uncertain smile in his direction. At least he wasn't alone in this unwanted attraction, he thought with satisfaction.

"You too, Major," she answered briskly, carefully avoiding touching him as she passed the infant back. She moved away jerkily, looking suddenly tired—and spooked, like she was ready to bolt.

He tucked the baby into the crook of his arm. "Cassidy?"

She paused in the process of pulling off the surgical gown and sent him a look over her shoulder, eyes wide and a little desperate.

"Yes?"

"You going to finish what you started earlier…before we were interrupted?"

Immediately a wild flush heated her face and her eyes widened as though she thought he was suggesting they finish their interrupted kiss. Her mouth opened but all that emerged was a strangled, "Uh…"

"I have another twenty-seven stitches," he went on, grinning wickedly at the deer-in-the-headlights expression that flashed across her face. Her mouth closed with a snap and her look of furious embarrassment had his soft chuckle following in her wake.

"Meet me in the ER in fifteen minutes," she snapped, and Sam got the impression she'd considered punching the smile off his face. He was suddenly glad he was holding a newborn.

Cassidy Mahoney, it seemed, was not a woman to be trifled with. And why that made his grin widen, he didn't know. Maybe he was an idiot, or crazy, like his family believed.

"What do you think?" he asked the infant staring intently up at him. The tiny girl blinked before surrendering to another big yawn, making Sam chuckle.

"Yeah," he snorted softly, "my thoughts exactly, sweetheart."

CHAPTER SEVEN

CASSIDY SENT FRAN GILBERT to the ER to deal with a hot, appealing SEAL, assuring herself she wasn't a coward. Besides, Gail's husband needed a status update.

She found Chip Sanders being fussed over by one of the older nurses on duty. The warm, motherly woman in her late fifties squeezed the new father's hand in silent support when they caught sight of Cassidy heading in their direction.

His expression was so painfully hopeful that Cassidy had to smile in reassurance as she announced that he had a beautiful baby daughter and that his wife's progress was promising.

Chip leapt up with a joyous whoop and Cassidy had to laugh when he caught her in a huge grateful hug. She briefly returned his embrace, cautioning that Gail was still critical and that she and the baby were being transferred to Spruce Ridge General.

After he rushed off to see his new family, she found herself smiling as she headed for the wards. There was nothing like making someone so happy they forgot all trauma and fear, she mused. Fortunately for Chip, everything had worked out fine.

Thanks to one overwhelming Navy SEAL. A man who seemed to have a really bad effect on her. Just the sound of his deep voice sent excited little zings into places that had no business zinging and she ended up losing a good portion of her brain.

Just as Cassidy was writing notations on the night roster, news came through that the chopper was five minutes out. After giving the night nurse a few last-minute instructions, Cassidy headed for Recovery to collect the patients for transport.

She...*they* had done everything they could to ensure Gail Sanders and her baby pulled through the traumatic incident. It was now up to the OB/GYN at Spruce Ridge General to ensure they stayed that way.

Heather was waiting for her and together they rushed the new family to the helipad, where the Medevac helicopter was already landing. While the paramedics transferred Gail and her baby to the chopper, Cassidy gave the Medevac doctor a rundown of the patient's condition and signed the release forms. With a nod, the guy sent her an appreciative smile and an over-the-shoulder thumbs-up as he loped off towards the waiting craft. Bare minutes after it had landed, the chopper was heading towards Spruce Ridge.

Beside her, Heather gave a huge sigh and sent Cassidy an elated smile. "Wasn't that just great? I love it when a bad situation turns out well, don't you?" She threw her arms around Cassidy and made her laugh with an exuberant hug. "Ooh, and wasn't the major just wonderful? With Gail's baby, I mean," she added hastily, when Cassidy drew back with a dry look. "I heard Chip was blubbering like a little girl," Heather chatted on. "Poor guy. He must have been terrified." She stopped to sigh dramatically. "Isn't he just dreamy?"

Cassidy eyed her sharply. "Who? Chip?"

Heather giggled. "No, silly. Samuel Kellan. Just wait until I tell the girls what happened. They're going to flip. Imagine, me getting to see him in action with my own eyes?" She squeaked and gave Cassidy another quick hug.

Then with a hurried, "You're the greatest, Doc," she turned and disappeared into the darkened hospital.

Cassidy shook her head at the departing nurse and turned to watch as the chopper's running lights rose over the dark mountains. With the *whup, whup, whup* fading into the night, she took deep breaths of cold mountain air and slowly let the tension of the night slide away.

"Well," she said dryly to no one in particular, "it seems Crescent Lake's hero has done it again."

She wasn't jealous that Major Hotstuff was getting all the credit for the night's work, she assured herself. He'd stepped up when she'd needed him, it was true, but you'd think he'd performed a miracle worthy of sainthood.

Laughing at herself, Cassidy went to tell Fran she was taking a break. Hoping to get a few hours' sleep before the next emergency, she headed for the quiet of her office.

The privacy hallway connecting the offices was in darkness but dim light eased its way through an open doorway. Cassidy's pulse gave a little bump and she paused as the scene brought back unpleasant memories. Fear clutched at her belly until she reminded herself that Crescent Lake wasn't Boston. Drugged-up vice cops didn't break into doctors' offices in small mountain towns, looking for prescription drugs. At least she hoped not.

Besides, in the few weeks she'd been in town the most dangerous thing to happen had been when she'd been escorted to the local jail to treat a hot, attitude-ridden Navy SEAL.

No, that wasn't quite true, she amended silently. *That* had been when he'd pushed her up against the ER wall and rearranged her brain synapses.

Heart hammering, Cassidy quietly approached the open doorway. She drew in a wobbly breath and peered around the door, half expecting to find crazed druggies ripping open drawers looking for their next fix. Her breath escaped in a whoosh when she found everything as it should be.

She was sliding her hand up the wall to turn off the
light when she realized the desk lamp was on and not the
ceiling fixture. Heading across the room, she reached over
the desk to extinguish the lamp when a soft sound had her
wide gaze flying towards the shadows. The sight of Crescent Lake's favorite son draped over the sofa with an arm
flung across his face, gave her a weird sense of déjà vu.

Straightening, Cassidy allowed her hand to fall away. It
seemed the man couldn't find anything big enough to accommodate his large body. She wondered absently why he
hadn't left, and took the opportunity to study him without
him being aware.

He was back in the faded jeans and she took a moment
to admire the way the soft material hugged his narrow hips
and long muscular legs while cupping more intimate places.
The black T-shirt fitted even more snugly, stretching across
his wide chest while straining the shoulder seams and the
sleeves around his big biceps.

It was only when she could see his lashes casting dark
shadows on the slash of his cheekbones that she realized
she'd moved across the room and was standing staring
down at him like an infatuated adolescent.

Darn, she thought, biting her lip, getting all excited
about some *guy* was the height of idiocy—especially one
who liked free-falling from high altitudes and blowing stuff
up. One who wouldn't be sticking around for long before
he was off again, saving the world.

Turning to go, she spied a blanket over the back of
the sofa and reached for it an instant before hard fingers
clamped over her wrist. In less time than it took for her
heart to jerk hard against her ribs, she was flying through
the air to land with a bone-rattling thud that knocked the
air from her lungs. She barely managed a strangled *oomph*
as a heavy weight rolled her across the floor.

They came to an abrupt stop against the solid desk with

Cassidy's wrists shackled over her head. A large hand clamped over her mouth, stifling her shocked gasp.

Blinking, Cassidy found herself staring up into a dark face lit with fierce gold eyes. For an awful moment she visualized him whipping out a knife and slicing her throat before she could draw her next breath.

She felt him everywhere—heat and hardness pressing her soft curves into the floor. During the tumble, one long, hard thigh had found its way between hers, effectively pinning her down. All she could do was gasp and stare into gleaming gold eyes as she waited for his next move.

One second she could see her life flashing before her eyes, the next he was cursing and rolling away to lie silently and rigidly beside her. The suddenness of the move stunned her and all she could do was try to calm her jagged pulse and smooth her ragged breathing. All she could think was, *What the heck was that?* It had been scary and…*darn it*…she hated to admit it a little exciting.

She was a sick person.

She felt rather than saw his head turn. "You okay?"

And he was insane.

Sucking in air, Cassidy lowered her arms and pushed her hair off her face before rearing upright to glare down at him.

"Are you insane?" she demanded furiously, then snapped her mouth closed when she realized that maybe it wasn't the most sensitive thing to say to someone suffering from PTSD—if that's what he had—but, *heck*, the man gave being trigger-happy a bad name.

Not surprisingly, he didn't look the least bit amused by what had happened. In fact, he looked mad—well, that made two of them—and embarrassed.

Embarrassed? What did he *have to be embarrassed about?* She *was the one who'd gone flying through the air.*

He scrubbed a hand over his face with a weary sigh and growled, "Sorry…" so softly she almost didn't catch it.

Her jaw dropped open. "Sorry? You're...*sorry*?" She was getting hysterical again and made an effort to lower her voice, even though she felt she was entitled to a little hysteria. "You can't attack people like that and just say sorry, Major."

He turned and scowled, his dark brows flattening across his forehead in a heavy line of frustration. "What the hell do you expect me to say? Besides, it was your fault."

Her eyebrows shot into her hairline. "*My f-fault?*" she spluttered, and when he smirked she had to get a firm grip on her temper before she gave in to the urge to smack it off his face.

"Hey, you were bending over me," he pointed out reasonably, as if he had women bending over him all the time. And after witnessing Heather's gushing infatuation, he probably did. *The jerk.* "What was I supposed to think? I thought you wanted to wrestle me to the floor. I was just being accommodating."

Cassidy stared at him open-mouthed for a few seconds as his words sank in then uttered a sound of disbelief. She drew up her legs and shoved her hands in her hair before dropping her forehead onto her knees. She snickered helplessly for a few beats. "You are such a liar," she said when she could talk without gasping.

He lifted the arm he'd slung over his face to crinkle his eyes at her, his poet's mouth pulled into a crooked smile. *God, that little grin was appealing.*

"Says who? *You?*" He made a rude sound. "For all I know, you *were* just looking for an excuse to roll around on the floor with me. *You* know, finish what you started earlier?"

"What *you* started, you mean," she retorted.

"*Me?*" He shook his head. "You have a defective memory there, Doc."

"And you're delusional. I ought to throw you out." Another mocking sound accompanied the *yeah-right* look he sent her and she narrowed her gaze. "You don't think I can?"

"Babe, I *know* you can't."

He sounded so arrogantly male that she straightened and stared at him. "Excuse me," she demanded frostily. "Did you just call me *babe*?"

He grinned and said, "Uh-huh," with the kind of look that had a bubble of laughter rising in her throat. *Darn*. She didn't want to find him irresistible, but there was just too much to like. Despite…well, everything.

Blowing out a breath, she dropped her head back against the desk, suddenly exhausted by her ping-ponging emotions. "Well, don't. It's demeaning."

"It is?" He sounded genuinely surprised. "Why?"

Cassidy snorted. "You ask that when you probably call every woman you meet *babe* because it saves you having to remember their names."

Sam was quiet for a moment, as though he was seriously considering her accusation, before finally shaking his head and saying, "That's not true. I don't call the ward sergeant at Coronado Med Center *babe*." He gave a shudder. "*Or* my CO's wife, for that matter. That's a surefire way for a guy to get court-martialed."

Cassidy caught herself smiling when she couldn't afford to. He was too big, too macho, too…*everything*. Everything she'd told herself she didn't want in a man. Everything she was finding alarmingly likeable.

She pushed out her lower lip and blew out a frustrated breath. "You're changing the subject, Major. It isn't normal for anyone to think they're being attacked in their sleep. I was just reaching for the blanket."

"That's what you say," he said, waggling his eyebrows at her when she rolled her eyes. Snagging her wrist, he tugged her towards him, tucking her body beneath his when she lost her balance. Cassidy once again found herself staring up into his darkly handsome face while his big body covered hers.

"What are you *doing*?" she squeaked, realizing his hard thigh was pressing against places that hadn't seen any action in a long while. It was mortifying to admit those places were turning liquid with heat.

"If you need to ask," Sam said, sliding his hand over her hip to rub his thumb into the crease her jeans created between hip and thigh, "you're not as smart as I thought."

She slapped a hand over his to stop him heading for forbidden territory. "I'm smart enough to know that whatever you're thinking is a mistake."

"*This*," he murmured, and dropped a kiss at the outer corner of her eyebrow, "is not a mistake." He slid his mouth to her ear. "SEALs carry really big weapons," he whispered wickedly. "Wanna see?"

Cassidy's gasp ended on a giggle at his terrible pun. *Yes, please. "No!"* She groaned silently. *No looking at his... weapon.* Or anything else.

"Major," she began, trying to sound firm, but her voice gave a little hitch as arousal sent heat skittering through her veins. "Let me up." If she stayed spread out beneath him like jelly on peanut butter, there was no telling what would happen.

His eyes had gone all dark and hot. He shook his head slowly. "I can't," he confessed, abruptly serious. Catching her hand, he brought it to his mouth, where he pressed a gentle kiss into the center of her palm. "I've tried. *God* knows, I've tried." He nibbled on the fleshy part of her thumb. "There's just no denying...*this*."

Her belly tightened and she let her fingers curl helplessly over his jaw, rough with a dark shadow that looked a good few hours past five o'clock. The rasp against her skin sent shivers of longing and arousal up her arm into her chest and a hot yearning set up residence in her belly. "Try harder," she gulped.

His smile was quick and sinful as his big hand smoothed a path of heat down the length of her arm, over her shoulder to her breast. "*Babe*," he drawled, brushing his thumb over the full bottom curve and drawing her nipple into a tight bud that had his eyes gleaming with satisfaction. "If it gets any harder I'll injure myself." He looked up from studying the hard tips of her breasts. "You're bound by oath to treat me then, aren't you?"

Cassidy slapped her hand over his with the intention of moving it to safer territory. "In your dreams, Major," she scoffed huskily, but her resistance was fast slipping away—right along with her mind. And she was having a hard time recalling why she should care.

"Sam," he corrected against her throat, and Cassidy lifted her chin to give him room, her eyes drifting closed with the lush pleasure of having his mouth on her. *Oh, God.* They needed to stop this before…before…

"Say it." A shiver raced down her spine, sparks bursting behind her eyelids as he opened his mouth to suck on a patch of delicate skin. She gave a little gasp and clenched her thighs around his, the pressure setting off tiny little explosions of sensation in forbidden places.

"Wh-what?" She tried to concentrate long enough to make sense of his words.

"My name." He abandoned her throat to kiss his way up to her parted lips. His thigh pushed harder against her. "Say it," he ordered softly, pulling back when she tried to capture his mouth with hers. A moan worked its way up from her throat and emerged as a growl before she could stop it. Tunneling her fingers into his hair, she tugged him closer and closed her teeth over his bottom lip in a punishing little nip.

"Don't make me hurt you, Major," she growled, and his answering chuckle was deep and dark and sent delicious sensations heating up lonely places. *Heck*, he was like a furnace, incinerating everything in sight—her resistance, her reservations...her *mind*—turning her to putty in his big, strong hands.

His mouth smiled against hers. "Say it," he taunted softly, applying a little hot, wet suction that made her moan. "Say it and I'll give you exactly what you want."

Cassidy heard a loud buzzing in her ears and in a far distant corner of her mind still capable of thought she acknowledged that he was right. She did want him and his name, "*Samuel*," emerged on a husky sigh.

With a growl, deep and low in his throat, he caught her mouth in a kiss so hot and raw that she felt it in the pit of her belly. He pulled oxygen from her lungs and a frantic response from her mouth. It was so good that Cassidy fisted her hands in his hair and opened her mouth beneath his, promising herself that she would stop. In a minute.

It was her last rational thought. The instant his warm hand slid over the naked skin of her belly, she lost all reason, all ability to think of anything but the sudden frenzy of his kiss. Excited thrills raced over her skin as her world narrowed and focused on his hot mouth, his eager hands. She tried to touch him everywhere at once—his shoulders, his wide back, his hard chest—as though she couldn't get enough.

She briefly acknowledged that she was in trouble—*big* trouble—when his hand slid beneath her jeans and cupped her through her panties. Thought slid away on a low moan as she arched into his touch, feeling perhaps for the first time the kind of hot, crazy desire people talked about. Too far gone to care that he was everything that was bad for her.

His touch felt too good, and the big erection pressing against her felt hard and powerful and welcome.

He shifted and before she knew it, he was whipping her T-shirt over her head. Grabbing a fistful of fabric at the back of his neck, he stripped off his own, sending both garments sailing over his shoulder into the shadows. Then he planted his big hands beside her head, and with their gazes locked he nudged her thighs apart before lowering his body slowly over hers until all that separated their good parts was denim and silk. At the press of his powerful erection into the notch between her legs he grimaced as though in pain and his eyes drifted closed.

"*Jeez*," he said, his voice so deep and rough it slid into her belly like dark sin. "*Cassidy…*" he breathed heavily, and stared down into her face with hot, glazed eyes. "You are so damn beautiful, do you know that? And I've had really carnal thoughts about your mouth for days," he growled. "It's driven me crazy, thinking about kissing you. Kind of like this." He bent his head and gave her a kiss, soft and sweet and hot. "*Oh, yeah*," he breathed against her mouth, sucking gently on her swollen lip. "It's lush and tempting and so damn sweet. It's all I can think about."

Then he opened his mouth over hers in a hard, hungry kiss that scattered her senses, and before Cassidy knew what was happening she was thrusting her hands into his hair and kissing him back, her mouth as hot and greedy as his.

Sam swept his tongue past her lips to taste the dark, sweet nectar within. She responded with a low hungry moan and closed her lips around his tongue, sucking hard.

Controlling himself with effort, Sam fed her hot, desperate kisses, tongue dueling and tangling while his hands streaked over her soft flesh, stripping off her clothing until she was left in nothing but a tiny triangle of teal silk.

Kneeing her smooth thighs apart, he settled his hips between them, pushing against her soft, wet heat until she was writhing restlessly against him.

"*Holy…*" His mind glazed over and he couldn't remember what he'd been about to say. Only knew that he wanted her more than he'd wanted anything. *Ever*.

"Samuel…" Her voice was a sweet, husky moan of desire that almost had him going off like a missile. He filled his big hands with her breasts and flicked at the hard little buds until a long, low wail tore from her throat and her back arched up off the floor.

Ignoring her entreaty, he dipped his head to scrape his teeth along her neck, nipping the delicate skin until she shivered as her palm slid down his belly. She pressed her hand against his button fly and he jolted like he'd been shot.

"*Sweet*..." he growled, grabbing her hand to pin it against the floor above her head. "Not yet, babe." He gave a rough laugh when a sound of frustration burst from her mouth. "Soon," he promised hoarsely, closing his mouth hungrily over one swollen breast. She gasped and his pulse spiked until all he could hear in the quiet room was the heavy thunder of his heart, the harsh sounds of their breathing and her soft, throaty whimpers.

She fisted her free hand in his hair and couldn't hold back the full-body shudder or the eager moan that ended with, "*Oh, my God*..."

Soothing her, he dropped a moist kiss between her lush breasts before heading south, stringing tiny, wet kisses across her abdomen. He paused to trace his tongue around her shallow navel, gently blowing against the damp skin until her belly quivered. His hum of amusement turned into a growl of pleasure.

With his mouth on her flat belly, Sam slid his hands up her long smooth thigh to hook his fingers into the narrow band of fabric at her hips. And before she could gasp out a breathless "*Wait*," he'd slid her panties down her legs and past her toes to send them sailing over his shoulder.

Grunting, he reared back onto his heels and looked at the woman sprawled like sin before him. For a moment he savored the tempting sight then dipped his head to run the tip of his tongue up the inside of her knee, chuckling when she shivered and let out a desperate whimper.

As though sensing the direction of his mouth, Cassidy uttered a squeak of protest and tried to clamp her legs together, fisting her hands in his hair to stop his upward progress. "No, Samuel," she cried breathlessly, "I don't—"

"It's okay," he murmured, sliding his big, rough hand over her quivering belly before wedging his shoulders between her thighs. He dragged damp kisses over her hips and stomach to the soft, sweet undersides of her breasts. Alternating stinging wet kisses with little swipes of his beard-roughened jaw that made her arch and moan, Sam gentled her with his hands and lips until her muscles went fluid and lax and she gave a long, lazy hum of pleasure.

The moment he felt her body shift languorously and turn liquid he moved and closed his mouth over her soft, damp folds. She tried to tug at him, her gasp of protest turning to a cry of pleasure as he pressed closer and did something with his tongue. In moments she was flying off the edge.

The force of her climax hit hard, and, eyes wide with shock, Cassidy could only lie there shuddering and think, *Holy cow...what was that?*

But Sam wasn't finished. He uttered a rough growl and reared up, yanking his jeans and boxer briefs down his legs before kicking them free. Then he slid up her body, dragging his tongue along the slick, damp flesh between her breasts and up her long slender throat until his fallen-angel face filled her vision. His molten-gold eyes locked with hers. She felt the bump of him against the tender flesh between her thighs and slapped a hand against his chest to keep him from thrusting home.

"Condom," she gasped.

He froze and swore, surging upward to reach behind him for his jeans. Within seconds he'd rolled the latex down his thick shaft before he positioned himself and, with one fierce thrust, buried himself deep.

The thick, solid invasion set off another series of explosions, sending Cassidy arching upward as her body stretched to accommodate him. It took a couple of thrusts but once he was buried to the hilt she let out a long low moan of pleasure and wrapped her arms and legs around his big body.

Softly murmuring her name, Sam slowly withdrew until she was lightheaded with the incredible explosion of sensations. Then he thrust deeper, his mouth closing over hers in a ravenous kiss that stole her breath and blew away what was left of her mind.

Applying the same light suction to her mouth that he'd used in more intimate places, Sam sucked the air from her lungs until she was dizzy, mindless with pleasure. Then he began to move in a slow, sweet rhythm. The sensations shooting through her ratcheted higher and higher until her blood caught fire and her world spun off its axis.

Before she knew it, she was straining against him, meeting his every hard thrust with one of her own, tongues tangling and clashing as her hands raced over him, greedy for the feel of his hot, tight flesh and the steel-hard muscles shifting and bunching beneath the smooth damp skin.

Helpless with sensation, Cassidy sank her fingers into his big shoulders and clung, her third climax catching her completely unawares as it ripped a low moan from her throat. Her body bucked and convulsed beneath his, the soft growl in her ear scraping at raw nerve endings and sending more detonations exploding through her blood.

Catching her hips in his hands, Sam dug his fingers into the smooth flesh to hold her in place as he increased his pace until he was hammering every hard inch, every powerful thrust into her as though he wanted to stamp his possession onto her very DNA.

Caught up in his desperate pace, Cassidy wrapped her long legs around him, and fisting her hands in his hair was lost to his driving rhythm. Hard and fast—plunging into her deeper and deeper—until, with a hoarse cry, he came.

CHAPTER EIGHT

THE BAD THING about disastrous mistakes was that no matter how hard you tried not to think about them, the more you did. It was this vicious cycle that gave Cassidy a headache and made her cranky in the week following…well, possibly the second-biggest mistake of her life. And even if she'd managed to forget for an instant that she'd had a one-night stand with someone so completely wrong for her, she just had to catch sight of her reflection and she was groaning in mortification.

Crescent Lake's favorite son had whipped her up, given her some seriously intense orgasms and when she'd thought he was sleeping and had tried to sneak away—they had been in someone's office, for heaven's sake—he'd tightened his hold on her and said in his deep sleep-rough voice, "Where are you going? I've just started."

Even hours later her skin glowed, her eyes sparkled and her mouth was bruised and swollen from his kisses. Anyone looking at her could see at a glance that she'd had her world rocked. And if that wasn't enough, she had whisker burns and hickeys in places that made her alternately smile and blush.

Except there was absolutely *nothing* to smile about. She'd rolled around on the floor—*and* the huge sofa—with a hot Navy SEAL whose idea of a relationship probably meant a couple of nights with a busty babe before he headed off to wreak havoc in some foreign war zone.

What had she been thinking?

Clearly she hadn't given a thought to where they were or the consequences of someone walking in on them. The last thing she wanted was to find herself hip-deep in another scandal. The last thing she needed was to get all worked up over some hot alpha SEAL with "temporary" tattooed on his sexy hide in eleven different languages.

Clearly the smartest thing to do was escape. Except every time she'd tried to slide out from under his big arm, he'd tightened his grasp, his sleep-rough voice murmuring, "I'm not finished with you yet."

Finally her brain had cleared and she'd told him she needed to check the wards. His heavy arm had reluctantly slid away but not before a big rough hand had smoothed a leisurely line of fire from her naked shoulder to her knee and he'd murmured, "Hurry back…" against her throat.

Resisting the urge to arch into his touch and purr with pleasure, Cassidy had rolled off the sofa, snatched up her clothes and bolted. Standing in the shower an hour later, she'd leaned her forehead against the tiles as steaming water had cascaded over her sensitized flesh and prayed that he'd be recalled to wherever he was stationed. Because there was no way she could ever look into his wicked eyes and not remember where he'd put his mouth and how he'd done things that had made her scream.

Okay, maybe not scream, she amended, but she'd made some pretty embarrassing noises that had her blushing whenever she thought about it. But as the days passed and the gossip mill in town had him harassing bad guys and helping little old ladies across the street—when he wasn't working behind the bar and chatting up the regulars—Cassidy realized he wasn't going anywhere. *Yet.*

And when the thought of him leaving made her feel

vaguely ill and a strange ache squeezed her chest, Cassidy began to get a very bad feeling that unless she got her head on straight, she was headed for heartbreak. Besides, he hadn't called or tried to contact her, which clearly meant he was done with her.

And she was done too—*really*. So why, then, did his absence feel like a slap in the face?

But that kind of thinking was not only ridiculous but self-defeating. Samuel Kellan had "temporary" written all over him and what had seemed like more than hot steamy sex—at least to her—had been nothing but a good time for him,

In the week since he'd toppled her to the floor and brought her intimate places out of deep hibernation, he hadn't been there to rescue her from falling off ladders or to push her up against any walls. And as she left the hospital eight days later and slid into her car, she firmly told herself she was relieved. She didn't need rescuing. And she didn't need a big, strong man with a wicked smile to rock her world.

Considering what she'd endured the past year she'd be really, *really* stupid to fall for another alpha male—even one with beautiful gold eyes, awesome biceps and the ability to reduce her to a mindless mess.

Except her confusion and uncertainty grew, along with the sick feeling that her emotions were deeper than she wanted to acknowledge, and that what she'd dubbed "just sex" had been anything but.

Frankly the smart thing was to pretend nothing had happened and wait for the churning in her belly to go away. Besides, there hadn't been time to develop deep lasting feelings for someone like him.

That would have been so utterly stupid when she'd already used up her quota of stupid on a man who lived on the edge.

* * *

The following week found Sam riding shotgun while Crescent Lake's sheriff droned on and on about something or other till Sam had been tempted to drive them both off a cliff. So he'd been a bit bad-tempered. *Big deal.* Instead of doing the job the government was paying him to do, he was driving around looking for truant kids and mediating between two old codgers who'd been fighting like toddlers over a toy truck for *fifty* years. And if that wasn't bad enough, the lean, mean badass SEAL had been dumped after the best sex of his life.

Okay, so maybe a *very* small part of his surliness was because he'd thought Cassidy Mahoney would be as eager as he was for a repeat of their night of passion. Instead, she'd escaped at the first opportunity. And all he'd done since then was think about her.

Like a damn girl—obsessing about what she was doing, who she was with and if she thought about him at all. Frankly, he was behaving like a pimply-faced nerd with his first crush. She'd slid her perfect body against his, put her lush mouth and her hands on him and made his eyes roll back in his head. Then she'd calmly risen from the sofa, collected her clothes and sauntered from the room without a backward glance.

Maybe in the past he'd encouraged it, but he really hated it that Cassidy had done it to him. Maybe it made him a hypocrite, but there was just something about her that made Sam lose his mind and act like a lovesick ass. It was baffling—and downright terrifying.

So he told himself to stay away. He was leaving and had no place in his life for the kind of relationship she probably wanted. His life was perfect…except he had to listen to Ruben go on and on about seeing a shrink so Sam could get back to protecting the nation because he was giving the sheriff's department a bad name by being a jerk.

And in the next breath he was telling Sam how great it

would be if he came home so they could run the department together.

Yeah, right. Like that would ever happen. Ruben liked being in charge and so did he. They would probably throttle each other in the first week.

Sam sighed—again—and wiped the already clean bar surface. Fortunately it was Sunday night and the bar was quiet except for a few die-hard regulars huddled in booths along the wall, and Sam didn't have to exert himself making conversation. Except it gave him way too much time to think—which was something he wanted to avoid like a tax audit.

The truth was he was bored. Bored with driving around harassing people during the day, only to serve them Buds and peanuts at night. So when his brother pushed through the front doors, Sam was ready to take his frustrations out on someone.

"I don't know who called you but I haven't beaten anyone up lately," he drawled, folding his arms across his chest and eyeing his brother darkly. "But I could always make an exception with you."

"No one called to complain," Sheriff Kellan said tiredly. "At least, not in the last three hours."

"Real funny. Beer?"

"God, yeah." Ruben pulled off his hat and tossed it onto the bar counter. He slid onto a stool and ran a hand through his hair. "I'm off duty. Sort of."

"How can you be 'sort of' off duty?" Sam demanded, sliding a bottle across the counter.

"I'm not here to hold up the bar and swap life stories with the barman," Ruben said tiredly, lifting the beer to his mouth.

"That's a good thing," Sam snorted. "I already know your life story, and it's about as exciting as a visit to the dentist. If you've come to nag me about my crappy attitude again I'm going to have to physically remove you."

Ruben smirked and lifted his brow in that superior big-brother way that used to drive Sam crazy as a kid. "*Right*," he snorted, and lifted the bottle in an ironic salute. "Like I'd let you." He took a couple of deep pulls before lowering the bottle an inch and fixing Sam with his dark gaze. "Got a job for you."

"In case you haven't noticed," Sam complained, "I already have a job. Hell, *three* if you count driving around in an air-conditioned SUV harassing innocent folk all day and serving beer to snarky sheriffs at night. You can do your own damn filing. Besides, I have to sleep some time."

Ruben snorted since they both knew Sam wasn't getting a lot of sleep. "Marty and Andy are back at work tomorrow and I'm tired of keeping you out of trouble. It's exhausting. Besides, with your attitude you're not exactly cut out for the sheriff's department."

Sam sent him a mocking look. "Just this morning you were telling me I should come home and join you fighting the terrible crime in Crescent Lake," he drawled. "Make up your mind."

Ruben shook his head. "Don't know what I was thinking."

"What changed your mind?"

"I need your unique skills."

Sam lifted an eyebrow. "You want me to kill someone? Blow something up? Infiltrate enemy territory?" He tutted and shook his head. "This from the man sworn to uphold the law."

"Not those skills, you moron. I'm talking about the medical degree you acquired on the taxpayer's dime. I need a doctor."

Sam arched his brow sardonically. "You sick? Your girlfriend find out she's pregnant with quadruplets?"

An irritated look crossed Ruben's face. "No, I'm not sick. And when do I have time to date?"

Sam shrugged, unconcerned with his brother's love life.

"How should I know? Most days you're so busy nagging I can't wait to get away from you. Besides, the idea of discussing your sex life is just disturbing. I don't want those visuals in my head. I have enough nightmares."

"Yeah, well, I'd like to have a sex life but I'm too busy protecting the innocent people of Crescent Lake from moody badass SEALs. Besides, I have a problem only you can solve. I just got off the phone. Doc Monty was run off the road up in Spruce Ridge. They had to cut him from his car and now he's in County Gen with concussion and a shattered hip."

"*Holy...* Is he all right?"

Ruben sighed and scrubbed a hand down his face. "I think so. Anyway, we need a doctor. Like now."

"In case you've forgotten, you already have a doctor. The one from Boston? The one Hannah says you have a thing for?"

Ruben's eyes glinted and his mouth turned up in a smirk that Sam was sorely tempted to remove. Ruben shrugged. "Well, she's beautiful, single and doesn't hold up bar counters in Spruce County. What more could a guy want?" He took a drink. "In fact, I was thinking of going over to the inn later and telling her about Old Monty. Maybe ask her out." And when Sam growled a warning low in his throat, Ruben snickered. "Maybe even stay the night." Then he burst out laughing. "*Jeez*," he gasped when he finally caught his breath, "you should see your face."

Sam folded his arms across his chest and narrowed his eyes, barely resisting the urge to reach across the bar and punch someone.

"You *do* remember I've been trained by the government to kill scum like you, don't you?" he drawled dryly, but that only made Ruben laugh even more until he was laughing so hard people from the booths in the back were craning their necks to see what was happening.

Sam ignored them and shook his head with disgust. "You're pathetic, you know that?"

Finally Ruben wiped his eyes and took a drink of beer. "No more than you," he snorted with a wide grin. "It's like you're sixteen again and mooning over Cheryl Ungemeyer."

"I did not *moon* over Cheryl. I was temporarily…um… distracted by her endowments. Especially the summer she wore that string bikini. I was young and impressionable and she was an older woman." He paused a couple of beats. "I'm neither young nor impressionable now."

"Cheryl's small fry compared to Doc Boston," Ruben told him, waggling his eyebrows. "Any idiot can see that."

"You keep your eyes, and everything else, off her endowments," Sam warned half-heartedly, pointing a finger at his brother. He knew Ruben was just yanking his chain, but it wouldn't hurt to warn the guy off. "She's a doctor, for goodness' sake."

Ruben shorted with disgust. "You should listen to yourself," he said, before finishing his beer in a couple long swallows. He set the empty bottle on the bar and rose. "I guess I'll have to look around for another medic, then," he said with an exaggerated sigh. "Maybe that guy from Redfern. The nurses all had a thing for him last time he helped out."

Sam snarled and reached over the bar to grab his brother's shirt. He yanked him close until they were nose to nose, before saying mildly, "You do that and you're a dead man." He let Ruben go with a shove. "Tell Doc Boston I'll see her in the morning."

Ruben laughed and smoothed the front of his shirt before reaching for his sheriff's hat. "Tell her yourself, stud," he said, slapping it onto his head as he turned to saunter from the bar, leaving Sam with the nasty suspicion he'd just been played.

* * *

It was past ten when a quiet knock at the door distracted Cassidy from the article she'd been reading about surgical procedures for head trauma patients. All very cutting edge and fascinating but she was having trouble concentrating.

Wondering who on earth could be visiting her at such a late hour, she tossed the journal aside and rose from the rumpled bed to pad across the floor to the door.

Expecting to see the innkeeper, she was unnerved to find a US Navy SEAL propping up the door frame, hands shoved into jeans pockets, radiating enough virility and attitude to give a woman bad ideas. Ideas she should be done with.

The shoulders of his jacket were damp and rain dotted his dark, ruffled hair. His eyes and most of his face were shadowed, leaving his left cheekbone and half his mouth and strong jaw illuminated by the hallway light.

Heat rose in her cheeks as his hooded gaze boldly swept from the top of her tousled hair to her bare feet. Her grip tightening on the door, Cassidy barely resisted the urge to slam it in his face or—worse—cover her breasts. And since he'd already seen every inch of her naked body, that, and slamming the door, would only make her look ridiculous.

It was the first time she'd seen him since he'd rocked her world and she couldn't help being conscious of her nudity beneath the thin tank top and long track pants she wore as pajamas.

"Major," she said coolly in greeting. A dark brow rose at her tone and his mouth kicked up at one corner.

"Doctor," he mocked, and after a few beats, during which he continued to study her silently, Cassidy gave in to the urge to flick her tongue nervously over her lips. His eyes went hot at the move.

Finally, when she could no longer stand the rising tension, she demanded, "What are you doing here, Major?"

"Invite me in and I'll tell you."

Wary of his strange mood, Cassidy eyed him suspiciously. "Why can't you tell me out here?"

A slow, wicked smile curved his mouth. "You want the entire floor to hear what I have to say, *babe*?"

Flushing at his reminder of the night they'd spent together, she narrowed her eyes and fought the urge to slam the door in his face-even if it did make her look like an idiot. He must have read her mind because he pushed away from the wall and stepped into her, forcing her back into the room to avoid coming into contact with his hard heat.

"Come in, why don't you?" she drawled dryly.

"Why, thank you, Dr. Honey," he mocked softly, "don't mind if I do." He angled his shoulders, intentionally brushing against her as he moved past. A shiver of awareness spread across her skin, tightening her breasts. Cassidy retreated while Sam continued into the room then turned to lean back against the door, hoping it would support her wobbly knees.

He simply took over her space with his presence, leaving Cassidy fighting twin urges to plaster herself against him or run like hell.

He shrugged off his battered leather jacket and tossed it over the back of an armchair, clearly intent on staying a while. She eyed the way his dark blue T-shirt molded to wide shoulders and a strong back and her hands tingled at the memory of running them over hard muscles covered with warm, satin-smooth skin.

Thrusting his hands on his narrow hips, Sam took his time looking around the room, making Cassidy painfully aware of her rumpled appearance and the large bed dominating the space. Glowing bedside lamps gave the room an intimate glow that had her recalling in perfect detail the last time they'd been in a room together.

He turned, catching her gaze over one broad shoulder. The hot, sleepy expression in his eyes told her his thoughts were moving along similar lines.

"You bailed." He sounded vaguely accusing, which surprised her since she'd thought they'd both wanted to avoid any "after" awkwardness. Talking about it now was not only redundant, it was…mortifying. She wanted to forget the whole incident. But if he wanted to discuss it, the least she could do was be honest.

"Look, Major, I'm not looking to start…well, anything. It…it was a mistake," she finished firmly.

His eyes darkened and his jaw flexed. "A mistake?"

Suddenly parched, she pushed away from the door and headed for the small bar fridge, determined not to let him distract her with memories of "the sofa interlude." It was over and she wasn't going there again.

She bent at the waist to grab a bottle of water and looked over her shoulder, only to catch his smoldering gaze on her backside. She straightened with a snap and "Can I get you something?" emerged on a breathless little squeak.

Unconcerned that he'd been caught ogling, Sam's brooding gaze traveled up the length of her body until his eyes met hers, heat and accusation in his expression. He shook his head. "I'm good."

Yeah, right.

She headed for the window with her bottle, hoping a little distance would help her breathe in the suddenly hot, airless room. She turned and propped her hip against the windowsill. "Why are you here, Major?" she demanded, twisting off the cap. "Are you ill? Find out your girlfriend has an STD?"

His lips twitched but he shook his head slowly, eyes scorching and intense as he watched her lift the bottle and drink thirstily. He licked his lips, his gaze travelling from her mouth, down her throat to her tight breasts. He didn't look sick, she thought a little wildly. In fact, he looked fabulous. And hot. *Dammit.*

"Is something…um wrong?" she asked hoarsely, before

clearing her throat irritably. "*Do* you need a doctor?" Her gaze checked him for blood and found none.

"Yes… No." He moved across the floor and her heart skipped a few too many beats when he came to a halt less than a foot away. His gold eyes studied her as though he'd never seen her before. "*You* do."

"I—what?" *What the heck was he talking about?*

"Monty had an accident on his way back from visiting his daughter. He's in Spruce Ridge General."

Cassidy gasped and felt her face drain of color. She tightened her hand on the plastic bottle. "Oh, God, is he all right?" She hadn't known the older man long but had come to like and respect him enormously.

"Shattered hip. He'll be out of commission for a while."

"You know as well as I do that he won't be back," she told him quietly. "After something like that the workload would likely kill him. Besides, he should be enjoying his retirement."

"He's been treating people here for the past forty-five years. Hell, he *is* the hospital."

"He still needs to enjoy his retirement."

"Tell that to him. Besides, Crescent Lake's tourism has soared over the past five years. The hospital needs someone younger who can cope with the workload." He paused. "So. You interested?"

Cassidy's heart skipped a beat but she knew enough not to read too much into his question. He wasn't asking because *he* wanted her to stay. "What about you?"

He sent her an impatient look. "I already have a job," he reminded her shortly.

"Yes," she agreed shortly. "Yelling '*boo-yah*' as you jump from high altitudes."

"That's right." His brows lowered and he folded his arms across his chest. "You make it sound like a kids' game."

"No, it's not and I appreciate that you risk your life with

every mission, but you're more than a SEAL, Major. You're more than infiltration, interrogation and demolition."

"Yeah," he agreed silky. "I'm damn good at my job."

"You'd have to be. But you can't be a SEAL for ever."

A dark brow rose arrogantly. "I can't?"

Rolling her eyes, Cassidy recapped the water bottle with an irritated twist. "You know you can't," she said flatly, slapping the bottle on the windowsill with a snap. He caught and held her gaze with an intensity she felt like a burn in her gut. "Eventually you have to retire or move up the ladder."

"Or come home in a body bag."

"Don't say that," she snapped, suddenly furious with his dry flippancy. The thought of him being KIA made her queasy. She gulped, pushing her hair off her forehead with unsteady fingers. "*God*, don't say that. Just…just…*don't*."

"Every soldier, every sailor thinks about it," he reminded her gently. "It's the reality of being in any country's armed forces. *Hell*, before every mission we write letters to our families and get our affairs in order."

Cassidy felt tears burning the backs of her eyes, pressure squeezing her chest like a vice. She pressed the heels of her hands against her eyes to counteract the sudden threat of tears. "That's… *Dammit*. That's not fair."

A slow, satisfied smile lit his dark features. "Sounds like you care what happens to me," he said cockily, the masculine confidence in his voice sending her belly dipping and her temper rising. She wanted to simultaneously slug him and wrap her arms around him.

"Of course I care," she snapped hotly, before realizing how he might interpret her words. "You're…you're a valuable member of the country's special armed forces. I'd care about anyone I knew going off to fight a dangerous war."

His looked skeptical. "*Riiiiight*." He stepped closer to plant his big boots either side of her bare feet and slapped both hands on the windowsill at her hips, effectively boxing her in. Then he leant down to brush his lips against the delicate skin beneath her ear.

"Are you sure you wouldn't miss me?" he demanded softly.

Cassidy gulped and her head spun with the warm, male scent of him. "I...uh."

"Not even a little?" he whispered, giving her earlobe a tiny nip that sent shivers of pure sensation spreading throughout her body. The back of her neck prickled, her breasts tightened and familiar heat pooled between her thighs. And when his mouth opened against her throat she moaned, tilting her head to the side to give him room. She wanted to beg him to stop one instant and the next—

"Samuel." Her voice emerged, husky and aching with a desire she could no longer deny. She wanted him. Needed the hot slide of his flesh against hers more than she needed her next breath. "This is a mistake."

"No," he rasped against her neck. "Inevitable."

She gave a breathless moan when his hands curled around her knees, pushed them gently apart to step between them until his heat and hardness pressed against where she ached.

"Admit it," he insisted softly, his hands smoothing a line of fire up her thighs to her hips. "Admit that you'd miss me if some scumbag terrorist took me out," he said against her mouth.

Dizzy with the force of her emotions, Cassidy slid her palms up his long muscular arms to his shoulders and fought the urge to clutch him close. She wondered briefly why she'd imagined she could ignore him, especially when he touched her like this. Put his mouth on her. Talked about dying.

"Yes," she breathed against his mouth, sliding her hands into his thick hair. "*God, yes*," and caught his mouth in a kiss that showed him exactly how much she would miss him. How much she'd come to need him despite her determination not to.

Sam growled deep in his throat and lifted her, yanking her hard against him. And when her legs snaked around his hips, he turned towards the rumpled bed.

"Show me, Cassidy," he growled against her throat. "Show me how much you'd miss me."

CHAPTER NINE

WHEN CASSIDY WOKE the following morning she was naked and aching in deliciously intimate places. *Again.*

Only this time *she* was alone and didn't have to scramble around looking for her clothes.

Sliding her hand over the bed where Sam's big body had heated up the sheets, she told herself she was relieved. But the truth was the hollow feeling in her chest made her feel like a hypocrite.

In the dark, intimate hours of the night she'd pressed her body to his, arched into his hungry caresses and moaned when he'd moved his hot, moist mouth over every inch of skin and thrust his body into hers. And when their ragged, harsh breathing had calmed and their skin cooled, he'd pulled her close and wrapped his arms around her as she'd slid bonelessly into sleep.

As if he'd never let her go.

He'd made her feel safe and protected as she hadn't felt in a long time—as though within his arms she'd found her shelter from the storm.

Which was ridiculous.

Samuel J. Kellan *was* the storm. He'd blown into her life when she'd been determined to hide from the world. He'd turned her inside out with his sexy smile and hot, seductive kisses that made her feel—things she didn't want to feel—and then he'd given her a glimpse of the caring, honorable man beneath the tough, broody SEAL exterior. *Worst* of all he'd made her admire him when she'd been convinced he was exactly like Lance Turnbull.

Okay, so she liked him too—a *lot*—but that was beside the point. He'd soon be back with his team, plotting mayhem and destruction in the world's hottest hotspots and she'd be…here. A world away.

Her one-night stand had just become two, and she didn't know what that meant, how she felt about it or if she wanted more. Heck, if *he* wanted more.

Fortunately, by the time she walked into the hospital she'd managed to get her wildly unstable emotions under control. Until she saw *him*—tall and darkly handsome—surrounded by animated adoring women and looking like a large hungry predator in a hen house.

As though his senses were attuned to her, Sam's head lifted and his eyes met hers across the room. The force of his gaze hit her like a sledgehammer, leaving Cassidy stunned and gasping for air because that look said he saw things she'd rather keep hidden. Things that had become painfully obvious last night when he'd talked about dying. Things she'd refused to acknowledge. Even to herself. *Oh, God.* Even with the truth staring her in the face.

Then his eyes crinkled in a private, evocative smile meant to remind her of hot, wet mouths and frantic, greedy hands. Her heart lurched in her chest before taking off like a crazed meth head fleeing from the cops.

Shocked and a little spooked by her reaction, she turned and hurried towards the hallway leading to her office, her palm hitting the door as though she couldn't escape fast enough. In reality she wanted to run for the exit and keep going until the feelings faded. But she had an awful feeling she couldn't run too far or too fast. Everything that had happened with Sam was burned indelibly into her mind—*heck*, her soul—and running would accomplish nothing.

Besides, she wasn't the kind of woman who got swept away by a couple of nights with a sexy Navy SEAL.

Was she?

Hyperventilating and angry with herself for making more of things than they were, Cassidy stormed into her office and yanked off her jacket. She flung it at the coat rack and tossed her purse into her bottom drawer with shaking hands, then gave the drawer a frustrated little kick.

What the hell was that?

"What the hell was that?"

Cassidy froze when the low, furious demand filled the room. A frisson of alarm skated up her spine as memories roared in of the last time she'd been cornered in an office by an angry man. Drawing in a steadying breath, she gathered her professionalism around her like an invisible cloak and turned to find him looking hot and annoyed and more than a little baffled.

Sam wasn't Lance, she reminded herself. And he wasn't a desperate, drug-crazed psycho.

"Excuse me?" she asked coolly, hoping he'd take the hint and back the hell off. With her emotions frayed and ragged, she wasn't up to a confrontation without exposing emotions scraped raw from panic.

Sam folded his arms across his chest, his dark brows a slash of irritation across the bridge of his nose. "You heard me."

Cassidy lifted her chin in challenge. "What was what?" She had the satisfaction of seeing a muscle twitch in his jaw. *Good,* she thought uncharitably, *I'm not the only unhinged person here.*

"*That,*" he snapped, pointing at her. "In here. Out there. It's like you're two different people. It's confusing as hell. I never know where I am with you."

All thoughts of poise and cool professionalism forgotten, Cassidy stared back at him frostily and ignored the way her stomach clenched. "I don't know what you're talking about."

"*Jeez,* Cassidy," he said roughly, his face harsh with some fierce emotion he seemed to be struggling with. "One minute you're all warm and sweet and sexy and the next… hell, you looked at me like I'm the Greenside rapist."

Wincing inwardly, Cassidy turned away, hunching her shoulders against the truth. She smoothed unsteady hands down her thighs. "You're imagining things. I was just a little surprised to see you, that's all. I'm—" She stopped abruptly when she turned to find him a couple inches away. Her eyes widened and she uttered an audible gasp. *Yikes.* The man moved like smoke.

She gulped and backed up a step. He was so close, so… *familiar.*

"That's bull."

"I beg your pardon?"

"You heard me," he growled, his deep voice scraping against ragged nerve endings. "I'm not some muscle-bound redneck you can intimidate with the frosty debutante routine."

Staring into eyes fierce with a confusing mix of emotions, Cassidy swallowed past the lump in her throat and sighed. "It's…complicated." She shrugged helplessly. "Just old, not-so-pleasant memories. Ancient history. Really."

After a long moment he lifted a hand and brushed his knuckles across her jaw. Surprise at the gentle touch added to her ragged emotions. Emotions she didn't want or need. Emotions that made her feel fragile and susceptible and long for something she couldn't have.

"Wanna talk about it?"

A strangled laugh escaped and she finally found the strength to move away from the temptation to lean on him, draw in some of his strength and heat.

"*God, no.* It's nothing, *really.*" She drew in a fortifying breath and turned, eager to change the subject. "So, what *are* you doing here?"

His gaze narrowed, probed. "I told you last night."

"You *did*?" Now it was Cassidy's turn to be confused.

"Yeah. I told you Monty had an accident and the mayor asked me to fill in until they can get someone else—or I'm recalled." He gave a one-shouldered shrug. "Whichever comes first."

Cassidy frowned as though trying to recall what he'd said last night. "You told me about the accident." She remembered him talking about body bags and dying and then— "You never said anything about filling in as medic," she added quickly, memories of what had followed flooding her with heat. *Yeesh. So not the time to be thinking about that.* "I would have remembered."

Sam eyed her flushed face silently for a few beats then his mouth slowly curved into a smartass grin that she wanted to simultaneously smack and kiss. "You thought I was here to take up where we left off last night, didn't you?"

She flushed. "Of course not," she denied instantly, smoothing her already smooth French twist with shaking hands. "That's…that's insane," she finished lamely, trying to hide her shock at discovering they would be working closely together. *Oh, boy.*

"You *did*." His grin faded into a harsh frown and his mouth twisted. She could feel him withdrawing. "I think I get it now. Negative reaction, ancient history. I reminded you of some scumbag stalker, didn't I?" Without waiting for a response, he swore and shoved his fingers through his hair. "What the hell kind of man do you take me for?"

"Th-that's ridiculous," she spluttered and turned to reach for the clean lab coat hanging on the back of her chair to give her hands something to do. "Why would I th-think that?" Large, warm hands dropped onto her shoulders and she tensed, abruptly sucking in a shaky breath.

"Hey." His voice, deep and rough, slid inside her chest

and aimed for her heart. "Is that what you think?" he demanded hoarsely. "That I would…hell…*could* hurt you?"

Cassidy looked up over her shoulder into his face and couldn't deny the sincerity behind the baffled hurt and anger. Sighing, she made herself relax and ignored the temptation to lean back against him, let him wrap his arms around her. Like he had during the night. But she couldn't. He might say he wouldn't hurt her, but he would. Not intentionally or physically. She didn't think he was capable of that. But he most definitely would hurt her. And soon.

"No, I don't," she denied, easing out from beneath his hands and moving a safe distance away. *Not really.* "A year ago I made the mistake of trusting…well, someone I shouldn't have."

She felt him come up behind her. "What happened?"

Cassidy sighed, admitting to herself that he deserved to know why she behaved like she had a multiple personality. "Lance is…*was* a vice cop. Charming, handsome…" Her mouth twisted wryly. "A hero. He…um…he was brought into ER after a drug bust went wrong."

"I sense that's not the only thing that went wrong."

Cassidy flushed with embarrassment, hating that she'd been so naïve. "He came to thank me for saving his life. An exaggeration, but he was sweet and…well—"

"Charming?" Sam demanded darkly, and when she remained silent he cursed softly. "And you fell for it."

Cassidy gritted her teeth. "I guess you could say that."

"But?"

"He had a habit of seducing women in the medical profession."

"Let me guess. He liked all the attention?" He sounded disgusted.

Cassidy shrugged. "That too."

"There's more?"

"He stole my security card and helped himself to the dispensary."

"*Holy cr*—! He stole drugs?"

"For which I was blamed. The cops were called in. Fortunately for me he was already under investigation and my testimony…well, suffice it to say he's no longer a cop."

"Good for you. I hope the bastard rots in jail." He was silent a moment. "You were exonerated?"

"Yes, but…"

"Again *but*?"

"Things got…well, *difficult* after that."

"They fired you?" He sounded outraged.

She shook her head. "No. But sometimes I think it might have been better if they had. There was a lot of gossip and jokes. Cruel jokes." She shrugged. "You know what it's like in hospitals. So…I eventually resigned and moved here." Cassidy abruptly became all business. "As I said, Major, ancient history."

A dark brow hiked up his forehead at her cool tone and his eyes darkened. "Are we back to that, *Doctor*?"

Cassidy sighed. "Look, last night was a—"

"Don't say it," he interrupted her shortly, taking a couple of long strides in her direction. Her eyes widened and she quickly moved to put the desk between them. He halted, shoving his hands on his narrow hips as he studied her, brows lowered in visible frustration.

"It *was* a mistake," she insisted, resisting the urge to roll her eyes since "mistake" was a major understatement. At least for her it was. It meant she could no longer blame her behavior on adrenaline. But he would still leave, and if she let her feelings develop, what then?

Sam was silent for so long she began to rearrange her desk to give her hands something to do. Just when she thought he'd finally taken the hint and left, a large hand covered hers.

She froze, staring down at the sight of her pale, slender hand engulfed in his. His hand was huge, tanned and broad with long skilled fingers that were capable of killing a man, bringing a baby back from the brink of death—and driving a woman out of her mind with pleasure.

The strength of it should have scared her but for some strange reason it just felt...right. *He* felt right. As though her hand had been fashioned to fit perfectly into his.

But that was a dangerous illusion and one she needed to get out of her head. He wasn't perfect, she reminded herself firmly. He was fighting demons as hard as he fought for his country. The combination wasn't healthy. For either of them.

"Why?" he demanded softly. "You didn't have a good time?"

Making a sound in her throat that was a cross between a laugh and groan, Cassidy stopped trying to escape and looked up over her shoulder into his fallen-angel face. She would like to say no, but she couldn't lie to him, not any more. So she said instead, "I refuse to answer that on the grounds that it may incriminate me."

Sam used his grasp on her hand to whip her around and tug her against him. "Then what's the problem?" His free arm snaked around her waist and his lips brushed her temple.

Cassidy pressed her palms against the hard heat of his chest and fought the urge to slide them up to cup his firm jaw, tunnel into his thick dark hair. "You. Me... Hell, I don't know. I just know it can't happen again."

His arms tightened as though he would pull her into him. "Why not?" He sounded baffled and frustrated. "You had a good time and I sure as hell did."

Cassidy sighed and pressed her face wearily into his throat, tempted to close her eyes and burrow deep. Until she absorbed his heat, his strength. Or he absorbed all of her.

"Lots of reasons," she murmured, drinking in his clean masculine smell. "One of which is that we're now working together. I don't sleep with colleagues."

"Glad to hear it," he drawled, smoothing a hand down

her back to her hip to press her closer. "I would have really hated punching Monty's lights out."

Cassidy grimaced and pushed away from him, feeling off balance like she'd entered an episode of *some adventure game show* dressed in a designer suit and four-inch heels. "That's disgusting."

"Besides, neither of us is married." He paused as though a horrible thought just occurred to him. "Are you?"

Cassidy gaped at him. "No!"

He shrugged but looked ridiculously relieved. "Then what's wrong with enjoying each other?"

"While you're here, you mean?"

He frowned and leaned back so he could look into her face. "Is that a problem?"

Sighing, Cassidy told herself she wasn't disappointed. She'd known from the beginning she was nothing more than a temporary distraction.

"I'm not built for temporary, Sam, and everything about you says your bags are packed and all you need is one phone call."

His hands dropped and she could see the truth in his eyes. Her heart squeezed, though she didn't know what she'd expected him to say. Deny it maybe?

Fortunately a voice from the doorway stopped her from humiliating herself further.

"Cassidy, Mrs. West is… Oh." Janice paused as if she sensed the tension in the room. "I'm sorry," she said, her eyes wide and curious. "I didn't realize you were busy."

"We're not," Cassidy said briskly, reaching out to snag the stethoscope she'd tossed onto the desk the previous night. "I was just on my way. Is Mrs. West in exam room one?"

"Yes, Doctor," the nurse said, wide eyes bouncing between Cassidy and Sam. "Hank Dougherty is waiting in two."

"Thank you, Janice," Cassidy said, looping the stethoscope around her neck. "I'll be right there. In the meantime, can you please hunt up a lab coat for Major Kellan and inform the staff that he's filling in for Dr. Montgomery?"

Janice beamed at Sam, and Cassidy could practically hear the woman's heart go pitter-pat. "I heard." Janice grinned excitedly. "Welcome aboard," she gushed.

And giggled when his "Thanks" was accompanied by a crooked grin.

Taking that as her cue, Cassidy headed for the door, desperate to escape before he remembered what they'd been discussing. His voice, dark as midnight and rough as crushed velvet, reached across the room and stopped her in her tracks. "I'm not him, Cassidy," he called softly, and her fingers tightened on the doorframe. She chanced a look across her shoulder.

"Not who?" she asked past the lump of yearning in her throat. A yearning she didn't want to analyze too closely.

"I'm not what's-his-name? Lance Full-of-bull."

"Today is senior citizen clinic day," she said briskly instead of replying to what was largely rhetorical anyway. "Hank Dougherty needs hip replacement surgery but he needs to get his smoking under control first. Don't let the old codger con you into thinking he's quit."

Removing the stethoscope from her ears, Cassidy smiled reassuringly at the anxious young mother hovering close. "Chest is all clear," she announced, "but this little butterball has a bad fever and her ears are inflamed."

She reached for a tongue depressor. "Open your mouth wide, sweetie," she cajoled gently, "I want to check if the bad germs got into your throat."

The child gazed back with huge, tragic eyes and held out the stuffed toy she was clutching. "Elmo first," she rasped, looking on intently as Cassidy examined Elmo's throat and made some doctor noises. "Do you think you and Elmo have the same bad germs?" Cassidy asked, hold-

ing out a new depressor. The little girl nodded and obedi-
ently opened her mouth.

"Uh-oh," she said, with an exaggerated look of dismay.
"Just as I thought. Have you two been sharing a toothbrush
again?" Jenny giggled around the thumb she'd instantly
shoved in her mouth and shook her head. "That's good
because Elmo needs his own toothbrush." She tapped a
little button nose and lifted the child into her arms. "And
you need to suck on something other than that thumb. How
about a magic lollipop?"

"Magic?" Jenny rasped shyly around her thumb.

"Uh-huh. One that'll chase away all those bad germs,"
Cassidy explained, reaching into a nearby cabinet. "And
make your throat feel better." She held out two antibacte-
rial lollipops. "There," she said, handing the little girl to her
mother. "One for you and one for Elmo." Returning to her
desk, she slid a handful of M&Ms into a small clear plastic
bag and wrote "Elmo" in permanent marker on the front.

"This is for Elmo but your mommy's going to have to
get your medication from the pharmacy," she explained
to the wide-eyed child. "Elmo is pretty bad at taking his
medicine. I want you to be a big girl and show him how
it's done. Can you do that for me?"

Jenny nodded solemnly as her mother smiled at Cassidy.
"Thank you so much, Dr. Mahoney. You're really good with
children," she said. "Are you a pediatrician?"

Cassidy shook her head. "I specialized in ER medicine.
And it's Cassidy."

"Thank you, Cassidy. And welcome to Crescent Lake."

Smiling, Cassidy sent the child a little wave over her
mother's shoulder as the two left her office, and had only
a couple of minutes to gulp down rapidly cooling coffee
before her next appointment arrived.

A clearly harassed Cathy Howard entered with a rowdy,
tow-headed toddler and sank wearily into the nearest chair.
Little Timmy Howard had been one of her first patients.

"Did I ever say I wanted him bouncing around again?" Cathy asked Cassidy with a grimace. "I would give *any-thing* for just *one* minute of peace."

Cassidy rounded her desk and looked into Timmy's big blue eyes, catching the wicked sparkle that would one day drive girls wild. Grinning, she swooped on him before he could escape, and plopped him down on the bed.

She laughed as he tried to wriggle free. "Come here, you little monkey. I want to listen to the engine inside your chest and see if all your spots have gone."

Timmy gurgled and pulled up his shirt, exposing his little pot belly. "See," he said, tucking his chin onto his chest and peering down at his tummy. "Gone."

"Are you sure?" Cassidy sounded dubious. "I think I see one here." She tickled him, making him squirm and chortle. "And here?" The noisy raspberry she blew on his tummy made him squeal and try to squirm away, but she held him firmly. "What about here?" He gave a great big belly laugh and caught her face in his hands before plant-ing a big wet kiss on her nose.

Cassidy laughed and brushed white-blond curls off his face. "I bet you do that to all the girls," she teased, lift-ing him onto his sturdy little legs. He wrapped his chubby arms around her neck and bounced happily while she lis-tened to his chest. Satisfied that he had no after-effects of the virus, she lifted him into her arms.

Turning to hand him to his mother, she came face to face with Sam. Her heart jolted and she sucked in a startled breath. They hadn't been this close since she'd told him she couldn't get involved with him.

"Oh. Major Kellan, you…you startled me."

"You got a minute, Doc?"

Belatedly noting his shuttered expression and the grim set of his mouth, Cassidy felt a prickle of alarm. A quick examination revealed blood staining the gray T-shirt be-neath his lab coat and her skin went ice cold.

"Samuel—?"

"You finished up here?" he interrupted, flashing a quick look over her shoulder at the room's occupant. "Hey, Cath," he greeted the other woman with a quick smile of familiarity. "How's Frank?"

"Hi, Sam," Cathy Howard greeted him back, her eyes alight with avid curiosity. "He's great. Thanks for asking."

"You need to come with me," he said to Cassidy, lowering his voice and backing into the hallway. "*Now*."

Dropping a quick kiss on Timmy's curls, she handed him to his mother. "Cathy, Timmy seems fine," she told the other woman, her attention on Sam's tense back. "If you're worried about anything, don't hesitate to bring him in. Keep him quiet for another day or two and be sure to give him a multivitamin and plenty of fluids."

She murmured a hasty goodbye and hurried after Sam, calling out to Janice at Reception that they had a code blue. Fortunately it was the midafternoon lull and she was certain Fran could handle the few patients that remained.

Cassidy hurriedly caught up to Sam, her pulse a blip of anxiety as she searched for injuries.

"Where are you hurt?"

His black brows came together over the bridge of his nose. "What?"

She drew level with him and gestured to his gray T-shirt and jeans. "Blood. Where are you hurt?"

He frowned down at himself. "It's not mine. A logger's just been brought in. Bad weather caused a cable to snap. He was in the way."

"Where is he?"

"OR. I can handle it if you're busy."

Almost running to keep up with his long strides, she sent him a sideways glance. "Fran's got the clinic. What's his condition?"

A muscle jumped in his jaw. His short reply, "Bad," sent an icy chill skating down her spine.

A white-faced Jim Bowen was already lying on the operating table, his shirt and jacket wet with his blood. Heather
Murray was at his side, holding a pressure bandage over
the wound, while a middle-aged man held his shoulders
and talked quietly to him. Another younger man hovered
nearby, looking like he was on the verge of passing out.
His relief when he saw Sam turned to confusion when he
spotted Cassidy.

"I thought you were getting the doctor?"

Sam's brow lifted and he sent Cassidy a wry smile. "I
did," he drawled. "This is Dr. Mahoney. She's an ER specialist from Boston."

Ignoring the skepticism in the young man's eyes, Cassidy moved towards the patient, noting his gray-tinged skin.
She lifted her head and caught Sam's gaze. "Heather, could
you please show the gentlemen out and get Spruce Ridge
on standby. Major Kellan and I will handle this until you
return."

Cassidy barely noticed the men leaving as she quickly
shed her lab coat and pulled on a surgical gown. Tossing another to Sam, she liberally sprayed her hands and arms with
disinfectant before grabbing two pairs of surgical gloves
from a nearby dispenser. She shoved her hands into one
pair and waited while Sam disinfected. There wasn't time
to scrub.

With swift, economical moves, Cassidy cut Jim's shirt
away while Sam inserted the stent and hooked up a saline
drip. For several minutes they worked together in silence,
cleaning the patient's chest and arm, positioning electrode
disks and hooking him up to the heart monitor.

Cassidy clipped on the saturation probe and frowned as
thready, irregular pulse beats blipped into the silence. Jim
had clearly lost a lot of blood and was going into shock.

"He's going to need an orthopedic specialist," Sam said,
tying Cassidy's face mask and shoving her hair under the

surgical cap as she gently eased pressure on the dressing to assess the extent of the damage.

Jim's arm had almost been severed at the shoulder and the instant she released the pressure, blood gushed from the jagged wound. "Can't wait," she said briskly, reaching for a clamp. "We're going to have to repair this artery first or he won't make the orthopod."

"Heather," she said briskly when the nurse returned, "find out his blood type and get the status with Spruce Ridge changed to code blue. What's our blood status? He's going to need at least six units."

"Four in total," Sam said from the refrigerator, "and they're all O positive."

They shared a look and Cassidy made a split-second decision she hoped she wouldn't regret. "We'll use them all and substitute the rest with blood plasma."

Sam's brow rose up his forehead. "And if he's AB negative?"

"We'll cross that bridge when we come to it."

CHAPTER TEN

CASSIDY STARED IN dismay at the ominous storm front that had rolled over the mountains while she and Sam had been in the OR. And if that wasn't bad enough, the helicopter pilot presently running towards them was alone. He wasn't even Medevac. A Forestry Services chopper had responded to their emergency.

Just great.

"Where's the Medevac crew?" she yelled, pushing her whipping hair off her face. The icy wind roaring down the mountain held more than a hint of snow and she had a feeling the storm was closing fast.

"You're it," he yelled over the noise from the engine and rotors. "Landslides and bad weather's already caused a major pile-up on the interstate to the northwest. They're stretched thin at Spruce Ridge General and when your call came through, all Medevac were engaged. You're lucky I was in the area."

"I'll go," Sam yelled, leaping into the helicopter with familiarity and an ease born of a well-conditioned body as he grabbed the collapsible gurney and pulled it inside. He slid it into place and hung the saline bag on an overhead hook before strapping the stretcher to the floor.

Cassidy felt her stomach clench into a tight ball of terror at the thought of flying through a blizzard. She'd heard stories about the late spring storms that often tore through the Cascades and wasn't looking forward to flying into it.

Swallowing her fear, she sucked in a lungful of cold air and shook her head decisively. Grasping the open door, she pulled herself inside before she could change her mind. "I'm the responsible physician at this hospital, Major," she yelled. "He's my patient. I can't let him go until I sign him over to another practicing physician." And when his dark gold gaze lifted and clashed with hers, she added a little more sharply, "My responsibility."

For a couple of beats Sam held her gaze then he gave a curt nod. "Fine. But I'm coming with you."

Ignoring the relief that slid into her stomach, Cassidy shook her head. "Not necessary. I...*we'll* be fine. I know you have other...plans."

He sent her a puzzled, narrow-eyed look that said he didn't know what she was talking about but wanted to demand an explanation. All he said was, "Be right back," before leaning forward to talk to the pilot, who was fiddling with the panel of overhead instruments. After a couple of beats the pilot nodded and Sam clasped the man's shoulder. Moving to the open door, he flashed an inscrutable look in her direction then jumped from the helo to lope across the helipad towards the building.

The rotors picked up speed and Cassidy swallowed hard. *Oh, God.* She hoped he hurried back before she changed her mind. Besides, she'd overheard a couple of nurses discussing meeting up with him later, which meant he was probably cancelling their date—or rescheduling.

And since he'd made it clear he wasn't in the market for anything long term and *she'd* made it clear she wouldn't get involved with a colleague, there wasn't much left to say.

Was there?

So why did she feel on the verge of tears? Why did she feel as though she'd just eaten a gallon of double-cream ice cream? Was she just having a panic attack at the idea of flying through a storm in a helicopter? Or was the queasy feeling in her stomach something else? But since she refused to consider the "something else" and wasn't some damsel in distress who needed to be rescued by a big, strong man, she didn't know where that left her.

She checked Jim's vitals in an effort to calm her nerves, tugged at the straps holding the gurney in place and fiddled with his shoulder dressing. After an anxious look in the direction in which Sam had gone, she flicked at a few bubbles in the IV line, hooked up another unit of blood, and then *re*checked his vitals, aware that with every passing second their window of opportunity for flying out was narrowing.

Finally, when her anxiety was at fever pitch, Sam reappeared. Without a word, he tossed her a thick parka, extra blanket and rucksack before leaping into the chopper. He pulled the door closed behind him, abruptly shutting out the worst of the rotor roar and the first snowflakes.

Cassidy bit her lip and slid onto the bench seat, pressing a hand to her roiling belly as he leant forward to tap the pilot on the shoulder. Without turning, the man lifted his hand in acknowledgement and in the next instant the engines screamed.

Cassidy dug her fingers into the bench seat beneath her. The craft shuddered and she squeezed her eyes shut in an effort not to freak out as the chopper lifted with a sickening lurch and the ground abruptly disappeared beneath her feet.

Biting back a whimper, her grip on the bench tightened until her knuckles ached and her fingers turned white. Something dropped around her shoulders an instant before Sam's heat enveloped her. He pressed his solid shoulder close as a big, calloused hand covered hers. Once he'd pried her fingers loose, he engulfed them in a firm, warm clasp.

With his rough palm sliding against hers, he laced their fingers together and gave her a comforting squeeze. Cassidy tightened her grip when what she really wanted to do was climb into his lap and hide her face against his strong, wide chest. She'd die of mortification later, she told herself, when her feet were once again firmly on solid ground.

His cold lips brushed her ear. "You can open your eyes now," he yelled, and she shook her head, unwilling to see the masculine amusement gleaming in his eyes.

God, she'd missed looking into those gold eyes...missed him more than she'd thought possible.

She felt his mouth smile against her temple and shivered as hot and cold goose bumps broke out across her skin. She was unsure if it was fear, the dipping temperatures or... or a desperate need for his touch—and terrified it was a combination of all three. For some reason his proximity always seemed to trigger a confusing mix of emotions that left her reeling.

"*Babe*," he said against her ear, and Cassidy could hear the smile in his voice before he gave her earlobe a gentle nip. This time she had no trouble identifying the origin of the shivers racing over her skin. "I won't let anything happen to you," he promised deeply. "I'm a SEAL. You're absolutely safe."

Cassidy turned to yell at him for calling her babe, only to find him less than an inch away. His gaze was hot, intense and a weird sensation of vertigo sent her stomach plummeting. For the second time in as many minutes her world tilted, and she was fairly certain it had nothing to do with being suspended above the earth in a flimsy aircraft.

Every thought fled save the sudden jumble of emotions she struggled to make sense of. Blood rushed from her head. Her lungs constricted and she was forced to acknowledge that she wasn't just hanging in space with a thin layer of metal between her and the jagged peaks below. Her heart was too—for an entirely different reason.

It quivered in her chest and before she could pull back from the edge or rip her hand from his and retreat to the opposite bench—*hell, throw herself from the helicopter*—

in an effort to protect herself, he lifted her hand to his lips and—*Oh, God*—pressed a kiss to her white knuckles.

A sob rose in her chest.

"I won't let anything happen to you," he repeated, with a reassuring smile that promised everything she'd told herself she didn't want and he couldn't possibly mean. And when she simply shook her head and squeezed her eyes shut, he cupped her jaw in his big, warm hand. He waited until her lashes rose before adding, "SEAL's honor."

Cassidy's heart clenched—his expression, and the heartfelt assurance, appearing more meaningful than a kiss. She sucked in a shuddery breath, suddenly terrified about what it could mean and blurted, "If we go down I'm going to kill you," as she battled with the shocking truth.

He laughed and her chest tightened painfully.

Oh, God.

She could no longer hide it from herself. She wasn't just fighting feelings for him. She was in love with Samuel J. Kellan, US Navy SEAL. A man who kept himself locked up tight, a man who didn't return her feelings, even though he wanted to be with her.

For now.

He'd wormed his way under her defenses and had settled next to her heart while making it perfectly clear she was a distraction. He didn't do long term and thinking she could matter to him was insane.

"Hey…" Sam's deep voice was laced with concern "…why the gloomy face?"

She dropped her lashes to hide her chaotic thoughts and bit her lip. Right, like she'd tell *him*. He already knew how to make her respond to him. She would rather die than have him guess how she felt.

Her pulse fluttered. He was such a beautiful man, strong, honorable and honest. He hadn't lied or made promises he knew he couldn't keep, and she couldn't imagine him taking a woman hostage after he'd been caught doing something illegal and realized he could no longer sweet talk his way out of it. He wasn't Lance Turnbull. He'd proved time and again that he could be counted on. That he was someone worthy of love. That he was worthy of her love.

Only thing was: he didn't want it.

She gave a wild little laugh and hoped he thought she was freaking out about flying. "You ask that when we're a thousand feet over the Cascades—in a tin can?"

His eyes crinkled and his mouth curled into a quick grin that had her breath catching in her chest. For the first time since that night in the jail cell he looked relaxed and... carefree. *Happy,* even.

"Isn't it great?"

Yes, it was, she admitted silently, but not the view out the window. With a sudden flash of insight she realized that he missed his team, his dangerous job. And she wondered for perhaps the hundredth time why he chose to be stuck in a small mountain hospital, treating runny noses and hypertension, instead of jumping from aircraft, yelling "*Hoo-yah*" as he took out the enemy. And if, for just a fleeing moment, she wished she'd been responsible for the dazzling pleasure lighting his gold eyes, Cassidy reminded herself that kind of thinking would only lead to heartache. Heartache she knew—with abrupt certainty—she would never recover from.

She loved him but would keep her heart safely hidden. For now she would simply enjoy the warm, masculine scent of him and the press of his body against hers, knowing it would soon be gone.

"You're insane," she yelled, and rolled her eyes when his quick answering grin flashed with wicked recklessness. And when his eyes dropped to her mouth, her blood turned hot.

An odd expression crossed his face and his eyes darkened. "Yeah," he agreed, wrapping a hand around her head to tug her close. Expecting his usual fiery mastery, Cassidy was stunned when his mouth touched hers gently in a kiss that was as sweet as it was unexpected.

And before she could remember that this was a very bad idea, she was sliding her hands up to cup his hard, beard-roughened jaw. She opened for him, tentatively touching her tongue to his, while she fought the aching need squeezing her heart.

He tasted of hot, untamed man and for once in her life Cassidy wanted to leap off the edge, uncaring where she landed. There was only *this*—this wild, exciting moment with this wild, exciting man.

Tilting her head to give him room, she traced the strong line of his jaw with questing fingers, ignoring the tiny voice of reason in her head that warned she was heading for disaster. She didn't care. She just wanted to feel what was suddenly the most significant kiss of her life.

If this was all she'd have, she would take it. But she had to remind herself they weren't alone. With supreme effort, she broke off to say, "Sam, we should stop," hoping he would make it easy for her, and hoping with equal intensity that he would not.

With a savage growl Sam leaned his forehead against hers and sucked in a ragged breath. His heart thundered in his chest like he was having a coronary, yet he felt more alive than he had in a long time. More intensely aware of his surroundings—as though electricity flowed across his skin and connected every atom in his body to the universe. To her.

Pulling back an inch, he stared into misty green eyes heavy with arousal and emotions he couldn't begin to identify, and wondered briefly what had made this kiss so different.

He was thirty-four years old, and he'd just had the hottest, wildest kiss of his life in a cold, noisy helicopter a couple of thousand feet in the air—with a woman who wasn't interested in a relationship and then kissed like she was searching for his soul.

Reminding himself that his time in Crescent Lake was running out—that this was just a fantasy interlude before he returned to his real life—Sam caught her mouth in a brief, scorching kiss. "Later," he growled, sliding his gaze over her face as though committing the soft confusion in her eyes to memory.

Damn, but she was so beautiful.

Suddenly her eyes widened and she pulled away so abruptly he cast around for the threat before he realized she was dropping to her knees beside Jim.

"He's crashing," she yelled, pulling at the straps securing the stretcher. Cursing himself for forgetting where they were, Sam leaned over to release the safety clip as Cassidy tore off the blanket to expose the patient's chest. She checked his pulse and immediately began performing CPR as Sam grabbed a headset to bark at the pilot.

Learning they were less than five minutes out of Spruce Ridge, he instructed the pilot to radio ahead with their ETA and to have a resus team waiting at the helipad. He tossed aside the headset and dug into his rucksack for the supplies he'd thrown there earlier.

He ripped off the plastic needle cover with his teeth and plunged the syringe into the vial of atropine. With a smooth one-handed move that might have impressed Cassidy if her patient hadn't been in trouble, he drew back the plunger.

"Get that into his vein," she ordered sharply, before stopping the chest compressions to begin mouth-to-mouth. The following minutes were filled with the urgency only experienced by medics concerned with saving a life, and by the time they landed and rushed him across the helipad, Jim Bowen's pulse was once again steady.

The ortho specialist was already suiting up when Cassidy followed her patient into the OR. The gray-haired surgeon's piercing blue gaze studied her over the top of his spectacles as he thrust his hands into latex gloves.

"Grant Sawyer, orthopedic specialist," he introduced himself brusquely. "Mahoney from Crescent Lake?" And when she nodded, he barked, "Fill me in."

Cassidy gave a succinct report of their intervention while the theatre staff prepped Jim for surgery. Sawyer listened and nodded as he skimmed through the patient's chart.

"Good job," he said with a brusque nod, and turned away to rap out orders for blood and instruments, leaving Cassidy with the impression that she'd just been dismissed.

She backed out of the OR, fighting the feeling that she should be doing something. *Anything* but stand around while others worked miracles.

Sam was waiting in the hallway. "You okay?" he asked, shoving off the wall he'd been propping up. Cassidy nodded absently and pushed the tousled hair off her forehead. "Why?"

"Resus says ER's swamped and could use some help. You up for it?"

"We're not flying back?"

Sam shook his head. "Storm's too bad. We're lucky we made it before all aircraft were grounded. Pilot's already gone and all roads into the mountains have been closed."

Cassidy's belly clenched. "So we're…stuck."

Sam placed a warm hand into the small of her back and sent her a crooked grin. "Just you and me, babe. Until morning."

Cassidy rolled her eyes at his use of the hated word that was strangely enough starting to grow on her. "And an ER full of accident victims."

"Yeah." He laughed dryly, steering her down the wide hallway. "And that."

* * *

Hours later Cassidy pulled off her latex gloves and made the last notations on her clipboard. Darkness had long fallen and the storm had turned the world beyond the hospital walls white and icy. Fortunately the number of casualties had dwindled to a trickle and she could finally take a break.

She was also starving.

Stretching tired muscles, Cassidy wandered out to the waiting room and handed the clipboard to the woman manning the nurses' station. "Finally packing it in, honey?" the nurse asked with a sympathetic smile.

"You're good to go," Cassidy replied, smoothing her messy hair off her face and twisting it at the back of her head, where she pinned it using a couple of pins someone had found for her. "Have you seen Major Kellan?"

"Big handsome hunk with the pretty eyes?"

Cassidy smiled at the woman's description. "That's him."

"I saw him heading towards the doctors' lounge with the ER manager about ten minutes ago," the nurse reported and eyed Cassidy with open envy. "You two…together?"

"Yes," she said with a small smile, and turned to head down the passage. They were together but not *together*. She didn't think any woman could say she and Samuel Kellan were…*together*. He didn't do together with anyone—which should have made her feel better but didn't, especially when she entered the doctors' lounge and found him surrounded by admirers.

Almost immediately he turned, a warm, intimate smile curling his lips when their gazes met and held. He quickly excused himself and headed across the room to wrap his hands around her upper arms and yank her against him. Her squeak of surprise was abruptly cut off by his open-mouthed kiss, and before she could react, he'd sucked out her brain along with her breath.

Several long seconds later Sam broke off the kiss and

lifted his head a couple of inches. "Hey," he murmured, his rough, deep voice sliding against her like a heated caress.

She gulped in a shocked breath and gaped at him. "Wh-what…?" Her mouth snapped shut on her stuttered attempt at coherence. Besides, they were standing in a brightly lit doctors' lounge filled with openly staring medical personnel.

"Work with me here, babe," he said out of the corner of his mouth. Baffled by his unexpected behavior, Cassidy opened her mouth again. "What…?" but Sam was tugging her into the hallway.

"*Hey*," she complained, and tugged against his grip. "Coffee. Now. Maybe even intravenously."

Sam grimaced. "Forget about that swill. I've got something better."

Her mouth dropped open and she stared at him in shocked silence before sliding her gaze down his hard belly to his crotch. *Did he…? Could he really…?*

"*Doc!*" Sam's eyes widened but he was also battling a grin. "You have a dirty mind," he accused, and when she just rolled her eyes he spun her around and hustled her back against the nearest wall, his body following.

Surprised by the slick move, Cassidy gave a startled squeak even as his mouth closed over hers, and then he was kissing her like he couldn't wait to get her naked. She slapped a hand against his chest and made a gurgling sound in her throat.

Sam reluctantly backed off, looking a little wild. Cassidy flushed and tried to shove him away but he leaned into her and rasped out, "Give me a minute." She opened her mouth to tell him he'd had his minute when she felt something large and hard poking her belly. She froze, her flush deepening, until she was sure she was glowing like a neon sign in the desert.

"What is it with you and walls?" she huffed out, secretly

grateful for the hard body keeping her upright. His gold eyes gleamed at her through thick dark eyelashes.

"If I don't take advantage of the nearest one," he growled, "you'd be practicing those sneaky evasion techniques you've perfected over the past few weeks."

Cassidy opened her mouth to reply when her stomach growled and she dropped her head back and closed her eyes in defeat. Sam chuckled and pushed away from the wall.

"Looks like you need more than coffee."

"I'm starving," she excused herself with a faint blush. "I wonder what the hospital cafeteria is serving."

Sam grimaced and stepped back, his hand sliding down to circle her wrist. "Nothing good, believe me." He gave her a gentle tug closer. "Let's go."

"Where? I'm starving."

His eyebrow rose at her petulant tone. "And I'm going to feed you," he promised. "Just not here. I managed to get us a room at a hotel a couple of blocks away."

Shock and panic moved through Cassidy. "*What? No!*"

Sam's brow rose. "No?"

"No," Cassidy said shortly. "I'm not sharing a room with you."

He sent her a chiding look. "Now, *babe*—" he began.

Only to have Cassidy interrupting with, "I beg your pardon?"

He grinned, leaving her head reeling at his abrupt mood changes. "You really shouldn't try that icy debutante tone with me, Doc."

"Excuse me?"

He leaned closer with a sinful grin that sent alarm and heat arrowing through her. "Makes me hot," he murmured against her ear, and Cassidy felt her cheeks heat. She could feel exactly how hot.

She edged away. "I can get my own room, Sam." No way could she spend the night with him and not expose herself.

Her feelings were too new, too raw—and she was terrified she would just blurt them out in the heat of the moment.

"No, Cassidy, you can't." And when she scowled he smoothed his hand down to the base of her spine and tugged her closer. "And not just because you didn't bring cash or cards. The hotels in the area are all full. I checked. I was lucky, *really* lucky to get that room."

His look was carefully casual. "So, dinner and the last room at the inn?"

Cassidy sighed and made a helpless gesture. "Sam—"

He captured her hand. "Look," he interrupted quietly, "I know you don't get involved with people you work with. But we're not colleagues here. We're just a man and a woman who are attracted to each other."

She looked up in surprise. "I thought—."

He shrugged out of his parka and wrapped it around her shoulders as he steered her towards the main entrance. "You thought what?"

Looking up into his handsome face, Cassidy recalled the conversation she'd overheard earlier that day. "I know you were planning to meet up with some of the nurses later."

His stopped abruptly. "What?"

She licked her lips and exhaled noisily, hoping he couldn't see how much the knowledge hurt. "I understand. Really. It's not like we're—" She stopped abruptly and looked away, unable to continue.

Sam folded his arms across his chest. "Not like we're what, Cassidy?"

She swallowed and smoothed her tousled hair off her face, looking anywhere but at him and feeling unaccountably flustered. "It's not like we're…well, together. Or anything," she ended lamely.

His mouth compressed into a hard line and a muscle jumped in his jaw. "Well, you apparently know more than I do," he growled. "*Jeez.* You don't have a very good opinion of men, do you? Or is it just me?"

Startled by his mercurial moods, Cassidy stared up at him. "What are you talking about?

His jaw clenched. "I'm talking about the fact that you think I'd have sex with other women just because you're avoiding me."

She flushed. Okay, so that's exactly what she'd thought. "Sam—"

"Cassidy," he mocked gently, and cradled her face between his warm palms. "It's just you," he murmured, his eyes a deep dark gold that had her heart lurching in silly feminine hope. Was he saying what she thought he was saying? "Since that night in county lock-up, it's been you."

For now, she wanted to add, but didn't want to ruin the fragile mood between them. Sucking in a shaky breath, she sent him a falsely bright smile and shored up the cracks in her composure. She'd take what she could and protect her heart later. When he was gone.

"I think you promised me dinner," she murmured, and his grin was quick and white in his dark face. Leaning forward, he planted a hard kiss on her mouth. "That's just the appetizer, *babe*," he promised quietly. "We have the whole night to savor the main course."

CHAPTER ELEVEN

CASSIDY WOKE ON a surge of adrenaline, abruptly and fully alert between one breath and the next. Heart pounding in her chest, she blinked into the darkness and struggled with a sense of disorientation.

Quickly taking stock, she realized she wasn't at home in Boston and she wasn't in her bed at the inn. But she *was* naked, which could only mean one thing…*Sam!*

Fear and a gut-deep knowledge that something was very wrong had her rolling over in the wide bed just as she heard it again—harsh, ragged. There was a heavy thud and something crashed to the floor, instantly followed by a litany of snarled curses.

Pulse spiking with alarm, she lurched upright and tried to recall where the bedside lamp was situated. His abruptly yelled, "*No! No!*" sent chills streaking up her spine, and a quick tactile reconnaissance of the mattress confirmed she was alone in the bed. Was Sam fighting some psycho who'd sneaked into their hotel room?

"He's just a kid, for God's sake. Let him go… *God*, let him go."

He? Who was he talking about? Heck, who was he talking to?

A low, threatening sound vibrated deep in his throat, making the hair on her body stand on end before a babble of foreign words filled the room, menacing and a little frightening.

Launching herself across the bed, she fumbled for the light switch, rapping her elbow on the bedside table and almost knocking the lamp over in her haste. She finally located the switch and blinked against the sudden light bursting into the room.

She didn't know what she'd expected but it wasn't Sam fighting an unseen enemy. *Oh, God,* she thought. Was he experiencing a flashback or having a nightmare?

A murderous bellow had Cassidy's heart rate spiking. She watched wide-eyed as he struggled violently, arms pinned to his side, tendons, sinew and well-defined muscles straining beneath acres of sweat-slicked skin.

He was gloriously naked, but for once she failed to appreciate the perfect lines of his hard body. Her gaze was locked on his face. His shadowed features contorted with fury as he lurched around the room, crashing into everything in his path. It was a wonder he didn't wake up with all the noise he was making and Cassidy wondered if he was reliving some actual or imagined event.

He suddenly stiffened, and with a hoarse, anguished *"No!"* he jolted like he'd been struck. Then he slowly sank to his knees, his breath coming in ragged dry heaves.

Biting back the cry that rose to her lips, Cassidy pressed herself against the headboard, wanting desperately to go to him. She *needed* to go to him—especially when he thrust his hands through his hair and she got her first good look at his face. He looked completely and utterly devastated.

No longer able to keep her distance, she slid from the bed and approached him warily, desperate to comfort him. A hoarse moan tore from his throat and the desolation in the sound lifted the hair at the nape of her neck. She halted a few feet away and dropped to her knees, the sight of his wet cheeks wrenching at her tender heart. Unbearable pressure squeezed her chest in a giant fist and before she could stop it from happening, her newly exposed heart quivered…and broke.

A sob rose in her throat and she reached out a hand, her trembling fingers sliding greedily over the rounded ball of his shoulder. His skin, normally so warm, was damp and cold to the touch and her medical training took over. She wasn't a psychiatrist, but working in ER she'd witnessed enough cases of psychological trauma to know shock when she saw it.

"Samuel," she said firmly, rubbing his wide shoulder in slow, soothing movements. For long moments he remained unresponsive, the room filled with nothing but his harsh breathing—his body shaking as shudders moved through him. "Sam. Wake up, you're dreaming."

His muscles turned to stone beneath her hand as he abruptly stilled. He slowly lifted his head, turning a gaze completely stripped of emotion in her direction. He looked at her as though he didn't know her and wasn't quite sure what she was doing there.

Tension radiated off him like a nuclear blast and she braced herself for his reaction. But after long tense moments he blinked as though coming out of a trance, confusion pulling at his dark brows.

"Cassidy?" His voice emerged, hoarse and a little rusty. Her shoulders sagged and her breath escaped in a relieved whoosh that left her trembling and dizzy.

Okay, she thought, *so far so good.*

Shifting closer, she carefully smoothed a line from his shoulder to his bulging biceps and curled her fingers into his inner arm where the satin-smooth flesh was clammy. A fine tremor twitched the muscles beneath her hand. Even in the dim light his pallor was evident, as was the fine sheen of perspiration, the dazed disorientation in his eyes. She pushed damp hair off his forehead with her free hand before cupping his hard, beard-roughened jaw in her palm.

Staring into his distressed eyes, she whispered, "It's

okay, Sam…I'm here," fighting the need to wrap her arms around him, to press her body close, share her warmth. Protect him from his demons. "I'm here."

After a couple of beats he lifted unsteady fingers to brush a light caress over her mouth. His tender touch, so at odds with the violence she'd sensed in him just moments ago, tore at her control, and a tear finally escaped, the accompanying sob a hot ball of razor-sharp emotions in her throat.

His eyes tracked the silvery tear before he caught it near her mouth with the tip of one long tanned finger.

"You're crying." He sounded baffled, concerned, as another tear escaped, then another.

Horrified by her slipping control, she covered his hand with hers and turned her face into his wide, calloused palm, choking back emotions that seemed to be rising faster than Biblical flood waters.

Get a grip, Mahoney. The guy needs your strength here, not tears and certainly not any declarations of love.

"I… It's nothing," she replied softly, nuzzling his hand, her gaze clinging to his as though he would vanish if she blinked. "Something happened. Tell me about it."

If Cassidy had blinked she might have missed the shield slamming down between them. Between one breath and the next his eyes cleared as he abruptly withdrew. All without moving a muscle. Then his hand slid out from beneath hers and he moved away, leaving her cold and oddly hollow.

The barrier was as tangible as a brick wall. Feeling suddenly exposed she hurriedly looked around for something to cover her nakedness. Spying his soft, well-washed T-shirt, she grabbed it and hastily pulled it over her head, surrounding herself with his familiar scent.

He was slumped back against the bed, wrists draped over his upraised knees, head bowed, breathing heavily as though he'd run ten miles in full gear up a steep mountain slope. His face was gray and emotional strain carved deep furrows beside the tense lines of his mouth.

Wishing she could comfort him and knowing it was the last thing he wanted from her, Cassidy felt raw emotion rise like a tide from her chest into her throat. She swallowed past the lump in her throat and wrapped her arms around herself to ward off the room's sudden chill.

"What happened?" she prompted softly.

A muscle ticked in his jaw and his face settled into a blank mask that squeezed her already bruised heart. For long moments he stared silently at the floor then exhaled noisily, thrusting a hand through his hair, the jerky motion dislodging a dark lock. She had to curl her fingers into her palm to keep from reaching out to smooth it away. Smooth his pain away.

After a moment he said flatly, "The mission was jinxed from the start. It was supposed to be quick. Drop in, find the hostages, blow everything up, go home. Instead there was a welcoming committee waiting at the drop site, as though they knew exactly where we were going to be." He pressed the heels of his hands against his eyes, looking unbearably weary.

"We barely had time to dive for cover before firepower erupted around us. Back-up was still miles away and we were pinned down from all sides. I remember thinking we'd bide our time, wait them out." He broke off with a bitter laugh. "Yeah, right. We'd expected maybe a dozen armed men. What we didn't figure was that our intel was compromised. There were maybe fifty heavily armed men. All with us in their sights."

He paused, face hard, hands curled into fists, as though he was reliving that night. After a few moments of silence he added, "Back-up was also taking heavy fire and before I knew it we were out of ammo and outmuscled. Finally they rounded us up and took us into the mountains, where we were questioned. Separately. Together—hoping we'd talk."

Cassidy had a feeling "questioned" meant tortured. She went cold at the thought and pressed a fist against her mouth to prevent a sound of distress from escaping.

"Did you?"

Sam's harsh laugh scraped at her ragged nerve endings. "Honey, SEALs don't talk. Ever." He took a couple of deep breaths before continuing. "They cut us off, took out our ground support and left us with no way to contact base command. We were on our own." He fell silent. "Then one night, about a week into our capture, they came for me," he said hollowly. "I remember thinking, *This is it, time to make peace with God.*" His eyes narrowed on some point in the past and he absently rubbed his wrists.

"What h-happened next?" Cassidy prompted softly, dreading what she sensed was coming.

He gave a heavy sigh. "They must have found out I was a medic," he said flatly, dropping his gaze between his large bare feet. "I was taken to a house in the village and told to treat some sick kid. I refused unless they let my team go." He snorted. "I had to try. Turned out they were waiting for a camera crew. An entire SEAL team is good leverage when you want scumbag terrorists released." He scrubbed his hands over his face. "I eliminated two guys before they…uh…subdued me."

Sick with horror, Cassidy tightened her grip on her arms. He didn't need to tell her what "eliminated" meant. She knew. Just as she knew "subdued" meant they'd probably beaten him senseless.

"Seemed they didn't want me dead. At least, not yet. Dead meant I couldn't save the kid, who was in pretty bad shape. I don't know how long I was out but by the time they emptied a bucket of water over me, they'd dragged in the team rookie and were holding a gun to his head. My eyes were practically swollen shut and my vision was blurring badly, but one look at him and I knew we were in trouble."

He muttered a few curses and wiped his face as though

he could wipe away the memories. "*Jeez*, they'd beaten Scooter until his mother wouldn't recognize him. But at least he was still alive. Anyway, I said I'd treat the boy if they let me patch Scooter up. They argued amongst themselves for a while before finally agreeing." He laughed bitterly. "I knew…God, *knew*…I shouldn't trust them. I knew it, but I—"

He broke off abruptly, shifting restlessly, leaving Cassidy dreading the rest of the story. She could guess what was coming and braced herself, knowing that despite his training he'd been helpless to save the life of his friend.

"I asked for my med supplies and removed the kid's appendix. Took a couple of hours for his fever to break but when he finally opened his eyes, the guy with the gun on Scooter just looked me in the eye and…pulled the trigger." He sucked in a ragged breath and then for the first time since he'd begun he turned to look at her—eyes bloodshot, devastated as he relived the nightmare.

"They shot him," he said blankly, as though he still couldn't believe it. "They laughed and shot him in the head like a rabid stray." Shoving his fingers through his hair, he looked away and struggled for control as Cassidy battled against the urge to hold him close, promise things he didn't want or need from her.

After a few moments he sucked in a ragged breath and added, "I went berserk. I took out everyone and secured the kid's mother before she could rouse the whole damn village. Then I went to get my team."

"Oh, Sam," she rasped, heartsick at how unbearably sad he looked, how unendurably weary. And she could no longer ignore the compulsion to touch him. But when she reached for him he abruptly turned away, as though he couldn't bear her touch. She bit her lip against the devastating hurt of his rejection and slowly lowered her hand.

"I'd do it again," he vowed softly, his tone deadly. "They tortured and killed half my team. Good men…my brothers, my friends…and I….they were my responsibility and I failed them. If I'd made my move sooner, Scooter would still be alive."

"Or maybe not," Cassidy offered softly. "Maybe you'd both be dead."

He rounded on her with a furious snarl, a white blaze of hot fury in his eyes. "It would have been nothing more than I deserved," he snarled, rising abruptly. "I'm a SEAL. Failure is *not* an option."

He looked around a little wildly, as though he'd found himself trapped. Movements jerky with suppressed violence, he snatched up jeans, socks and boots and dressed in simmering silence. He'd shoved his arms through the sleeves of his flannel shirt and grabbed his jacket before she realized he was leaving.

"Samuel, wait." She reached out to tangle shaking fingers in soft flannel before she realized she'd moved. He stilled but didn't turn, his stiff posture broadcasting louder than words that he was barely hanging on to his control.

"Where are you going?"

"Out."

Feeling him slipping away, she did the one thing she'd promised herself she would never do. She begged.

"*Please*, Sam, don't go. Stay. Talk to me."

Ignoring her plea, he silently reached for the door, and before she knew she was moving, Cassidy slipped around his body to press her back against the door. He looked momentarily surprised, even retreated a step before his features hardened and his laser-bright gaze sliced her to ribbons.

Ignoring the aggression pumping off him in waves, Cassidy locked her wobbling knees and bravely held his gaze, aware that she was shaking inside. She had a feeling if she let him go she'd never see him again.

For a long tension-filled moment he stared at her, eyes blazing with emotions so raw and violent that she had to force her body not to step into his. "Stay, Sam…just *stay*," she pleaded hoarsely.

A muscle flexed in his jaw and she realized with shock that he was shaking too. She wanted to go to him but was held in place by the invisible *keep out* signs radiating off him. Finally he gritted through clenched teeth, "There is nothing to say. Now move out the way, Doc. I don't want to hurt you."

Doc? He was calling her Doc after everything they'd shared?

Swallowing a bitter laugh, Cassidy drew in a shuddery breath and tried not to show how much his words—heck, his attitude—hurt. "I…love you Sam," she whispered hoarsely.

His gaze sharpened as though he'd heard her but intended to ignore her ragged confession. "It's just a walk, Cassidy," he said roughly. "I need some air." And when she held out her hand, his coldly furious "I don't need a goddamn nursemaid, for God's sake. I just want some damn air. Is that too much to expect?" had her jaw dropping open in shock.

Recovering quickly, she stepped forward to flatten her palm against his naked chest, hoping her touch would somehow get through the impenetrable wall he'd built around himself. "I… Let me help you, Samuel," she blurted out before she could stop herself. "Please, don't go. I…I love you. I love you, let me help."

His reaction was swift and shockingly direct. Jerking back as if she'd slapped him, he stared at her in silence for a couple stunned beats before his expression turned into a remote mask, rejection clear in every tense line of his body.

Cassidy's heart sank and she pressed a shaking hand against the hard cold ball of misery forming in her throat. "Sam—?"

"I'm sorry," he interrupted impassively, frowning at her as though he'd never seen her before, and the cold ball of dread dropped into her chest, lodging right where her heart should be.

Two words, *I'm sorry*, were suddenly the most devastating of her life. More devastating than anything that had happened in Boston. "You're…s-s-sorry?"

He gave a heavy sigh. "Yes." His handsome face was carved with cold disinterest, his once beautifully glowing eyes flat and detached—as though she were a stranger. A stranger he didn't particularly like the look of. "I'm flattered, of course, but I thought you understood I wasn't…" He made a sound of annoyance. "Well, I'm sorry you believed otherwise. Now please step aside, I don't want to hurt you."

Cassidy didn't remember moving, could only watch as he opened the door and walked out without a backward glance. Hours later, when a firm knock sounded at the door, she flew across the room, wild hope and relief shriveling along with her heart when she opened to find not Samuel but the Forestry Services pilot.

Once the pilot left, Cassidy moved around the room like an automaton, gathering her clothing and dressing in stunned silence. She carefully washed and dried her face, ignoring the white-faced stranger in the mirror as she pulled her hair off her face and secured it at the nape of her neck. Then with her raw, bleeding heart carefully locked away behind a coolly professional façade, she left the hotel and headed for the hospital to check on Jim before taking the elevator to the helipad.

She scarcely remembered the flight back to Crescent Lake. Staring sightlessly out the window, she was impervious to the cold, the stunning scenery, the curious man at her side.

Nothing. She felt absolutely…*nothing*.

By the time the chopper touched down, Cassidy was grateful for the numbness. She even managed to aim a small smile of thanks at the pilot before alighting from the helicopter. The ground was slippery with ice as she carefully picked her way to the building.

Fran Gilbert took one look at Cassidy's face and the blood drained away from her face, leaving her pale and concerned. "What's wrong?" she demanded. "Are you okay? Is Jim okay?"

Drawing her professionalism around her like a cloak, Cassidy paused to reassure the older woman. "He's holding steady," she said. "I checked on him before I left and spoke to his doctor. He seems cautiously optimistic about Jim's recovery."

"I'll call his wife," Fran said with relief but kept her gaze sharply on Cassidy's face then voiced the question Cassidy had been dreading. "Where's Samuel?"

Cassidy wrapped her arms around herself and forced herself not to react. "I... He had to leave suddenly."

Fran looked surprised, confused. "Leave? Where did he go?"

Cassidy shrugged as though her heart wasn't a bloodied, pulpy mess. "I don't know," she admitted, pressing trembling fingers against her aching temple. "His message didn't say."

Fran digested the news in silence before saying, "You look awful, honey, and you're frozen to the bone. Are you sick?"

Cassidy didn't believe her attempt to smile fooled the other woman but she was beyond caring. She was barely holding onto her composure as it was and Fran had just given her the perfect excuse. "I think I've caught a bug," she croaked, instantly ashamed when Fran looked concerned.

"Oh, honey, do you need someone to drive you home?" Fran asked, gently rubbing some warmth into Cassidy's frozen arms. But she had a feeling nothing would ever make her feel warm again.

She shook her head and resisted the urge to drop her head onto Fran's shoulder. If she did, she would shatter into a million pieces and she couldn't do that until she was alone.

"I can't leave, Fran," she croaked, her control slipping fast. "Now that…um…" She swallowed hard and drew in a shaky breath. "Now that the major is gone, I'll need to pull double shifts." Besides, being busy would keep her from thinking too much.

"No, you won't," Fran reproached firmly. "You'll go home and get into bed. We'll handle things today." And when Cassidy opened her mouth to argue she said, "No arguments. I promise to call if we have an emergency."

Cassidy stared into Fran's gentle blue eyes and finally pulled away. The woman knew. *Oh, God, was she that obvious?*

"I'll get my purse and jacket."

Cassidy let herself into the inn, aware that she was shaking uncontrollably as if she'd contracted some kind of jungle fever. Sweat slicked her skin and she had to wipe her damp palm against her thigh several times before she could shove the key into the lock.

Sudden dizziness swamped her one instant, the next her stomach cramped violently and the hand that she'd flung out to grab the doorframe slapped over her mouth instead. She made a mad dash for the bathroom at the end of the hall, barely slamming the door behind her before she lost the meager contents of her stomach.

When the retching finally stopped, she dragged herself to her feet. Moving to the basin to rinse her mouth, she caught sight of herself in the mirror and couldn't hold back a horrified gasp. She was paper-white, hollow-eyed and looked like she'd just survived a major disaster. No wonder Fran was concerned, she thought, eyeing herself dispassionately. She looked like hell. And felt much worse.

Unfortunately, the numbness that had got her through the past six hours was fading and the awful truth of what had happened was finding its way through the cracks in her composure.

Her eyes and her throat burned with unshed tears and her heart felt like he'd ripped open her chest and savaged her. Hurrying back to her room before the dam burst, Cassidy shoved the door closed and she was finally—*finally*—alone.

She sank back against the door, her knees buckling as a ragged sob escaped and the first scalding tear eased over her lashes to carve a fiery path down her cheek. By the time her bottom hit the floor, keening sobs racked her body and the tight leash she'd kept on her emotions finally snapped.

It was over, she told herself. *Over.* When she'd finally admitted to feelings she'd never intended to feel.

Dropping her forehead onto her updrawn knees, she choked back a ragged cry. Samuel J. Kellan had rocked her world then walked away without a backward glance. As if she meant less than nothing.

He'd made mad, passionate love to her then coldly, dispassionately, told her he was sorry she loved him. He was flattered—*flattered*—but thought she'd understood he wasn't looking for a relationship. *I'm sorry you believed otherwise,* he'd said, slicing her to the soul. And then, when she'd stared at him, her shattered heart exposed for the world to see—for *him* to see—he'd calmly told her to step aside because he didn't want to hurt her.

He'd calmly crushed her heart…and left.

CHAPTER TWELVE

CASSIDY ENTERED BERNIE'S supermarket and exchanged a few hurried greetings of "Hello, how are you feeling today?" and "Don't forget to bring the baby in for his next checkup." As much as she enjoyed stopping to chat, she hoped she could get in and out as quickly as possible.

She had a long list of items to get for a bachelorette party, in…she quickly glanced at her watch…*yikes,* less than two hours. She also had to get back to the inn and shower and change out of her jeans and stained scrubs top.

She was heading down the snack aisle, tossing things in her trolley, when she caught sight of the sheriff's car drive past and pull in across the street. Turning away with an irritated mutter, Cassidy checked the next item off her list.

She'd thought she was getting over being dumped in a Spruce Ridge hotel but then she'd heard Ruben Kellan's voice down the passage in ER. Her heart had sped up and stopped at the same time, which was not only impossible but alarming.

Her knees had turned to jelly and the blood had drained from her head so fast that Mrs. Jenkins—whom she'd been examining at the time—had shoved her into a chair and called for a nurse.

Cassidy had blamed the episode on lack of food and long hours. No one had said anything but she didn't think they believed her. Later Fran Gilbert had pulled her aside and handed her a pregnancy test. Cassidy remembered gaping at the other woman and dismissing the idea since Sam had used protection, but when she'd had a chance to think clearly, she realized she couldn't remember her last period.

So she'd panicked.

But when the results had shown up negative she'd cried, great big gulping sobs that hadn't made a bit of sense. She didn't *want* to be pregnant—at least, not like that—by a man who'd made mad, passionate love to her one minute, as though he couldn't get enough, then the next had walked out like she was nothing.

Except it had proved to be a turning point of sorts. She'd emerged from the bathroom bound and determined to get over him. She'd thrown herself into the community, introduced a monthly clinic day for the local schools and a mothers' support group that she hoped they'd continue after she was gone.

During her visit to the middle school she'd met art teacher Genna Walsch, and they'd become close friends. It was Genna's bachelorette party Cassidy was on her way to.

Whipping through the store, she piled items into her trolley before heading for the refrigeration section. She selected a few bottles of chilled champagne and then added fruit juice for pregnant guests.

Next she headed towards the deli, where she'd arranged to pick up a few roast chickens, and had to squeeze past two women studying the selection of cold cuts and chatting.

"I heard Patty Sue from the sheriff's office tell everyone he's coming back," the thirty-something blonde told her friend. "No one knows for sure if it's for good but rumor says it is. I've been surfing the net for obscure symptoms that will get me some quality time with him." She shivered dramatically. "I heard he's *real* good with his hands and I can't wait to play doc—"

The second woman caught sight of Cassidy and nudged her friend into silence, making her wonder what they'd been discussing. Or rather *whom* they'd been discussing. Just then the server turned with a welcoming smile and a "What can we do for you, Dr. Mahoney?" and Cassidy pushed the conversation from her mind.

She knew the county had hired two new doctors that were expected to start at the end of the month. She also knew she would have to make a decision about where to go once *her* contract expired.

As much as she told herself she was over Sam, Cassidy was honest enough to admit that living in the same town as his family meant it was fairly reasonable to expect him to visit occasionally. The longer she stayed in town, the greater the possibility of seeing him, and quite frankly she wasn't sure how she'd feel, or react, if she saw him again.

She'd made several enquiries and had received a couple of good offers—one of which was Spruce Ridge General—but she couldn't make up her mind. Frankly, she didn't want to leave. For the first time in her life she felt part of a community, like she was making a difference in people's lives. She liked feeling needed and appreciated, and she really liked seeing their health improve under her care. It was so much more satisfying than treating nameless masses day in and day out.

She thanked the server and turned, checking chicken off her list. And walked into a wall. Of muscle.

Opening her mouth on an automatic apology, she was instantly assailed by a masculine scent that was all too familiar. Barely an inch from her nose was a wide, hard chest covered in soft black cotton. She knew without looking up past the long tanned throat, strong jaw and poet's mouth to sleepy golden eyes, that she was inches away from the one person who was able to scramble her brain.

Samuel J. Kellan.

Her stomach clenched into a hot ball of dread and joy, and her heart squeezed in her chest. Taking a hasty step in retreat, she tightened her grip on the strap of her shoulder bag. The dimly lit aisle, the illuminated display cases behind her, the couple discussing what to have for dinner, *everything*…faded.

It was as if the universe had suddenly narrowed to just the two of them. Her skin hummed, her ears buzzed and it was only when her vision grayed at the edges that she realized she was holding her breath.

Expelling it on a shaky whoosh, Cassidy's gaze hungrily traced his handsome features. He'd lost weight and he looked tired. There was a healing laceration on his jaw and a bruise darkened his sharply defined cheekbone and the skin around one eye.

Despite his features being in shadow, he appeared tanned and amazingly fit. He looked…wonderful, even if the gaze he'd locked on her face was hooded and unreadable.

Her stomach clenched and her chest felt like a giant fist was squeezing the breath from her lungs. So many times over the past weeks she'd imagined seeing him again. Had even practiced what she would say. But nothing, *nothing* could have prepared her for the stark reality of being this close to him again after she'd convinced herself that she was over him.

Her spirits sank. She'd clearly miscalculated. And with the knowledge came a swift rise of self-directed anger. Okay, she was angry with him too. The jerk had made mad, passionate love to her and when she'd told him she loved him and *begged* him not to go, he'd ripped her heart out and told him he was sorry. Yes, well, she was sorry too— sorry she'd been stupid enough to fall for him.

Yet despite all that, she was glad to see him. Relieved he was alive and in one piece.

He was the first to break the awkward silence.

"Cassidy." The sound of his voice, as deep and rough as she remembered, brushed against jagged emotions and tugged at something deep and raw within her.

She swallowed what felt like ground glass in her throat. "Major," she said, inordinately pleased when her voice emerged coolly polite, as though they were nothing more than casual acquaintances.

His eyes narrowed and his face tightened before his features assumed an impassive mask. He widened his stance and folded his arms across his chest in a move that emphasized his wide shoulders and the bulge of his biceps straining the sleeves of his T-shirt. He was carelessly masculine in a way that made her heart speed up and her knees wobble. And it was suddenly all too painfully obvious that she wasn't going to get over him.

Ever.

She gulped. She'd been fooling herself. He was *it* for her. And nothing she did would stop this soul-deep yearning for him, this ache of knowing they weren't meant to be. That *she* wasn't meant to be—at least not for him.

And didn't that just…*suck*.

The urge to leave was suddenly overwhelming but his big, tough body blocked her way and the potent cocktail of pheromones and testosterone he exuded made her feel lightheaded. Oh, wait, that might be caused by food-shopping on an empty stomach. A stomach that was suddenly queasy.

Biting her lip to keep from falling apart, she turned and had to abruptly alter her course to evade the hand he lifted. Thinking he meant to touch her, she stumbled backwards and froze. She sucked in a startled breath and her gaze flew from the hand suspended in the air between them to his face. Something flashed in his gold eyes—something that looked like pain. But he recovered quickly, a shutter slamming down over his features, and she thought maybe she'd been mistaken. His arm dropped to his side.

"How have you been?" he asked softly, and Cassidy's eyes widened. She clenched her jaw to keep it from bouncing off the floor.

He was asking how she'd been? *Really?* After he'd emo-

tionally savaged her in a hotel room then disappeared for
five weeks without a word?

She stared at him for a long moment, tempted to just
walk away, but a closer inspection of his features revealed
lines of exhaustion and uncertainty. Uncertainty?

Yeah, right, she thought with a silent snort, and folded
her arms beneath her breasts. "Um…great," she rasped,
before clearing her throat and saying with a little more
composure, "I'm fine. You?"

His forehead wrinkled as though her behavior baffled
him and Cassidy couldn't prevent a little spurt of satisfaction. He was baffled by her behavior? *Well, tough*, she
thought, straightening her spine as though the sight of him
didn't make her want to simultaneously punch him and
throw herself in his arms. Besides, he'd given up the right
to be baffled by anything she did.

"Um…yeah, fine," he said absently, his eyebrows pulling his face into a scowl.

Ignoring the urge to trace the arrogant arch of his
brows with her fingers, she nodded. "That's…good," she
said vaguely. "Your…um, family must be relieved you're
home safely." And after an awkward pause during which
his intense stare sent flutters dropping into her stomach,
she added lamely, "Well, excuse me."

She stepped around him and escaped towards the checkout counter. This time he didn't try to stop her. Instead, he
followed, looking big and bad and deliciously dangerous.

He waited while she paid for her purchases, chatting
with the checkout clerk. And before she could object, he
hefted her packets, announced, "I'll walk you to your car,"
and headed for the exit. As though expecting her to follow.

She did, quickly, trying to head him off. "That's not necessary," she told him, and grabbed for the carry-bag handle. They engaged in a brief tug of war until Sam gently
removed her hand and repeated quietly, "I'll walk you to
your car," his gaze as implacable as his words. His mouth

tightened when she seemed about to argue, then he stepped around her, turning to wait patiently for directions.

She stood indecisively for a few moments, wondering if she should just leave her groceries and bolt. But that would only prove he still had the power to affect her.

Shoving an errant curl off her face, Cassidy sighed impatiently. "This really isn't necessary, Major," she said huffily. "I can manage a few grocery bags and I'm sure you're busy. So…I won't detain you."

He studied her silently for a few moments before transferring all the bags to one hand. The other he wrapped around her arm and steered her out into the early evening.

Hunching her shoulders against the cool mountain air and the curious looks they were receiving, Cassidy sighed and stepped through the doors. The last thing she needed was him walking her to her car. She was hanging onto her control by her fingernails as it was.

"Where's your car?"

She shifted nervously and adjusted her shoulder bag. "Major—"

"We need to talk," he said quietly, implacably, and Cassidy welcomed the surge of anger that followed his announcement. *What the hell?*

Suddenly furious with him, and with herself, she swung to face him. "There's nothing to say, Major," she said tightly, coolly. "*Nothing.* In fact, you were more than clear about your feelings the last time we…spoke. I get it. I'm not stupid, recent behavior to the contrary. I can read between the lines. Now, if you'll give me my damn bags, I'll be on my way." She grabbed her bags and yanked. This time he allowed her to take one. The others he held out of reach. Growling, Cassidy spun away and headed purposefully for the stairs leading to the parking lot. He snagged her arm in a tight grip.

"Cassidy…"

And suddenly she'd had enough. More than enough,

actually. *"Don't!"* she snapped, ripping her arm from his grasp and turning away abruptly. She sucked in a ragged breath. "Just...*don't.*" Furious tears pricked the backs of her eyes and she swallowed past the lump of emotion threatening to choke her. She needed to escape before her rigid control snapped. "I...I have to go. G-goodbye, Major."

Sam followed silently and watched as she fumbled in her purse for the car keys. Locating them, she pressed the remote and even in the gathering dusk he saw her fingers tremble.

Feeling his gut clench, he reached out and closed his hand over hers. She jolted as though he'd prodded her with a shock stick. Her skin was cold to the touch and his grip tightened when she tried to yank away.

Dammit, I screwed up and now she can't even stand my touch, he thought, when that was all he wanted. He wanted to press up against her curvy body and bury his face into the soft, sweet hollow beneath her ear. He wanted to lick her smooth skin and breathe in her special fragrance— warm, slightly fruity and smelling of clean mountain air. A scent he'd craved with every breath he'd inhaled every second of every day he'd been away.

She hurriedly stepped away and waited tensely while he unlocked her car and stowed her bags on the backseat. He then opened the driver's door and held out her keys. She reached for them, careful not to touch him, and would have slid into the car if Sam hadn't abruptly pushed her back against the cool metal, knowing he couldn't let her go like this. Not after the past weeks. Weeks of hell when he'd missed her like an absent body part.

At first he hadn't understood what the hell was wrong with him. Even his commander had ripped him a new one after he'd blown off the psych eval.

He was supposed to be an invincible SEAL but he'd fallen apart—shared his nightmares and his guilt with her, for God's sake. He hated her knowing he was a cold-blooded killer. Okay, he'd killed to save himself and the rest of his team—but he'd killed in a cold rage. And he hadn't been able to bear the compassion, the sympathy in her eyes. He didn't deserve any of it. He didn't deserve her.

He didn't remember much about that night in Spruce Ridge, but he did remember what he'd said to her. And he felt ashamed.

Everyone thought he was still PTSD but Sam knew that wasn't why he'd been a basket case after that night.

Okay, he was still PTSD but that wasn't the problem, and it had taken him a couple of long weeks to realize exactly what *was*. He was missing something more important than his sanity. His heart. And *she* was his heart.

But all he could think about now was the feel of her soft curves against him. *God*, he'd missed this. Missed having her curvy body pressed against his—like he was finally home.

She made a sound of distress and tried to push him away, but Sam manacled her wrists and pressed them against the cool metal beside her head. Then he took advantage of her shocked gasp and swooped down to crush her mouth with his.

God, he thought, thrusting his tongue deep, hiding out in a desert cave, he'd thought of nothing but the feel of her in his arms, the taste of her in his mouth.

Her heart pounded as hard as his and she struggled to free herself but he wasn't letting go. Not now that he was finally where he belonged. For long moments she remained stiff in his arms, and then with a long throaty moan her body melted against him.

Heart pounding, he released her hands and abruptly broke the kiss, pressing his erection against her. *God*, he wanted—no, *needed*—her more than he'd wanted anything.

Resting his forehead against the roof of her car, he

gulped in air and prayed for control, but then she whispered his name, "Samuel," and the sound of it on her lips blew him away.

He thrust his hands onto the wild silvery mass framing her face and the next instant he was devouring her with a hot, hungry desperation he'd never realized he was capable of. It burned him up, a raging wildfire that swept away every thought, every need in a wave of hot primal craving.

His emotions, unrestrained and frantic, burned hot and fierce. His hands streaked over her in a desperate attempt to feel all of her—her soft silky heat, her firm, smooth flesh—and it was a moment before he realized her hands weren't trying to pull him close but push him away.

"Stop," she cried hoarsely. "*Samuel! Stop!*"

Shocked, he froze, his chest heaving with the effort of drawing air into his lungs.

"Stop?" he croaked, not believing he was hearing right. *"Stop?"*

A ragged sound of misery escaped her throat and she flattened her palms against his chest and shoved. Sam was so surprised that he staggered back a couple steps until his back hit the neighboring car.

"Wha—?"

"Leave me alone, Sam," she croaked, and with one desperate look she dived into her car, slammed the door and shoved the key into the ignition before he could move.

The engine engaged in a roar and the car shot out of the parking lot, barely missing a battered Ford truck and a shiny new SUV parked beneath the streetlight.

The last image he had was of her white face streaked with tears, and the knowledge that he'd caused them made his gut clench in sick shock. He'd made her cry. *Again.*

Sam watched as her taillights disappeared, feeling at once numb and devastated. Gutted, like he hadn't felt since he'd let his team down. And just like that night, his rage turned outward. A red tide of primal fury he knew he couldn't let loose on the good people of Crescent Lake.

Shoving his hand into his pocket, he palmed his keys and headed towards his SUV. He might not want to let his rage loose on his friends, but he knew exactly where he *could*.

The sheriff hit the doors of the Crash Landing with the heel of his hand and strode into the bar, expecting to call in for a dozen body bags.

After a crappy week, he'd gone home armed with a six-pack and a giant pizza topped with the works, hoping to relax in front of his big-screen TV. Seattle was playing San Francisco. It was just his luck the call from Dispatch came through as Seattle slammed the first puck into the opposition's net.

Expecting to wade into World War Three, Ruben halted three feet into the bar and blinked in the dim light, aware that his jaw had dropped open. About a dozen men were propped up against the bar, tossing back tequila like they were practicing for a Mexican showdown and singing off-key enough to make tone-deaf ears bleed.

Pushing his hat up his forehead, Ruben shoved his hands on his hips and gaped at the spectacle. Sam was in the thick of things, arm slung around Chris Hastings as though they were bosom buddies when Ruben knew damn well and good they'd been enemies in high school. He'd never seen a sorrier bunch of idiots.

He strode up to the bar and pushed his way through the throng. The owner, watching the proceedings from behind the counter with an unreadable expression, nodded when he saw Ruben.

"Sheriff," he said. "Can I get you something?"

"Coffee, Joe. Strong, black with plenty of sugar."

Joe Montana lifted a brow and grinned. "One cup or two?"

"Make that two. And don't skimp on the sugar."

By the time Joe slid two coffees across the counter the men at the bar had left or wandered away, leaving the brothers alone.

"Go away," Sam growled, and defiantly lifted the last shot to his mouth. Ruben hastily removed the glass and shoved the coffee at him.

"Drink," he said shortly. "And then tell me what Crescent Lake's newest doctor is doing practicing for *America's Got No Talent.*"

Sam grimaced at the cup in front of him. "Real funny."

"Not when I've been called away from a game where Seattle scored the first point against 'Frisco. Not when my *brother* is propping up Joe's bar and making people's ears bleed." Sam opened his mouth to argue but Ruben beat him to it. "Drink the damn coffee before I slap your ass in jail for disturbing the peace."

Sam scowled at him through bleary eyes for a couple of beats before he gave a heavy sigh and complied. "I was ready to quit anyway."

Ruben waited until Sam had consumed half the cup's contents before he said mildly, "Care to tell me what's going on?"

Sam shoved a hand through his hair and stared down into his half-empty cup. "Nothing." *Everything.* He'd glimpsed that flash of pain in Cassidy's beautiful green eyes and he'd gone a little crazy.

He'd shoved her up against her car and sucked her breath from her lungs and then she'd cried. The memory of her white, shocked face still had the power to make him feel like the worst kind of monster.

"Uh-huh," Ruben said mockingly.

He loved her, *dammit.* More than being a SEAL. More than his miserable life. More than he wanted to draw his next breath. And she'd told him to stop and had then fled as though she couldn't stand the sight of him.

"Nothing," he repeated wearily, shoving his hands through his hair and propping his elbows on the bar. He'd messed up and now he didn't know how to fix it.

"So," Ruben said, absently stirring his coffee, "this has nothing to do with a certain doctor you were seen practically inhaling whole in Bernie's parking lot, then?" Sam turned to glare at his brother. Ruben's sigh was as weary and heartfelt as Sam's had been a minute ago. "You're an idiot," Ruben said.

Sam straightened and opened his mouth to ream his sibling a new one, then shut it with a snap and looked away. No use denying it. He *was* an idiot.

"I messed up," he confessed roughly, swallowing past the lump of misery stuck in his throat like a burning lump of self-loathing.

"So fix it," Ruben said, his voice laced with steel and something that sounded like impatience-laced sympathy.

"Don't know if I can," Sam admitted quietly, shoving a shaking hand through his hair. "She hates me."

Ruben made a sound of irritation. "You're an embarrassment to Irishmen everywhere, you know that, Kellan?" he snapped, and when Sam's gaze flew up he added, "And here I thought your SEAL motto was 'Adapt and Overcome.'" He pointed a finger at Sam. "So get over yourself, and go do some adapting and overcoming."

"She doesn't want anything to do with me."

"You're a SEAL," Ruben reminded him ruthlessly. "Go be a SEAL. No obstacle too big and all that."

For long tense seconds Sam glared at his brother. He finally gave a sharp nod and downed the last of the god-awful coffee. He slapped the cup back in its saucer and shoved away from the bar.

"Pay the man," he ordered, before turning towards the door. "I've got something to do."

Groveling sounded about right, he admitted with a grimace. *And when I'm finished she's going to know she's mine—and that I'm hers.*

Failure was not an option. Not this time.

CHAPTER THIRTEEN

CASSIDY PUSHED OPEN the glass door to the sheriff's department, recalling the last time she'd been there. And like that night, Hazel Porter was once again manning the front desk.

The deputy peered over her half-spectacles and an odd expression crossed her face. She cleared her throat loudly once, then again, and abrupt silence fell over the room as a dozen pairs of eyes swung in her direction.

Forehead wrinkling in confusion, Cassidy approached the desk, suddenly feeling as nervous as a newlywed outside the honeymoon suite.

"Evening, Mrs. Porter," she greeted the deputy. "Dispatch said you…um…had a medical emergency?"

"Glad you could make it, hon," Hazel rasped, and turned to snag a bunch of keys from the board behind her. "We have a…situation."

"A situation?"

Hazel headed around the counter and made shooing gestures at the group of young deputies watching Cassidy with big toothy grins.

Cassidy frowned. "What's going on?"

Hazel shook her head. "Ignore 'em, hon, they're just a bunch of idiots with nothing better to do than stand around grinning like loons." The last she said loudly, scowling at the deputies who instantly tried to pretend they were busy.

Cassidy opened her mouth but the desk sergeant barreled on. "It's been a real slow week and nobody in this town can keep their noses out of other people's business."

Brow wrinkling with concern, Cassidy asked, "Are you all right, Mrs. Porter? You seem a little—"

"Call me Hazel, hon," the deputy interrupted, "everybody does. And I'm fine." Then she muttered something that sounded like, "Or I will be once all the hoo-hah is over," leaving a clueless Cassidy to follow her down the hallway towards the holding cells.

Muffled laughter and scuffling sounded somewhere behind her and she glanced over her shoulder. Several deputies were pushing and shoving each other to peer around the door—like they were in junior high.

They grinned and gave her the universal thumbs-up sign. *Weird,* she thought with a mental eye-roll, and turned back to follow Hazel's diminutive figure.

"This way, hon," the deputy said, unlocking the door and gesturing as if they hadn't done something similar a few months earlier. Stepping cautiously through the open doorway, Cassidy paused, wondering why every hair on her body was standing on end like a freaked-out cat.

Biting her lip uncertainly, she looked at the deputy and found Hazel staring at her with the oddest expression in her dark eyes.

"Don't be too hard on him, hon," Hazel murmured softly. "He's an idiot, but we love him."

Alarmed, Cassidy opened her mouth, certain now that Crescent Lake's sheriff's department was under some kind of Rocky Mountain madness. "Mrs. Porter—"

"It's Hazel, hon," the deputy interrupted cheerfully, and gestured to the large lump occupying the narrow bunk— in the same cell she'd entered before. "Now, in you go, everything's already set up. Holler if you need anything."

Squaring her shoulders, Cassidy stepped into the dimly lit holding area, vaguely aware that the cell doors were all ajar—and empty. *That's odd.* The outer door slammed shut.

She gave a startled squeak and told herself she was letting everyone's *weirdness* affect her.

Inhaling an unsteady breath, Cassidy tightened her grip on her medical bag and headed for the occupied cell. Stepping through the open doorway, she sensed movement behind her and whirled, using the momentum to swing her medical bag at the intruder. With a surprised curse, he ducked and lifted his forearm in a lightning-fast move that caught her wrist and sent the bag flying.

Squeaking in alarm, Cassidy scrambled backwards and stumbled over her own feet. She fell, landing hard, and for just a moment saw stars. Gasping for the breath that had been knocked out of her, she blinked and realized a man—*God, he was huge*—was bending over her…reaching for her.

She saw his mouth move but heard nothing over the blood thundering in her ears as she scuttled out of reach. But his big hands closed over her shoulders and before she could squeak out a protest, he'd hauled to her feet like she weighed nothing.

Intent only on preventing every woman's worst nightmare, Cassidy lashed out with her hands and feet, unaware that she was screaming until she heard a familiar voice calling her name.

"*Jeez*, Cassidy, stop. Stop it. *Cassidy!* Dammit. *Calm down!*"

She froze, gulping in great big sobs and stared into the dark face above her. It took her a couple of seconds to recognize the familiar masculine scent, the wide gold eyes staring at her as if she'd lost her mind.

She croaked, "*Samuel?*" and her knees abruptly buckled. He yanked her against his big warm body, hard arms keeping her from sliding to the floor.

"*Jeez,* woman," he growled into her hair, his arm an iron band across her back as she fisted her hands in his shirt and pressed her face into his warm throat. Her heart raced at warp speed. His free hand cupped the back of her head and she breathed in the comforting scent of heat, clean male and crisp mountain air.

By the time her heart dropped from stroke level to a mere freaked out, Cassidy remembered that she was furious with him—hell, he'd just scared a decade off her life.

Acting on impulse that was triggered by fear, fury and relief, she shoved him back and rammed her knee into his groin in one smooth move. With a startled yelp, he jerked away from the unexpected attack and dropped like a stone. Suddenly free, Cassidy hastily backed up until the cold steel bars bit into her shoulders.

"*Holy...*" Sam wheezed after a couple minutes of gasping like she'd gutted him with a scalpel. "*What...the...hell... was...that...for?*"

Shocked by her own action, Cassidy could only gape at him and stutter. "You... I... *Dammit!*" Her knees gave out and she slid down until her butt hit the cold floor. When her vision finally cleared and she could speak without stuttering, she opened her mouth to apologize and "You scared the *crap* out of me, you...you *dufus!*" emerged instead.

Sam stilled for a long moment then a rough sound emerged from his throat, sounding like a mix between a laugh and a groan. Moving slowly like he was in severe pain, he sat up and sank back against the bunk, one leg drawn up tightly to his chest. In the dim light his mouth was a tight white line in his green complexion.

Appalled by what she'd done, Cassidy rose on shaky legs, took a couple of wobbly steps and dropped to her knees beside him.

"I'm...I'm sorry," she gulped, lifting a hand to brush an errant lock of dark hair off his forehead. For a moment she enjoyed the feel of cool, silky strands between her fingers before admitting shakily, "I don't know why I did that."

His rough, gravelly laugh was abruptly cut off as he sucked in an unsteady breath and wiped his face with shaking hands. After a long silence he finally opened his eyes and stared at her.

"Dufus?"

She blinked. "What?"

"You called me a dufus."

Cassidy grimaced and sat back on her heels. "Yes… well…um. It was the best I could come up with in the heat of the moment."

His mouth curled into crooked smile and the expression in his eyes made her gasp. Before she could even begin to interpret it he said, "Come 'ere," and wrapped his fingers around her wrist.

With a gentle tug he pulled her towards him. She gave a startled squeak and found herself in his lap. His arms, his warmth, his scent surrounded her and she was tempted to wrap herself around him too. Just to prove to herself that he was here. Fortunately, she recalled his behavior of the previous night and pushed away. Sam tightened his arms with a deep, rough sound of pain.

"Don't…move," he rasped in her ear. "Just…gimme… a minute."

Realizing her bottom was planted right where she'd kneed him, Cassidy froze until she remembered that she was supposed to be treating an injured prisoner. *Him?*

"Where are you hurt?" she asked quietly, resisting the urge to run her hands, her lips over every inch of him.

He stilled and there was a moment of stunned silence. Then he lifted his head to gape at her. "*Really?* You do *that* and then ask where I hurt?"

A scalding blush rose into her cheeks and she bit back a hysterical giggle. "I'm s-sorry," she said in an unsteady voice. "But you deserved it for scaring me."

His snort told her what he thought of her apology. "I'll be lucky if you haven't permanently destroyed any chance I have of fathering future Kellans."

Reminded that he wasn't interested in making those

future Kellans with her, Cassidy snapped, "That's not my problem," and tried to scramble away. He yanked her back.

"Stop that," he ordered, clamping his hands on her hips and pulling her closer. "It *is* your problem." And then he murmured something that sounded like, "Or it will be…I hope."

Confused, Cassidy pulled back to look into his face. His color had returned but he still looked a little worse for wear.

"What's going on, Sam?" she demanded, lifting her hands to examine the bruises on his face, before probing his shoulders and chest. "The dispatcher called for a medic."

"Who just about crippled me. What's with the ninja attack, by the way?"

"Sam…"

He sighed. "Look, you're right I am a dufus. In fact—"

"Sam."

"Just let me finish, okay," he interrupted quickly, his hands clenching on her thighs and sending little shivers of heat and arousal through her. "I need to say this."

Sighing, Cassidy studied him closely for signs of PTSD or at least an answer to his behavior. "All right," she said quietly, ruthlessly squelching the urge to squirm against him. "I'm listening, especially to the part where I'm right."

His mouth quirked up at the corner then tightened as he exhaled heavily. He looked nervous but Cassidy dismissed it as her imagination. He was a SEAL. The notion that he might be nervous made her want to smile. He'd survived being captured and tortured, for goodness' sake. Samuel J. Kellan didn't do nervous as much if not more than he didn't do relationships.

But something was clearly up and it was starting to make *her* nervous. "What are you doing here?" she asked quietly when the silence finally became unbearable. "Aren't you supposed to be parachuting into hostile territory and wiping out bad guys?"

"I quit," he said quietly, his gaze intense and unreadable on hers.

She blinked. "You...you...*what*? But...wh-why?"

He was silent for so long she didn't think he intended to reply but his gaze turned fiercely possessive when he finally admitted, "*You.*"

"Me. *Me?*" Her voice emerged as a squeak. "*What do you mean, me?*"

Sam's mouth lifted at one corner but his eyes were serious. "I mean I was on a mission and all I could think about was you. That's dangerous, Cassidy. For me *and* the team."

This close, Cassidy could see the individual muscles in his throat as he swallowed. Not knowing where to put her hands, she smoothed them down her thighs to disguise the fact that they were trembling.

"I messed up," he admitted softly. "I was five miles above the earth in a HALO jump and closing fast when my chute failed to deploy—"

Her head went abruptly light. "*Oh, my God,*" she gasped out, clutching at his shoulders and shaking him. "Tell me..." she demanded hoarsely. "Tell me you're okay." His hands reached up to grab hers before she ripped his shirt.

"Hey." His grip tightened. "I'm here, aren't I?"

She stared at him wide-eyed for a couple beats then pulled a hand free and punched him—hard. "*Dammit,* don't...don't you *dare* scare me like that."

He winced and wrapped long fingers around her wrist. "If you'll just let me finish," he said gently.

Cassidy swallowed a sob and grimaced. "Sorry."

He absently lifted her hand to plant a kiss on her white knuckles in a move that stunned her. "Well, there I was," he continued, "falling at a hundred miles per hour..." Her gasp earned her a chiding look. "As I said, a hundred miles per hour, with the earth rushing up to meet me, and I thought, This is it. I even relaxed, thinking it was nothing more than I deserved for failing my team." He paused and drew in a shaky breath. "Failing you. I heard someone yelling in my head and…*hell*…I was all ready to go out in a blaze of glory. Arm the grenades and aim for the target instead of the drop site…just blow everything to hell and back."

"*Oh, God, Sam no*," Cassidy cried out, slapping a hand over her mouth to hold in the ragged sound of shock and horror. Her eyes burnt with unshed tears and he tugged her close, smoothing a shaking hand over her messy ponytail to her back. "I was reaching for my stash, voices yelling in my ears, and the next second…" He pushed her away to look into her eyes. "The next second everything faded— like I'd blacked out—and I…I heard you…yelling at me to get my butt into gear." He paused and swallowed. "Then you said…*I love you Samuel, please*…please *don't go*."

Stunned, Cassidy jerked back, fighting to free herself from his hold, but Sam's grip tightened, banding around her like steel, as though he couldn't bear to let her go. "*Don't*," he said hoarsely. "Don't pull away. I know I deserve it, but…just let me finish. *Please?*" He waited until she stilled, her face buried against his wide shoulder, tears dampening the soft, warm cotton.

"I saw your face, Cassidy," he said tightly against her temple. "As clear and real as you are to me now. And in that instant I knew… *Jeez*. You're right, I am a dufus. It took almost dying to realize that I…that I…" He halted and sucked in a sharp breath.

Cassidy froze and when he continued to breathe heavily she pushed away from him and lifted her gaze past the muscle twitching in his jaw. "That you what, Sam?"

His mouth twisted into a half-smile but his eyes glowed with an emotion Cassidy was too afraid to interpret.

"I was on a collision course with disaster. I blamed myself for living when my friends died. And when my chute failed I thought, *It's nothing more than you deserve.* But you rescued me, Doc, and even though I hurt you…didn't *deserve* you…I suddenly couldn't bear the thought of never seeing you again. That I hadn't told you." He inhaled shakily. "My mind was suddenly clear, like I was finally seeing the world for the first time. I sent up a prayer and yanked that damn clip.

"For a couple seconds nothing happened…and then… and then it deployed." He gave a ragged laugh and lifted his hands to cup her face. "Other than seeing your beautiful smile," he told her softly, "it was the most welcome sight I've ever seen."

"*Oh*," was all Cassidy could manage, her voice low and raw.

"I love you Cassidy," he said solemnly. "Tell me it's not too late. Tell me I didn't dream those words. Tell me you didn't rescue me…my heart…only to break it."

"Oh, *Sam*," Cassidy said again, too overwhelmed to think past the jumble of emotions rioting through her. "You're…sure?"

"That I love you? Dead sure—"

"*Don't say that*," she burst out, placing a hand over his mouth. He paled, looking appalled. "Don't say that I love you?"

She let out a little giggle. "No," she said, smiling, leaning in to replace her hand with her mouth in a soft, sweet kiss. "You can say *that* as often as you like. In fact, you need to say it again."

Inhaling shakily, he thrust his fingers into her hair, his gaze falling to her mouth. "I love you," he groaned, his lips dropping to brush against hers. "God, you have no idea how much I love you."

Dizzy with happiness and wanting nothing more than to sink into his kiss, she throatily ordered, "Kiss me, then." But he pulled back, grinning at her growl of frustration.

He shook his head. "Not until you tell me."

"Tell you what?" she demanded huskily, leaning forward to catch his sculpted bottom lip between her teeth. She gave it a punishing nip and wriggled her bottom against him.

God, she'd missed this. His scent, his touch and the taste of him in her mouth.

"Aw, c'mon, babe," he groaned, pulling back to scowl at her. "Don't keep me in suspense."

Her mouth dropped open. *"Babe?"*

He gave her a hard shake. *"Dammit,* Cassidy," he growled. "I'm dying here. Rescue me, Doc...*please.*"

Palming his tense face, Cassidy stared into his deep gold eyes, all humor abruptly disappearing. "I love you, Samuel Kellan," she murmured, her eyes soft on his before she caught at his mouth, and clung, like she'd never let go. "Don't you know? Don't you *know* yet how much I love you?"

A beautiful smile bloomed across his dark face and the next thing Cassidy found herself lying flat with his body, huge and heavy, pressing her into the cold floor. And before she could squeak out a protest, he slid a hand up her thigh to cup her bottom and pull her against him.

She thought he murmured, *"Thank God,"* and the next thing his mouth opened over hers in a kiss so hot and wet and *hungry* she nearly combusted.

Clutching at him, she sent her hands racing over his wide shoulders and back, down his arms, reveling in the solid feel of him beneath her palms. Her eyes drifted closed in delight and she gave herself over to his hunger.

For long moments Sam's mouth ravished hers as though he was starving for the taste of her, like he'd gone years instead of just weeks without her. She hummed her own hunger deep in her throat and marveled at the lights exploding behind her eyelids.

By the time they came up for air, she was gasping, dizzy with a pleasure she'd found only with him, and frustrated that they were still fully dressed. More than anything she wanted to feel the heated slide of skin against damp skin.

It was a few moments before she was able to open her eyes, only to discover a circle of curious, grinning faces peering down at them. Clutching Sam, she gave a startled squeak and felt her eyes widen as she recognized the young deputies who'd given her the thumbs-up earlier. Then the sheriff's face appeared overhead and then another…Sam's *sister?*

Oh, my God.

A hot blush rose in her cheeks. "*Sam,*" she squeaked, ducking her face into his throat.

"Yeah," he said in her hair, his voice strangely tight. "I know."

"Do you two need a room?" Hannah Kellan asked mildly, and laughter burst around them.

Sam stiffened, finally realizing they weren't alone. "What we need," Sam growled dryly, "is some privacy."

A moment later he rolled off Cassidy and drew her to her feet in one smooth move. He yanked her back when she made a move to bolt and tucked her against his side. He shook his head at their captive audience.

Hannah propped her shoulder against the open doorway and folded her arms beneath her breasts. "Well?" she asked cheekily, her elegant dark brow lifted in a way Cassidy recognized as pure Sam.

"Well, what?" he demanded, clearly annoyed by the interruption.

"Did she or didn't she?" Ruben demanded impatiently, and Cassidy nearly giggled at the way everyone's gaze jumped from one person to another in a ridiculous parody of a tennis match.

"I haven't asked her yet."

Hannah snickered and to Cassidy's embarrassment said, "What, too busy shoving your tongue down her throat?"

Sam growled threateningly and everyone laughed. "I'll be shoving you all out the door if you don't give us some space," he told her. "*Jeez*, can't a guy propose without the whole damn zoo turning up?"

Cassidy's head whipped up. "P-propose?" she squeaked.

His gaze turned possessive but to Cassidy's amazement he flushed. "Of course. What did you think I meant?" he demanded with a scowl.

"Well…I—"

His voice dropped. "You rescued me, Cassidy. You saved me when I didn't realize until it was almost too late. I love you. You're everything I want, everything I didn't realize I was looking for."

Cassidy's eyes misted and the buzzing in her ears almost blocked out the snickers of *"Aaaaww, isn't that sweet?"* coming from Sam's siblings.

"But…but what about your job?"

"I told you I quit."

"I don't know," she said slowly, ignoring the sharply inhaled breaths around them.

Sam froze and panic flashed across his face. "What do you mean, you don't know?"

"You haven't asked me yet," she reminded him gently, and reached up to kiss the corner of his mouth when he gusted out a relieved breath.

Turning her in his arms, he wrapped a hand around her neck and pressed his thumb beneath her chin, lifting her face to his.

"Cassidy Maureen Mahoney, will you rescue me one last time?"

Tears filled her eyes and her breath hitched in her throat. "Oh, Sam—"

"Will you marry me?" he continued in a voice deep and clear and filled with emotion. "And spend the next sixty years loving me as much as I love you? Will you raise a family with me here in Crescent Lake and work by my side at the hospital, keeping the nosy locals healthy? Especially people who don't know when the hell to take a hint."

Her breath hitched. "Oh," she sighed, staring up at him with damp eyes until he couldn't stand the suspense.

"Say something, babe," he whispered pleadingly. "You're making me look bad in front of everyone."

She giggled and a sudden hush fell as every ear strained for her answer. "Yes…" she whispered into the hushed silence, and wild emotion burst into Sam's eyes.

"Yes?"

"Yes," Cassidy said a little louder. "Yes, I'll marry you." And when he gave a whoop she put up a hand. "But…." He stilled, the panic on his face priceless. His mouth dropped open and there was a smattering of snickers. "But?" He looked suddenly nervous and wary. "But what? I have to give up a kidney? Done. My family? With pleasure."

Cassidy's mouth curled in a private smile. "I want to know all your secrets."

"All of them?" And when her eyes narrowed he said quickly, "They're yours."

"Great. Now, what's the J for?"

He blinked. "Huh?"

"In your name," she explained, curling her arms around his neck and burying her hands in his thick, silky hair. She watched as a slow, sexy smile bloomed. He leaned closer to whisper in her ear and Cassidy pulled back, wild color blossoming in her cheeks. "I don't think so." She giggled. Sam sighed then tried again and when he finally pulled back, he let his brow rise questioningly.

Cassidy rose on her toes to seal the promise with a kiss. "Samuel James Kellan, nothing would make me happier than being your wife."

A deafening cheer rose to fill Crescent Lake's jail cells. Sam ignored the loud congratulations and celebratory back-slaps to wrap his arms around the woman who'd rescued him from a life of nightmares.

"I love you, Doc Honey. What do you say we find someplace more private?"

A smile lit her face with love and anticipation and she blushed adorably. "I know just the place, Major Hotstuff."

He grinned. "Lead the way *babe*."

And she took his hand.

* * * * *

LET'S TALK
Romance

For exclusive extracts, competitions
and special offers, find us online:

 facebook.com/millsandboon

@MillsandBoon

@MillsandBoonUK

Get in touch on 01413 063232

For all the latest titles coming soon, visit
millsandboon.co.uk/nextmonth